THIS BOOK SHOULD BE RETURNED ON OR BEFORE THE LATEST
DATE SHOWN TO THE LIBRARY FROM WHICH IT WAS BORROWED

**AUTHOR**

ROSE, L.

**CLASS**

F

**TITLE**

Heaven

D0432353

# HEAVEN'S DOOR

*Also By Lynda Rose*

Kingdom Come

# HEAVEN'S DOOR

## Lynda Rose

**HEADLINE**

First published in Great Britain in 1997 by
HEADLINE BOOK PUBLISHING

10 9 8 7 6 5 4 3 2 1

British Library Cataloguing in Publication Data
Rose, Lynda
    Heaven's door
    1. Lottery winners - Fiction
    2. Pastoral theology - Fiction
    I. Title
    823.9'14 [F]

ISBN 0 7472 1855 2

Typeset by Palimpsest Book Production Limited,
Polmont, Stirlingshire
Printed and bound in Great Britain by
Mackays of Chatham PLC, Chatham, Kent

HEADLINE BOOK PUBLISHING
A division of Hodder Headline PLC
338 Euston Road
London NW1 3BH

For Dominic, Josephine and Christabel.

# Chapter One

The Reverend Casaubon's lips set in a thin, angry line. 'I am not going to talk about it,' he said, 'and that's final.'

Across the kitchen table Pippa glared at him angrily. 'How can you say that?' she blurted, before she could stop herself. 'Honestly, Mark, I sometimes think you just don't care. I want a baby!' The corners of his lips went white but he said nothing and, even more incensed, she shouted, 'You know that's what I want. I'm so fed up! We've been married eight years. What's so wrong with having tests?'

She was near to tears as she screamed this, and she could have kicked herself. She knew this was the wrong way to handle Mark. A clergyman of twelve years, his invariable response when confronted by anything he disliked was to clam up. She could never understand it. Every Sunday he would get up in the pulpit and talk about loving and sharing, and the importance of openness and expressing one's true feelings, but, as soon as it came to talking about anything really important between themselves, it was as if some steel security shutter plummeted down and a great big sign went up, 'Warning – Keep off!'

When they were first married, they had both been determined to start a family. Mark had been thirty-three to her twenty-six and, although they were still young, she had been acutely conscious even then of the biological clock ticking away. She wanted a large family. She always had, perhaps because she herself was the sole product of a broken marriage and her mother had always been so down on family life. But Mark had shared her feelings, and the fact that they had no money, apart from his stipend, had seemed irrelevent. God, they were both convinced, would provide. And, in the radiance of unshakeable faith, she had decided not to work, which had delighted Mark, devoting herself instead to being the perfect vicar's wife.

The trouble was, the children they had longed and planned for had failed to materialise. In the eight years they had been married, there had not been the slightest sign of a child. Pippa could not understand it. She had always been so healthy and normal. It had never occurred to her that they might have problems conceiving a child. But they did.

At first everyone said how wise they were, giving themselves time to adjust, and then, after a couple of years, even her mother had started to drop mild hints that maybe it would be quite nice to have a grandchild after all. When Mark had taken up his first full incumbency, the churchwardens and appointing committee had stressed how much the church wanted a 'family' man, and that they would not be at all averse to seeing a whole string of little Casaubons as soon as possible. They might even, they said, be willing to give some extra help financially if that was what had been deterring them. They had declined this – a full incumbent's stipend had seemed like wealth after the comparative poverty of being an assistant priest. But Mark had said that the offer was a sign, and that perhaps God had simply been waiting for them to get settled and more financially secure so that they could more fully enjoy family life and give their children the best possible start. Pippa had felt sure he was right and they had redoubled their efforts with vigour. But still nothing had happened. And after another couple of fruitless years, Pippa had begun to feel that the young mothers in the church were looking at her pityingly and making comments behind her back.

If her biological clock had been ticking before, it was positively thundering now and as she approached her mid-thirties, she began to feel real panic. The idea of a baby seemed to obsess her. It was all she could think about. She read every book she could find on how to increase their chances of conception. She kept temperature charts, and threw away all Mark's old underpants in favour of boxer shorts, because she had heard somewhere that restriction of the scrotum could reduce the sperm count. For her own part, every day she tried consciously to relax, until she felt like screaming with so much relaxation. And all the while she bombarded God with requests, promising spectacular sacrifices and acts of devotion if only he would help.

But still nothing happened, and she began to wonder if it was a judgement of some kind. She said as much one day to Mark, and it was around that time that she felt he began to withdraw. It was only little things at first. He stopped telling her about what he was doing, or about the people he had met, and gradually she began to feel pushed out and alone. Outwardly he was still the model husband of course, but whenever the topic of children was raised, or she told him dismally that yet again they had failed, he seemed to flinch, and it was as if another brick was added to the wall that was slowly growing up round him, which she was powerless to breach.

Mark threw himself into his work. He seemed to be at meetings all the time, always taking up causes, always looking for a soul to save. But between himself and Pippa there stretched a gulf of frigid non-communication. Pippa tried to talk to him. But each time, her resolutions to be gentle and patient ended with their having a blazing row, and the gulf yawned ever bigger. She began to think that the only possible answer to all their problems now would be the birth of a child.

Finally she went to the doctor and asked for an examination. She did not tell Mark because she knew he would not approve. Five years ago she would not have dared. She had fully imbibed evangelical doctrine and would have seen such a small strike of independence as rebellion and betrayal – a wife, after all, must be obedient to her husband, as to the head of the house. But things were different now. She was desperate. And she felt, too, that something huge and clammy and amorphous was coming between them, and it had to be driven off somehow. She believed that if the problem was hers then maybe steps could be taken to rectify it.

Mark, she knew, would never agree to any of the IVF treatments that were around, though for herself she was feeling so desperate she was beginning to consider anything. Yet it occurred to her that if it was simply a matter of something like blocked tubes then the doctors could unblock them, surely, and everything would be OK. So she had the tests, and Dr Forrest had told her, with a huge smile, that everything was fine, and that there was absolutely no reason at all why she should not conceive that very day. Pippa's face had fallen. This was not what she had wanted to hear at all. She wanted remedies, not assurance. And then Dr Forrest had said gently, 'Maybe your husband has a problem . . .' which was what had provoked the angry exchange this morning over breakfast.

The tests would be just for reassurance really, she had explained, because the doctor had said that sometimes just knowing everything was all right helped a couple to relax so that conception could take place. Somehow, in the doctor's surgery, it had all sounded so very reasonable, but Mark had hit the roof.

'Do you really mean to say you went behind my back?' he demanded through clenched teeth.

Pippa swallowed. 'It wasn't behind your back,' she replied. 'I just wanted to know if there was anything wrong.'

'So that you could put the blame on me!'

'No,' she protested. 'It wasn't like that at all. I just want us to have a child. And they're making such marvellous advances these days . . . Lots of couples have this kind of problem. The doctor explained . . . It's just giving a little bit of help.'

Mark's eyes blazed. 'You know I don't agree with that kind of thing.'

'But it may not be "that kind of thing"! I'm not suggesting we have IVF. But they may be able to do something like boosting your sperm count.'

He glared at her as if she had just given voice to some kind of obscenity – which was what had finally provoked his total refusal to discuss the matter any more. Now, pushing away his half-eaten bowl of cereal, he said frostily, 'I'm going to be out all day. I have a meeting of the anti-lottery campaign this morning, and this afternoon I'm going to pick up Tom from the airport. I thought I'd bring him back here tonight.'

She flushed angrily but, with an immense effort of will, managed to bite back the retort that sprang to her lips. 'You never said you were bringing Tom back here,' she said levelly.

Mark looked at her reproachfully. 'We need to discuss the mission he's going to be doing here next weekend,' he said. 'He's flying into Heathrow this afternoon from the States. Then he's up to Blackpool tomorrow. This is the only opportunity we'll get. It makes sense for him to stay here overnight. Besides which, I want him to meet Canon Brierly – I've managed to get him on to the anti-lottery committee, and I think he and Tom will hit it off.'

Pippa swallowed. 'I'm sure you're right,' she said. 'But I do think you could have mentioned that you were planning on inviting him back tonight.'

Mark contrived to look injured; no great feat at that precise moment. 'I'm sure I mentioned three weeks ago that he'd probably stay over tonight.'

'No you didn't.'

They glared at each other and, once again, Pippa's heart sank. At last Mark said, 'Am I to take it you don't want Tom to come here?'

Defeated, she looked down. 'No, of course not,' she muttered. 'I'd just like a bit of warning, that's all.' Her mind leapt ahead to the empty fridge. She would need to go shopping now, she realised, and she had promised Maggie, the editor of the parish magazine, that she would help assemble that month's contributions in the afternoon. Damn, she thought furiously; her carefully planned day had once again been upended. She would have to shop this morning, do the magazine in the afternoon, then dash back before five to get on a meal and sort out the guest room. Somehow she would have to tidy the lounge and kitchen too, because they both looked as if a bomb had hit them after the inroads of the parish steering group the night before.

Mark pushed back his chair and rose to his feet. 'Good,' he said, 'we should be back about six then. We'll need to eat straightaway because Canon Brierly's coming round about half seven. Then we're going on to this meeting over at St Peter's to discuss the deanery response to the commemoration plaque to that Indian chappie, Sri Sugnam. The council say they want to put it up on

4

the bell tower in the square. I think we've got a real battle on our hands here.'

Wooden-faced, Pippa stared after his retreating back as he disappeared through the door. Sometimes, these days, she thought she almost hated him. Still, there was no time to waste if she was to get through everything she had to do in time for Tom's arrival tonight. Chucking everything in the sink to be cleared up properly later, she hurried off down to the shops.

Tom Dragonar had been at college with Mark some fifteen years before. He had started off reading physics but, halfway through his course, had undergone a rather dramatic conversion and had confounded everyone with the announcement that he rather thought he was being called to serve God. Unlike Mark, who at the time was already reading theology and had decided on his future life's course, Tom had chosen not to go into the ordained ministry but to try and become a kind of media evangelist and youth guru instead. He had held a couple of appointments at churches in the north as a roving youth missioner and had then decided to try and go freelance, inspired by the example of a couple of American youth leaders that he had met on a three-month trip to the States. To Mark he was a figure of tremendous inspiration.

In recent years Mark had felt his own ministry was going nowhere. Indeed, he felt his life was going nowhere. He had never told Pippa, but he loathed the five rural parishes where he had ended up. He felt like some kind of peripatetic caretaker and, deep in his soul, he yearned for something a bit more ecclesiastically important – something, as he phrased it, at the cutting edge of faith. He knew he had a whole treasure house of untapped resources, but somehow they were never called upon and, casting around for someone or something to blame for all this non-utilisation, he began, rather unfairly, to feel it was all Pippa's fault. She was dragging him back, he decided. With her desire for security and her constant harping on about family life and their nonexistent children she had, from the moment they married, been like a millstone about his neck, preventing him from taking, like Tom, that giant and spectacular leap of faith. But when Mark was with Tom, he felt he was young again, with a whole realm of elusive potentiality spread at his feet.

Rather unfortunately, but perhaps unsurprisingly, Pippa, dimly aware of Mark's feelings, disliked Tom. She felt very guilty about this and did her best to disguise her feelings, but whenever he was around she felt her flesh crawl. It was not simply that Mark seemed to find him so wonderful, there seemed something rather oily about him, and insincere. She did not entirely trust him.

She was not thinking about Tom, however, as she dashed around the supermarket. Her thoughts were still on Mark and the stormy state of their marriage. As she banged the trolley viciously down the side aisle, looking vainly for tomato puree, resentment boiled afresh in her blood. He had not told her of Tom's visit, she was sure of it. She never forgot things like that. She was efficient. But what really rankled was Mark's utter casualness. As Pippa saw it, he had simply delivered his requirements for the day and then announced that he was off, as if she was no more than the hired help. Sri Sugnam indeed! She flung a bag of sugar into the trolley and had the satisfaction of seeing an assistant jump in surprise. The anti-lottery campaign! A packet of coffee followed the sugar, and the assistant stared at her. Pippa ignored her.

It occurred to her, not for the first time, that this was all Mark ever did now. Good causes and committees! But what good did it all do? she demanded of herself furiously. At the end of the day, would the people he was supposed to be looking after know God any better? Was it going to add numbers to his dwindling flock? She was so angry that, not looking where she was going, she banged up hard against a small box-like contraption jutting out into the aisle.

'Damn!' said Pippa. The trolley leapt back and gave her shin a nasty crack, as if in revenge for having been so badly driven. Aggrieved, Pippa looked at the unwitting cause of the accident. The thing really should not have been there. In fact it had *not* been there the last time she had been in. And feeling fully justified indignation at having at long last an external cause for her rage, she peered at the obstruction more closely.

She discovered it was a small counter for filling out lottery tickets. On a panel at the top was a long list of instructions and then, immediately underneath, a small ledge with unmarked forms packed neatly into two compartments. Pick six numbers, she read. Place a heavy vertical mark in each chosen box number.

A little demon seemed to materialise at Pippa's side. 'Why not?' it inquired.

Pippa did not need much urging. She was still seething from her encounter over the breakfast table, and it seemed to her now that buying a lottery ticket would be the perfect revenge. Not thinking, she picked up the pen lying invitingly in front of her, and resolutely pulled out a form. She found herself staring at neat boxes of red numbers, and her mind went blank. Which ones should she choose? And then inspiration struck. She would choose number one, because there was one God; three, because there were three persons in the Trinity; seven for the seven churches of Asia addressed in Revelation; twelve for the twelve apostles; thirty because that was the age of Jesus when he began his ministry, and ... She hesitated, caught between thirty-three, Jesus's age when he died, and forty, the number of

6

years the Israelites spent in the wilderness and the duration of Jesus's temptations.

Her hesitation lasted only a minute and then, very deliberately, she crossed through the forty. Long tribulation and hardship seemed, somehow, fitting. Then, without giving herself time to think, she went straight over to the desk and paid her pound.

'Didn't think you'd ever buy a lottery ticket,' remarked the girl, who did not go to church but nevertheless recognised Pippa. 'Thought you lot all disapproved.'

Pippa had the grace to blush. 'We simply condemn the misuse,' she said defensively.

The girl looked unconvinced. 'Well, good luck anyway,' she said. 'I won ten pounds a couple of months back.'

Perversely, Pippa felt awful the whole way home. She felt as if she had committed some fundamental act of betrayal, whether against Mark or against God she was unsure. But she comforted herself with the thought that she would never do it again, and after all, Mark need never know – which just left God to worry about. Unlike Mark, however, who was always so certain about what he believed, Pippa was not sure whether the lottery was a sin or not. She certainly disagreed with the size of the prizes, and she knew that some people spent money they neither could nor should afford, but she was unsure whether or not the lottery in itself was wrong.

She was still pondering this question as she turned into the vicarage drive and immediately spotted Elaine Dufrayn, the wife of one of the churchwardens, sitting crying on the front doorstep. 'Elaine, what's wrong?' she exclaimed.

Elaine sniffled and then, registering who it was, let out a howl. 'Everything!' she announced tragically.

Elaine was one of those confident, very smart women who always filled Pippa with secret dread. The two of them were about the same age but, unlike Pippa, Elaine always looked so neat and capable, with everything in exactly the right place. Her husband worked as an investment banker in London and they had a lifestyle to match. Yet what most aroused Pippa's envy was not Elaine's so obviously affluent and successful life but her two boys of eleven and thirteen.

Quickly Pippa ushered her into the kitchen and sat her down in front of a cup of steaming coffee. Elaine ignored it. 'I'm so sorry,' she said, 'I don't want to be a nuisance, but I just wanted to talk to you.' She began to cry again, and a long streak of mascara trickled down her cheeks.

'You're not a nuisance,' said Pippa robustly, 'but what's wrong? Has there been an accident or something?'

Elaine shook her head and brushed a hand across her eyes, but it was some minutes before she could speak. 'Nothing like that.' A fresh paroxysm of crying followed this announcement, and Pippa waited quietly till she could go on. 'It's Paul!' Elaine brought out at last. She gave a loud sniff and looked down at her hands, now clenched tightly together in her lap as if she dare not let them go. 'He's having an affair.'

Pippa gaped. In the wake of this pronouncement, the ticking of the hall clock sounded inordinately loud and the whole house seemed to freeze in shocked disbelief. A picture of Paul, long, loose-limbed and genial, sprang unbidden to her mind. In the way of parishes, she and Mark did not have many friends in the villages. Mark had told her when they first married that it would be like that. They had to be available to everyone, he had explained. But Paul had seemed to be the exception to the rule for Mark. The banker had discovered, soon after their arrival, that Mark had a passion for golf, and so he had arranged for his membership at the local club at a much reduced rate. Mark could never have joined otherwise and he had been overjoyed. Since that time, they had played together regularly and a kind of male camaraderie had sprung up between them. Paul had always seemed outwardly to be a model of Christian virtue – always polite, a devoted family man, full of church plans.

Pippa felt absolutely floored. 'Surely not, Elaine,' she managed as the silence grew and she became aware of the other woman staring at her.

Elaine sprang to her feet. 'Oh, there's no mistake,' she said bitterly. 'I know exactly what you're thinking. The perfect Paul Dufrayn! But it's all a front. He's told me all about it. I even know her name. Melanie! I've even spoken to her.'

There was another silence as Pippa digested this. 'I don't know what to say,' she said at last. And then, 'Is he leaving you?'

Elaine's face contorted afresh. 'No,' she said, with such anger that Pippa involuntarily flinched. 'He cares too much about what people think – especially you and Mark! His plan, he says, is that we carry on living together – perfect Paul has to be part of a perfect couple! But our marriage as such is over. He says he wants carte blanche to carry on with Melanie. Little slag!' And then, after a short pause, she added, 'He's moved into the spare room.'

# Chapter Two

Mark was at Heathrow by three o'clock. Tom's plane was due in at twenty past, but in the event it was delayed by one and a half hours, and it was almost five thirty by the time Tom finally emerged through customs. 'Would you believe it?' he said irately as he pushed his way through the barrier. 'They searched my bags! I mean, what a nerve! Do I look like I'm a smuggler or something?'

Mark said nothing, but actually Tom did look rather odd. He had grown a droopy moustache and he had on an ice-cream coloured jacket and maroon trousers that had both seen better days. What really drew the eye, however, of seemingly everyone within a ten-yard radius was the floppy paisley hankie that dangled artistically from his top pocket. Tom, Mark remembered, had always had a rather questionable dress sense but in recent years this had grown even more bizarre as he attempted to cultivate what he called an 'accessible' style. By this he meant a style that would appeal to the young. Unfortunately, however, his hairline was receding, while his girth seemed to be increasing in direct proportion. This, combined with the rather battered looking Panama hat that he had pulled down low over his forehead, gave him the look of a distinctly dodgy art dealer. In itself this might have been all right, but Tom was always quick to assert that you had to be upfront with your faith and, in line with this belief, he was at this moment clutching an extremely large Bible across his chest like some kind of talisman. All in all, Mark was not at all surprised that he had been stopped.

He seized Tom's bag. 'You're terribly late,' he said, rather curtly. 'Pippa's expecting us for six.'

Pippa may have been expecting them for six, but by ten to she was in a positive frenzy, chucking food into the oven and praying they would be late. Elaine had stopped for a good two hours, and throughout that time she had cried continuously. By the time she finally left, her face had looked like some kind of ravaged moonscape.

Melanie worked in the bank, Elaine had explained between sobs. She was twenty-three, and obviously flattered by the attentions of her boss. It had all started a couple of months back. Elaine confided that she had suddenly realised that Paul seemed to be working all the time. He never seemed to get back before eleven at night and when she asked him where he had been he would never say, brushing her aside with muttered excuses about increased workload and the need to maintain his position. He had even, she said, made her feel guilty by implying that his job was under threat and that he needed to work such long hours in order to stay on top; and that he was only doing it for her and the boys.

Pippa was appalled and instantly thought about Mark.

One morning, Elaine went on, she discovered old theatre tickets in the pocket of a suit that she was taking to the cleaners for him, and something in her knew instantly. She stayed up for him that night and confronted him as soon as he came in. To her utter devastation, he immediately confessed. At least, she amended, he did not exactly confess, because he showed not the slightest trace of remorse. He simply admitted that he had taken his assistant, Melanie, and that they had enjoyed several such outings in recent months.

But there was worse to come. It was not long after this, Elaine said, that the phone calls started. Paul was perfectly open about them and more recently he had even begun to phone Melanie back. A short time after that he had announced that, as far as he was concerned, the marriage was finished. But what really shocked Pippa was Elaine's casual revelation that Melanie was simply the latest in a long line. The only reason she was now getting so upset, Elaine confided, was because this time it seemed to be more serious and she had not the slightest idea what to do. Paul had always liked his bit on the side but before, she insisted, it had always seemed to help the marriage and he had been discreet. But now he had simply dropped all pretence in front of her and seemed to expect her simply to stand quietly by while he did whatever he pleased. Even the boys had noticed, she said.

Pippa was riveted. She found it hard to believe that she knew this man Elaine was talking about. This was Paul, she reminded herself, who regularly helped her organise the children's services for Mark, and who had so warmly praised Mark's scheme to set up a course of meetings on the enrichment of family life.

And then Elaine said slowly, 'Something similar did happen five years ago. He got obsessed with the wife of a colleague. She wasn't interested, of course, but he wouldn't leave her alone. He was always phoning her, buying her presents. It only stopped when her husband came round one weekend and they had a fight. Paul ended up with a black eye. It looked really funny!' She looked down, biting her lip and crying softly. 'It wasn't really funny. It almost ruined our marriage. I only stayed because of the kids. And Paul almost lost his job over it all. He was really scared for a while. I thought at one point he was going to have a breakdown, but he pulled through, with a lot of help – that I gave. But you know, Pippa,' she looked up suddenly, 'he really did begin to try after that. He really began to work at the marriage, and I thought it was all going to be different. And then you and Mark came, and you were so nice, and Paul became really involved with the church. It was around then that he became churchwarden, if you remember. I thought he'd turned over a new leaf!'

'Maybe it's just a phase,' said Pippa.

'Maybe.' Elaine looked at her mournfully, and Pippa wondered what she would do if she were in this position. Infidelity had never seriously occurred to her before.

'I can't leave him,' Elaine said. 'Not now. A lot's happened to me these last five years too. I don't particularly want to, but I really believe all that stuff in the Bible. And it says, doesn't it, marriage is for life.'

'Yes,' said Pippa, and she felt suddenly that it was a reminder to herself.

'That's why I spoke to Melanie,' Elaine went on. 'She phoned up one night and I answered. She wanted to speak to Paul of course, but I couldn't help myself. I asked her why she was doing it. I said Paul was happily married.' A shadow crossed her face, and then her mouth suddenly contorted and she gave a loud sob. 'Do you know what she said? She said I ought to talk to Paul, and then she laughed. She laughed at me.'

All Pippa had been able to think of doing was to pray with her, and shortly afterwards Elaine had left, sniffing bravely, and saying that she would cope. At the door, however, she had paused. 'Pippa,' she said solemnly, half turning, 'you've got to promise me you won't tell anyone. Please. Not even Mark.' Then, seeing Pippa's face, she explained, 'While it's all hidden away, there's hope. Paul's tremendously proud. He keeps up this front of being so good, and it matters to him. He couldn't bear it if people knew. If he thought they'd found out, that would be it. He'd leave. So promise me, please.'

And then she had gone, leaving Pippa feeling as if a tank had just rolled over her. She was so angry with Paul, she felt she could have hit him. After that, the day had somehow simply refused to get back on course. She had dutifully gone round to Maggie's house in the afternoon, and done her bit with the magazine, but then Maggie had wanted to talk too and, try as she might, she had been unable to tear herself away. Which was how, come quarter to six, she had still not managed to get the dinner in the oven.

For once, however, God seemed to hear her prayers. Mark and Tom did not arrive back until ten past seven, and by then she could say virtuously, 'Where on earth have you been? The dinner's all cooked!'

Mark, still smarting from the morning's exchange, sniffed disdainfully. 'No time to eat now,' he announced. 'Canon Brierly will be here in a minute, and then we've got to go. We'll eat later.' He did not add, 'Will that be all right? Will the food keep?' and Pippa's hackles rose. But Mark did not notice. He had taken the chance to have a moan on the long journey back and was now feeling rather good. 'She's saying it's my fault!' he had spluttered to Tom. 'She went and had tests without asking me!'

Outrage had almost choked him at this point and Tom had looked at him sideways. Whatever Pippa felt about him, he actually liked her. He always had, even at university when Mark had first started going out with her. He was not married himself, but he liked women, especially pretty ones, and Pippa was, undeniably, very pretty. He could not understand why Mark was making so much fuss. 'Perhaps you should do as she asks,' he said carefully.

Mark was so astounded, he almost drove off the road. 'You can't be serious?' he spluttered.

'I don't see that a chat with the doctor can hurt,' said Tom reasonably.

Mark was furious. 'She's trying to say it's all my fault. She'll be wanting to do something next. Donor insemination or something! I wouldn't put anything past her.'

'I think you're maybe being a bit unfair,' said Tom mildly. 'You could just talk to her about it, after all.'

Mark appeared not to hear him. 'There is absolutely nothing wrong,' he said, staring woodenly ahead through the windscreen. 'It has simply not been God's timing yet. I will not be humiliated by undergoing a lot of irrelevant and highly offensive tests!'

'Quite,' said Tom drily.

By the time they got home, Mark had convinced himself that he was entirely right and that Pippa was not only wrong, but in imminent danger of spiritual collapse. She had to be, because otherwise she would be happy to leave the matter in the hands of God. A warm glow of self-righteousness had engulfed him. He would talk to her later, he decided, as Tom had suggested. He would tell her how wrong she was.

Pippa, detecting his smug self-satisfaction, felt even more furious. A fact noted by Tom, who took the opportunity to give her a big hug and planted a sloppy kiss on her cheek. 'Pippa!' he said. 'Looking wonderful as ever.'

Pippa restrained herself, with difficulty, from pushing him away. She looked at him tartly, but he only smiled at her and gave her another hug. 'You do,' he said. 'Absolutely gorgeous!'

Something in his manner alerted Mark, and he looked at his wife suspiciously. Not for the first time he wondered if Pippa dressed in a way that was entirely suitable for a vicar's wife. She was quite tall and slender, with long red-gold hair, and she always wore clothes that he was sure other vicar's wives would not. It was not that she spent a lot of money on clothes. They could not have afforded it anyway. But somehow she always contrived to look a little bit racy. Alluring, Tom had once called her. Mark sniffed. Something else to speak to her about. At that moment, however, they were mercifully interrupted by the arrival of Canon Brierly.

By the time they left, some five minutes later, Pippa could have wept with frustration. She had wanted desperately to voice just a tiny bit of the concern she was feeling about Elaine as they sat over dinner. She had thought that she could put out the pie she had made and then casually drop into the conversation that Elaine had been round earlier, and that she had seemed a bit down. She had absolutely no intention of breaking the promise she had made but she thought that perhaps just a few words would alert Mark to the fact that something was wrong. He might then, she reasoned, as a part of his pastoral concern, mention the fact to Paul. And perhaps that would be enough to end the affair, without anyone ever being the wiser. She sighed. That would have to wait now till Mark and Tom returned.

Fate, however, remained perverse. When they finally got back, just after ten, they still had Canon Brierly in tow. 'There'll be enough for Michael, won't there?' Mark said airily. 'He hasn't eaten yet tonight either, so I said to come on back here and have something with us.'

Pippa inwardly seethed but pinned a smile to her face. 'Of course,' she said. Still smiling, she dished out three pieces of pie and then sat them all down at the dining room table, determined, if at all possible, to raise the topic of Elaine. The opportunity did not arise.

'So kind,' said Canon Brierly, taking the plate from her hand. 'I'm not married myself, you see, and I'm afraid it would just have been bread and cheese again tonight, had it not been for your husband's kind invitation.' He smiled at her gently. He was in his fifties, with grey hair and eyes that seemed to see a lot more than what was in front of them. Pippa felt ashamed of herself. 'It's perfectly all right,' she said sincerely. 'We can't have senior members of the clergy starving to death.'

Tom was watching her throughout this exchange, a curious little smile playing about his mouth, and Pippa felt suddenly uncomfortable.

'We're really pleased you're giving your support to the lottery group, Michael,' said Mark, sitting opposite him.

13

Canon Brierly nodded, in the act of raising a forkful of pie to his mouth. 'Not at all,' he replied equably. 'It's totally immoral. People are spending far too much each week, and with very little chance of winning. In fact the odds must be infinitesimal, when you think about it, but it is so addictive. And it's decimating the giving to charity. Many now are facing real financial hardship. And it's all happened since the lottery began.' There was a small silence, and then he went on reflectively, 'But the worst problem of all, I believe, is that it's encouraging a spirit of covetousness and greed, and that has got to be bad, both for the individual and for society.'

Pippa, in the act of spooning out more broccoli, was extremely conscious of the ticket in the front compartment of her purse upstairs. In spite of herself, she blushed. Tom noticed. Drat the man, she thought, catching his look. He seemed to be staring at her all the time tonight, and that knowing little smile was driving her mad.

To her intense chagrin Tom smiled at her even more broadly. 'It's families that are the real victims, aren't they, Pippa?' he said, addressing her directly. 'You know what I mean. Wives and,' he gave the slightest pause, 'mothers.'

Unable to help herself, she glared at him, and when she went out into the kitchen, he followed her. 'You look tired,' he remarked, watching her as she began to put things away.

She gave him a quick glance of irritation and then shrugged. 'It's been a long day.'

'So I understand from Mark.'

Pippa, transferring some butter back to the fridge, froze. 'What do you mean?' she asked carefully.

Tom came further into the room and leant up against the kitchen table. A horrible feeling of dread trickled down Pippa's spine. 'What do you mean?' she said again distinctly.

Maddeningly, Tom pursed his lips and looked down. 'Only that Mark said you were having some problems . . . He said that you'd had a bit of a row this morning.'

Pippa could scarcely believe her ears. She felt outraged. From the other room she could hear the low murmur of Canon Brierly and Mark's voices. The words 'moral irresponsibility' floated through to her and then a low laugh from Mark. At that moment, she felt she could have killed him. How dare he talk about their personal problems to Tom like that. She felt violated. Tom, however, seemed oblivious. Very carefully he pushed the kitchen door quietly to with his foot, and then came forward till he was standing directly in front of her, a look of painful concern on his face. 'You can always talk to me, you know, Pippa,' he said softly. 'I'm not just Mark's friend.' She was so outraged she could have choked, but the next moment,

14

to her complete and utter astonishment, Tom raised a hand and laid it caressingly against her cheek. 'I'd like to help you, if I can.'

At Tom's touch Pippa went rigid and then just stood there stupidly, unable to think of anything to say or do. She was so taken aback she just wanted him to go and the next moment, as if divining her thoughts, Tom did, rather abruptly.

If Pippa had not been so intensely angry she would have laughed, but amusement was an emotion that felt rather alien to her at that moment and instead she collapsed shaking against the fridge door, her brain whirling. Her first conscious thought was positive fury that Tom had dared touch her like that. Involuntarily, her hand went to her face. It had all happened so quickly, she wondered suddenly if she had imagined it. But she could still feel her skin tingling where his fingers had been and she felt a fresh burst of anger, not against Tom but against Mark. It was all his fault. These stupid men! He had complained to Tom and asked him to have a word with her, make her see sense, and now here they were, treating her like a child. Sympathy but firm handling! She could even imagine Mark's voice. He always said something like that when faced with a particularly knotty pastoral problem. The theory was fine. But Tom, like so many men, had got it horribly wrong. He had misjudged it with his heavy-handed blundering, and the result was they had both ended up embarrassed.

She wondered what exactly Mark had confided to Tom. Had he gone so far as to share the details of their ailing sex life? She would not put anything past him. And in that instant, she felt as if something precious had been contaminated.

'Oh God,' she said aloud. 'This simply isn't fair!'

Outside, in the hallway, Tom was also reeling from the encounter. He had not actually intended to touch Pippa at all. It had simply seemed to him that to offer her support now was the Christian thing to do. But somehow, standing beside her in the kitchen, the full force of the attraction he felt had surged up and throttled him, and he had been seized by a quite irrational desire to be close to her. It had been all he could do to restrain himself from folding her in his arms then and there. But then he had seen the shocked expression on her face and he had been so unnerved that he had fled.

As he stood in the hall, however, catching his breath, it came to him that this analysis of his feelings was actually mistaken. What he had just experienced was not carnal desire (which he had thought it was), but a movement of the Spirit. At least, he thought, determined now to be scrupulously honest, he had experienced carnal desire, and he had quite properly felt guilty about this, but the underlying reality had actually been a surge of God's love towards Pippa, who was obviously suffering. His mistake had been to get diverted by his own feelings, and the proper course of action now was clearly to purge all thoughts of lust towards Pippa from his mind and try and help her in the pure light of God's love.

After this, Tom felt better. Noble even. His two old friends were quite clearly going through a very difficult time and would need a lot of help if they were to come through the crisis unscathed. Tom knew he had to try and give that help. It was the Christian thing to do. He knew, too, that he could only give that help if he was on hand.

He gnawed at his moustache, pondering the dilemma, and came to an abrupt decision. He was due to lead the parish youth mission at St Saviour's in a week's time anyway. So then . . . He would juggle his timetable round so that he could stay at St Saviour's throughout the coming week. And that way, maybe, just maybe, he could help them get this frightful mess they seemed to have got themselves into sorted out.

Tom announced his changed plans to Mark the following day. 'Look here,' he said, 'I know I've got to go up to Blackpool today but, looking at my diary, I find I could easily come back on Saturday and base myself here next week, if you think that would be helpful. That way we could give a lot more thought to this mission.'

Mark looked at him gratefully. He had actually been dreading being alone in the house with Pippa. He knew she would try and talk to him again and, despite all his bombast when with Tom, he felt scared. 'Marvellous, Tom,' he said, with genuine enthusiasm. 'And tell you what, do you fancy a game of golf on Saturday? I'm doing a round with Paul, our churchwarden, in the morning. He's a nice chap. You'll like him. He won't mind, and I've got an old set of clubs you can borrow if you want.'

# Chapter Three

Spring had come late this year and, even now, it seemed uncertain whether or not actually to commit itself to staying around. True, the daffodils were poking their heads through the earth and there had been a slight rise in temperature, but so far the actual flowers had resolutely refused to emerge. They stood in the gardens and hedgerows like so many rows of frozen green sentinels, nodding their heads in the breeze as they waited for the weather to change.

Paul Dufrayn, coming out into his garden early on Saturday morning, felt he could detect a definite stirring. The air was more mellow, and overhead the clouds spread like a kind of thin white haze, barely covering an azure sky. It looked as if it might be warm later, he thought. But for the present it was still very cold, and he found himself shivering as he advanced slowly out to inspect his domain.

Behind him the old thatched farmhouse where he and Elaine lived sprawled like some rambling but immoveable outcrop of the land. It was a large old house, very solid, and with its rough-hewn, laburnum-covered walls and steeply sloping roof, indescribably pretty. Paul had spent a lot of money on Gentillesse. Everyone said it was money well spent, but although they had been here all of ten years now, Paul still felt alien, like some kind of passing guest that the house put up with but would never acknowledge as its own. It was different for Elaine, he thought. She spent all her time down there in Little Wakenham and had worked hard at becoming part of the community. But somehow he always felt like a visitor. He would have liked to move back to London, but Elaine would not hear of it. And at the thought of his wife's obstinacy, his face twisted and he kicked viciously at the grass.

Truth to tell, Paul was still smarting from the scene he had had with Elaine the night before. She had dared give him an ultimatum – an extremely loud ultimatum which he was petrified had been heard the length of the lane. 'That slut Melanie, or me!' she had screamed. 'Choose!' But Paul was not ready for that yet. He was unsure what he wanted. All he knew was that there was a great space of emptiness at the centre of his life that nothing seemed able to fill. Five years ago, and after his disastrous non-affair with Rhona, he had thought that the gap might be God and that if he 'got religion', as he put it, everything would come right; that remote being who he vaguely felt inhabited some nether part of the sky would leap gratefully in and fill the void. But though he had thrown himself into church life with gusto, that had not happened. God, the supreme deity, had remained as elusive as ever. And lately nothing seemed to go right. His work bored him. Elaine seemed simply to regard him as an open chequebook and, to cap it all, he had recently lost a lot of money (which he had not told his wife about) on an ill-judged gamble on the Stock Exchange. In fact, taken all together, it felt to Paul as if his life had atrophied and God was simply looking the other way.

Paul hunched his shoulders and gave the grass another kick. It was at that moment that he became aware of the boots. They were protruding from under the hedge, battered toes pointing defiantly up towards the sky. As far as he could tell, they seemed to be inhabited. A sense of outrage swept over him. Someone was lying under his hedge. Without thinking, he bent down and gave a sharp tweak.

'Hey, watch it!' came an enraged cry. The next moment there was a loud rustling and grunting, and then a black head poked itself through the leaves. Paul almost fainted. The darkly gleaming face staring up at him was surrounded by wild dreadlocks, and on top of the young man's head was perched what looked suspiciously like a brightly coloured knitted tea cosy. 'There's no call to do that,' said the young man in a broad Liverpudlian accent. 'I'm not hurting nuthin'!'

'Who on earth are you?' said Paul.

The young man looked at him. 'Stripe,' he answered.

'Pardon?' Paul wondered if he had misheard, or if this was some abstruse term of abuse.

'Stripe,' repeated the young man obligingly. 'I said me name's Stripe.'

'Really?' Paul stared at him nonplussed. Apart from annoyance at having been disturbed, the young man gave every appearance of feeling there was absolutely nothing wrong at being found in his present position. 'Well, what are you doing under my hedge?' said Paul at last.

Stripe looked at him measuringly. 'Well, if you want the truth,' he said, 'I'm on the run. There's some real heavies after me. They said I welshed on a deal. It's all lies. But I had to get away.'

Paul had the distinct feeling he was losing control of this conversation. 'Come out,' he said abruptly. 'I can't talk to you under there.'

Stripe obligingly wriggled his way out and stood up. He was about six foot three, very obviously of West Indian origin, and wore tattered black jeans and a battered denim jacket. 'Where are you from?' asked Paul helplessly. 'How did you get here?'

'Liverpool,' said the young man. 'I'm from Liverpool. I'm a musician.'

He said this as if it explained everything, and Paul gaped at him. Whoever this young man was, he decided, he did not want him in his garden. He sounded like trouble. There were the boys to think of. 'Well, you can't stay here,' he said at last. 'This is private property. You're trespassing.'

'I've not got nowhere to go,' said Stripe. 'I was only having a kip.'

'Not under my hedge,' said Paul firmly.

Stripe looked at him. 'Well, could y'at least give us some brekkie?'

All of Mark's pontificating about homelessness and the treatment of those in need came back to Paul. In spite of himself, he felt guilty. 'Oh, I suppose so,' he said tetchily, half turning. 'Come on up to the back door.' Then, as an afterthought, he flung over his shoulder, 'But I don't want you inside.'

When Paul pushed his way into the kitchen he found Elaine quietly crying into the toaster. Sebastian and Harry were ignoring her, riveted by a cartoon on the TV. 'There's a down-and-out outside,' said Paul abruptly. 'Give him some breakfast, Elaine. Then we'll tell him to push off.'

The boys looked round, their attention immediately caught. 'What do you mean, a down-and-out, Dad?' inquired Sebastian. 'Where's he come from?'

'I found him under the hedge,' said Paul, and then, as they looked as if they were both about to leap up to go and see, 'Stay inside, both of you. No need to make a fuss.'

But it was too late. Both the children had catapulted through the door. 'Gosh!' said Harry, pulling up short as he took in the full glory of Stripe, standing patiently waiting just inside the yard. 'Who are you?'

'Stripe,' said Stripe. 'Watcha!'

When Paul came out five minutes later, bearing a mug of steaming coffee and warmed rolls and jam, Stripe was sitting on a low stone wall with the two boys, holding forth about something that, quite obviously, had got them both enthralled. 'Dad,' said Sebastian breathlessly, 'Stripe plays in a band. He's made a record.' Paul grunted. 'He says he'll send us a tape.'

'How interesting.' Paul smiled coldly and then, feeling something more was required, added, 'So what's the name of this group of yours?'

Strike accepted the food gratefully. 'Thanks, man,' he said, 'I haven't eaten in two days.' He bit voraciously into one of the rolls, tearing at it with his teeth.

Harry sniggered. 'Mummy says we mustn't eat like that. She says we've got to break it first and then butter it.'

Stripe continued to munch. 'Quite right,' he agreed. 'Manners!' He slurped some coffee loudly and then turned back to Paul. 'We're called Dreadlocks.'

'Gosh,' said Sebastian, round-eyed. His vocabulary appeared to have become severely limited. 'Is that because of your hair?'

'Yeah. We're into reggae, garage, that kinduv stuff.'

This was utterly meaningless to Paul, but the boys were obviously tremendously impressed. 'Just eat up,' he said uneasily. He did not add, 'And then go!' but he was thinking it, and Stripe obviously divined his thoughts. He smiled.

'Don't worry,' he said equably, 'I won't be around long. I've got things of me own t' sort.'

Back at the rectory, life was not all sweetness and light either. Pippa had finally heard the news of Tom's projected early return late the previous night and, predictably, had almost hit the roof. Mark had been putting off telling her for as long as possible. In fact, he had been putting off talking to her at all as long as possible, and had contrived to be out of the house all day. But by Friday night the conversation could be avoided no longer because Tom had said he would be with them by ten on Saturday morning.

Pippa's reactions entirely lived up to Mark's expectations. 'Don't keep doing this!' she shouted at him. 'Don't just keep springing people on me and expecting it to be all right! I need some notice.'

'But I am giving you notice,' he said defensively. 'I'm telling you now. He doesn't get back here till tomorrow.'

Very ostentatiously Pippa looked at her watch. 'It's eleven fifteen,' she announced sarcastically. 'Even Seven Eleven is shut now. What am I supposed to do?'

It had been on the tip of Mark's tongue to say 'Go to bed' and smile with false concern, but he had decided that that would perhaps be unwise and so instead he had hung his head. Pippa continued to stare at him balefully for another minute, during which time Mark prayed devoutly that that would be it, and then she said, 'I've been wanting to talk to you all day.'

'Oh Lord, no!' Mark said, before he could help himself. 'Not now. It's too late. We'll discuss it tomorrow.' And before Pippa could say another word, he bolted into the study and shut the door. Pippa sat down heavily on the nearest chair and burst into tears.

She had spent the most awful night. Mark had come up to bed

over an hour later, and had then pointedly ignored her. This in turn had made her feel even more angry, and she had spent the entire night tossing and turning, and wondering grimly whether to kick him out of bed in revenge. She had not, and when she got up the following morning she was rewarded by a terrible headache. Black coffee and two aspirins had done nothing to help and, when the doorbell rang just before ten, she went to answer it feeling absolutely dreadful. She found herself confronted not by Tom but by Paul. He looked strained.

'Can Mark come?' he said without preamble. 'We've got a problem.'

Pippa's heart transferred itself to her mouth. 'Elaine?' she asked.

Paul shook his head. 'No,' he said, 'far worse. I think we've been invaded by a creature from another planet.'

When Mark heard all the details about Stripe, he immediately agreed to go back with Paul to Gentillesse and see what he could do to help. Tom, who had arrived by now, said that he would go too. Mark took the golf clubs with him. 'Sympathetic but firm,' Pippa heard him saying as they went out through the front door.

An hour later Elaine phoned. 'Oh Pippa, you've no idea,' she wailed, 'we're having the most dreadful time!'

'What's happening?' Pippa asked curiously.

'He won't go,' said Elaine. 'He said he's going to squat in the flat over the garage.'

'Who?' said Pippa incredulously. 'This young man Stripe? He can't do that. How does he know about the flat anyway?'

'The boys told him. They say they want him to stay. They gave him the keys. They're all in there now!'

Pippa digested this. 'What's Paul doing about it?'

'Nothing! He's gone off to play golf with Mark and Tom.' Elaine sounded bitter. 'He said a lot before he left, of course. He said he wanted him out by the time they got back. He said he'd call the police. But then he just went and left it all to me! Men!'

'Yes,' agreed Pippa feelingly.

There was a tearful sniff from Elaine at the other end, and then she said, 'Pippa? You couldn't come round, could you? I don't know what to do . . . I can't cope.'

By the time Pippa got there, the sound of loud tribal music was pounding out from over the garage. The windows of the flat were open, and the air seemed to throb. 'It's been like that for the last hour,' screamed Elaine, trying desperately to make herself heard above the din. 'Harry took his music centre over. It's very powerful!'

'Yes!' shouted back Pippa. 'I can tell!'

Together they advanced on the garage, and Elaine hammered

21

on the door. 'Come down!' she screamed. 'Immediately! Open this door!'

'One woman, one way . . .' wailed the music.

Over the hedge Pippa could see the affronted face of Colonel Duke, the Dufrayns' neighbour. She smiled apologetically. Elaine hammered on the door with both fists, and then added a kick for good measure. 'Open this bloody door!' she shouted.

The music was turned off. In the sudden silence, Elaine looked stunned. Then there was a sound of footsteps coming leisurely down the stairs, and the door was drawn slowly back. 'Wot's up?' said Stripe. 'D'ye want me?'

Pippa goggled. She had never seen so exotic a creature as Stripe in the village of Little Wakenham before. Come to think of it, she had never seen so exotic a creature as Stripe anywhere. He looked as if he ought to be wandering down some Caribbean beach, propositioning the tourists. Behind him she could see Sebastian and Harry, their faces flushed with what looked like a mixture of excitement and pride. She became aware of Stripe staring at her. 'Hi,' he said pointedly. 'Who are you then?'

'She's the vicar's wife,' said Elaine tartly. 'Now come out of there, young man. We want to talk to you.'

Stripe looked at her consideringly, and then turned back to Pippa. 'OK,' he agreed.

Slowly he came out into the garden. 'You can't stay,' squeaked Elaine, as soon as he was out of the door. 'You must see that. You can't just take over our property.'

Stripe looked at Sebastian and Harry. 'They invited me,' he said laconically. 'They said it was empty and that I could hang out for a while.'

'But you can't!' again squeaked Elaine.

'Why not, Mummy?' piped up Sebastian. 'It is empty, and the vicar's always going on about how we ought to share.'

'Be quiet, Sebastian!' snapped Elaine. She turned imploring eyes back to Stripe. 'Please, we don't want to get nasty about this, do we?'

He ignored her. 'What's your name then?' he asked Pippa.

'Pippa,' said Pippa.

'I'm Stripe. How d'ye do.' He held out his hand and, in spite of herself, Pippa smiled. She felt he was playing a game with them.

'You really ought to go, you know,' she said. 'It's not fair otherwise.'

He continued to stare at her. 'There's some men after me,' he said at last. 'I just want somewhere to 'ang out for a few days.'

'Heaven help us!' said Elaine. She looked from one to the other of them and came to a sudden decision. 'Look, come into the

22

kitchen and have some coffee, and let's discuss this like rational human beings.'

Out on the golf course the three men were enjoying their round of golf. Paul was in no doubt that Stripe would be gone by the time they returned home because as they had left he had shouted up to the young man, in no uncertain terms, that if the situation remained unchanged by the time they got back, he was going to phone the police. The music had started up some fifty seconds later but he did not know that; by then, he, Mark and Tom had left. Now, as Mark teed off, he was saying, 'Firm handling. That's what these types need.'

'Ye-es,' temporised Tom. He was acutely aware that of the three of them only he, as a youth missioner, had any experience of working with the minority group to which Stripe belonged, and he was keen now to parade his expertise. 'You know, young people really do respond to this kind of thing.' He turned to Paul. 'Look at your two kids. They were absolutely captivated by Stripe. He's an anti-authority figure for them. And there's a tremendous pull in music.'

Paul looked at him drily. 'Well, I'd just like him to go and exercise his pull somewhere else.'

All three stared down the fairway as Mark's ball sailed into the air and then disappeared into a clump of trees. 'Blast!' said Mark.

'Bad luck, old boy,' said Paul.

But Tom was not to be deflected. 'You know,' he said, 'if we had someone like that who was a Christian, we could do enormous good. He speaks to the kids. We've seen that already. His music attracts them . . . Just think, if that was combined with evangelism! Tremendous!' He waved a club in the air. 'Can you imagine, an evangelistic concert!'

'I imagine,' said Paul witheringly, 'that it would be extremely expensive. Also we have the slight problem that young men like Stripe are very rarely Christians.'

A dreamy look had settled on Tom's face. 'If we could convert him,' he persisted. 'And if we had the money . . .'

Mark snorted. 'Not very likely.' He felt depressed by all this talk of converting people. He had never actually converted anyone in his life. 'Come on, Tom,' he said wearily. 'Your shot. Get a move on!'

Stripe's whole attention was fixed on Pippa. He explained in great detail that he had been set up by heavies who insisted that he had sold them some bad crack. At this point Elaine banished the boys. Stripe seemed hardly to notice. It had actually been the drummer,

23

he said, not him at all. But there had been a lot of confusion between them and, overall, he had thought it wiser to disappear for a time. Particularly, he added reflectively, as somebody had turned over his flat in Toxteth and set fire to it. Pippa could only stare at him fascinated. Elaine asked briskly how long he thought it would be necessary to lie low. Only a few days, he assured them. The drummer, he knew, had fled back to Barbados. It could only be a matter of time before the whole truth came out, and then he could go back.

'All right, you can stay for one week,' Elaine said firmly. 'During that time you are not to play loud music, and you are not to talk to the boys about any of this. For my part I will not tell the police that you're here. I'm sure,' she added grimly, 'that whatever you say, you would prefer them not to be involved. And the condition is that at the end of that time you leave *without any trouble*.'

Stripe grinned. It was not a particularly nice grin. 'OK,' he agreed, 'you've got a deal.' He turned back to Pippa. 'Do you really believe all this God lark?'

Paul could hardly contain his anger. 'She said he could bloody stay,' he spat angrily into the phone. He was talking to Melanie. 'The woman's an idiot! We'll never get him out like this.'

Melanie sympathised, but she was becoming bored with the topic of Elaine. 'Never mind,' she urged, 'let's talk about something else.'

Paul decided she was a bit dim. He could not even think, let alone talk, about anything else. He was consumed with rage. Elaine, he felt, had let him down. In fact, it had even crossed his mind that she had done it to spite him. Unwisely, he said as much to Melanie, who responded by getting really angry.

'I don't care about your sodding wife!' she snapped. 'Why do we always have to talk about her?'

'We don't,' said Paul, affronted.

'Yes, we do. It's all Elaine this and Elaine that. I'm fed up with hearing about Elaine!'

Paul digested this. 'I'm sorry,' he said.

Melanie was instantly mollified. 'I just want to talk about us,' she said. 'I've really missed you this weekend.'

'I couldn't get away.'

'You promise that next weekend I'll come on that trip to Milan?'

Paul squirmed. 'Yes of course,' he hissed. 'But watch what you're saying. She may be listening on the other phone. She doesn't know about it yet.'

It occurred to Melanie that yet again they were talking about Elaine, but she restrained herself from making any comment. He had given his word now, and she really wanted to be a part of the trip to Milan. She had been uncertain whether or not she was going to be allowed to go – it was bank business certainly, but it was not really her area, so there was no obvious reason why she should be included. But now he had said yes. She hugged herself in delight. 'You angel,' she cooed. 'I won't say another word.'

Paul rang off, uncertain what he had just committed himself to. The Milanese trip was to confirm reciprocal arrangements with the Banco Feliciano. He had known for ages that Melanie wanted to go but he had been hesitating, unwilling to commit himself to crossing that particular Rubicon. Melanie, he knew, was after something more permanent in their relationship but he wasn't sure. She was very young, he thought. She was undeniably fun, but he had to admit that she was also something of a bimbo. He found Elaine dull, and it was true she sometimes irritated him beyond measure, but did he really want to let her go? Could he afford it? He stood there in the middle of their bedroom, chewing the tip of his finger, wondering what on earth he ought to do.

At the rectory, Mark and Tom had just sat down in front of the television. 'We really ought to watch the lottery draw,' Mark said, 'to get a better idea of exactly what it is we're up against.'

In spite of herself, Pippa came in too. She told herself it was all nonsense, and very, very wrong, but even so, she thought she ought to see. That way, in five minutes she could throw away the wretched ticket that she had bought and vow never ever to do it again. 'Coffee?' she asked, seating herself behind the pot on the small table. A kind of uneasy truce had settled between herself and Mark after the fiasco earlier at the Dufrayns'. Mark had clearly been just as annoyed as Paul at what he saw as female idiocy, but by the time they got back, Stripe had returned to his eyrie over the garage and had proved totally impervious to all further requests to come down.

'Yes, please,' said Tom.

Mark smiled thinly as Pippa handed him his cup, but was spared the necessity of saying anything by the music for the lottery programme choosing that moment to strike up. A woman in a skimpy dress sang. A clairvoyant floated above her ball, and announced that the winner would be a raven-haired male whose name began with a W, living in the Staffordshire area. Mark hooted in derision. Then the moment they had all been waiting for arrived. Pippa sank lower in her seat.

'And first out tonight,' shouted the commentator, 'is . . . number thirty. A popular ball this, ladies and gentlemen. It's been out of the machine five times in the last seven weeks!'

Pippa swallowed. Thirty, that was one of her numbers.

'And number two tonight is . . .' the voice laughed, 'number *one*! Lucky for some!'

Oh God, thought Pippa, surely not. But you had to have three numbers to win a prize. She remembered distinctly. And there were still five more to go.

'Number twelve,' boomed the voice.

Pippa hastily took a gulp of coffee as Tom looked at her. 'Ridiculous, isn't it?' he said. She nodded.

'Next one out is number forty. Another old favourite, ladies and gentlemen. We've seen this one quite often in the past.'

Pippa shut her eyes. This, she thought, could not be happening. She had just won a prize.

'Number seven!' shouted the voice.

Pippa's mouth felt dry. Oh God, she began to pray, please, no. You can't let this happen. I can't win!

There seemed the faintest of tremors in the air. 'The sixth ball tonight,' positively bellowed the voice, 'is number *three*. Another old favourite, I don't believe this!'

Neither did Pippa. She did not hear the last number. She had shut her eyes in blank shock, her brain reeling. She could hardly take it in, but it seemed she had just won the lottery. What had they said the prize was this week? The presenter's voice floated back to her. 'A massive fourteen million pounds!' It was obscene. What on earth would she do with all that money? She wondered if she had won it all, or if there were others. What would Mark say? She steeled herself to glance over in his direction and found that he, like Tom, was now staring at her too.

It had actually just struck Mark how very pretty his wife looked tonight. Maybe he was being rather hard towards her. As the numbers had started to come up, he had noticed her close her eyes in prayer and it had struck him what a really good person she was, and how devout. As he stared at her, he thought how very lucky he was that they were man and wife. Now, on impulse, he got up and went and sat beside her. 'I know,' he said, 'it's awful, isn't it?'

For one paralysed moment Pippa had the dreadful feeling that he knew. She gave a shaky laugh.

'Good old Pippa,' said Tom admiringly. 'That's what we all ought to have been doing during that disgusting spectacle. Praying!'

# Chapter Four

The next few days for Pippa were agony. In disbelief she kept examining the ticket, as if expecting to find that she had made a mistake and that it was all untrue. But the numbers, maddeningly, remained the same and at last she was forced to face the terrible truth. She had just won the largest jackpot ever on the lottery and, as far as she could make out, she was the only winner. By Thursday, stories were beginning to appear in the national press. Who was the mystery winner? the papers kept asking. Why had he or she not come forward? Speculation was rife, and then the next day one of the more lurid tabloids began a campaign. 'Find the winner,' it blazoned across its front page, 'and we'll give you the holiday of a lifetime!'

Throughout the week, Mark, as if trying to make amends for having been so horrible to her before, was exceptionally nice. Tom noticed this and, quite irrationally, felt put out. Whenever Pippa was around he began to ooze sympathy, and kept raising his eyebrows and smiling at her meaningfully, as if to imply that Mark was not to be trusted. Pippa wanted to hit him. The superiority in his manner seemed to suggest all the time that Mark was a fool, and she found she resented it.

She felt hopeless. She was overjoyed at the change in Mark's attitude towards her and wanted desperately to raise the question of tests again. While he was being so nice, he might even say yes. But – there always seemed to be a but – each time, when it came to it, she simply could not bring herself to broach the subject. The trouble was she felt so horribly guilty. She knew he would be furious if he ever found out she had played the lottery, and she felt it would be taking advantage. But what to do?

She thought at first that perhaps she would do nothing and just leave the prize unclaimed. But then the little demon that had whispered to her that there could not possibly be any harm in buying a ticket in the first place again raised its head, and suggested to her that she could claim the prize in complete anonymity, and Mark need never know. She had, she remembered, read of people before who had refused all publicity when they won. At the time she had wondered why. Now she felt she knew. Then it occurred to her that, even without publicity, it would be very hard to disguise the fact that she had fourteen million pounds in the bank. Although she knew the win itself was not taxable, at some time in the future there would inevitably be returns and disclosures of income to be made, and Mark always handled that. She could not possibly keep it secret from him, and anyway, she would want to spend some of it! Even Mark, she thought, would not believe she had been able to save for luxury holidays entirely out of the shopping money. He would notice any new clothes too. And she certainly could not initiate any grand schemes to help the homeless or anything of that kind because, again, he would quite properly want to know where she had found the money.

To make matters worse, as the week went on and her thoughts became more and more chaotic while she tried vainly to come up with a solution, she found herself being inexorably sucked into the vortex of activity that seemed suddenly and inexplicably to have sprung up around the mission. As the time for it drew near, the house seemed to be turned upside down. People seemed to be dropping in and out every moment of the day; asking what to do, where to get things from, where to put them when they had got them. Pippa was never entirely sure who she was going to find in her kitchen next. Then one night three jars of coffee and five packets of biscuits disappeared, to be replaced by twelve dirty cups and little mounds of crumbs on the floor. She never discovered who had consumed it all. Mark, when she asked him, was vague, and Tom just shrugged. 'Haven't a clue,' he said.

Pippa felt irritated, but that was nothing to what she felt when Mark informed her she was supposed to be organising somewhere to stay for Tom's music group. They would be arriving, he announced, on Friday. 'How many are there?' she asked, horrified.

'Ten,' said Tom. 'They need somewhere with a bit of space because most of them will have their instruments with them and they'll want to practise. But they'd prefer to eat together, if that's all right. They like to pray together and share what's been happening during the day too. So can you provide meals for them here at the rectory?'

In panic, Pippa rang round every available person she could think of who might possibly be able to help out. Then she began to try and work out three days' worth of meals for thirteen people. The absurdity of it all only hit her when she realised how impossible it was to keep within the budget of twenty-five pounds that Mark had set as being all they could afford. I could phone up caterers, she thought hysterically, and just get them to send it in. Why am I doing all this? In disgust she flung her pen down on the kitchen table.

At this moment Stripe arrived at the kitchen door. 'Oh,' she said unenthusiastically, 'it's you.' She had not seen him since the previous Saturday and, since Elaine had not called, had simply assumed that all was well and that very soon he would quietly disappear. Something in his manner now, however, made her question that assumption, and she looked at him warily.

'That's not a very nice welcome,' he said. 'Can I come in?'

She shrugged. 'I suppose so, everyone else has.'

Stripe grinned. He came in and settled himself down on the small chair opposite her. 'It does seem a bit busy round here,' he remarked. 'What's going on?'

'The youth mission,' she said drily. 'It's this weekend.'

Stripe looked interested. 'What's that?'

Briefly she explained. 'It's all a way of bringing young people to Christ and getting them involved,' she finished. 'That's Tom's ministry. He's a youth evangelist. He does this all the time.'

'Does your bloke do that too?'

Pippa laughed. 'No,' she said, 'he's not really "in" to young people, I don't think. He's more your traditional parish priest.'

Stripe did not appear particularly interested in this. 'I like this place,' he announced suddenly.

Pippa looked up, surprised. 'Do you?'

'Yeah.' He nodded. 'It's a bit different to Toxteth. I like the village. It's pretty. I could feel at home here.'

Something in his tone made her glance at him sharply. 'You'd better not!' she said.

Stripe laughed. 'I thought you Christians were supposed to love everybody.'

'Loving people is not the same as being taken in by them,' Pippa responded tartly.

He looked at her for a few seconds, surprised, and then said, 'Ye know, you're different from the rest of them. You're honest. An' you're real.'

The words made her writhe inwardly and her face froze, but he was staring at her, expecting a reply. 'Oh, we're all real,' she said lamely, laughing uneasily. 'It's just that we don't always like the reality.'

He continued to stare at her, a puzzled frown on his face, and then said at last, 'You're not very happy, are you?'

She felt it was the understatement of the year. 'What on earth's happy?' she demanded, before she could help herself. 'As far as I can make out, life is about surviving and putting up with things. Emotion just gets in the way.'

'Is that what your God teaches you?'

Startled, Pippa looked up. 'No, of course not,' she said, and then she flushed uncomfortably. 'Don't take any notice of me, I'm just tired.' She pulled a face. 'There's so much to do.'

29

'Yeah.' Stripe looked down at his fingers on the table. 'Your mate Elaine's not very happy either. You should 'ave 'eard 'em last night. Thought they were going to do for each other.'

That at least caught her attention. 'What do you mean?' she asked.

He shrugged. 'Dunno really. But they were 'avin' a real argy-bargy. She was shoutin' about some bird called Melanie, an' 'e kept tellin' 'er to mind 'er own business.'

Pippa swallowed. 'Oh dear, that sounds awful.'

'Never did like 'im,' remarked Stripe inconsequentially. 'Slimy git! 'E thinks the world's got to bow down three times when 'e comes in the room. That's one reason why I took over 'is garage.'

Pippa stared at him. 'What on earth do you mean?'

He shrugged. 'Oh, the story's true enough, but I didn't 'ave to stop 'ere now, did I? I was just passin' through on me way to 'Olland. I've got mates there, see. I can join another band over there. I was fed up with the old one anyway.'

There did not seem anything very much to say to that, so instead she asked, 'Are you any good?'

Stripe glared at her, as if she had touched a raw spot. 'Yeah,' he said angrily, 'I am. I'm bloody good, me. I'm going to make it to the top – if I live that long.'

'Ah yes, you mean if your heavies don't catch up with you.'

He did not blink. 'That's exactly what I mean.'

As soon as he had gone, Pippa phoned Elaine. 'How are you?' she asked cautiously.

There was a long silence, and then at last Elaine said in a whisper, 'Not too good. I found out he was planning to go to Italy with her.'

'With Melanie?'

'Yes. This weekend, on a business trip, he said. Only now he's not going because he says he can't go away with Stripe here.' She sniffed. 'We had a terrible row last night. He blames me. He says if I hadn't let Stripe stay, none of this would ever have happened. And he says he's fed up with me.'

'Paul said that?' said Pippa incredulously.

Elaine gave a bitter laugh. 'Oh, that was the least of the things he said. He accused me of doing it all to get even with him.' She laughed hysterically. 'I mean, I didn't even know he was planning on going away, so how could I have tried to stop him! He's such a bastard.'

There was a pause, during which Pippa could hear Elaine quietly crying. 'Please talk to Mark,' she begged. 'I'm sure he could help. Paul respects him.'

But Elaine refused. 'No,' she said, 'I've told you before, if he ever thought Mark or the rest of the church knew, that would be it. I'd never see him again.'

'Paul's a wonderful chap!' Mark said that night. 'He's given us one hundred pounds to put towards the cost of the youth mission. We can afford to hire a proper sound system for Tom for Saturday night now.'

All week, while Pippa had been trying to organise the practical side, Mark and Tom had been going round the local youth clubs and schools, giving talks and inviting all the kids to a fun night to be held on Saturday at the old army hall which they had hired for the night. The Garrison, as it was known locally, was a huge, rather tinny barn-like place that looked, since the army had moved away, as if it was in imminent danger of collapse. But it was cheap and Tom said it was ideal. The idea was that Tom should stand up halfway through the night of music and entertainment and tell the kids the good news that Jesus loved them. He would invite any who wanted to make a commitment to stand up and go forward. He and Mark would then pray with each person individually while the music programme continued. The service in church the next day was to be the grand finale. The trouble was, when they had tried out the church's sound system in the hall, it had proved woefully inadequate and it had looked for a while as if the event was going to be a disaster. But now Paul, with his open chequebook, had stepped into the breach.

'Yes,' Tom agreed, 'he's a really good chap.'

Pippa pulled a face but said nothing. 'What's up?' chided Mark, catching the look and giving her shoulders an affectionate squeeze. 'You like Paul. Remember?'

'Umm . . . yes,' said Pippa, noncommittally. Mark laughed and, before she could help herself, she added, 'Elaine seems a bit down at the moment.'

'Is she? Oh dear.' Mark helped himself to a strip of carrot from the chopping board and then remarked, 'If you ask me, she's a bit of a manic depressive.'

'Who's this?' asked Tom.

'Paul's wife.' Mark seemed totally unconcerned. 'She's always banging on about something. Always feeling low. You know the type. Too much money, too much time, so she has problems instead.'

'Ah,' said Tom sagely, 'yes, I do know that type.'

'Perhaps,' Pippa said tartly, 'she has cause!'

Both men turned and stared at her. 'Cause?' said Mark. 'Don't be ridiculous, Pippa! The woman's got everything she could possibly want. That's the trouble. She's got too much. And she always seems

31

to be whingeing on about it not being enough.' He turned back to Tom. 'She's one of those closet feminists, if you ask me. Always moaning about how unfair things are to women and always trying to take things over. She's so pushy!'

'How bloody typically male!' flared Pippa, unable to stand any more. 'Don't any of you ever think before you speak? Why don't you try actually looking at Elaine sometime, and her so perfect husband! Ask yourself what's really going on!' And with that she burst into tears and ran from the room.

Mark and Tom looked at each other, stunned, and then Mark said, 'Poor Pippa, time of the month, I think.'

'She's been doing rather a lot, too,' ventured Tom.

The phone rang. Out in the hallway, Pippa, in mid-flight, stopped and picked it up. 'Yes,' she said, sniffing loudly into the receiver.

'Is that St Saviour's?' asked a voice tersely. 'Can I speak to Tom?'

She went and got him.

Tom listened, his face going white. 'Yes,' he said, 'I see . . . of course not . . . no, stay there . . . it's all right . . . we'll manage.'

Mark came into the hall and stood beside Pippa. They both stared at Tom. He put the phone down and remained for a minute, facing the wall. Then, very slowly, he turned round.

'It's the worship group,' he said hoarsely, 'they've had an accident. The van's a write-off. The keyboard player has broken two fingers, and five of the instruments have been wrecked.'

It was Pippa who suggested Stripe. 'He is a professional musician,' she pointed out reasonably. 'And he says he's good. Surely he could help.'

'But what does he play?' asked Mark.

She did not know.

'Well, I suppose we can at least go and see,' said Tom. He seemed to have shrivelled in on himself, as if the news had knocked all the stuffing out of him.

'Surely God will provide,' said Pippa hopelessly. She had never seen Tom like this before and discovered she felt rather sorry for him.

'Yes,' agreed Tom. He sounded unconvinced.

They called on Paul and Elaine first, because Mark said they could not possibly approach Stripe without first getting Paul's agreement. Paul was not happy. 'He's supposed to be going on Saturday,' he protested. 'If he stays on for this, who knows when he'll leave.'

Elaine, hatchet-faced, glared at him. 'Perhaps it's our Christian duty to put the *mission* first,' she said pointedly.

Paul ground his teeth but did not respond. 'Well, I'm coming over with you,' he said at last. 'If he does agree, I want a cast-iron assurance that he's going when it's over.'

Together they trooped, like a little delegation crossing the Berlin Wall, to the garage. Stripe had replaced all the lights with red bulbs and, from a distance, the flat now gave off the air of a rather upmarket brothel. He was cooking something that smelt very spicy when they arrived, standing in front of a large saucepan on the hob and stirring gently. Two flame spotlights cast a dusky glow over the cooking area, while beyond, the room seemed alive with huge shadows. Elaine stared around in consternation. The once perfect kitchen no longer looked like something out of the design section of *Good Housekeeping*. Unidentifiable things had been hung over the once streamlined walls and there were dishes and pots everywhere. 'Good God!' said Paul. 'He's turned the place into a sty!'

The whole flat was wreathed in layers of softly undulating smoke. It wrapped itself round them as they walked in and seemed to take hold of their clothes. At the same time, combined with the spices from the cooking, there was an overriding scent of geraniums. 'What an odd smell,' said Elaine. 'What on earth is it?'

Stripe ignored her. 'Yeah,' he said, continuing to stir, 'wot d'ye want?'

They all five stood in the doorway and Mark cleared his throat. 'We've got a slight problem,' he said loudly. 'We wondered if you could help.'

Paul muttered, 'Be the first bloody time if he does.'

'I 'eard that,' said Stripe.

Sensing trouble, Tom stepped forward. 'Look,' he said hastily, 'the problem is, my music group has had a bit of an accident. They're not going to be able to get here in time for the mission. At least, three of them might be able to, but most of the instruments have been destroyed. Also one of them's been hurt, and the rest of them really need to stay with the van and try to get things sorted out.'

'So?' said Stripe.

Mark and Tom looked at each other, and Paul said, 'What did I tell you?'

'Oh, come on,' said Pippa. She pushed abruptly past the three men and walked into the kitchen. 'What they're trying to say is, could you help with the music?'

There was a long silence, during which Stripe continued to stir his saucepan and apparently ignore them. They looked at each other helplessly, and then Stripe suddenly shrugged. 'Dunno,' he said. He looked up. 'Depends wot ye want me to do, and wot do I get out of it?'

All five of them now advanced further into the room. Elaine was still staring around in dismay. Then, as if unable to take in any more, she sat down heavily on the nearest bar stool. 'What do you play, for a start?' asked Mark.

Stripe considered this. 'Keyboard,' he announced, 'and drums. I can play harp too.'

Mark and Tom looked at each other and nodded. 'Can you, um,' began Tom, 'can you play any sort of music? Can you play unseen?'

Stripe looked at him witheringly. 'I'm a pro, man. I can play anything.'

'Ah!' Tom exhaled loudly and now also sat down. Elaine was still looking numb, but there was an air of hopeful excitement about Tom now. 'So do you think you could do it?' he asked.

In the dim light, Stripe's eyes gleamed amber. 'I could,' he said. 'The question is, why should I?'

Unable to contain himself any longer, Paul pushed his way forward. 'Because if you don't, sunshine,' he said menacingly, 'I'll kick you out, here and now!'

Stripe put down the spoon. 'Try it!' he said.

'Paul!' shrieked Elaine, jerked out of her state of numbed shock. 'For goodness sake, stop it!'

It was some moments before calm was restored, but when at last they were all sitting down and Stripe had consented to put on another light, Mark said, 'Of course we'll make it worth your while. We understand you wouldn't be doing this out of any commitment.'

''Ow much?' said Stripe.

'Thirty pounds,' said Paul promptly.

Stripe made a sound midway between an express train and a baboon. 'Thirty pounds! You've gotta be jokin'! I don't play nowhere for thirty pounds.'

Pippa's heart sank. Money again, she thought. This was stupid. She had had the silly idea that Stripe might be glad to help. She had thought he seemed rather nice in the kitchen, earlier today. She had thought he might even say he would waive any fee, and she still felt he might respond positively if asked nicely. But every word Paul now uttered seemed to be like acid, producing an immediate adverse reaction. He and Stripe seemed to be once again squaring up to each other for a fight.

'How much then?' snarled Paul.

'For goodness sake,' interjected Pippa, 'calm down. This isn't exactly the way to ask a favour of anyone.'

Paul breathed heavily and Elaine laid a restraining hand on his arm. Tom leant forward. 'How much would you be prepared to do it for?' he asked quietly.

Stripe looked around at them consideringly, and then stared

straight at Pippa and smiled. 'I take it you'd be providing the instruments?' he inquired.

'Of course,' said Mark and Tom together.

The musician's smile broadened as he weighed in his mind exactly how much he could get away with. It would be nice to see that slimy banker pay. 'Two 'undred pounds,' he said, looking directly at Paul.

'Plugh!' spluttered Paul.

'Done!' said Tom.

But Mark was looking concerned. 'How?' he asked. 'We're already running over budget. I was going to make an appeal in church on Sunday. How on earth can we raise another two hundred pounds?'

'Plus instrument hire,' pointed out Pippa. 'That won't be cheap.'

There was a small sound from Elaine. 'We'll pay,' she said suddenly. She leant forward and held out her hand to Stripe, chin raised and very pointedly not looking at Paul. 'Deal?'

'Deal,' said Stripe. He closed his hand over hers, and shook it firmly.

# Chapter Five

On Stripe's advice they hired a keyboard that did everything, including sounding like the London Philharmonic when he pressed a certain stop. Stripe pronounced himself well satisfied, especially with this latter facility, and promised them a performance they would never forget. He seemed to be in his element and spent the whole of the next day at the Garrison tinkering around, producing strange and wonderful sounds that had any passing members of the mission team riveted. He was, as he had said, extremely good.

Halfway through the day Tom produced some worship music of his own. 'I wonder if you could practise some of this?' he asked apologetically.

Stripe glanced at it and then handed it back, sniffing disdainfully. 'Don't need to,' he said. 'I can play that stuff standin' on me 'ead.'

Tom looked concerned and Stripe glanced back at him. 'Give us it 'ere then,' he said, relenting. He took the music and spread it on the keyboard and Tom looked even more apprehensive. He was used to members of his music group being rather more orderly than Stripe was. By and large they tended to stay where they were put, but Stripe had a disconcerting habit of wandering around while he played. Sometimes he sat on the stool provided but, more often, he stood, swaying and undulating in time to the music, playing with his eyes closed. Tom was beginning to have serious doubts about the wisdom of having asked Stripe. The next minute, however, his jaw dropped in astonishment because Stripe, after the briefest of glances at the music, flicked back his dreadlocks and then, without pause, began to play. He played tune after tune. Faultessly, and with absolute familiarity. More than that, he seemed to inject a depth of feeling that Tom had never noticed in them before.

'You know this music,' he said incredulously when Stripe paused, 'don't you?'

'Yeah,' Stripe nodded. 'Me mam's very big on God. I play for her lot sometimes. They use most of this stuff. Some of the tunes are OK, but some are a bit naff. I won't play them.'

By Saturday night there was a mood of suppressed excitement that seemed to have affected all of them. All of them, that is, except

Stripe. He seemed to be taking the whole event in his stride. He had made no more mention of leaving Little Wakenham, and Mark and Tom had forbidden Paul to say anything until after the mission concert was over, in case Stripe took offence and left prematurely.

Pippa, meanwhile, had managed temporarily to push the problem of what to do with the lottery jackpot to the back of her mind. She felt she would have liked to have talked to Elaine about it, but she knew that, in the circumstances, that was impossible. So instead she refused to think about it at all, promising herself that she would address the question again once the weekend was over.

The three undamaged singers from Tom's worship group turned up without warning on Saturday morning, and announced that they would sing. Since news of the accident had first broken, it had been assumed that none of the group would be able to make it, and so Pippa had done nothing further to sort out arrangements for them. For the next few hours, therefore, she found herself scuttling round trying to get their accommodation sorted out, and preparing a huge amount of food. By seven she was utterly exhausted and would have given anything just to crawl into bed and go to sleep. Mark, however, appeared to be expecting her to go along to the concert. 'You never know, Pippa,' he said, 'there may be some counselling needed, and you're ever so good at that.' So reluctantly she dragged on her coat and trailed off after them through the door.

The atmosphere at the Garrison, when they arrived, was electric. Kids were streaming in from everywhere, and the stewards on the doors looked flushed. 'It's incredible,' said Derek, one of the youth group from St Saviour's who had been pressed in to help. 'There must be about four hundred already! Where are they all coming from?'

On the stage Stripe was already in place and was playing softly. As usual his eyes were closed and he was swaying gently, totally lost in the music. 'Wow!' Pippa heard a young boy say. 'He's terrific. I never knew Christians were like that.'

By the time they were ready to start, the hall was packed. News of Stripe seemed to have leaked out to all the kids round about and they had come, Pippa suspected, more to see and hear him than to listen to the Gospel. 'Doesn't matter,' Tom said blithely, when she voiced this thought to him. 'They're in here now and, like it or not, they'll listen. It's tremendous.'

When at last Tom stood up to welcome everyone and introduce the evening, he seemed to be on fire, and when it was time for him actually to preach, he seemed inspired.

'Gosh,' said Mark, standing with Pippa at the side, 'he's terrific, isn't he? I'd never realised.'

It was the music, however, that really caught everyone. Stripe played as if giving form to some eternal harmony that sprang straight from God. The music flowed from him and, at his side, the three worship singers joined in with gusto. By the end, when Tom asked if anyone would like to make a commitment, everybody sprang to their feet and cheered wildly, and there were cries of more. Tom looked momentarily nonplussed, and then shouted into the microphone, 'If you'd like to come forward . . .' There was a mad stampede for the stage which was halted only when Stripe leapt to his feet, seized the microphone from Tom's nerveless hand and bellowed, '*Sit down!*'

There were more whistles and cheers, but the kids checked, and then obediently turned and went back to their seats. Stripe gazed at them like some disciplinarian head teacher who has just had to sort out a particularly unruly class. 'That's better,' he shouted, once they were all sitting down again. 'Now stay quiet an' I'll play one last number. An' then you can all go 'ome an' come to church tomorra!'

'Will you be there?' shouted a voice. Stripe waved.

'But, Stripe,' muttered Tom, unnerved, 'what about my altar call?'

'Fogerrit, man,' advised the musician. 'They'll swamp us. Do it tomorra at church. I'll make sure they come. Jus' let them listen tonight.'

Tom looked as if he was about to protest, but the next moment Stripe launched into a thundering crescendo of shimmering sound, his fingers rippling without pause over the keys as if he and the music were one, and everyone jumped up and cheered. 'More!' came shouts. 'Give us more!' Then the building began to shake as the entire audience began to stamp and whistle and cheer.

Tom swallowed. He had never encountered a reaction quite like this before. 'I think you'd better give it to them, Stripe,' he muttered uneasily.

But that was not what Stripe had in mind. 'If ye want to 'ear more,' he shouted into the microphone, 'cum to church tomorra! But that's all fer now! I'm tired. Good night, and God bless!'

'This is preposterous,' said Paul the next morning. He had come round early, furious that Stripe had announced his intention of coming to church.

'Why shouldn't he?' asked Pippa, clearing away the breakfast things and staring at him coldly.

'He's in my flat,' spluttered Paul. 'He said he'd go.' He appealed to Mark. 'You've got to see this can't go on. I'm worried about the boys as much as anything.'

'Did they come to the concert last night?' inquired Tom.

'Yes, they did. They haven't stopped talking about it since.' He

39

flung up his hands. 'You see, that's the problem. They're totally besotted with him. It's as if he's cast a spell over them. Sebastian is even talking about growing his hair!'

Tom chuckled sheepishly. Now it was all over, he was beginning to regard the concert as a personal triumph. He felt responsible for Stripe. 'He was rather good,' he pointed out.

'But he's not going to stay in my flat!' exploded Paul.

'Look,' said Mark, 'let's discuss this after church, there's a good chap. I'm going to be late at this rate.' He planted a quick kiss on Pippa's cheek. 'See you in a bit. Don't be too long. I must get off now. Coming, Tom?' Tom nodded and, grumbling, Paul picked up his jacket to go with them.

'We might have quite a good crowd this morning,' said Tom hopefully. They disappeared through the door.

'Quite a good crowd' turned out to be a wholly inadequate description. When they got there the church was packed, and a huge crowd spilled out into the churchyard. St Saviour's was an old church. It had been founded in the twelfth century by Alfred the Hermit, and had been a centre of worship ever since. It had been a haven during the plague, a refuge during the civil war, and a place of tranquillity and prayer ever since. This morning, it was difficult even to push a way through, and there seemed a huge number of press men and photographers clustered around the door. 'Morning, Vicar,' said Mrs Jenkins who was on duty handing out books. 'We've run out of 'ymn books, and there's 'alf o' the regulars as can't get a seat!'

'Oh dear,' said Mark, but his eyes shone. 'What a splendid crowd!'

A sea of young faces turned expectantly towards him. 'They came,' said Tom, in tones of greatest surprise. 'That must be why the press are here. They must have heard about the concert last night. Do you think we can get Stripe to play again for us this morning?'

Stripe himself at this moment appeared, and all over the church kids leapt to their feet and cheered. 'Mornin',' he said. 'Good turn-out.'

Paul glowered at him. 'Now see here—'

'Not now, Paul,' Mark said firmly. 'I've already said we'll discuss it later.' He took Stripe's elbow and began to steer him up the nave. 'Would you like to play?' he asked. 'I'm afraid our keyboard isn't quite up to the standard of the one you were playing last night, but it's quite good.'

'If ye like,' said Stripe. 'Yeah, I'll give it a go. Why not?'

Pippa arrived a few minutes later and had to run the gamut of the St Saviour's Ladies Club. There were nine members in all, aged between sixty-five and eighty-nine, and each one had her own particular seat. Arriving at church two minutes before the service was due to start, they had found their seats filled. Even worse, they could not get in through the door. 'It's not good enough,' Mrs Stibbins complained loudly. 'Who are all these people?'

Pippa promised she would see what she could do. 'Excuse me,' she said, pushing her way past a photographer. 'Why are you here anyway?'

The photographer looked mysterious. 'You'll see, love,' he said, 'in a minute.' He winked.

Pippa pushed her way to the front, but try as she might there was nowhere she could squeeze in the Ladies Club. She was obliged to report her failure, and was rewarded by a stream of muttered abuse. Raising her eyes heavenward, she pushed her way back to the front, and then squatted on the floor in the side aisle. One young boy, with unusual chivalry, said, 'Here, would you like my seat? Mum says I ought to stand up for older people.'

Pippa sat down, and the service began. Into the rustling quiet, Mark spoke the traditional words of welcome. There was a stirring at the back, and then a woman came forward, followed by a small cluster of photographers and rather seedy-looking newsmen. She seemed to be looking for someone; her head kept swivelling back and forth and her eyes raked the congregation. Pippa recognised the assistant from the supermarket. 'That's her!' screamed the girl suddenly, coming to a stop and pointing directly at Pippa. 'She's the one wot bought the ticket!'

Cameras flashed and a babble of excited voices broke out. To her horror, Pippa found a microphone pushed under her nose. 'Congratulations!' said a voice. 'Any comment?'

Mark stood on the dais stunned, and then he stepped forward, outraged. 'What on earth is the meaning of this?' he thundered.

There was another blaze of cameras, this time in his direction. 'You 'er 'usband then, mate?' inquired one of the newsmen. He turned back to the girl, 'You did say 'er 'usband was the vicar, didn't you?' She nodded.

Mark went purple, while all around people rose noisily to their feet, craning to see. 'I repeat,' shouted Mark, ignoring the newsmen and striving to make himself heard above the hubbub, 'what is the meaning of this?'

There were some sniggers, but quiet fell. No one had a clue what was going on but whatever it was, they did not want to miss it. Pippa, with rather more understanding, shut her eyes. As it turned out, this was perhaps wise, because the girl from the supermarket chose that moment to tear off the coat she was wearing. Underneath she had on the skimpiest of scarlet swimsuits. 'She's won the lottery!' she shrieked. 'I sold her the ticket. I remembered the numbers 'cos of who she was!' She gave an explosive giggle. 'And now I've won the dream holiday for finding her!'

Pippa opened her eyes and gaped, aghast, as the girl flung her arms round her neck and planted a big kiss on her cheek. The cameras flashed again. The newsmen were enjoying this. 'Bit more leg, please, Tracy luv!' one of them shouted.

Tracy obliged, and the cameras flashed yet again. 'I'm going to the Seychelles,' she confided breathlessly to Pippa. 'Wiv me boyfriend!' Then she pulled back slightly and shouted out, so that the whole congregation could hear, 'Blimey! I said good luck when she bought it but I never thought she'd win. Wot a turn-up!' She turned exultantly back to Pippa. 'We've both won now, 'aven't we?'

From his position at the top of the chancel steps, Mark reflected that women often had difficulty making themselves heard in a large church but that unfortunately this did not seem to be a problem for Tracy. Her strident tones reverberated through the building and, to his intense chagrin, from somewhere at the back someone cheered.

One of the newsmen shoved the reporter with the microphone violently. 'Look, mate, this is a *Globe* story. Get your nose out!'

'Up yours!' retorted the other, in rather more refined tones. 'You haven't got a premium on this, you know. We'll have the story out by this afternoon!' He seemed inclined to follow up this observation with a shove of his own, and there ensued a slight but unseemly scuffle.

Pippa turned her head slowly and became aware of Mark staring at her. She had thought for one dreadful moment when it all began that she was going to pass out. There had been a curious singing in her ears, and the whole world had seemed edged with black, but now she felt as if she was slowly returning from a great distance.

The reporter with the microphone managed to jostle his rival out of the way. 'Would you care to make a comment?' he asked again, panting slightly from his exertions and now planting himself firmly in the way.

'No,' whispered Pippa.

Mark came down a step and held out his hands beseechingly. 'Pippa,' he said hoarsely, 'tell them it's not true. You can't have won the lottery. Tell them we don't approve of this sort of thing. It's gambling!'

'He doesn't approve!' shouted one of the delighted newsmen. 'I'll bet he didn't even know!'

There were more flashes from the cameras and then everything went quiet as everyone again turned expectantly to Pippa. She swallowed. 'I . . . I'm sorry.'

42

It was all she could manage. Unable to stand any more, she tore herself from the suffocating embrace of Tracy and began roughly to try and push a way past and escape. But the reporter with the microphone was standing directly in front of her and behind him the rest of the clamouring newsmen were blocking the aisle. All of them seemed to want to talk to her.

'Sit down!' suddenly bellowed Mark, as if her movement had released him from some terrible spell. He seemed to be fighting a battle with himself, and it was some moments before he could go on. Finally, however, he drew himself up and managed to bring out, 'This is a house of God! We are in the middle of a service. Whatever the truth of all this is, I will not have the service disrupted in this way! Sit down, all of you. Whatever you wish to ask must wait until after the service is over.' And with that, in the most terrible voice, he bellowed, 'All things bright and beautiful. We will sing. *All things bright and beautiful!*'

Stripe obediently, though with a few embellishments, struck up on the keyboard, and the rest of the congregation now also rose noisily to their feet. In utter misery, Pippa turned back to her seat and the newsmen, after a moment's indecision, stayed where they were. Mark, however, would have none of that. Under cover of the music, he strode towards them and gestured to them roughly to go. 'Wait outside,' he said furiously. 'This is not right.'

'But if we do that, mate, she might get away!' complained one of the photographers.

'There *is* no other way out,' Mark snarled. 'Now go, before I have you ejected!'

Muttering, they withdrew.

'Is this true?' Mark hissed at Pippa.

She stared at him fearfully. 'I'm so sorry,' she said again.

There followed an hour of utter misery for them both. Mark hardly knew what he was doing. He repeated his parts of the service woodenly and, when it came time for Tom to speak, he sat down heavily, not hearing a word. He seemed stunned. Pippa, for her part, was consumed by an agony of shame. She felt that the entire church were staring at her – as indeed they were. Never in her wildest dreams had it occurred to her that something like this might happen. She felt as if some malignant spirit had taken a hand and twisted fate. Then she thought that God himself might have done it, to pay her back. As the service ploughed on, she wanted to scream with rage at the unfairness of it all, but she felt terror too. She had an overriding sense of urgency that she *must* speak to Mark. She had to explain, to try and make him understand somehow why she had done it. She felt that something terrible was about to happen. All through the service she kept looking at him glumly but, after their hissed exchange when

43

he had expelled the reporters, he did not glance at her again, and she felt his anger like a wall of shocked hate.

As the service went on, Mark came to a decision. He felt immensely disappointed in Pippa. She was clearly not what he had believed her to be but, even worse, by her actions she had made him look a fool. She had obviously done it to spite him, and it was clear to him now that she was in a state of acute rebellion against God. The way ahead, therefore, was clear. There would be no talking about it. As head of the household and therefore responsible for the spiritual welfare of his wife, he would simply inform her that she must renounce the prize. And it occurred to him that if she obeyed him in this, as indeed she would have to, not only could he save face, but her public repudiation of the lottery would have the most tremendous impact in registering his disapproval to the country at large. He began to think that, although Pippa was quite clearly an extremely weak vessel, perhaps after all God had had a hand in all of this and would use it for good.

While Mark was turning all this over in his mind, a curious change seemed to have come over Tom as well. Like everyone else, he had been stunned when the reporters had burst in and then, seeing Pippa so overwhelmed, his initial impulse had been to rush to her side and defend her. He had been restrained only by the thought that that was Mark's prerogative. When Mark had failed to do this, he had been caught by an agony of indecision, which had been brought to an end only by the resumption of the service. Once the reporters had gone and he felt Pippa was, for a while at least, safe, he had forced himself to turn his attention back to the crowded church and an idea began to take shape at the back of his mind.

As he sang the words 'All things wise and wonderful', he remembered that the jackpot prize was a massive fourteen million pounds. If the newsmen were right, and Pippa was indeed the sole recipient of this sum, she was an extremely wealthy woman. Tom was not actually a greedy man, and he was not at this moment being driven by thoughts of personal gain, but the acquisition of adequate financial resources for his work had long been a major problem, and he would hardly have been human if it had not occurred to him that a very small part of Pippa's winnings would fund his work for a good few years to come. It had been but a short step then for his imagination to make a quantum leap. A slightly larger portion, he thought, and he could put in place an evangelistic campaign the like of which England had never seen before!

Over the past few years, Tom had spent quite a lot of time in the States, and he had been impressed by the huge, mega-buck church organisations over there. In particular he had been impressed by their appeal to young people, and by their use of the new media technologies to further their aims. It occurred to him now that with funding he could do exactly the same. And as he stood there, his eyes alight as they swept over the upturned faces, before finally coming to rest on Stripe, it further occurred to him that God had not only provided the financial means for the realisation of this vision but that in the timing of the mission, the accident to the worship group, and Stripe's totally unforeseen arrival he had provided a very powerful sign. God, Tom decided, wanted them to inaugurate a new ministry!

When it came time for him to stand up and preach, he gripped either side of the wooden pulpit, took a deep breath and then proclaimed loudly, 'If you love the Lord, he will supply your every need!' Then he turned and looked straight at Pippa and announced, 'Brothers and sisters, we have the example of this in our midst today. Our sister here loves the Lord, and she has been obedient to him. And because of that, he has entrusted to her the means of spreading abroad his grace.'

Pippa's jaw dropped open and Mark's head jerked up and round. They both stared at Tom in astonishment. Mark had just been thinking to himself that since Pippa had been so *very* disobedient, she ought not only to renounce the win but also publicly repent, and he had been in the process of working out the best way of doing this. The last thing he had been expecting was a thundering affirmation from the pulpit that her win was a sign of grace. In agitation he half rose to his feet. Tom, however, seemed oblivious of the effect he was having. He turned back to the congregation, his face alight. 'Come to the Lord!' he cried. 'Open your lives to him, and receive in like manner the riches of his grace!'

St Saviour's had never had an altar call before. Mark had always felt, given the nature of their congregation, that it would be rather out of place. They had one that morning, however, because Tom finished up his sermon by inviting all those who would like to receive the wealth he was talking about into their lives to come forward. It only needed then for Stripe to begin to play softly, and almost the entire church stood up. 'Excuse me,' said the young boy sitting next to Pippa on the floor, 'can I get past? I want to go up. I want to receive all that now, just like he says!'

It was half past one before they finally got away. One hundred and seventy-three young people and five of the regular congregation had given their names and said they wanted to make a commitment. Tom had insisted that he and Mark pray with every one of them, and had given a promise that each one would be contacted during the course of the following week. Stripe had played throughout. Indeed, he seemed to have lost all consciousness of where he was after about the first ten minutes, and had launched into a stream of rather strange harmonies, but the effect had been not unpleasant, and Tom had been well pleased.

45

When they finally emerged from the church, he, Mark, Paul and Stripe formed a little phalanx around Pippa, in an effort to protect her from the waiting reporters. 'Run!' shouted Paul as they got to the door, and they took to their heels. Pursued by a crowd of jostling pressmen and half blinded by the barrage of flashes that greeted them as they emerged, they ran through the churchyard, dodging around headstones, jumping over the graves. By the time they got back to the rectory they were all out of breath. Without pause they flung in through the front door, and then Mark slammed it shut.

When he turned round, his face was black. 'What the hell were you playing at?' he snapped, rounding on Tom. 'How could you have said that that win was a sign of grace?' His face twisted and he turned on Pippa savagely. 'And what on earth were you thinking of to buy that wretched ticket in the first place?'

They all stared at him amazed. Tom was the first to recover. 'Hang on a minute, Mark,' he said, 'that's a bit over the top, isn't it? Just calm down.'

'The lottery is the work of Satan!' spat Mark.

Pippa hung her head. 'I'm so sorry,' she said again. She began to cry.

'Now look what you've done!' said Tom. He put an arm round her shoulders and hugged her.

'She's my wife!' said Mark furiously. 'Leave her alone. This is between her and me. She's done wrong!'

'Did ye really win?' said Stripe suddenly. Startled, they all turned and stared at him. They had not realised that he had come in too. Stripe grinned. 'It's great if ye ask me!'

There was a moment's silence after this and then, through gritted teeth, Mark said, 'No one did ask you.'

Stripe was unperturbed. 'If my old lady won, I think I might be pleased. I think I might be nice to 'er, too.'

'Yes,' said Paul. 'Come on Mark. You're being a bit hard. She's only won the lottery, for God's sake. She hasn't been found at an orgy.'

Mark breathed heavily. He seemed scarcely able to believe his ears and stared from one to the other of them, confounded. Tom took full advantage of the situation to hug Pippa again, and she was so upset that she buried her head in his shoulder and began to sob. 'There, there,' said Tom approvingly. He turned back to Mark. 'Look here, old man, so maybe she shouldn't have bought the ticket.' He raised a hand as Mark looked as if he was about to explode. 'All right! All right! So she shouldn't have. But she did. And she won!' He squeezed Pippa protectively. 'Has it occurred to you to wonder why?'

'Someone 'ad to,' remarked Stripe.

They all ignored him. 'What you're really saying,' said Paul slowly, 'is that you think God planned all this. Is that right?'

'Right!' Tom turned to him excitedly. 'What are the odds of winning the lottery? A million to one? Pippa buys one ticket one week, and she wins.'

'Huh!' snorted Mark.

'Stop it, Mark,' said Tom. 'Just listen.' He turned back to Paul. 'That one week and she wins. But look what else has happened this week.'

Paul's face darkened as he glanced at Stripe. 'Absolute bloody chaos, if you ask me,' he muttered.

'Right!' said Tom again. 'At least, not chaos, but you're right, Stripe arrived. The mission began, all those young people turned up. It all fits together.'

'How?' asked Mark suspiciously. In spite of himself, his attention was caught.

'God's showing us the way ahead,' said Tom patiently. His manner suggested that he was dealing with a particularly obtuse class of six-year-olds. 'He's given us a taste of what it's like to bring these kids into the Kingdom. But more importantly now, he's given us the means to carry that on.'

All three men were staring at him, and Pippa now also raised her head and looked at each of them in turn. On Mark's face was a dawning light of unwilling excitement, while Paul looked as if some particularly attractive business deal had just been laid on his desk. Stripe just looked bemused. 'And you're here, Paul,' continued Tom, turning to him excitedly. 'Can't you see? To have any chance of success, we also need someone with the necessary financial skills to take over and direct the business side – and God's taken care of that too!'

'Ye – es,' said Paul, 'I see.' He stroked his chin, considering the idea. 'You mean you need a financial adviser who knows what's what.'

But Tom was going on. 'Even if all those things weren't enough by themselves, look at the response this morning. Not only was the church packed, but almost two hundred people have made a commitment. It was like something out of Acts! When did that last happen at St Saviour's, Mark?'

'Never,' said Mark.

'Exactly!' exclaimed Tom.

Silence fell after this, and they all looked at Mark. He stood there irresolutely, and it was obvious he was being torn by inner debate. Conflicting emotions flickered across his face, and then finally, very slowly, he said, 'We've won because God has a mission for us.' He looked up at Tom. 'You really believe this?'

Tom nodded. 'Yes,' he said fervently, 'I do.'

There was another silence, then Mark said, 'I've been hasty.

47

God moves in mysterious ways, but I didn't understand . . . It's Nebuchadnezzar's gold, isn't it?' Tom nodded again. 'Oh, how could I have been so blind!'

Pippa stared at him incredulously. She could not believe she was hearing this. *She* had just won the lottery, and here were these men, these men who disapproved, talking as if the win belonged to them! She seemed to have entirely disappeared from the picture. She was so shocked she was speechless.

Tom released her and went forward and hugged Mark. 'It's all right,' he said, 'we all make mistakes. We just have to have the humility to recognise that.' He turned back to Pippa and drew her towards them. 'Mark,' he said firmly, 'maybe you need to say sorry to your wife.'

Obediently, Mark turned to her. 'I'm sorry, Pippa,' he mumbled. 'I didn't understand. I'm sorry I spoke to you the way I did.' Then he put his arms awkwardly round her and hugged her. 'Do you forgive me?' he asked.

She felt she could have throttled him, but Tom was smiling at her benignly, and she knew exactly what was expected of her now. 'Of course,' she mumbled back, biting her lip.

'There!' said Tom, satisfied.

# Chapter Six

Paul was not happy. Tom had put it to him that Stripe had to stay, that his continued presence was vital to the operation of God's plan. 'But I don't see why he's got to stay over my garage,' Paul protested.

Patiently Tom explained to him that Stripe needed his own space, and that the flat over the garage was the only suitable space available. 'He says he likes it,' Tom added. 'He says he's only prepared to stay on for a while if he *can* stay there.'

'But I don't want him there!' Paul said belligerently.

In the circumstances, Tom did not consider Stripe's removal an option. He had spent a long time talking to the young man and had had an unexpectedly difficult time persuading him to stay around. 'I don't want to, man,' Stripe had said. 'I'm not into all this religion an' stuff. I don't like it.'

Tom had pleaded with him. 'It could make you big in Christian circles,' he said. 'You could become a star!'

This had not seemed to hold any great appeal for Stripe. 'I don't need all that,' he said. 'I'm goin' to be a star anyway. I don't need all these Christian types!'

'Five hundred a week,' Tom said desperately.

Stripe looked at him. 'A thousand.'

Tom swallowed. 'Seven hundred?'

'Eight hundred and fifty, and I stay rent-free at the garage.'

'Done!' Tom said.

It was difficult, however, to persuade Paul that this was a good deal, and Tom was driven at last to say, 'OK, we'll pay his rent. Whatever you want.'

Paul named an exorbitant sum. But he was still not happy. He did not want the disruption to his life that Stripe represented, all the more so since he was having such a difficult time with Elaine.

Elaine had felt hopeful when Paul had finally come home late on Sunday night and told her all that had taken place. Since he had not come back for lunch and had not phoned, she had been imagining him with Melanie all afternoon and had been growing increasingly angry the later it became. When he finally came through the door and told her where he had been, relief had swept over her like a flood. 'Pippa's won the lottery?' she repeated incredulously. Paul grunted. 'And the press were there?' Paul grunted again. 'Lucky Pippa,' said Elaine enviously. 'I wish something like that would happen to me.' If such a thing ever did happen to her, she thought suddenly, the first thing she would do would be to leave Paul.

The idea popped into her head out of nowhere, and she recoiled from it, shocked. Her life was here, with her husband and with the boys. She hated what Paul was doing; his adultery was so blatant, and he showed such little regard, but it could not go on for ever, surely. He would tire of Melanie eventually or maybe Melanie would tire of him. She must cling to that hope. After all, if Pippa could win the lottery, anything was possible!

The papers on Monday morning were plastered with photographs of Pippa and Mark. Some had Pippa looking astonished, being hugged by Tracy, and others had Mark striking a pose like some Old Testament prophet, and looking annoyed. The lottery company phoned Pippa and asked her if it was true that she had the winning numbers. She replied that it was, and they said could they present the cheque to her at a big reception at the Savoy? Pippa said no, and Mark approved. But later Tom said that the publicity would serve the cause of the Lord. So three hours and a lot of argument later she phoned back and said, 'OK then. When?'

It was arranged that the cheque would be presented to her three days later, and that a Rolls-Royce would come and collect her and Mark and drive them to London. 'What we'd really like,' said the voice at the other end of the phone, 'is some footage of you and your husband going round the shops and picking out some new outfits. We'll pay for all that of course, because it's publicity for us. Though it goes without saying that we'd like to choose the outfits. Then if you'd like to come back to the Savoy later for a reception, we'll get one of the big soap stars – Tony Cromper maybe – to present it to you. And we'll have all the press there too.' Pippa did not reply, and after a second he went on, 'And then of course we'd like you to be our guests overnight at the Savoy . . . and maybe you'd like to take in the theatre too?'

Pippa put down the phone stunned. 'I'm not sure I want to go through with this,' she said.

'You must,' said Tom firmly. 'Trust me. We can use this for a bit of publicity of our own.' He went away muttering about getting in touch with a friend of his called Jack. 'He was one of the team I was working with over in the States,' he explained. 'He's really good at handling publicity. If we could get him on board, it would be great.'

Jack arrived the next day, and Paul arranged to have a solicitor friend of his draw up a contract. Jack then phoned the lottery people and told them that Chalice Ministries – the name Tom and Mark had come up with for their new enterprise – had some suggestions to make about how the reception should be handled. Pippa was not consulted on any of this and was rather surprised, as she walked through to the kitchen, to overhear Jack saying that she would agree to drive to London in the Rolls-Royce but that instead of shopping for the cameras she then wanted to do a walkabout among the homeless that they would have gathered for the event in Leicester Square, talking and distributing chicken nugget meals and Christian tracts.

'We've got to drum up some down-and-outs,' he announced, as soon as he was off the phone. 'This will be a terrific photo opportunity. We can present you,' he looked at Pippa, 'like a kind of latter day Mother Theresa. That way we can publicise the work of Chalice Ministries at the same time as you receive the prize.'

'But I thought Chalice Ministries was going to be outreach to the young,' said Pippa, bewildered.

'Of course,' said Jack patiently. 'Young homeless is simply another aspect. It'll all help create a big launch!'

'It's all right, Pippa,' said Tom, catching her look of unease, 'Jack knows what he's talking about. He's done this kind of thing before. He's simply trying to get us a high public profile.'

On Wednesday morning, Jack went through Pippa's and Mark's wardrobes and picked out what they were to wear. 'We've got to present the right image,' he explained. He turned to Mark. 'We want young but mature; stylish but dependable. A visionary with integrity. The kind of guy you'd want to talk to if you were young, because you felt he was on the same wavelength, but who you'd also want to baptise your kids when you got a bit older. We want an image that says "faith is fun" to the kids, but "safe" to the mums and dads. Hey!' he checked suddenly. 'I like that, we can use it.' And then, seeing their puzzled expressions, he said again, 'Faith is fun! We can work it into our logo.'

Pippa decided she did not like Jack. He was tall and skinny, with long dark hair and gold-rimmed glasses, and he obviously felt that he personified exactly the image that he was trying to project on to them. He turned to her and looked her up and down appraisingly. 'Good body,' he announced, 'but we're a bit ageing hippie, aren't we? Let's see what else you've got in the clothes line.' He rifled through her wardrobe three times and then said despairingly, 'This lot's useless. The current look for wives is glossy. You can't wear this stuff!' He thought for a minute and then announced, 'We'll have to go shopping. You can leave the hair . . . I think . . . for the moment. I rather like that long, unstructured look, but we're

51

going to have to get you something that looks as if it hasn't come from Oxfam. Stylish but—'

'I know,' said Pippa drily, 'dependable.'

'Good idea,' said Tom approvingly, when he heard. 'Jolly important, image.'

Mark looked worried. 'I'm not sure we can afford it,' he said.

'Don't be silly,' said Tom. 'She's going to have fourteen million pounds tomorrow.'

Jack bore Pippa off for a shopping trip to London. He seemed to know exactly the right places to go, and in no time at all she found herself kitted out with a long, gently flaring A-line skirt and fitted jacket, both of which bore the name Armani, and the most exorbitantly expensive shoes she had ever seen. 'You need some make-up too,' he said. 'Over in the States the wives are real icons. The other women all copy them. They look really good.'

'We're not in the States,' Pippa said crossly. 'Why can't I just be me?' But it was no good, because the next instant she found herself being taken to a discreet little salon down a side street and taught how to apply make-up most effectively for publicity shots and the media.

'Good,' said Jack, well satisfied at the end of the day. 'Now just make sure you look like that tomorrow, and we'll be away.'

Tom gave a low whistle when she walked in, and Mark looked appalled. 'She can't go like that,' he said. 'Vicar's wives don't look like that over here!'

'Don't be silly, Mark,' said Tom patiently. 'We're image creators, not followers. Pippa's going to be the model for Christian women throughout the UK.'

'But people are going to look at her,' said Mark. 'Men are going to look at her.'

'Yes,' said Tom approvingly, 'they are, aren't they?' He winked at Pippa and then turned back to Jack. 'Have you managed to prepare those forward projections I mentioned to you?'

Jack nodded. 'You can have them now if you want. I think we need a nucleus team of eight. You and Mark as our upfront evangelists; Paul to take care of the financial side; me for publicity. You say you've got this Stripe character for music, and then of course we've got the worship group too.' He bit his lip. 'But I really think, top priority, that we need a conference organiser to get a programme up and running as soon as possible, together with a head of counselling to start arranging follow-up work. And lastly, of course, very importantly, we need a handyman type who can drive the bus we're going to have to get, to trundle all our equipment around.'

Jack and Tom disappeared into the next room to talk over plans, and Pippa and Mark were left alone. Apart from going to bed at night, they had not actually been alone since the news of the win had broken, and now Mark looked slightly embarrassed. 'Yes, well, I suppose I'd better go and see Paul,' he said. 'See if he's going to be around tomorrow too.'

'Why?' asked Pippa. She was nervous about how he would respond, but she felt she had to try. 'Why can't you just stay and talk to me for a while?' she pleaded.

Mark shuffled uneasily and looked down at his feet. 'I don't really know what to say,' he brought out at last.

She looked at him for a minute longer, but he refused to look up. 'I'm so sorry,' she said softly, unable to think of anything else. It was all she ever seemed to be saying to him these days. 'I really didn't mean any of this to happen.'

It was as if she had touched a nerve. His head jerked up. 'Why, Pippa?' he demanded. 'Why did you do it? Why did you buy that wretched ticket in the first place?' But then, before she could reply, he shrugged bitterly. 'It doesn't matter now anyway. It's too late. It's happened.' And with that, he spun on his heel and flung out of the door.

She wanted to call after him that it did matter, and that it wasn't too late, whatever might have happened. But he had gone, and she found herself staring into empty air. Glancing up, she caught sight of herself in the mirror over the fire and for a second checked, startled. She did not recognise the beautiful but rather remote woman looking back at her. Then she realised it was herself and her face crumpled, because inside that radiant shell she could feel only a cold and empty space.

The next morning, when she got up, she felt terrible, but obediently she dressed and put on all the make-up Jack had told her to apply, and then went downstairs. Mark, she discovered, was already out. He had gone over to the church, Tom told her blithely, but he had said he would be back by ten, when the car was due. She did not reply but, like a little girl in a party frock, sat down to wait.

Mark had actually gone over to the church to try and pray. He had been distraught ever since his brief exchange with Pippa the night before but did not know what to do. He wanted desperately for things to be right, but he felt he did not know what 'right' was any more. As he sat in the cool gloom of the church, he felt as if his head was going to explode. He had been such an idiot, he thought, ever to have trusted Pippa. But then he remembered that her win was going to fund his new ministry, that it was going to make possible the realisation of his dreams, and he felt even more confused. If the win really was God's will and right, why did he feel so bad about it all? Why did he feel as if he had been betrayed? And why did he feel such unease deep inside him with all the excited preparations that were going on? He truly did want to do God's will, but he had to acknowledge that he was finding it very, very hard. He felt like the prophet Hosea, discovering the adultery of his wife and told by God to take her back. But he was not sure that he could manage it. Maybe this was God's will, he told himself, but what Pippa had done had seared his soul. He was not sure he could forgive her.

When he got back to the rectory, just after ten, he found the car already there. Pippa, Tom and Jack were all waiting for him. There were a couple of other people there too whom he had never seen before, but they looked perfectly at home in his front room and Tom explained that they were going to hold the fort while the rest of them were away. 'Anything might happen,' he said enthusiastically. 'It's vital that we have someone on hand to take calls so that we can respond straightaway. We're in the big league now!'

Mark looked at him, but said nothing. As he clambered into the car beside Pippa, Jack was busy talking into a mobile phone. 'Yes,' he said, 'that's right . . . Get as many as you can there . . . Try the night shelters . . . No, we don't want the Jesus Army . . . Yeah! OK . . . See you later.' He rang off. Mark had not the slightest idea who he had been talking to, but Jack looked extremly pleased with himself. 'It's looking good, Mark,' he announced. He levered himself into the car and scrambled across their feet, heaving himself into the seat in the far corner. 'This is going to be a launch like you've never seen before!'

Throughout the journey Jack maintained a steady stream of the same monosyllabic calls. He spoke to Crichton, Wanda, Ben, someone who sounded like Oogi, and at great length to an individual who remained unnamed. At one point Mark thought he heard a giggling female laugh, but he was not sure, and he could not rouse himself sufficiently to ask who any of these people were. He had the oddest sense that all this was happening to someone else and that he would wake up at any moment and discover it had all been no more than a rather unpleasant dream. He stole a quick glance at Pippa, but she was sitting with her head averted, staring blankly through the window at the landscape flashing past.

The chauffeur drove quickly, and within the hour they were beginning to nose their way through the London suburbs. By eleven fifteen they had hit the Marylebone Road and Jack was beginning to glance at his watch distractedly. He made one last call, to Bernie.

'Food vans in place?' he asked. There was a long buzzing sound from the other end. 'Police been alerted? Yeah, OK.' He nodded his head decisively. 'Right, get them all ready. We'll be with you in ten minutes. We want high impact as we come in.'

As they turned into the approach to Leicester Square, a wall of faces suddenly rose in front of them, like some undulating, chaotic wave. Almost as if there had been a prearranged signal, they began to cheer and shout, and in the same moment Pippa became aware of cameras and newsmen running alongside the car. 'Good grief!' she said. 'What is all this? What's happening?' She felt she had never seen so many people before, and was suddenly rather scared.

Jack, however, was jubilant. '*You're* happening!' he said triumphantly. 'This is the reception committee!'

Pippa stared at the sea of faces. Close to, she saw that they were all about the same age – late teens, early twenties. But there was an air of sad scruffiness about them all, as if they had been cast into the sea of life rather too early and then been chucked out like flotsam. Some looked like travellers, with their hair tightly braided and brightly coloured, wearing defiant clothes; but others looked sad and worn, with dirty grey sweaters and unkempt hair. 'Who are they?' she asked.

'They're homeless,' said Jack triumphantly. 'We've brought them in from the streets and from every hostel around London. You're going to meet them.'

Tom was impressed. 'This is really great, Jack,' he said. 'You've done a terrific job here.'

Jack smiled modestly. 'That's what you're paying me for, Tom.'

Pippa could only stare appalled. 'You can't be serious,' she said as the car turned into the square itself and glided to a halt.

But Jack had already sprung from the car. 'Hurry up,' he chided, 'we're on a tight schedule here. Twenty minutes to distribute the chicken nuggets and chat – good opportunity for photos here . . . and don't forget to smile! Then we've got to get over to the Savoy for twelve thirty for the presentation. We've got this guy Tony Cromper due at twelve forty, and apparently he doesn't want to hang around. We didn't particularly want him,' he added irrelevantly. 'He's not Christian. But Fantasy were very keen to use him, and this way we get a TV interview later too.'

Pippa would have liked to protest but before she could open her mouth, she found herself bundled out of the car and five neat little packs of chicken nuggets were thrust into her hands. Jack gave her a shove forward. 'There you are,' he said. 'Now do your stuff. Talk.'

She found herself immediately surrounded by a crowd of noisy and rather smelly down-and-outs. She held out a packet of greasy nuggets to the nearest. He was a scrawny young man of about twenty, with dirty dark hair and ragged stubble on his chin. Through it, Pippa could see his skin, chalky and white, and there was a hunted look about his eyes. He looked confused. 'Here,' said Pippa, 'have something to eat.' He stared at the packet uncomprehendingly and she felt suddenly sick.

'No use givin' it to 'im!' said a girl. ''E's out of 'is 'ead, 'e is. Don't know what day it is.'

'Dear God,' said Pippa. 'What's wrong with him?'

The girl looked contemptuous. ''Eroin,' she said. ''E's done 'is 'ead in.' She grabbed one of the packets out of Pippa's hand. 'But I'll 'ave some. I'm 'ungry, I am.'

There was some good-natured bantering and Pippa found herself being borne forward by the crowd. When she looked back, the young heroin addict was still standing there, the same dazed expression in his eyes, but he was staring straight at her, and there was so much pain in the look that she felt she wanted to cry.

'That geezer over there said you won the lottery!' someone else said to her.

She turned. 'Yes, that's right.'

There were whistles, ''Ow much you won then?'

'Fourteen million,' said Pippa. 'I think.'

'Blimey! Fourteen million, and all we get's a bag of bleedin' chips!'

'They're not chips,' said someone else. 'Can't you tell the difference?'

A huge young man in a grey tweed coat caught round the waist with a piece of string thrust himself forward. 'Where you from then?' he asked in a broad Irish accent.

Pippa pulled up short. She found herself staring into a pair of dead, coal-black eyes and, in spite of herself, she shivered. 'Little Wakenham,' she replied without thinking. 'It's a village just beyond . . .'

As if from nowhere, Jack suddenly materialised at her side. 'Yes, well,' he said, 'must press on, I'm afraid. Tight schedule. Running late.' He took hold of Pippa's arm. 'Just smile one more time for the cameras.' He planted himself firmly between Pippa and the Irishman. 'Don't let people know where you live,' he hissed. 'We're not ready for that yet.'

Throughout all this Mark stayed miserably over by the car. He felt as if he had just been catapulted into some kind of mad circus and he did not like it. Also he felt that he was rather superfluous to requirements, and the first faint stirrings of jealousy began to stab at him.

'Jack's done us proud,' remarked Tom, coming now and standing beside him. 'And Pippa's doing marvellously. She really gives the impression that she cares. She's so warm.'

'I think it's pathetic,' said Mark contemptuously. 'The whole thing's a sham. They'll be getting her to sing next.'

Tom glanced at him but said nothing. Finally he said softly, 'It's getting us launched, Mark. We'll be on the map after this.'

By the time she returned to the car, Pippa felt shattered. She could not believe she had just talked to so many people, and with each contact she had felt more and more drained. She had felt she wanted to stay and find out something more about them all, but Jack proved a rigorous task master. He would not allow her to delay and, each time she showed signs of staying longer than a minute with any one group, he inserted a hand under her arm and propelled her firmly forward. At the same time he marshalled the cameras and pressmen, and each time she looked up, there was a little flurry of flash-lights. 'Well done,' he said when he finally delivered her safely back to the car. He gave her elbow a squeeze. 'Wasn't too bad, was it? Now for the presentation!'

Pippa had never been to the Savoy before. She was unsure what to expect, and felt daunted when the car pulled up before the main entrance and they discovered more newsmen awaiting them.

'Oh good,' said Jack, glancing round with satisfaction as they alighted, 'we've got Carlton and the Beeb here now.'

They found themselves being filmed as they walked in. At the top of the steps a small group of very polished looking men and women stood waiting for them. An urbane man, in what Pippa judged to be his early fifties, detached himself and came forward. He held out his hand to her. 'On behalf of Fantasy Products, let me welcome you here to receive this wonderful prize.' She found her hand firmly shaken.

'How are you feeling then?' shouted a voice. Half turning, Pippa recognised one of the reporters from Sunday.

'Marvellous!' Jack shouted back. 'She's feeling terrific!'

Then she found herself being swept on and up. 'Tony Cromper isn't here yet,' said a glossy young PR falling into step beside her. 'Do you want to come and tidy up?'

Jack looked the girl up and down and then said, 'Yes, it's OK, Pippa. Good idea, why don't you do that, and I'll make sure everything's laid on OK in the hall.'

'The Riverside Room,' corrected the girl. She lifted her chin and stared at Jack, and he glowered back at her. Then he shrugged and smiled.

'Of course,' he said.

Pippa's sense of unreality increased. She found, when she finally emerged from the huge cloakroom that the PR had taken her to, that she felt even more sick than she had done earlier. Her hands were shaking, and she could feel her skin prickling with cold sweat. 'I just love your suit,' said the girl, noting her nervousness and trying to help her feel at ease. 'Where did you get it?'

Pippa smiled, but found she could not reply. Stepping into the packed room where the reception was to be held, she cast round quickly for Mark. He was nowhere in sight. She pulled at her hair nervously, feeling about fifteen years old again and at her first dance. She would have given anything, just at that moment, to have her husband at her side – but he was still so angry with her. She wondered if he was avoiding her deliberately. The thought made her cross, which achieved what the good-natured PR had been unable to manage by being nice. Someone shoved a glass of champagne into her hand and, unthinking, Pippa took a gulp. She found it relaxed her. Pinning a rigid smile on her face, she stepped forwards and into the crowded room.

'You look great,' said Jack admiringly, attaching himself to her as she came through the doors. 'Come and join your husband and Tom. They're talking to the Chairman of Fantasy.'

The mobile phone, Pippa noticed, had now gone and, in its place, he had acquired a little walkie-talkie which he kept glued to his ear and kept muttering into intermittently.

She drank some more champagne. She did not really want to, but she felt so nervous, it was something to do.

'Who are you talking to?' she asked, as Jack guided her deftly across the room.

'Oogi,' he responded briefly. 'He's keeping me posted for when Tony Cromper arrives.'

Pippa found a plate of salmon and another glass of champagne pushed into her hands. She had not realised the first was empty. 'Congratulations!' people kept saying, 'Well done . . . how are you going to spend the money?'

'She's going to use it for the Lord,' Jack kept replying. After the fifth time he said this Pippa began to feel annoyed. It was as if she was incapable of answering, she thought . . . and besides which, nobody had actually asked her before. They had simply assumed. She found herself drinking more champagne, and her thoughts became more belligerent. Tom and Mark had come up with this brilliant idea, she thought, and ever since they had been acting as if the money was theirs! She took another gulp, and little thoughts of rebellion began to rear in her head. How would *I* like to spend the money? she wondered. What would *I* like to do? A world cruise might be nice. What would they all say if I just announced that now? But the next moment she suddenly found herself wedged on the dais between Tony Cromper, who had just arrived, and the chairman of Fantasy, and her alcohol-stiffened nerve failed.

'Come on up,' said the chairman jovially to Mark. 'Come and stand beside your wife!'

Pippa became aware that Mark was standing only three paces

away. He glared at her. She had not the slightest idea why. She smiled reassuringly and, sullenly, he came up the shallow steps and took his place at her side. 'Hi,' said Pippa tipsily. Then she noticed that he had chosen to wear his biggest and stiffest clerical collar, the one he said always made his neck hurt, – and she added reprovingly, 'You shouldn't have worn that. It looks silly. I don't like big collars!'

'For God's sake, eat something,' Mark whispered.

This struck Pippa as an extremely odd thing to say, but after all, he was her husband, and so obligingly she stuffed a large piece of smoked salmon into her mouth and smiled idiotically. Mark raised his eyes heavenwards.

'It gives me very great pleasure,' began the chairman now, 'to give this cheque to Mr Tony Cromper to present to our charming winner . . .'

Pippa stopped listening. She was not at all used to alcohol and that, combined with the turmoil and the fact that she had not eaten all day, was beginning to make her feel decidedly queer. For some reason the room would not stand still, and everything looked slightly lopsided. '. . . all that remains,' droned on the chairman's voice, 'is for her now to give me the winning ticket.'

Pippa swayed slightly. In the silence that fell, she suddenly became aware that the chairman had turned and was looking at her expectantly. She smiled at him, uncertain what was going on. 'The ticket?' he prompted.

She stared at him blankly. 'Umm, what ticket?'

His smile slipped slightly. 'The winning one.'

Mark nudged her. 'Give him the ticket,' he said. 'Now!'

Something in his manner pierced through Pippa's alcohol-fuddled brain and she stared at him attentively. 'I haven't got it,' she said. 'I never thought. I didn't bring it with me.'

The whole room went quiet. 'Where is it?' asked Mark.

She noted with interest that his face had paled. 'It's in my purse,' she said, 'at home.' She smiled. He was speaking to her again. That was nice, she thought.

The chairman looked confused and Tony Cromper turned away in disgust. 'Don't tell me the silly cow's forgotten it!' he muttered.

A low murmur ran through the room. Jack leapt up on to the podium and pushed his way to her side. 'Where is it?' he hissed in her ear.

She smiled at him too. What a nice young man, she thought, but he seemed a trifle agitated. She could not think why. 'It's at home,' she said sweetly. 'I put it somewhere safe.'

'Where?' he hissed again. He had his mobile out. She watched closely as he punched in the numbers for the rectory.

'It's no good,' she said, 'we're all here.'

'No,' he said briefly, 'I've got Wanda back there She's covering any in-coming calls. Remember?' He bit his lip as the phone rang. 'Where is it, Pippa?'

Something in the way they were all looking at her made her feel cold. She shook her head, trying desperately to clear her thoughts and said, 'In my bag, in the bedroom. It's in the front compartment of my purse.'

Jack looked at the chairman. 'How will it be if we fax it?' he asked. His lips were taut. 'You have got a fax?' he added to Mark. Mark nodded glumly.

The chairman went pink. 'Fax it?' he repeated, aghast.

'Yeah,' said Jack, 'you know.' Then he began to speak into the phone. 'Hi, Wanda, it's me. Bit of a panic. We've forgotten the ticket. Pippa says it's up in the bedroom . . .' He looked at the chairman. 'OK?' he mouthed.

The chairman nodded dumbly. 'I suppose so,' he began. 'I don't know. We've never had this happen before.'

'You've got it. Good. Go into the study,' Jack mumbled into the phone, 'and fax it to . . .'

He looked at the chairman, who looked across at his PR, who said, 'Hang on, I don't know the number here. I'll go and check.' She was back two minutes later and reeled off the number.

'Great,' said Jack. He repeated the number into the phone and then clicked it off. 'Can we all go up to the hotel office?'

They went in a body, the chairman leading the way. It was on the fifth floor and there was an unseemly scramble for the lifts as everyone tried to crowd in. Nobody wanted to miss the big moment. Pippa found herself wedged between Mark and Tom. Both of them looked annoyed. She found she was still clutching her champagne glass and so, unable to think of anything better to do, she fortified herself with a quick swig. Somehow, it did not have quite the same effect any more. She felt miserable.

The doors of the lift opened and they poured out. Jack almost ran down the corridor ahead of them. He was speaking into the mobile again, and Pippa heard him gasp, 'Yep, almost there. Get ready!'

They streamed into the office and clustered expectantly round the fax machine. It obligingly buzzed and then whirred, and then nothing happened. 'What's up?' said Jack into the mouthpiece. 'What do you mean it's stuck? Then unstick it! I don't care if it is too small! Try again!'

The machine began to whirr again and then coughed slightly, and then, very slowly, a crumpled piece of paper began to emerge. The fax appeared to be sticking at both ends. They all craned forward to see and Jack began to read off the numbers aloud. 'One, three

. . . seven . . . twelve . . .' His voice began to rise in excitement, and he almost tore at the paper as it paused. Then, 'Thirty! Forty!' he shrieked.

The chairman looked at him witheringly but said nothing. He looked affronted. He waited for the paper to come fully through and then said sourly, 'I suppose we can proceed with the presentation of the copy cheque here, since the press are all present. But we shall require the actual ticket before we hand over the cheque itself!'

'Of course,' said Jack.

The chairman looked at him again. 'Who is this person?' he asked.

'He's Jack,' said Pippa.

The chairman smiled thinly. 'Quite,' he said. He nodded at Tony Cromper, who was still clutching the large presentation cheque.

'Yeah, OK,' agreed the star. He looked around to make sure the film crew and all the photographers were ready and then flashed on a treacly smile. 'It gives me great pleasure to present this lucky lady with her winning cheque.'

Cameras flashed as he leant forward and planted a huge kiss on Pippa's cheek, and the next moment she found herself clutching an extremely large cardboard cheque. 'OK. So you get the real one when we get the ticket,' the chairman hissed again. Pippa smiled.

# Chapter Seven

Pippa awoke the next day with the most terrible head. 'Aah,' she said, sitting up and gingerly opening one eye. The world slid sideways, and then very slowly righted itself. As she came more fully awake, she recalled the events of the previous day and cringed. The sudden movement was unwise, because it sent pain hammering through her head. 'Oh God,' she said despairingly.

Misery swept over her. She felt she had behaved extremely badly. Mark had certainly said as much although, amazingly, the news report that had been on television later the same night had simply presented her as being bubbly and rather fun. The reporter who had fronted the item described her as a refreshing breath of life for the Anglican Church, and said what tremendous value she was. Jack, who had been watching throughout critically, breathed a sigh of relief and then said, 'Endearing. That's what they're making you out to be. I think we've got away with it.'

He had worked extremely hard. Once the photographers had finished snapping away at the presentation, he had driven as fast as possible back to Little Wakenham to get the ticket, collected it, and then hared back again. Pippa shuddered to think how many traffic offences he must have committed, but he had achieved the entire journey in just under one hour fifty minutes. During the wait, Mark had first poured two very strong cups of black coffee down her, and then insisted that they all go and eat a proper lunch. She had had chicken and Perrier water, which was all he would allow her, and by the end she had felt depressingly sober. She had rather felt by then that she preferred the former state.

Tony Cromper had disappeared almost immediately after the presentation, and the newsmen, having got their story and lost their star, had also withdrawn. She had imagined then that she would be allowed to relax, but it was not to be. As soon as Jack rejoined them and the actual cheque was in their possession, he looked at her carefully, appeared satisfied, and then announced, 'We've got to be at River Radio for three.' Luckily, when they got there, Mark and Tom did most of the talking, doing their best to promote Chalice, and Pippa took the opportunity to slump down in her chair, and pray. She did not pray for anything in particular, she just asked Jesus to come in and sort out the mess into which she appeared to have plunged them all.

When they had finally got back to the rectory later that night, Tom said to Mark, 'I've had the team put together a couple of conference projections. One for a mission to Solihull, and the other centred on Cambridge. I've called a meeting for nine thirty tomorrow over in the church hall. OK?'

Mark nodded. He seemed as surprised as Pippa, but he merely said, 'How many are going to be there then?'

Tom responded, as if the question were of no importance, 'Six, I hope. But I'm not sure if Oogi can make it yet.'

Now, remembering all this, Pippa glanced at the clock. Nine forty-three ... She listened carefully, but the house remained reassuringly quiet and so, very cautiously, she slipped her legs over the side of the bed and stood up. The hammers pounded again through her brain and she flinched, not daring to move till the pain subsided. Then, very slowly, she began to dress.

By the time she got downstairs it was almost quarter to eleven but after a cup of coffee and the slice of toast that she forced herself to eat, she began to feel slightly better. Just as she was finishing, there was a knock at the door. 'Come in,' she called, 'it's open.'

Elaine came in. She looked pale. 'Hi,' she said. 'I just thought I'd come and see how you were. I saw you all on the telly last night. How did it go?'

'Awful,' said Pippa. And then she added, 'They're all at a meeting over in the hall.'

'I know,' said Elaine. 'Paul's gone.'

Pippa grunted, then poured Elaine a mug of coffee and pushed it towards her. 'Do you want to see fourteen million pounds?' she inquired.

Elaine goggled. 'Why? Have you still got the cheque here?'

Pippa nodded, and then very carefully got up to get it. 'My head hurts,' she explained. 'I think I've got a hangover.' She laid the cheque on the table in front of Elaine and they both stared at it.

'Funny,' said Elaine. 'It doesn't really mean very much. I can't actually visualise fourteen million pounds.'

'No,' agreed Pippa. 'Stupid, isn't it? Apparently we're going to go and put it in the bank this afternoon. Mark and Tom say they've got to be there too because of this trust thing we're setting up.'

'That must be why Paul's over at the hall this morning.'

They sat companionably. Pippa noticed for the first time that Elaine looked as rough as she felt and, after a moment, she said, 'So how's it going with you?'

'Bloody,' said Elaine. She breathed deeply and then went on,

'Three more phone calls in the last couple of days. She knew very well he wasn't there, I think she was just gloating.'

Pippa did not have to inquire who 'she' was. 'Has Paul said anything?' she asked.

Elaine shrugged. 'No, not really. He says he doesn't want to talk. He's still absolutely furious with me that Stripe's there. Though at least,' she added, 'it's meant he's been at home a bit more. I think actually that's why Melanie keeps phoning me. I think she's cross and blames me.' Elaine pulled a face. 'It's nonsense, of course. I don't insist Paul's got to stay around all the time – he wouldn't listen even if I did – but he says he's worried about leaving the house with Stripe there. He says he might murder us all in our beds.' She gave a snort of derision. 'Do you know, he's even arranged for a security firm to come and update our alarm system!'

Pippa shook her head. 'I still wish you'd talk to Mark,' she said at last.

'Why?' said Elaine. 'Do you really think he'd listen to me? He'd just shoot straight round to Paul. Paul would deny it, and then they'd both agree that I was going loopy.'

'Of course he wouldn't!' said Pippa indignantly. But she remembered Mark's comments to Tom earlier in the week and fell silent.

'Yes he would,' said Elaine bitterly. 'No offence, Pippa, but you know what they're like, these male clergy. They're totally incapable of keeping a confidence when it comes to something like this. I think they just imagine women don't know what they're talking about. It's all in the mind, we're hysterical, we've got to be looked after. And if he did believe me, my God!' She rolled her eyes. 'No, Pippa, I couldn't do that. Not unless I was absolutely sure that there was no hope left.'

Tom had invited Stripe to join them in the hall at eleven, after the meeting, so that he could meet the team. Stripe was half an hour late, but as it happened the meeting had dragged on because none of them been able to agree on whether or not to target Christians or non-Christians first, and Jack had said that anyway he didn't like Solihull, and it made much more sense to start in Cambridge. Somebody else had then promptly disagreed and said no, it ought to be Solihull, and then somebody else had said that they didn't think either place was a very good idea, and why couldn't they start with Carbery instead. It had been at this point that Tom had said ominously that they ought to pray, and they were just finishing as Stripe joined them.

The musician pulled over a chair and sat down, and Tom announced, 'We're planning an evangelistic tour . . .' He looked round threateningly, as if daring anyone to say anything, but they all remained silent. He was about to go on when Stripe spoke up.

'I'm not goin' nowhere near Liverpool.'

Tom blinked, surprised. 'Er, no,' he said uncertainly. 'We hadn't really got Liverpool in mind anyway yet.'

'Good,' said Stripe. 'I don't want to go nowhere near there at the moment.'

Paul snorted loudly and rose to his feet. 'That's all we need,' he said, 'a dope-crazed junkie having histrionics!'

Stripe was indignant. 'It's jus' for the good of me 'ealth, that's all.'

'Hum!' said Paul. He began to gather his papers. 'If you'll excuse me, everyone, I think my bit of the meeting's concluded, and I've already met this gentleman.' He shot a quick glance at Mark. 'I'll see you at three, Mark, if you'd like to pop round with Pippa, and then we can get all this sorted out properly.' He snapped shut his briefcase, nodded curtly and headed for the door.

'There was some bird round your place this morning,' said Stripe loudly after his retreating back. 'Said 'er name was Melanie something.'

In mid-stride, Paul halted. 'What?' he said, turning back.

'Said she was lookin' for you,' said Stripe coolly. He tilted back his chair and began to inspect his nails. 'Said she was a good friend of yours.'

Paul flushed. 'Ah, yes.' He cleared his throat loudly. 'I know who you mean. Miss Jenkins. She works at the bank.'

'That's wot she said,' agreed Stripe.

Paul ran a finger round the inside of his collar. 'I expect she was bringing some papers for me to sign,' he announced to the room at large.

'No,' said Stripe, 'I don't think it was that. Leastways, if it was, she didn't 'ave no briefcase with 'er.' He looked up and smiled at Paul; a hard little smile that left his eyes cold.

'Yes, well,' said Paul, flustered, 'I expect they were in the car. I would imagine she wanted to find me first before she got them out.'

'Maybe.' Stripe looked unconvinced. 'I'd 'ave said meself it was more of a chat she was after.'

The rest of them, puzzled, looked at each other, wondering what on earth was going on. Mark watched Stripe and Paul with concern. There seemed something more than usually aggressive in the way they were skirting round each other, and he began earnestly to hope that there would not now be an open row between them. Not for the first time, he wondered at the wisdom of Stripe's continuing to live over the Dufrayns' garage. Perhaps, he thought, the young man should come and live at the rectory instead. He must, he thought, talk it over with Pippa. And then he remembered that he was not talking to his wife about anything, and sighed. 'See you later, Paul,' he said. 'At three.'

Paul looked at him gratefully and, not replying, hurried through the door. Stripe stared after him and then remarked, inconsequentially, 'Funny that, 'e seems a bit upset.'

Paul was a bit upset. He was horrified at the idea that Melanie should have come down to the village to find him. He felt that he was being checked up on, and it occurred to him that if she encountered Elaine now, there would be the most frightful row.

He had not brought his car, and so now he almost ran back to Gentillesse. As he turned into the lane leading down to the house, he saw Melanie's black Golf was parked in his drive, and she herself leaning up against the side, arms crossed pugnaciously across her chest. Paul swallowed and broke into a run.

Melanie was an attractive, if rather angular young woman, about five foot eight and with very short, shiny black hair. She adopted a streamlined, rather severe style and, as he drew close, he saw that she was wearing what was, for her, a typical dark charcoal suit, while her hair seemed to glitter with a kind of odd metallic lustre in the sun. She looked rather out of place, he thought, framed by the soft prettiness of Gentillesse behind.

'What on earth are you doing?' he panted, scrunching his way noisily up to her on the gravel. 'I've told you before not to come here.'

She turned and stared at him, her face inscrutable. Then, after a second, she smiled sweetly and said, 'I came to find you. There's been a phone call from Milan.'

'What?' said Paul, aghast, wondering instantly if he had made some blunder in his dealings with the Italian bank.

'Not really,' said Melanie, relenting. She stepped forward and slid her arms round his neck, and then planted a long, lingering kiss on his mouth. 'I came to see you, darling. I've missed you.'

At her first touch Paul had gone rigid, and now he leapt back like an affronted hare. 'Melanie, please!' he said. 'Not here. Someone will see.'

Her eyes grew hard and, almost imperceptibly, she tightened her grip on his neck. 'Who? Like Elaine? I think people ought to see.'

He removed her arms with difficulty. 'No . . . yes. This isn't the right time.'

She continued to stare at him measuringly and then said, 'When is the right time, Paul?'

His only thoughts now were on getting her away. 'Look,' he said hastily, 'this isn't the right place. We'll talk about it later. I promise.'

His eyes darted round, and he was relieved to see nobody seemed to be about. 'Where's Elaine?' he asked.

Melanie shrugged. 'Haven't a clue. She's not here. I've already tried the door. I did meet your Stripe character though.'

'I know,' said Paul, 'he told me.' He was thinking fast. 'Look, come away now. I'll buy you a quick lunch or something if you want before we go back to the office. But you must go before Elaine gets back.'

Melanie seemed disinclined to move. 'I think I'd rather like to hang around, if it's all the same to you,' she said coolly. 'I'd like to meet Elaine. I want to talk to her.' Her chin lifted, and she looked Paul straight in the eye. 'After all, one of us has to tell her.'

'She already knows,' said Paul bitterly. 'You've made sure of that with all your phone calls.'

'I don't mean that. I know she knows, but I mean she needs to know it's over.'

It was a threat and Paul knew it. He licked his lips. 'Look,' he said again, 'let's talk about this. There are things to consider.'

'Not for me. It's all perfectly simple for me.'

Paul was beginning to feel trapped. 'But it isn't for me,' he said urgently. 'There's the house to think about, and the boys. I can't just leave. There's a lot of money tied up here. You're going to be the loser too if I just walk out without getting all this properly settled.'

Any appeal to emotion would have cut very little ice with Melanie, but the financial problem made perfect sense to her. She was a girl who liked her creature comforts, and Paul was right. She would not like him half so much poor. 'OK,' she said slowly, 'but make sure you *do* sort it. I've had enough of being a bit on the side, and if you don't tell her soon, I shall. Or it's over. OK?'

'OK,' said Paul thankfully. He gripped her elbow and began to propel her none too gently towards her car.

'Watch it,' said Melanie indignantly. She twisted away from him, affronted, and then slid into the driving seat. 'What was this meeting you were at this morning anyway?'

Paul, still worried that Elaine would at any minute return, muttered distractedly, 'It's this lottery win there's been all the fuss about. The Vicar's wife was the one who won. They're setting up a trust. The bank's going to be handling it.'

A strange expression flitted across Melanie's face and she glanced at him quickly. 'You mean the fourteen million?'

'Yes,' said Paul.

'Really?' Melanie appeared to consider. 'You know, I could work on that account. It sounds interesting.'

'Yes,' agreed Paul hastily, 'whatever you want. Just go!' The sound of voices floated over the hedge and he slammed the car door. 'I'll see you at the office this afternoon.'

As Melanie turned out of the drive, Elaine walked in. 'Who was that?' she asked, gazing after the car.

'No one,' said Paul. 'At least . . . someone from the office, dropping some forms round for the Chalice account.'

Elaine looked from the car to him then back again to the car. 'I see,' she said.

The team Tom had so far assembled professed themselves intrigued with Stripe. He was, they all agreed, sent by God, and Jack caught the first faint glimmerings of a publicity campaign. Following on all the argument, it was finally decided that they should after all begin by going to Carbery, and Oogi undertook to find a suitable venue and liaise with churches. Mark said he felt that they needed to plan things very carefully, but Tom said that they should not waste time and that they should capitalise on the publicity from the win, and so they fixed on a date only two weeks away.

They bought a small bus, and had it sprayed white, with a huge gold chalice on the side; and a synthesiser and sound system for Stripe. Then Tom announced that he and Mark should both have larger and better cars, because people would expect it of them now, and so they both went out one day and bought a Mercedes apiece. Pippa gaped when she saw them and said they must be mad. But Paul said that they were tax deductible as capital assets . . . Whatever her protests, she discovered that nobody anyway seemed to listen to her any more. She found herself given a brand new chequebook for the brand new account, and lectured by Paul on financial responsibilty.

More and more people arrived at the rectory, and the phone seemed to be going nonstop. Mark announced that they needed full-time secretarial help. He took on a lady in her fifties called Agnes, who was overjoyed to find her typing skills of use once again (she had been made redundant a couple of years before), and who seemed to be constantly under Pippa's feet. Then Tom announced that Pippa herself should become more involved. She would have to speak, he said, in Carbery, before he and Mark went on. Her testimony would be inspiring. Mark attempted to demur. He was not sure he wanted his wife to play so prominent a role, but Tom assured him that over in the States the wives did it all the time. They were still under the authority of their husbands, he explained, but they had their own ministries that people looked up to and appreciated. Pippa, Tom said, could be just like them. She might even in time become an evangelist, given half a chance. Mark continued to look grim, but then Tom reminded him that although the money was now in a trust account, by rights it still actually belonged to Pippa, and so, reluctantly, he gave way. Pippa was told she was going to speak. 'It doesn't have to be anything very long,' Tom said. 'Just tell them how it all happened. How God guided you.'

Pippa swallowed. 'I'm not sure that's such a good idea,' she brought out at last.

Tom would have none of it. 'Of course it is,' he said. 'It's your testimony. It'll be inspiring for others.'

Ever since the win, Tom had become increasingly attentive to Pippa. More and more, he had noticed how Mark seemed to ignore his wife and it had begun to annoy him. Mark, he felt, did not deserve her. Tom began to trail after Pippa. At night when she went into the kitchen to prepare their meal, he would be there. Afterwards he would clear away, and then help her load the dishwasher and get the kitchen straight. At least, he said he was helping, but more often than not he would just stand there and chat, until Pippa felt that if he did not move she would scream. If anything, she was irritated by him, but as the days passed and Mark seemed to become increasingly distant, she found herself encouraging Tom in an effort to win her husband's attention. When that did not work, she tried talking to him.

'Hasn't this gone on long enough?' she said one night as they were getting ready for bed.

'Don't start,' said Mark wearily, 'I'm too tired.'

Pippa bit her lip. 'I'm not starting,' she said, 'I simply want to talk.' He did not answer, and after a moment she went on, 'Look, I really am sorry about the ticket. But it's not my fault I won and maybe, like Tom said, it's actually a gift from God . . .' Mark shrugged and pulled off his socks. 'Don't you care?' she said desperately. 'Doesn't it matter to you about us any more?'

Mark breathed heavily, but only continued to stare woodenly at the carpet.

'For God's sake, why can't you say something?' exploded Pippa, her patience snapping. 'How many other men would just sit there like you do? You're like a deaf mute!'

Mark glowered. Carefully he folded his socks, laid them on the floor, and got into bed. 'Put the light off,' he said.

The day before they were all due to go over to Carbery, Pippa bumped into Dr Forrest in the village. 'Did you speak to your husband?' he asked, stopping to chat.

Pippa smiled ruefully. 'I tried,' she said, 'but he's not too keen.'

The doctor looked at her. 'Some men,' he remarked casually, 'think it's all a bit of a challenge to their virility. Some of them can even get quite cross.' He looked at Pippa closely. 'Of course, I'm not saying your husband's like that . . . clergyman and all the rest of it . . . Vicars don't get cross, do they?' He laughed. 'But all the same, it can be a bit bumpy.'

'He won't talk to me,' said Pippa in a rush. She had not intended to, but somehow, in face of Dr Forrest's concern, she suddenly found the words just spilled out. 'He was fearfully angry when I first mentioned it, and then things seemed to get a bit better, and I thought he was coming round. But then I won this wretched lottery and he's hardly spoken a word to me ever since.'

'Ah yes, the lottery. I heard about that.' Dr Forrest looked thoughtful. He was a kindly man, only some two years off retirement. He liked Pippa, he always had, and he guessed accurately that a lot of people came and poured out their troubles to her but that she had no one in whom she could similarly confide. He chewed his lip, at a loss. 'Good fortune can sometimes be quite difficult to contend with,' he remarked at last, 'especially when you already feel threatened.'

'It's not that,' said Pippa. 'He thinks I've betrayed him. He set up this anti-lottery group. He says I've made him look a fool.'

'Ah, I see.' He watched her walk away down the street, and scratched his head. He was not a particularly religious man, but just at that moment he found himself uttering a prayer. He felt that the Vicar and his wife needed it.

Sebastian and Harry announced that they wanted to go along to the youth rally too. 'Please, Dad,' begged Sebastian. 'We'll be quite safe. After all, the Vicar and his wife are going to be there, and Tom. And it is supposed to be evangelistic.'

Paul glowered. Two weeks of living in close proximity to Stripe had done nothing to alleviate the concern he felt. 'I don't like you hanging around anywhere where that young man's going to be,' he said. 'I seriously doubt if it would ever be safe where he was. Even if the Archangel Gabriel was there too!'

'Please, Dad,' chimed in Harry. 'Some of the kids from school are going along. Caldwell's mother is going to take him and Freestone.'

'You might as well say they can go,' remarked Elaine. 'I'm sure they'll be all right. After all, a Christian concert is hardly going to turn into a drug-crazed rave.'

'Oh, all right. I suppose so,' said Paul grudgingly.

The boys let out whoops of delight. 'Cool! We'll go and tell Stripe,' yelled Harry. 'Come on, Seb!'

They pelted out through the door and Elaine looked at Paul. 'They'll be all right,' she said. Then, 'Look, can we talk?'

Alarm flew across Paul's face. 'Not now,' he said hastily, 'I've got some things to do . . . said I'd meet Mark over at the hall.' He fled.

71

The boys meanwhile had burst in on Stripe. 'Dad says we can come,' said Sebastian jubilantly.

'That's great,' said Stripe. He was lying full length on the couch with his eyes closed. In the ashtray on the floor at his side was a half-smoked cigarette, the smoke wafting in a gentle spiral up into the darkened air. It gave off a pungent smell.

'What are you doing?' asked Harry.

'Nuthin',' said Stripe. 'Just 'avin' a fag.'

'Mummy says we're not supposed to smoke,' remarked Harry.

They both came in and settled themselves down on the floor. 'Can I try it?' asked his brother.

'If yer want,' said Stripe. He waved a languid hand. ''Elp yourself.'

The boys needed no further urging. First one, then the other, took a long drag. Harry collapsed coughing. 'Gosh,' he gasped, his eyes watering, 'that's really strong. What is it?'

'Nuthin',' said Stripe. He shrugged. 'Weed. Try some more.'

Cautiously the boys tried it again. 'It makes me feel a bit funny,' said Sebastian. 'I'm not sure I like it really.'

Elaine found them half an hour later. She had been calling them to come in to bed, and when they did not respond she went in search of them. They were nowhere in the garden or down at the boat house, and so finally she went over to the garage. Finding the door open, she did not bother to knock, but simply went in, calling out as she went up the stairs, 'Hello! Anyone there?' At the top, at the door leading into the living room, she paused, and then peered in. The sight that met her eyes made her pull up short. Stripe was lying inert on the sofa, but Harry and Sebastian were both crawling round the floor, giggling inanely. Sebastian, for some obscure reason, had a towel about his head. 'Boys,' said Elaine, startled. 'What's going on?'

Harry looked up and giggled. 'It's Mummy,' he said happily. 'Hello, Mummy.' Sebastian began to laugh too.

A horrible suspicion began to form at the back of Elaine's mind. Stepping quickly in, she flicked on the light.

'Hey, watch it!' said Stripe, waking up. He raised his head and peered at her blearily.

'What's going on?' repeated Elaine. She sniffed the air. 'Oh my God,' she said. 'Stripe! You haven't?'

He had the grace to look guilty. 'No,' he protested, 'I never. They 'elped themselves!'

He flinched under the look she gave him. 'Get up!' she said grimly to the boys. She stooped down, picked up the ashtray, together with the tobacco and papers lying at its side, then walked quickly into the bathroom. There was the sound of the lavatory being flushed.

72

'Hey!' exclaimed Stripe indignantly. 'That's private property, that is!'

Coming back into the room, Elaine glared at him. 'You thank your lucky stars,' she said, 'that I don't take your private property to the police!' Then she reached down and grabbed Sebastian with one hand, and Harry with the other, and began to drag them up. 'Whatever happens,' she said grimly, 'for God's sake don't tell your father.'

# Chapter Eight

Pippa's journey to Carbery was grim. Once again she found herself with Mark, Tom and Jack. They travelled in the new Mercedes that Mark had bought. It was a kind of dull metallic pink, with cream leather upholstery and a roof that curled up and tucked itself neatly away when you pressed a button. Mark and Tom both hooted derisively at this facility, and said how stupid people were who took such interest in cars, but all the way down, one or other of them kept pressing the switch and then guffawing loudly at the envious expressions on the faces of other motorists as they sailed past. By the time they were halfway through the journey, Pippa felt heartily sick of them both and when Jack, sitting beside her in the back, looked at her and pulled a face, she found herself raising her eyes heavenwards in a kind of shared commiseration.

'Let's open her up,' said Tom, as they hit the motorway. 'Let's see what the old bus can do.'

Nothing loath, Mark obligingly put his foot down on the accelerator and the car sprang forward. 'Whe-hay! Light speed!' shouted Tom, as Mark slid smoothly out into the fast lane. The finger on the speedometer moved gently up. In the back Pippa gazed at it with a feeling of alarm. To her disordered senses, they now seemed to be travelling so fast that cars in the other lanes seemed almost to be standing still. She felt a thrill of fear.

'Attaboy!' shouted Tom.

Mark put his foot down a bit more. The engine purred gently, and beside them slower cars whistled by in a blur of speed. It was shortly afterwards that they became aware of the siren. 'Can you hear anything?' asked Jack.

Mark glanced in his rearview mirror. As Pippa stared at him, his face seemed to drain of all colour, as if someone had flicked off a switch. 'Oh no!' he said.

Alarmed, Pippa twisted round in her seat and peered through the back window. Screaming up behind them, lights flashing like some angry hornet, she saw a police car. Abruptly Mark transferred his foot to the brake and pulled over to the inner lane. The police car drew alongside and Pippa saw the policeman in the passenger seat gesticulating to them to move across. The next second a disembodied voice boomed, 'Pull over, sir. Now!'

As if by common consent, Pippa and Jack slid down in their seats, and Mark pulled over on to the hard shoulder and brought the car to a stop. The police car drew up behind, and then the officer driving sprang out and strode up to Mark's door. He rapped smartly on the window and, as it went down, snapped, 'Do you have any idea what speed you were doing just then, sir?'

Pippa knew exactly what speed they had been doing. The needle on the gauge had been at 130. She did not volunteer this information. Mark had apparently decided to feign ignorance. 'Eighty-five?' he hazarded.

The policeman glared at him. 'We have you down at one hundred and thirty, sir,' he spat. 'We've been trailing you on camera for the last twelve miles!'

Mark cringed, and wished suddenly that he was not wearing his clerical collar. The policeman's eyes fell on it. 'Thought we'd take a short cut to heaven, did we?' he inquired sarcastically. 'Or are you merely trying to put the fear of God into other motorists?'

Mark mumbled something incoherent and the policeman gazed at him stonily. 'May I see your licence and insurance, sir? I take it that this vehicle is yours.' His tone expressed incredulity and Mark flushed, but the next second his embarrassment had gone, chased away by a look of alarm. He swallowed uneasily and then said, 'This *is* my car, officer, but I'm terribly sorry, I don't think I've got my licence and insurance with me.'

The policeman was already filling out a ticket. 'You are required to present your licence, insurance, and all relevant documents pertaining to ownership of this vehicle at your nearest police station within the next seven days.' He tore off the ticket and held it out to Mark, his eyes hard. 'You are being fined for speeding. Failure to present your documents will be an offence under sections 164 and 165 of the Road Traffic Act 1988 and will render you liable for prosecution.' Then he leant forward and hissed, 'And think yourself very lucky, matey, that I'm not doing you for dangerous driving too!'

It was a subdued little group that drove on after that. For the rest of the journey Mark kept rigidly to the speed limit, and when they finally got to Carbery, it was going on for four o'clock. They should have been there at three. In silence Mark drove straight to the town hall, which they had hired for the event, and dropped them there while he himself went to park the car in a multi-storey car park nearby.

The three of them tumbled out on to the pavement, and found themselves immediately engulfed by the swarms of people shambling by. A group of Japanese tourists, eyes glued to their cameras, began busily filming the street. It was not a particularly attractive street, as far as Pippa could see, and just at that moment it was full of cars, but obviously something had caught their interest, and it was all she could do to push her way through. She caught up with Jack and Tom, who were inspecting a large poster stuck to the wall. 'Faith is fun!' she read, and then in smaller letters underneath, 'Come and discover the truth with Chalice Ministries tonight.'

'Looks pretty good, doesn't it?' said Tom approvingly. 'You've done well, Jack.'

Pulled up on the kerb a little further on, they found the Chalice van. Stripe came bounding down the steps of the town hall as they came up. He looked as if he was enjoying himself. 'Hi!' he said, at their approach. 'What kept ye? We thought you'd be here hours ago. We've almost finished now. The keyboard and sounds are all set up, but we haven't done lighting or anything yet.'

Jack and Tom headed off to supervise and Pippa said, 'You look as if you're having fun.'

'Yeah,' he responded, 'it's jus' like a gig. I like performing.' He glanced at her. 'You don't look too happy though.'

'No,' she agreed. She pulled a face. 'Mark just got a ticket for speeding.'

Stripe stared at her and then burst out laughing. 'There ye go,' he said. 'Boys with their toys!'

When Mark finally joined them, he did not seem in the best of moods. 'We need to eat,' said Tom briskly, 'and then we ought to call a prayer meeting for everyone, to get us ready for tonight.' Mark grunted unenthusiastically, and Tom went on, 'Why don't we phone out for some pizzas? That way we can stop here and we won't get distracted by anything. We need to focus on the Lord now.'

As Jack was busy ordering the pizzas, Pippa sidled up to Mark and slipped a hand through his arm. 'Don't worry,' she said encouragingly. 'It could have happened to anyone.'

He pulled away from her as if he had been stung. 'But it didn't,' he said bitterly. 'It happened to me. Just my luck! Why do things always seem to go wrong for me?'

It was on the tip of Pippa's tongue to suggest that perhaps he should have kept to the speed limit, but wisdom prevailed and she forbore. 'It was just one of those things,' she said mildly.

Mark glared at her as if somehow, inexplicably, it was all her fault. 'Stop trying to be so bloody reasonable,' he spat. 'Stop pretending you care!' He pushed her roughly aside and strode away, leaving her staring after him with her mouth open in dismay. Tom, who had witnessed the exchange, came up and slipped an arm round her shoulders. He gave her a quick hug. 'Never mind, Pippa,' he murmured. 'He's just finding it all a bit much. He's nervous, that's all.' Unexpectedly, the scent of her perfume wafted up and seemed to hit him squarely on the nose, almost like a blow. It was so hard and so sudden, it felt almost physical, and he reeled, his senses swimming. It was all he could do to stop himself from kissing her there and then. With a tremendous effort of will he merely lowered his face into her hair, drinking in the scent and nuzzling the side of her head.

Pippa did not even notice. 'I just can't get through to him, Tom,' she was saying plaintively. 'Nothing I say to him has any effect. He won't talk to me.'

Tom swallowed. 'I know, Pippa,' he said hoarsely. His other arm was creeping up and round her, but the next second Pippa pushed violently away. It was not that she was reacting against him, she was just so upset by Mark.

'I simply don't know what to do,' she wailed.

Tom recovered himself and stared at Pippa. She was standing not two paces from him, wringing her hands, a distraught expression on her face. As he gazed at her, he suddenly realised how close he had been to casting all restraint aside and telling her how much he loved her. And in the same moment he felt he no longer cared. He took a step towards her. He felt he wanted to tell her that he understood, and that Mark was a swine, and that if she would only come away with him now, he would never treat her like that. He felt he wanted to tell her that she could have a dozen babies if she wanted, and he would be only too happy to help make them.

'Where do you want the speaker's mike?' said Stripe suddenly, coming up behind them. 'Jack said to come and ask you.'

The spell was broken. With a start, Tom recollected himself and Pippa turned away. She did not want anyone else to see her distress. But in that moment she felt very, very grateful to Tom. She glanced quickly at him and gave a watery smile. 'Thank you,' she whispered.

The city churches had worked very hard in the preceding two weeks. They had marshalled from their congregations every available boy or girl under the age of twenty that they could find. They had put posters in the local schools, and they had blitzed all the local youth groups. The result was that they had assembled an audience of young people who, in the main, already came to church. They had also succeeded in capturing a fairly large number of parents who, despite the protests of their offspring, had come along because they wanted to see what was going on.

Five minutes before they were due to start, in the prayer meeting that Tom had called backstage, Pippa burst into tears. A spotty young man had just been proclaiming, 'We claim this hall for you, Lord!' and there had been various little oohs and aahs of support, when a sudden flood of absolute terror had swamped her. 'I can't do it,' she hiccuped through her tears. 'I simply cannot stand up there on that stage and tell people how wonderful it's all been.'

'This is all your fault!' snapped Tom, glowering at Mark.

'My fault?' said Mark, enraged. 'What do you mean?'

'I mean you ought to try being nice to her for a change!'

'Nice? I am nice!'

'No you're bloody not!'

'Stop it! Both of you!' Pippa exclaimed. 'What's it matter whose fault it is? I just can't go on like this!'

'There!' said Tom.

'I think she's nervous,' whispered someone else.

'I think we should pray for her,' offered Jack.

Pippa could have screamed, but the next moment five pairs of hands descended on her head and a loud male voice began, 'Father, we want to lift Pippa up before you here. In her frailty she's feeling very weak and insecure, and we ask you now to strengthen her and give her peace . . .'

'Come on, Mark,' said Tom.

Two more pairs of hands descended on Pippa's head. 'You ought to pray for her too, Mark,' Jack chipped in. 'She's your wife.'

After a moment, very grudgingly, Mark began, 'Lord, we ask you to help Pippa now. Give her what to say, Lord, and strengthen her. Amen.'

'There,' said Jack, as the hands were removed. 'Do you feel better now?'

Pippa did not dare say no. She was afraid that if she did they would start praying again. 'Yes,' she said hollowly, 'much better, thank you.' She looked at Mark, and he grimaced and turned away.

'Look,' said Tom softly, sitting down beside her, 'don't worry. Just stand up and tell people what you think God's doing. It's easy. Just tell the truth.'

They trooped out on to the stage and Stripe, now sitting nonchalantly at the keyboard, led them in worship. Amazingly, it seemed again as if he was born to it. The words of encouragement between the songs seemed to come easily to him and, as he played, the music seemed to flow out and up in a great rolling tide of love, warmth and forgiveness. Dotted around the audience, here and there, people began to cry, and then others stood with their arms upraised and, quite spontaneously, people began to pray aloud. The music flowed on, and then in itself became a prayer; a voiceless cry for help.

When at last it was Pippa's turn to stand up to speak, she found that she was no longer afraid. Her own concerns and hurts seemed temporarily to have been blotted out by some great and enveloping spirit of love. She could feel it almost tangibly, as if something huge and beautiful was there, something that was working to its own purposes. She felt awed. That others could feel it too, she knew, and she suddenly imagined she could almost see a huge, brilliant angel, with a curved flashing sword in its hands, battling against all the chaos and pain that seemed to be surrounding them all. She gave herself up to the great gentleness that seemed to flow over her, and began to speak. She heard herself tell people how she had bought the lottery ticket because she had been so upset and angry. She told them how she had picked the numbers, with absolutely no expectation of winning, but as an act of defiance to an uncaring world. She told them of her shame. And then she told them of God's all-conquering love. She did not say anything more, and there was a silence as she finished, then people began to cheer and stand up, and from all sides there were cries of 'Alleluia!' and 'Praise the Lord!' Stripe began to play.

Pippa felt tremendous. She felt as if God himself had spoken to her, as if he had given her a promise that, although things seemed such a mess, he *was* there, and he was in control. She turned round and looked for Mark, her eyes glowing, sure that he must have felt it too. But as her eyes raked over the little group behind, she received a shock. His chair was empty. He had gone.

Totally humiliated, Mark had fled from the stage halfway through his wife's address. How could Pippa stand up and say all that? The knowledge that it was the truth did nothing to make him feel better. He felt yet again that she had betrayed him. True, she had not specifically mentioned the fertility tests that had been the original cause of their dispute, but she had spoken of deep personal hurt and pain, and of relationship problems with those whom she held most dear. Mark had felt at that moment that every eye turned on him accusingly.

His attempts to leave the hall, however, were frustrated. The back exits were locked, which meant the only way out was through the main body of the hall. Angrily, he flung himself down on a rickety chair in the little room immediately behind the stage, and settled himself to wait. Moments later, he heard Tom begin to speak. 'If I have not love,' he heard his friend proclaim, the words echoing with the suppressed emotion that seemed to ring through every syllable, 'I am but a clanging cymbal! A noisy gong!'

Mark almost choked. He felt he could take no more. He had to get away. Staring round distractedly, his eye alighted on a small window set high in the wall. It was only about eighteen inches square and it was so grimy it looked as if no one had opened it in years, but he was by now so desperate, he felt it was worth a try. Dragging over the chair, he stood on it and, reaching up, gave a sharp push. The chair swayed and he put out a hand to steady himself, but the next moment his efforts were rewarded because, with a low groan of protest, the window pushed up. A rush of cold air flooded into the room and Mark breathed it gratefully. He felt he had been suffocating in the hall. Then, very carefully, he swung himself up on to the sill and thrust out a leg.

He found a drop on the other side of about seven feet, but he had come so far, he was not to be deterred now. Giving one last shove, he heaved himself out through the window and almost catapulted into the dark alley beneath. As he landed, his foot caught a can and sent it scuttering noisily across the uneven paving. The dark seemed to pulse with the echo, and from somewhere off to the right a cat howled angrily. Then all fell silent.

Mark looked about uncertainly. Now that he had flung himself out from the safety of the hall, he rather wished he had stayed inside. The alley was very dark, and there was a forlorn feel about it. It was not, he decided, very safe. He glanced up at the window, thinking that perhaps he would go back, but it was too high. The only way he could get back into the hall was by going round to the front and in through the main doors. He had scrambled out to prove a point. He had wanted, he realised, to hurt Pippa, but now he was outside the full stupidity of his actions hit him. He peered about himself in the dark. He felt almost as if he had tumbled into some kind of Stygian hole, and for an instant he had the oddest sensation that there was very little hope of escape. He shook himself angrily, trying to free himself of the thought. He did not hold with imagining.

Ahead of him were some iron stairs leading upwards, and beyond them was a door. The alley then went on for some fifty yards, at the end of which he could see street lights. But between their reassuring glow and himself there seemed to be a great distance, with a couple of shadowy recesses on the way that filled him with unreasoning dread. Behind him the alley ended in a wall. If he was to get out, he had to go towards the street.

He listened. All was quiet. All, that is, except for the unnatural beating of his heart. Castigating himself for being such a fool, he set off carefully in the direction of the light, hugging the side of the building as if somehow it afforded him protection. He promised himself that when he got back inside the auditorium he would go straight to Pippa and say how sorry he was for behaving so badly. Only another twenty yards to go. Just as he was passing the last recess and congratulating himself on being almost there, a hand suddenly launched itself out of the dark and fastened on his shoulder. 'Where you going then?' said a voice.

Mark froze. His stomach knotted and the bones of his legs turned to jelly. 'What?' he brought out.

A figure detached itself from the dark and came forward. The hand did not move. 'I said,' said the voice, 'where you going?'

Mark swallowed. 'Ugh . . .' He shook his head stupidly, paralysed by fear. 'Back inside.'

'Bit odd, isn't it?' said the voice.

'What?' said Mark.

'Well, we wus watching you.' Mark became aware of another figure just beyond the first. 'We saw you jump outta that window. Seemed a bit odd, it did.'

'I . . . I just wanted some air,' Mark managed at last. 'I'm going back in now.'

The two men regarded him. He could feel their gaze, cat-like, fixed on him in the dark. 'Who are you then?' said the first man. 'You some sort of vicar, are you?'

Mark detected a familiar Liverpudlian twang. 'Yes,' he said numbly. 'We've got a rally on in the hall.'

Both men advanced further into the light, and Mark found himself looking at two individuals whom he instinctively felt to be villains. One was black, and one white. They were both very tall and very solid looking. As far as he could make out, both wore perfectly ordinary jeans and leather jackets, but they seemed to ooze menace, and the one who was gripping him by the shoulder had on a pair of tight-fitting leather gloves. 'We heard about that, didn't we, Marty?' said the black man. His teeth flashed in the dark. 'We thought that maybe a friend of ours might be in there.' He said the word *friend* with peculiar emphasis, and Mark felt that, whatever their intentions were, they were not good.

'W-who?' he brought out at last. Even to his own ears his voice sounded odd.

The men looked at him measuringly and then the first one said, 'Stripe. 'Is name's Stripe.'

'Oh,' said Mark. 'Really? What an odd name.'

'Yeah,' agreed the second man. 'It is, isn't it? Do you know 'im then?'

Mark shook his head; he felt the less information these two had, the better, and he ought, in all decency, to warn Stripe.

The first man moved closer, and Mark could feel his breath on his cheek. He shook his head again, too scared to speak, and the man looked at him as if he was examining a fly he was about to swat. 'You see,' he said softly, oozing menace, 'this mate of ours, who you say you don't know, 'e's got something wot belongs to us. And we want it back, see? So, if you did know 'im, even though you say you don't, the Christian thing to do would be to tell 'im to give it back – before someone gets 'urt. Like you maybe.'

Suddenly the hand that was on his shoulder transferred itself to his neck, and Mark found himself bodily lifted off his feet.

'Don't you agree?'

Mark could hardly breathe. 'Yes . . . yes!' he gasped.

The second man gave a low laugh, and the next moment Mark found himself tossed aside up against the wall. He fell heavily, banging his arm and shoulder, and then collapsed on the ground as his feet slipped. The two men turned and walked away. The last Mark saw of them was their dark silhouettes disappearing into the light. 'Oh God,' he muttered. He sat up and gingerly rubbed his neck and shoulder, and pain shot through him. Feeling dizzy, he clambered to his feet, and found he could not straighten his left arm. 'Oh God,' he said again weakly. Almost reeling with the pain, he began to stagger down the alley, his one thought now to get back inside. Stripe, he thought, he had to warn Stripe.

# Chapter Nine

'I've already told you,' said Stripe, 'I didn't do it. I can't give back wot I 'aven't got. They're just a couple of nutters.' He, Mark and Tom were sitting together in the study at the rectory.

Mark leant forward. 'They,' he said, with emphasis, 'are under the distinct impression that you have got it. Whatever it is. And they want it back.'

'But I told ye,' protested Stripe, 'it's the drummer wot did it. An' 'e's done a runner!'

Tom looked perplexed. 'Exactly what are we talking about here?' he asked. 'Did what?'

Stripe took a deep breath. 'Look, I'll be 'onest. They're pushers. Jimmy was dealin' for 'em, see. At least, 'e should 'ave been. But 'e lost the stuff. So 'e took off.'

Tom was still puzzled. 'So why do they think you've got it?'

Stripe breathed heavily. 'Because Jimmy told them I nicked it.'

'Did you?' asked Mark.

But Tom was still bemused. 'Nicked what?' he said, impatiently.

Stripe rose to his feet and crossed over to the window, staring out of it, his back hard. 'Look . . .' he began again, 'me an' Jimmy, we go back. We wus kids together. I found out 'e wus dealing. Round the clubs, when we were doin' gigs. Stupid, it was. It cud 'ave landed us all in it.' He shrugged. 'We 'ad a row.' He paused, still staring out of the window, and then said quietly, 'Heroin. That's what they're after. An' they think I've got it because Jimmy told them I had.' He swung round suddenly and stared at them. 'But it's not true. It fell into an incinerator.'

There was a stunned silence.

'Jesus help us,' said Tom. 'This is all we need. You're trying to tell us that you took some drugs off this friend of yours which you then destroyed. Your friend's so frightened he's gone into hiding in the Caribbean and so now these men are after you. Is that it?'

Stripe appeared briefly to consider this, and then shrugged. 'Yeah,' he agreed, 'yer cud say that. Yeah, that's about it.'

Mark and Tom stared at each other helplessly. 'But you must

85

go to the police,' said Mark at last. 'If you're telling the truth, they'll help.'

'I don't think so,' said Stripe.

'But why not?' asked Mark.

Stripe gave a snort. 'Because they wouldn't believe me. Look,' he said, coming and throwing himself back down in the chair, 'I'm sorry you got involved in all of this. I didn't want this to 'appen, but I did warn ye. But don't worry, I'll sort it.'

'How?' demanded Mark.

'I'll go and see them,' said Stripe immediately. 'I'll explain.'

Mark wasn't convinced, but he had no idea what to do: a terrible inertia was gripping him. He looked blankly out at the grass of the rectory lawn, still waiting for its first cut of the year. Here and there dandelions poked through, and over to the right a tabby cat was inching its way through the overhanging bushes, stalking an invisible prey. 'Oh dear,' he said heavily, 'I've got a bad feeling about all of this.'

'So have I,' said Tom. He leant forward and stared at Stripe intently. 'To be blunt, I'm not particularly concerned about you because I think you can take care of yourself, but Mark has already had a run-in with these people and he got hurt, and there's the rest of the team to consider. And Pippa too. Are we all going to be safe if you're still around?'

Stripe's eyes were veiled as he stared back at him. 'It's a chance you're going to have to take, man, isn't it? If you want me to stick around.' And with that, he got up and left.

Mark was not at all sure that he did want Stripe to stick around, in fact he would have been greatly relieved if Stripe had simply disappeared. But ever since he had been told about the two men, the musician had been manifesting a disconcerting desire to want to stay, almost as if he had decided there was no longer any point in trying to hide and that he might well be safer with them.

They had been back from Carbery all of three days, and Mark's shoulder still ached, though the X-ray at Carbery's hospital had shown nothing was broken.

Mark had been genuinely terrified when he had rushed back into the hall after the assault, and had been utterly astounded to discover that Pippa was angry with him. 'What were you doing out in the alley anyway?' she had demanded. And then, glancing at his ripped trousers and muddied jacket, she had snapped, 'How did you get out there?' When Mark admitted that he had climbed out through the window, she and Tom had both looked at him as if he was mad.

To make matters worse, the entire team had been positively bubbling with their success. In fact, he had seemed to be the only one who felt at all bad and, over the next few days he had become heartily sick of people coming up to him and telling him how wonderful Pippa had been, and wasn't he fearfully proud of her. He did not feel proud at all. He simply felt depressed. He had a feeling of heaviness that nothing seemed able to shake, a kind of inner conviction that something was terribly wrong, not just with what was going on, but with something unidentifiable at the heart of his life. The Stripe problem, coming on top of all of this, was simply another burden to be borne. More than anything else now, he wanted desperately to talk to Pippa, but he felt that she no longer wanted to talk to him, and when he did feebly make the effort, it was as if his tongue clove to the roof of his mouth, and he found himself unable to say a word.

For Chalice, however, things seemed to be going from strength to strength. There was undeniably something of a backlash from the anti-lottery group which felt that Mark had betrayed them, but *Church News* had phoned early on the Monday and asked if they could come down and interview Pippa and the rest of the team for a centrefold spread to be included that weekend. Then they had found themselves inundated with inquiries from Christian groups up and down the country, asking sometimes for advice but more often for money. Agnes, Mark's new secretary, for so long displaced in the world of work, blossomed with the importance of it all. She was tart with requests for finance and superior with pleas for help. Then four churches phoned and asked if the Chalice youth team, and Pippa in particular, would come and lead a mission. Agnes was offhand with them all, and told them rather sniffily that the team director would get back to them in due course. To her intense chagrin, however, Tom immediately said yes to every one. She would have liked to have kept them all waiting, and then informed them by letter that they could maybe fit them in in a year's time. Agnes harboured dreams of glory.

She took instruction, however, with as much grace as she could muster and, looking in his diary this morning, Mark had been astonished to discover it seemed full. What had been blank spaces reserved for prayer, sermon preparation and visiting the sick were now covered with neat tiny writing. Tuesday, the fifth, he read – Strathclyde, lunchtime consultation. Return flight booked, three o'clock. Wednesday, the sixth: Porthcawl, Church of Wales Missioners . . . and so it went on. Turning the pages, appalled, he discovered that almost every spare moment he had for the next three months had been pencilled in, and he had had the oddest sensation that he was caught in a vortex of spiralling activity that was rapidly spinning out of control. He had summoned up the energy to voice his concerns to Tom, but Tom had been jubilant with the apparent success of it all. This, he said, was exactly the way it ought to be, and if Mark wanted to move into the fast lane, then he had better get used to it.

Mark looked at Tom now, and wondered whether there was any point in raising the subject again, but Tom was already on his way out.

'Got to get on,' he said, cheerfully. 'I've got a meeting with Jack that started ten minutes ago. Don't worry. We'll sort all this out later.' The door banged on his retreating back.

Left alone, Mark sighed and turned to his lectionary to look up the readings for Sunday. He had a family service to prepare for St Saviour's; Holy Communion for St Adelph's in Crendon; and a shortened morning prayer for St Mary the Virgin in Appleton. Mark did not like going to Appleton. The churchwardens, verger and organist were all ardent Freemasons and they looked on him with disapproval, so that he always felt he had to be careful what he said. But at least Tom had taken from him the responsibility for evensong back at St Saviour's. 'How about we try something a bit different this week?' he had suggested. 'To welcome all those young people we've got coming now. How about we have a youth service in church?' Mark was not entirely convinced of the wisdom of this just yet, he was not sure how his usual congregation would take it, but he felt so battered by everything that had happened over the past few days that he had accepted gratefully. Anything to lighten the load.

As he left the rectory, Stripe was not in the best of moods either. For all his apparent assurance, he was actually extremely worried. Reason told him that the safest course now would be simply to disappear again. But he rather felt he wanted to hang around. He thought there might well be something in all of this for him, even a record deal if he could play his cards right. And then there was the priest's attractive wife, too. Stripe liked older women, and he thought there might well be hidden depths to Pippa that he would quite like to plumb. He had wondered, too, if he might be able to use some of her money to work out some kind of a deal that would free him from the unwelcome attentions of his friends. When Mark had described the two men, he had known exactly who they were and felt a thrill of fear. He was only puzzled that they had chosen to send him a warning rather than simply jumping him and extorting what they wanted to know by force.

It was entirely true that Jimmy had been dealing, but the drummer had entrusted the gear to Stripe and then, rather inconsiderately, got himself knifed. He might have survived the first attack, but his assailants had followed the ambulance to the hospital and had there finished off what they had begun, slashing him repeatedly as he lay on the trolley in the rather grubby casualty corridor where he had been left. Before he died, Jimmy told them that Stripe had the gear.

Stripe had been entirely honest in saying that he himself did not like hard drugs, and at first he had indeed been tempted to destroy Jimmy's package. But fear had restrained him, and instead he had fled, taking the package with him. Jimmy had told him the drugs had a street value of a hundred thousand, and while he had them he felt they were some kind of insurance policy. It had crossed his mind simply to give the package to the men who were following him, but although he knew who the two men were, he had no idea who they were working for. It occurred to him that the drugs might not actually belong to them at all, so handing over the package to them would not necessarily guarantee his health. But while he had the gear, and they did not know where it was, he felt he had a margin of safety until he could work out a satisfactory deal. But he did not think he had much time. They had let him know they knew where he was, that much was clear. But Stripe felt they were waiting, maybe as unsure of him as he was of them. He decided there was someone he had to go and see, back in Liverpool; but meanwhile it occurred to him that as a top priority he had to move the gear. At present it was stashed in the lavatory cistern back at the flat over the garage. But Stripe knew that would be one of the first places the men would look if they decided to take matters a step further and break in.

As he turned into the drive, he was surprised to note again the black Golf that he had seen there once before. As he came up, Melanie was just uncurling herself from the driving seat. This time she had a briefcase with her, and Stripe looked at her with interest. He had not come across Melanie's particular type before, though the fact she was associated with Paul inclined him to dislike her. 'Hi,' he said, coming up behind her. 'You're back then?'

Melanie jumped, and then turned and looked at him coldly. 'Yes,' she agreed, 'I am.'

'He's not here,' said Stripe.

'I know that. He sent me to get some papers.'

Stripe regarded her, his eyes watchful. 'That's an odd thing to do,' he remarked.

Melanie sniffed disdainfully and began to walk towards the house. 'You'll probably see me again,' she said casually over her shoulder. 'I'm working on the Chalice Trust now, you know. I'll be around quite a lot, I should think.'

Stripe watched her as she paused on the step and rang an imperious summons on the bell. There was going to be trouble there, he thought, and it might well be amusing, but right now he had more pressing concerns. He shrugged and ambled off towards the flat.

Elaine, busy stripping beds, hurried down the stairs to answer the door feeling flustered. There seemed to be no end to the interruptions this morning. She had already taken three calls for Paul and at last, annoyed, had put on the answerphone. Then had come the rings at the door. Janice from church wanting to know if she could have the keys, because the toddler group wanted to borrow a banner; a rather suspicious young man who claimed to be selling brushes for a work scheme, and now this. Feeling harassed, she flung back the door, and pulled up short.

Melanie smiled at her sweetly. 'Paul sent me,' she said maliciously. 'He forgot some documents for the Chalice account.'

Elaine gaped at her. She knew instantly who it was and felt certain that the girl was lying. Paul, she knew, would want to avoid confrontation at all costs, but Melanie seemed so assured that she felt thrown. 'Why didn't he come himself?' she asked abruptly.

Melanie raised an eyebrow. 'Well, I am working with him on this.' She laid peculiar emphasis on the *with*. 'And he has given me responsibility for the day-to-day administration of the account.' Uninvited, she stepped in through the door and turned critical eyes over the hall. 'How interesting,' she said.

Elaine turned on her heel. She felt compliance would be the quickest way to get rid of her unwelcome visitor. 'Wait there,' she commanded, 'I'll go and get them.'

She set off towards Paul's study, but Melanie followed in her wake. Elaine, picking up the papers from Paul's desk and turning back, jumped to find her close behind. 'What on earth are you doing?' she demanded frostily, intercepting the tail end of Melanie's appraisal as her eyes swept round.

Melanie came further into the room. 'I thought you might need some help,' she said. 'I thought you might not know which papers they were.'

'I'm perfectly capable of reading, thank you,' said Elaine tartly. She held the papers out. 'Are these what you want?'

Melanie hardly glanced at them. 'Yes,' she said. 'Thank you.'

'What are you really doing here?' asked Elaine.

Melanie turned and smiled at her. 'Well, since you ask,' she said, 'I wanted to meet you face to face. And I wanted to see where Paul lived.' She paused, and Elaine almost felt the unspoken thought, 'and where I'm going to live'. Melanie looked her up and down, and Elaine felt acutely conscious of her faded jeans and untidy hair. 'You're older than I thought you'd be,' Melanie remarked. 'Quite attractive, I suppose, but you've let yourself go . . .'

'Get out!' said Elaine, her voice shaking with anger.

Melanie only looked at her contemptuously. 'You can't win, you know,' she said softly. 'Why don't you just acknowledge defeat now, while you've got a bit of dignity left? He doesn't love you. He never has.'

'That's not true.' Elaine found she was shaking. She felt her home, even her person, was being violated. The phone calls had been bad enough, and she had often wondered about the woman at the other end, but nothing had prepared her for this. She felt indescribably wounded that Paul should have chosen this hard-faced, immaculately painted young woman. She felt she could not compete.

Melanie smiled again. 'I will get him, you know,' she said. 'And I'll get all this too, if I want it.'

'Over my dead body,' Elaine snarled. 'Get out, you little slut!'

'Keep your hair on,' said Melanie nastily. 'I've seen what I want to. I'll go now, but I'll be back.'

Elaine heard the click of her heels as Melanie walked out over the stone flags in the hall, then she heard the door close. Not loudly, but softly, as if the other woman, having made her point, did not need now to make too much noise. For one frozen moment more Elaine continued to stand there, and then she gave a single sob and crumpled into an ungainly heap against the wall. Her whole body felt numb, except for a kind of remote tingling on the back of her hands. She wondered if she was going to be ill. She felt unable to think clearly, but somehow, coming face to face with Melanie, she felt another nail had been driven into the coffin of her hopes. Paul had not sent the girl, she was certain of that, but the fact struck her as irrelevant. She felt that Melanie was pursuing her own devious schemes, and that she had just come face to face with a very deadly foe.

For her part, as she strode back to the car, Melanie was jubilant. She had not known exactly what she wanted to achieve when she had first stepped out of the office over an hour before, but she had wanted very much to see Paul's wife so that she might, as she told herself, know what she had to contend with. Paul himself was up in Scotland today, and so she had manufactured an urgent need to see some papers that she knew he would have left at home.

Now that she had seen Elaine, she felt on very much firmer ground. In Melanie's eyes, Elaine was middle-aged and frumpy. The archetypal and boring, middle England housewife, regularly cheated on by her spouse. And Melanie felt she knew why. Elaine looked unimaginative and dull; she deserved to be made a fool of. The only pity was, Melanie thought, that it would not be more of a contest. She rather enjoyed a challenge. Still, she reflected, in this particular case, the acquisition of the prize was far more important than the chase.

As she got into her car, she smirked. Overall, things were going rather well. All she had to do now was take full control of the Chalice account, which did not seem too great a problem, and her business future, too, would be assured. She might even end up as Paul's boss!

# Chapter Ten

'I think it's disgusting,' announced Mrs Stibbins. She shoved another chrysanthemum into her flower arrangement and then stood back to scrutinise the effect.

At her side, little Miss Ellis twittered distractedly and held out the scissors. 'I'm really not sure we ought to judge,' she said timidly. 'After all, the Vicar *is* simply trying to do his job.'

'Humph!' said Mrs Stibbins. She snipped viciously at a stray leaf that had dared interfere with her line, and then again stood back. 'It's not him I blame so much as that wife of his. It's all her fault.' In Mrs Stibbins's opinion, everything that had been at all wrong in the parish over the last fifteen years was the fault of the Vicar's wife. She was rather irrational in her dislikes, and completely ignored the fact that Mark and Pippa had not been at St Saviour's for fifteen years – Pippa's influence, she seemed to imply, exercised a retrospective effect. Unfortunately, Mrs Stibbins wielded tremendous influence over her cronies in the Ladies Club, with the result that all of them now also disliked Pippa and similarly blamed her for everything that went wrong.

The two women were in church, arranging the flowers for Sunday. Mrs Stibbins always arranged the flowers. In fact, she prided herself on her displays, and resented it if someone else had the temerity to put themselves forward, as she saw it, with an offer to help. Miss Ellis, however, she did not mind because Miss Ellis simply trailed respectfully after her, holding the flowers, or the watering can, or the scissors, and by and large agreed with everything she said. But Pippa had long ago aroused Mrs Stibbins's wrath when she had taken it upon herself without permission to do the flowers one Sunday, shortly after she and Mark had arrived. Mrs Stibbins had got to church on the Friday morning at ten o'clock, as she did every week, clutching a mixed box of antirrhinums and nasturtiums that she had thought would look rather nice set against the green altar cloth, and had discovered to her intense chagrin that the flowers were done. Shocked inquiry had elicited the information that the person responsible was the Vicar's wife, and her hatred had been confirmed when she had overheard someone remark that the flowers looked so sweet and unassuming, just like Pippa herself. On that occasion she had written a stiff letter to Mark, pointing out that she had arranged the flowers at St Saviour's every week for the last eight years, and that if they were dissatisfied or thought her deficient, she would quite understand, but that she did think someone should have had the courtesy to come and tell her so first.

Pippa had been horrified. In their last parish, everyone had hated doing the flowers and they had had endless trouble trying to arrange a rota. She had simply assumed that the same situation prevailed at St Saviour's and had thought she would be doing everyone a favour by taking upon herself the task for that week. She had immediately gone and abjectly begged forgiveness, but by then of course the damage had been done. In Mrs Stibbins's eyes she was an irredeemable upstart; a parvenu rival who from that moment on had to be kept firmly in her place. In fact, even without the incident of the flowers, she would probably have disliked Pippa intensely, because Pippa did not conform to Mrs Stibbins's idea of what a vicar's wife ought to be like. The skirmish, however, had given her a peg on which to hang the grounds of her disapproval, and she had taken full advantage of it ever since. Now she had another peg.

'She shouldn't ought to have won all that money!' Mrs Stibbins declared self-righteously. Mrs Stibbins had always bought a lottery ticket herself, ever since the national lottery had first been set up, and had in the past simply ignored Mark's urgings to the congregation to stand aloof. She had said then that he was stupid and that he didn't know what he was talking about – and he certainly wasn't going to put her off a chance of winning, thank you very much. This had changed, the minute it became known that Pippa had won. Overnight Mrs Stibbins had become a confirmed opponent of all forms of gambling, and had waxed self-righteous on the greed that made people want such large wins. She had also made several comments to the effect that she bet none of *them* would benefit.

She tweaked at a trailing frond of ivy, pulling it closer round the iron pedestal. 'And I don't hold with any of these goings-on' she said sanctimoniously. 'With all these guitars and things! As for this youth service thing that they want to introduce! I tell you, if it doesn't stop I'm going to write and complain to the Bishop. And Mrs Stuck-up Casaubon ought to take her nose out now and do something useful like having a baby. No wonder her husband always looks so harassed, poor man! What kind of a family life does that woman ever give him? If she thought a bit more about her Christian duty instead of all this gadding around she does, he'd be a lot happier.' Mrs Stibbins put the scissors in her bag and stood back satisfied. 'I think we've about done here, Dolly,' she announced. 'Fancy a cup of tea?'

The two of them went out. In the shadows behind the pillar where she was sitting, Pippa put her head down between her hands and tried

94

to suppress the urge to cry. She had come into the church earlier to pray and had been there all the while. When the two women had first come in, she had drawn back further into the shadows, hoping they would not see her. It was not that she disliked them but she felt totally unable to cope with the presence of another human being, just now.

Ever since the stupidity of the mission to Carbery, she had felt a deep kind of pain that seemed to be gnawing at her soul. She had tried repeatedly to pray, but every time she sat down, it was as if a great tide of grief surged over her, and she could never get beyond the opening words, 'Lord, help.' She wondered if she was under some kind of judgement for the sin she had committed in buying the ticket in the first place, but she had not the slightest idea how to put things right.

The church felt cool and still. In pain, Pippa stretched out her hand and ran it along the rough stone wall at her side. But instead of comfort, it seemed to exude only a great weariness, as if it had seen it all before. Years ago Pippa had read that during the plague in the Middle Ages the villagers had taken refuge in St Saviour's, trying to turn aside from their community, by prayer, what they saw as the wrath of God. Twenty-eight villagers, it was said, had died, but by some miracle the rest had survived. Their deliverance had been recorded. 'This twenty-first day of June, by the grace of God, we have been delivered from the shadow, by the coming of the angel.' The words had intrigued Pippa. She had felt they masked indescribable suffering and fear, but she had been caught, too, by the reference to the angel. What did the words mean? Were they just some pious form of thanksgiving, or did they mean that the villagers really thought an angel had come and turned aside the dreaded spectre of disease? Now, sitting there in the quiet, Pippa wished she could meet that delivering angel. But the church remained depressingly still and, try as she might, she found she could not keep back the tears.

It was not the conversation of the two women that had upset her so much, although their words had certainly hurt, but the injustice of being so continually judged by others to be in the wrong when she knew that she tried so hard to do what was right. And, on top of that, to be condemned for her apparent refusal to have a child was like a knife twisting in her gut. All the old pain and longing flooded through her, and in that moment she felt a deep and welling anger against God.

It was in this condition that Tom found her half an hour later. He had come in to have a quick look at the church to see where he could best place the video screen, cameras and sound system for Sunday evening. He had big plans to make the occasion memorable and wanted to transform the interior so that it would lose its medieval calm and take on more the air of a nightclub. He thought the young people he was hoping to draw along would relate more easily to that. He was just wandering down the centre aisle, thinking to himself that if he draped a large curtain across the Lady Chapel they could set up a light show using lasers, when he became aware of Pippa's huddled form crouched in the pew. 'Good heavens, Pippa!' he exclaimed. And then he realised that she was crying. 'My dear! What on earth's wrong?'

In a trice he had crossed over to her, all thoughts of the service forgotten, and had gathered her in his arms. 'Pippa,' he said again, 'what's wrong?'

In response she burst into a fresh flood of tears and, unable to think of anything else to do, Tom sat there, quietly rocking her backwards and forwards and kissing the top of her head, as if he was comforting a small child. 'I'm so sorry,' she said at last. She pulled herself away, at the same time groping for the soddened rag of her hankie, and blew her nose. Then she sniffed, her eyes fixed on the floor.

Tom waited another moment and then said gently, 'My dear, what is the matter?'

She shrugged. 'Nothing . . . everything.'

'Is it Mark?'

She nodded, and tears again welled up in her eyes, but this time she fought them back and after a second whispered, 'Oh Tom, I just don't know what to do any more. Everything seems to have gone so horribly wrong, and I don't know why. He won't talk to me any more. I'm sure it's my fault.' Tom demurred, but she ignored him. 'I've pressured him, Tom, I know, but it's as if he's gone behind this thick shell, and I can't get through it. I'm just not sure he cares about me any more. And he seems to have become such a prig.' She looked up then. 'I bought the ticket to spite him, you know. He was being so horrible, and so "good", with that wretched group he'd set up. He just never seemed to listen to anybody and he was always so certain he was right, so I went and bought that ghastly ticket. But I never dreamt it would win.'

There was a silence and Tom bit his lip. He could think of absolutely nothing to say that would be right. He knew what he ought to say. He knew what he ought to do, but somehow, faced with the reality of her presence, all he could think about was her. He could smell again the delicate perfume of her skin, and the white of her neck looked so fragile . . . He ached to touch her. He knew that Mark was her husband, but just at that moment he genuinely believed that his friend had forfeited all rights by the complete idiocy of his behaviour. He was tempted, almost beyond measure, to reach out and fold her to him, and assert his own claim. He felt sure that in that moment she would respond. Not from any smouldering passion, he did not delude himself as to that, but because she felt so forlorn and alone, and because he could see she was wracked by guilt.

Something stopped him. Even afterwards he was not sure what it was, but it was as if a hand was suddenly laid on his arm and he had the oddest sensation of, not a voice, but meaning, pure and strong, that rocked him to the centre of his being. 'No.' That was all, but it was enough to halt him.

He became aware that Pippa was speaking.

'You're so good, Tom. You've been such a friend to us both, though sometimes I've felt so jealous of you.' He shook his head wordlessly and she went on, 'You look so shocked. Do you hate me for saying I bought that ticket out of spite?'

'No, Pippa.' He shook his head vehemently, incapable of adding more, his brain still reeling.

'Oh, that's good,' she said. 'I've been feeling so awful, especially with everything that's happening now. I thought maybe it was judgement.'

That got to him, and at last his voice was unlocked. 'You must never think that, Pippa,' he whispered, and now he felt like crying. 'God loves you very much, you know. All this with Mark will sort itself out. You'll see.'

She looked indescribably sad. 'I'm not so sure, Tom. Sometimes I've thought I loved Mark too much, and that was why God had refused us a child – because that's what it feels like, you know?' She looked up suddenly. 'I've wanted and longed and prayed for a child, for Mark's child. And it feels just like God has said no. I even went and had tests.'

'I know,' said Tom.

She flashed him a look and then gave a watery smile. 'Of course you do. Mark told you, and you tried to help then too, didn't you, just like you always do for us.'

Her words were like a knife going through him and he shook his head in denial. She reached out and took his hand.

'Tom, I don't know what I've done by having those tests. Mark was so hurt. And then this awful lottery business on top of all that. I don't think he'll ever forgive me.'

'Yes, he will,' whispered Tom hoarsely. 'Just wait. You'll see.'

Stripe saw them coming out of the church together a few minutes later. Tom's arm was round Pippa's shoulders and she was leaning against him heavily, almost as if she was having difficulty walking. From behind the gravestone where he was crouched down out of sight, Stripe stared at them curiously. His first thought was that there was something going on between them, and he felt jealous, but looking at them more closely, he was not so sure. There was something oddly still about them both. Tom looked very sad, and Pippa looked as if she had been crying. He wondered if something had happened. He watched them walk down the gravel path and out through the gate, and then slowly rose to his feet as they disappeared from view. Once out of sight, however, they also went from his mind. In his left hand was a bulky white package, sealed in plastic, about six inches square.

He was still looking for a hiding place for the drugs, and it had occurred to him that burying the gear in the churchyard might be a very good idea. Stripe rather liked St Saviour's graveyard. It was large and green, overhung by trees that he did not know the names of, and bordered by untidy bushes. The graves, he had been told by Mark, dated back to thirteen hundred, and he had looked once, trying to find some evidence of that, slightly over-awed by the thought that people who had lived so long ago were under his feet, wondering what they had been like. He had trailed around all the older looking stones but found that their lettering had long since crumbled away, obliterating the inscriptions and pious hopes that had been engraved there, and leaving only rather lopsided, anonymous stumps. It had saddened him rather, but for all that, it was a nice place, he thought. A good place to end your days.

Now, as he began to move slowly across the grass, his gaze darting this way and that, it struck him afresh how tranquil the place seemed. He decided he liked the way the graves were all higgledy-piggledy and squashed together, with the stones slanting this way and that. He liked the way the ivy had grown over some of the tombs, so that they stood like huge green tables dotted around the grass. And he liked the trees; they seemed to him to whisper of peace.

To find a hiding place in the midst of all that leafy tranquillity, however, was easier said than done. When he had tried to scoop out a hole, which had been his first thought, he had found that the earth was too hard. So now he thought that he would maybe stuff the package behind the ivy on one of the tombs, but he found that it was difficult to wedge it, and when he stood back to survey the effect, he discovered he could still see the plastic behind. Cursing softly, he retrieved the bag, and again looked round.

He decided the churchyard afforded little chance of concealment, and so he turned his gaze instead to the church. All was quiet as he crept stealthily up the path. Overhead a pigeon cooed quietly, and there was a rustling of disapproving wings in the trees. Stripe paused in the porch and listened. The heavy oak door was slightly ajar, and inside he could hear only silence. Glancing round to make sure he was still unobserved, he gave it a quick push and slid inside.

He stepped into a silence so profound it was almost tangible.

Breathing heavily, he halted, feeling momentarily suffocated, and allowed his eyes time to adjust to the gloom. No one. Again he listened, head to one side. But the silence was complete. Carefully he shut the door behind him and then advanced down the aisle.

Stripe felt unnerved to find himself alone in the church. The light had a kind of shady, gentle feel to it, but he could not rid himself of the feeling that he was being watched. As he stole down the nave, he kept glancing behind, almost expecting to see someone there. Once he thought he caught the shadow of movement, but when he looked more closely, there was only the quiet gloom of the font. Apart from himself, the church was totally empty, but still he felt on edge. He wanted to get out, back into the open air and away from all these feelings of watching shadows. But he forced himself to continue. Surely, somewhere here, he would find a hiding place.

Just beyond the priest's stall in the chancel he paused, his attention caught by a monument set high up in the wall. It was of grey marble, with ornate milky-white carving around the top and sides. The writing was feathery and, to Stripe, totally incomprehensible, but it was not that that interested him. What had caught his eye was a slight gap between the left edging and the wall. If you just glanced at it quickly you would not notice it was there and, even staring intently, Stripe was not sure what he was really seeing.

Crossing quickly, he clambered up on to the heavy stall and then, reaching up with his hand, felt along the inner edge. The heavy scrollwork jutted out over his head and obscured the edge, but he was right; his fingers found a definite space. Quickly he explored it. He discovered a gap about six inches long and one inch wide. The scrollwork curled over it, but behind he thought it widened out. How far back it went he had no idea, but his fingers, when he thrust them in, encountered only space. Looking round one last time, he took the package and thrust it roughly into the gap. It was a tight fit but he managed to get it in. By the time he had finished, he was sweating and felt slightly giddy. When he sprang down and looked up, there was no sign of the package. A feeling of relief flooded him. That was his insurance policy safely stowed away. They would never think to look here in a million years. Now he had some people to see.

# Chapter Eleven

By five o'clock on Sunday afternoon, with the enthusiastic help of the team, Tom had transformed the interior of the church. They had hired lasers and a lighting system that would have done justice to a professional production of *Henry V*. The younger members of the team had also unscrewed the pews, promising Mark faithfully that they would reinstate them the following day, and had then draped long black sheets over the medieval wall paintings. Oogi, who was artistic, had scattered the sheets with stars, and they flashed and glittered in the light like some kind of twinkling Disneyesque firmament. But even that was not the end to the changes. The team had then built a kind of ramp going up to the altar in alternating bands of colour, like a rainbow, and at the top of that they had removed the usual medieval oak table that served as an altar and installed a huge wooden cross. In the main body of the church there was now a wide, open area – for dancing and praising, as Tom explained – then a kind of kaleidoscopic hill and then, overarching all, like some kind of cosmic rudder plunging through time, the cross. Stripe had his own little dais off to the side, bathed in light, so that as people came into church their attention was immediately drawn to him.

Tom was pleased. Mark had taken one look and then shut his eyes. 'What about our usual evening congregation?' he demanded, aghast. 'Where are they going to sit?'

'Oh, they'll have to stand,' said Tom airily. 'They won't mind, not this once. Not when they see all the young people joining in. And if it really takes off, well, we could have a regular slot every Sunday night but move it to nine or something, after evensong. That way we could keep everybody happy.'

Mark was not convinced, but it seemed too late to demur, and so instead he took himself off to his study and prayed. Miracles that night, however, seemed to be in rather short supply. The first person to arrive at church was Mrs Stibbins, with Dolly Ellis in tow. 'What's going on?' she asked suspiciously, seeing the young people clustered round the door. And then, as she stepped through the porch, she let out a cry.

'What is it, dear?' said Miss Ellis, rushing to her side. She too

101

pulled up short and stared around. 'H-has there been some kind of accident?' she faltered.

A young girl thrust song sheets into their hands. 'No,' she said cheerfully, giggling, 'of course not. Tom's going to lead a youth service tonight, that's all.'

Mrs Stibbins looked ominous. 'It wasn't,' she said, 'in the parish magazine.'

Paul was the next to arrive, and even he looked taken aback. 'What's happened?' he asked Jack, whom he managed to buttonhole as he rushed through carrying a theatre spotlight clutched to his chest.

'A praise service,' said Jack cheerfully. 'Great, isn't it?'

Paul did not look as if he fully agreed, but he said nothing. He was still smarting from his latest row with Elaine and lacked the energy to protest. Not so Mrs Stibbins.

'Where are we supposed to sit then?' she demanded of Jack.

'Well, you're not,' said Jack uncertainly. 'This is an informal service tonight. So the idea is you stand or, well, if you really want, I guess you could sit on the floor.'

Mrs Stibbins went puce. 'Sit on the floor?' she repeated.

Jack, looking at her ample curves tightly encased in her beige Crimplene dress, swallowed.

'I'm not sitting on the floor,' she went on, 'and neither is Dolly! We're too old for that kind of malarky, thank you very much, young man.' Her gaze swept round. 'And where are my flowers? They should be over there by the . . .' Mrs Stibbins's eyes fixed on the huge cross and her mouth dropped open in astonishment. 'Where's the altar then?' she demanded.

'Er, we've moved it,' said Jack. 'Only for this evening,' he added hastily. 'It'll be back tomorrow.'

Mrs Stibbins thrust him aside. 'You can't do that!' she almost shrieked. 'Where's your respect, young man? It's holy, the altar. You can't just up and cart it off when you feel like it, like a sack of potatoes.'

At that moment, Pippa arrived. She had not yet seen the inside of the church, though she had heard Tom giving instructions to Jack and Oogi earlier, and had rather wondered about the wisdom of so abrupt a change. But Mark had said nothing and so she had assumed it would all be all right. She, too, was taken aback by the sight that met her eyes.

'I suppose this is all your doing!' said Mrs Stibbins, rounding on her. 'Always have been jealous of my flowers, haven't you? Well, it won't do.' She glared at Pippa malevolently. 'We're not just going to stand quietly by while you turn our church upside down, even if you have won all that money and think you can do whatever you want. We won't have it, will we, Dolly?' She appealed for support to Miss Ellis, who looked as if she was about to faint.

'No, dear,' whispered that lady, who deplored the changes but felt that Mrs Stibbins was going too far. She gave every appearance of wishing the ground would open up and swallow her.

'There!' said Mrs Stibbins triumphantly. 'You see? Even Dolly is upset.'

Pippa looked at Jack, who was beginning to edge away. 'Er, I've got to make sure this gets put up,' he said apologetically. Then he ran and Pippa found herself facing the enraged Mrs Stibbins alone. 'So what are you going to do about it then?' demanded that worthy. 'We're not going to sit on the floor, you know.'

'Right,' said Pippa faintly. She stepped forward uncertainly. Clouds of incense wafted in front of her nose, and to her right, stuck into the wooden covering of the font, she saw a line of joss sticks, the smoke curling up into the darkened air in lazy spirals. She shut her eyes and uttered a prayer, then opened them and went resolutely forward. Stripe was playing some kind of dance music she had never heard before, and the young people already assembled were beginning to sway, while a couple of the more extrovert were dancing in the space directly in front of the ramp. Pippa set off in search of Tom. He was responsible for all this, she thought angrily, so it was up to him to sort it out.

She found him in the vestry, trying on a pair of sunglasses and rumpling his hair, attempting vainly to see his reflection in the tiny mirror that hung over the desk beside the rusty safe. Like the safe, the mirror had seen better days, and its surface was now so pitted and pockmarked that at best all you could see was a kind of ghostly half image that stared back as if trapped in some kind of gloomy nether world from which there was no escape. Tom was further hampered in his endeavours by the three pews that had been stacked up on top of each other between the desk and the door, leaving a space of only some two feet for officiants to change and generally prepare themselves. 'Hello, Pippa,' he said cheerfully, looking round as she came in. 'Do you think I should wear the glasses or not?'

'What on earth for?' she demanded tartly. 'It's so dark out there, if you wear glasses you won't be able to find your way to the altar. Speaking of which,' she added grimly, 'where is it?' She became aware of Mark standing miserably behind the door, wearing his usual vestments and academic hood, and with difficulty suppressed the urge to give an hysterical laugh. Instead she rounded on him. 'I might have guessed you'd be skulking back there,' she said savagely. 'Have you any idea of the effect all this is having on the usual congregation?'

Mark blanched. 'What do you mean?' he asked. 'Has anyone said anything?'

'Said anything?' repeated Pippa. 'No. Not exactly. A more accurate description would be to say that Mrs Stibbins and Miss Ellis are having apoplexy over by the door.'

'Oh dear,' said Tom, 'don't they like it?'

Pippa gave him a withering look. 'No,' she said, 'they don't. Mrs Stibbins wants to know where her flowers, the altar, and the pews are. In that order.'

Mark and Tom looked at each other, and Tom attempted a laugh. 'Well, they're all over in the hall,' he said, 'except for these few pews here. There wasn't room for them.'

Pippa turned back to Mark. 'You can't seriously expect Mrs Stibbins and Miss Ellis to sit on the floor,' she said. 'And the rest of the Ladies Club will be here soon, too. They need somewhere to sit. That is,' she added darkly, 'if they stay.'

Mark cleared his throat. 'Oh dear,' he said unhappily. The folly of having trusted to providence in this particular situation was beginning to have its full impact upon him. 'What do you suggest?'

She glared back exasperated. 'Well, for a start, I think we'd better give them somewhere to sit.' She turned and looked at the pews. 'These'll have to go back.'

'But they can't!' protested Tom. 'They'll spoil the atmosphere. The whole idea of tonight is that it's informal. Not churchy.'

'That's all very well,' retorted Pippa, 'but you've done this completely without warning. You're going to alienate everyone who usually comes even more. And they're already annoyed.'

Mark swallowed and stepped forward. 'I think we'd better do what Pippa suggests, Tom,' he said. 'Some of them can be a bit difficult.'

Tom looked as if he was about to explode. 'Mark, we can't. It'll ruin it.'

Mark looked even more miserable, but he nodded to Pippa. 'Go and get Oogi and Jack and ask them to take back these three pews.'

Outside, Mrs Stibbins was slightly mollified. 'That's better,' she announced, as the first pew reappeared. She had ploughed her way in and was standing in the exact spot where she usually sat, two rows back on the left. Exactly how she had managed it, Pippa was unsure; it was as if she had radar. 'Over here,' she said imperiously. 'No, no, not back there. We want to sit in our usual places.'

Oogi, who had been making his way towards the back and out of sight, looked annoyed. 'You can't sit there,' he protested. 'You'll be right in the middle of the praise area if you go there. And the lasers will be fixed on you too.'

Mrs Stibbins sniffed. 'Well, at least we'll be able to see then,' she said haughtily. 'We want it here, right where we usually sit!'

From that position she would not be moved. Unhappily, Oogi and Jack set the pew down where she directed and then, muttering to himself, Oogi screwed it to the floor.

'We won't all fit on this, you know,' said Mrs Stibbins as he fixed the last screw. 'There are about sixteen of us usually. We'll all need somewhere to sit.'

Oogi made it perfectly clear that he disapproved, but obediently he and Jack went and fetched the other two pews. When they had finished, Mrs Stibbins and Miss Ellis settled themselves down, right in the middle of the floodlit dance area, which was now effectively destroyed. Stripe, who had been watching the entire proceedings with interest, chose this moment to strike up 'Onward Christian soldiers', but played with a kind of mocking flourish that produced titters from the back.

'Oh God,' said Tom in the vestry, 'that's all we need. Who'd have thought he'd have known that!' He looked at Mark despairingly. 'Shall we start?'

Mark nodded. His expression seemed to say, let's get it over with. He was preparing to process sedately out in his normal fashion when Tom suddenly exploded forward and began to bound down the church, waving his arms and shouting 'Alleluia, everyone. Let's go!' He had on a radio mike, so that his voice boomed through the building, and wild shrieks and alleluias greeted his appearance. Almost running, he took the ramp at a leap and then, spinning round, flung his arms wide. 'God welcomes you! Bless you all!' he cried.

Mark, still standing half in, half out of the vestry, gaped at him appalled. He became acutely conscious of Mrs Stibbins's behatted head rearing itself on her puffy neck, and then swivelling 180 degrees in his direction. Around her sat the Ladies Club, and he was certain he heard little gasps of affronted horror from them.

'Put your hands together,' shouted Tom, oblivious, 'for our rector and brother in Christ, Mark!'

To Mark's complete astonishment, from all over the church applause broke out, and a spotlight suddenly swivelled and fixed itself upon him. He stood riveted in the light. The clapping and cheers continued, and then Tom shouted, 'Come on up here, Mark. We're waiting for you!'

Wishing he was anywhere rather than there, Mark set off down the church. He had never before processed into a service to the accompaniment of whistles and cheers, but he did so that night, and discovered that from the vestry to the cross was a very long way. Blinded by the light, he could not see for certain how many people were there, but from the stamping and cheers there seemed to be a lot. As he drew abreast of Mrs Stibbins and her entourage, he paused and glanced at her. He wished he had not; Mrs Stibbins's eye was fixed upon him in a way that was not at all nice.

They began with worship songs, and then Tom read from the Bible. It was from 1 Corinthians 13, Mark noted, the passage about love. Rather forlornly, he wondered if Mrs Stibbins was taking it to heart. And then, just as Tom was finishing, breathing reverently into the microphone like some demented American evangelist, 'This is the word of the Lord,' there was a commotion over by the door. 'Why can't we come in?' demanded a voice. 'We want to come to the service. Like everyone else.'

In vain Mark strove to see what was going on, but in the flickering candlelight that was the only illumination beyond the lasers, he could make out hardly anything at all. Then a man broke roughly through the ranks of tightly packed bodies into the central area immediately behind the pews, and there seemed to be some kind of scuffle going on in his wake. Mark stared in consternation, and then he saw Jack appear at the young man's side and try to take his arm. He was elbowed roughly aside for his pains and fell, so that the crowd seemed to waver and then again rise. Others swarmed forward, and it looked as if a fullscale fight was about to break out.

Mark looked at Tom, but he was standing rock still, looking as shocked as Mark felt, and seemed uncertain what to do. Mark felt sick. He wondered if this was to be the end of his career as a priest, and found himself speculating what the Bishop would say. An angry cry from the well of the church recalled him abruptly to the present. Hesitating no longer, he stepped forward. 'All right, everyone!' he shouted, with far more authority than he felt. 'Calm down! We don't want anyone to get hurt here. This is the house of God.' He took three short steps down the ramp and then pushed his way through to the little knot of flailing bodies. All around him silence fell. 'What's going on?' he demanded.

Breathless, Jack thrust up his head. His shirt was ripped and his right eye was swelling. 'It's this lot,' he said. 'They're trying to disrupt the service.'

Mark took another step forward and peered at them more closely. A measure of calm seemed to have been restored and the little group of dissidents now stood to the side, looking ruffled and offended but not, he thought, very threatening. They did look rather strange, however. They were wilder and more unkempt than the other young men and women already here. In fact, to Mark, they looked rather like outcasts who had stepped straight from the pages of some intertestamental history, with ragged, once-brightly coloured, clothes and hair that looked in need of a wash. One of them, he noted, even had a dog. 'It's not fair,' said a girl, panting slightly and pushing herself forward. 'We don't mean no harm. We was only trying to get in.'

'There's no room,' said Jack immediately.

Mark held up his hand. 'Who are you?' he asked.

'Roseanne,' said the girl. 'We was in Leicester Square when that Chalice woman came and gave out the chicken nuggets. Someone said you was a religious group, and that you prayed wiv people.'

Mark tried to smile but discovered, to his consternation, that his face felt frozen. Pippa suddenly materialised at his side and, relieved, he turned to her but she ignored him. 'Were you really there?' she asked the girl. 'In Leicester Square?'

'Yeah.' Roseanne's face broke into a smile. 'Hey, you're her, aren't you? You're Chalice.'

'Yes.' Pippa came forward. The light fell on the golden sheen of her hair and in that moment she seemed, suddenly, to be wreathed in bright shining light. A hush fell. Behind Roseanne there was a sudden flurried movement and then a young man broke through and fell on his knees before her. Pippa thought he looked familiar. She peered at him more closely, taking in the grey woollen sweater with its ragged cuffs and frayed neck, and the trousers that looked too big, held in place by a piece of string. His hair, she saw, was long and dirty, and she found herself wondering if he had lice. Then he looked up at her, and she found herself staring into a lacerated, child-face, full of pain. 'Help me,' he said, 'please.'

In that instant she recognised the young heroin addict, and she stared at him appalled, not knowing now what to do.

'This is Daffyd,' said Roseanne. 'He begged us to bring him to you. He said you could help.'

For one frozen second longer Daffyd stared up at her, his face a voiceless plea for help. Then suddenly he half crumpled, half launched himself at her and wrapped his arms round her ankles, burying his face against her feet. She felt hot tears on her skin, and then his shoulders began to heave with sobs.

'We'll leave him with you then,' said Roseanne. 'He'll be all right now, won't he?'

Pippa stared down at the young man. 'Yes,' she said, 'leave him here. We'll help.' She had not the slightest idea what any of them could do, but she knew she had to respond. Immediately Roseanne's face broke into a huge smile, and only then did Pippa realise how frightened the girl had been.

'Thank you,' Roseanne said softly. She stooped quickly down, wound her arms round Daffyd's neck and gave him a quick kiss.

'You were right,' Pippa heard her whisper, 'you'll be OK now.' Then she sprang away and the next second she was gone, the whole group with her, leaving only Daffyd.

Reaching down, Pippa began gently to pull him up. 'Come on,' she said softly, 'come with me. I'll look after you.'

'Where are you going to take him?' asked Mark.

'Back to the rectory,' she said briefly. 'You carry on with the service. I'll see you later.'

As she led Daffyd stumbling down the lane, a voice cried out, 'Pippa! Pippa, hang on!' Elaine came panting up behind. 'I was in church,' she said. 'I saw what happened. Can I do anything? Do you want any help?'

'Oh yes, please,' said Pippa gratefully. She was finding the burden of Daffyd rather difficult. All his strength seemed to have deserted him. She had slung one of his arms across her shoulders and was bearing most of his weight. Daffyd was skinny, like a kind of animated bag of bones, but he was also tall and gangly, while Pippa was rather small.

Elaine grabbed his other arm, pulled him upright and supported his other side, clamping his arm firmly to her shoulders.

'You look like you've done this before,' panted Pippa.

Elaine grunted. 'I have,' she responded. 'My father was an alcoholic.' They went slowly down the lane. Close to, Daffyd did not give off a very pleasant aroma, and Elaine's nose twitched slightly, but she said nothing. 'Where are you taking him?' she asked after a moment. 'Back home?'

Pippa nodded. She had no energy for more.

It took them about ten minutes to complete the hundred yards that lay between the church and the rectory. To Pippa it could have been a hundred miles. With each step Daffyd seemed to drag more heavily, so that her shoulders under the weight of his arms, even with Elaine's help, felt strained almost to breaking point. By the time they reached the back door he had given up all pretence of walking, and just hung like a lump of lead, his feet dragging in the dust. Wedging him up against the wall, Pippa fished in her pocket for the key, shoved it in the lock and, in one swift movement, kicked open the door. All three of them tumbled through into the kitchen, and Daffyd fell heavily into the nearest chair.

Elaine went straight to the kettle, filled it, and plugged it in. 'Coffee,' she announced.

Of the three, she seemed least affected. Some sort of fighting spirit seemed to have resurrected itself within her, and she bustled around, opening cupboards and drawers, searching for what was needed. Pippa was rather amazed by this new side to Elaine. Gratefully, she sank into a chair opposite Daffyd and looked at him appraisingly.

'Right now, young man,' she said, 'suppose you tell us what's wrong.'

Immediately, his face contorted. 'Something told me to come,' he whispered. 'Something just seemed to say to me that you'd help.'

Pippa and Elaine exchanged glances. 'Why?' Pippa asked.

His eyes were huge, limpid pools that seemed to be all pupil, with just the thinnest band of colour at the edge. 'I can't get free,' he whispered. He glanced around, as if frightened someone, or something, might overhear. 'It's there all the time.' His voice dropped still further. 'I try to hide, but it comes looking for me. It hurts me.'

Elaine shoved a mug of coffee under his nose. 'Drink that,' she commanded briskly. 'You'll feel a bit better.'

Dutifully he put his hands out and wrapped them round the mug, but he made no attempt to lift it to his lips. Instead he just continued to stare at Pippa. 'Something else came,' he said softly, 'after I saw you . . . something nice . . . It said to come to you, and that you'd help.'

As soon as the service was over, Mark raced back to the rectory, leaving Tom to stay behind and talk. It had occurred to him that he might have let his wife go off with a psychopath, and he had been seized with dread. In agony he had joined in the choruses and prayers, which that night had seemed interminable, all the while just wanting to rush after Pippa to see that everything was all right. Never had Tom seemed so slow as he did that night. 'Let's sing it one more time!' he kept saying as they came to the end of a song, and then, 'Let's take time now to wait before the Lord.' Then, when there was total silence, he stood up and shouted, 'Lord, we're begging you to send your Spirit. Speak, Lord, your servants are listening!' Still nothing, and Tom gazed round for a couple of minutes, before saying hopefully, 'Are you sure no one here has a picture or a word?' Mark felt he could have throttled him.

As soon as the last chorus ended, Mark tore off his robes and dived for the door, but Mrs Stibbins was waiting for him in the porch. 'This really won't do, Vicar,' she said, catching hold of his arm. She never called him Mark. 'My Harry would turn in his grave if he could have seen the goings-on here tonight. All these lights, and that music! It's not respectful.'

'I'm very sorry, Mrs Stibbins,' muttered Mark, 'but if you'll excuse me . . .' He tried vainly to disentangle his arm, but Mrs Stibbins refused to let go.

'And where are my flowers? That's what I want to know.'

Mark had not the slightest idea where Mrs Stibbins's flowers were and he cared even less. 'Not now, Mrs Stibbins, please!' he said, determinedly wrenching away his arm. 'Come and see me tomorrow.' And with that he ran off down the lane.

'I shall,' floated Mrs Stibbins's enraged tones after him. 'Make no mistake!'

Mark did not care. He had become convinced that Pippa even now was being bludgeoned to death. He tore the short distance down the lane and flung into the kitchen, where he could see a light. But there he pulled up short. Pippa and Elaine were sitting companionably at the small table, a mug of freshly made coffee in front of them both and a half-empty bottle of nit lotion on the table between them.

'Where is he?' panted Mark, casting wildly around. 'Has he gone?'

'No,' said Pippa tranquilly, 'he's in the bath.' She looked tired. 'We've just deloused him. His hair was alive. Elaine went and brought some lotion from home. She always keeps some spare,' she added, seeing his look of confusion and misinterpreting it, 'for the boys.'

'Nits seem to be a regular occurrence these days,' said Elaine conversationally, 'so I always keep a bottle by. Just as well really, tonight.'

Mark stared from one to the other. 'Well, what are you planning to do with him?' he asked stupidly. At that moment Daffyd himself appeared. His hair was tousled but looked clean now, and his skin looked as if it had been scrubbed. But it was what he had on that caught Mark's attention. 'He's wearing my pyjamas,' he said, outraged.

'Yes,' agreed Pippa. 'He didn't have any of his own, and we've burnt what he was wearing. That was alive too.'

Pippa put Daffyd to bed in one of the spare rooms and Jack, who had been sleeping there, found himself dispatched to the local hotel. 'I would offer to have him,' Elaine said apologetically, 'but with Stripe already staying with us, I don't think Paul would stand for it.'

Mark began to feel an unexpected sympathy for Paul. 'But we can't have him staying here, in the house!' he protested. 'We don't know anything about him. He might have a disease.'

Pippa looked at him witheringly. 'What would you prefer?' she inquired. 'That I put him under the hedge?'

Tom, when he eventually returned home, was equally unsympathetic towards Daffyd, though for different reasons. 'You know,' he said, 'I think we need to be a bit careful exactly who we take in like this. We could get inundated with all sorts of undesirables. They could divert us if we're not careful.'

Mark looked slightly alarmed.

Pippa ignored them both. 'Thanks for the lotion, Elaine,' she said. 'Do you think we used enough?'

'Think so,' said Elaine. 'But you need to make sure his hair gets combed with the nit comb for at least the next three days. If I were you, I'd do it myself. I always do with the boys, otherwise it doesn't get done properly, and then we find we're back at square one.' She rose wearily to her feet. 'I'll leave the bottle here anyway, just in case. I hope the boys'll be in bed when I get back.' She looked at Pippa. 'Would you like me to come round tomorrow?'

Pippa nodded. 'Yes,' she said. 'I'm hoping we can talk properly to him then. I'd like it if you were there too.'

# Chapter Twelve

There was something feline about Melanie, Paul decided. He was not entirely sure that he liked it, but now that they had come so far, he was finding it almost impossible to break free, or even to put a little distance between them. She was like a drug in his blood, he thought. Each time he made a resolution to draw back from the relationship, a hot longing for her seemed to spurt up inside of him so that he could hardly think straight till the longing had been assuaged. Now, moodily watching her through the glass partition of his office, the familiar and disorientating craving seemed to creep up on him, making him want to rush out and pin her to the desk while there was no one around and take his pleasure fast. A part of him knew that she would enjoy that, that she would laugh and find the risk exciting, and he found that attractive too.

But he was angry with Melanie. As well as the phone calls, she had taken to faxing him now, and Sebastian had picked up the last one. 'Who's Melanie, Dad?' he had inquired, coming into the kitchen where the family were gathered. 'It's marked urgent, and she says her loins are yearning for you.' He looked puzzled. 'What does she mean? Is it some sort of a joke?' Elaine, who had been standing at the breakfast bar juicing oranges, froze.

Paul laughed embarrassedly. 'Yes,' he said, a shade too heartily, 'that's it. It's a joke. She works in my office. Tremendous sense of humour!'

'I'll bet,' Elaine had muttered and viciously twisted another orange.

A kind of frozen no man's land seemed to stretch between them now. Elaine was icily polite but, in so far as she could, she refused to address Paul directly. After Melanie's visit, she had told him that if the little slut ever came round again, she would not be responsible for her actions. Paul had been surprised how very upset she was.

Now he found himself wondering, with despair, if he would ever again be able to thread a way across that wasteland where howling gusts of icy hatred seemed to blow. Melanie, he decided, had known exactly what she was doing when she had descended on his house like that. The situation, he realised, had moved to a different level. But this was alien ground to him, he no longer knew the rules by which

113

he was supposed to play. He still found Elaine boring, but there was a dawning conviction inside him that he did, after all, want to remain married to her. She seemed to represent a kind of stolid domesticity and order that he knew he did not want to be without. A part of him even despised himself for this weakness, and yet he knew that it was so. He wanted his family. He wanted the boys. He even, God help him, wanted Elaine – to carry on with her extravagance and her visits to the fitness club, and her role as the perfect society wife. But just for the moment he also wanted Melanie. His hand reached out to the intercom and he pressed the buzzer. 'Come in here a moment, Melanie, please.'

She glided in through the door, perfect knees just showing beneath the perfect band of her skirt. She took one look at his face, glanced quickly round, and then wriggled on to his knee. 'Yes?' she breathed. 'Can I do something for you?' Her hand slid up his chest, and he felt a small, betraying knot of excitement uncurl in his stomach.

'Not now, Melanie,' he said hastily, restraining himself with difficulty. 'I want to talk about the Chalice account.'

She pouted but obediently slid from his knee and stood up.

'We've got a general investment trust here, so I want some of the money to start working, and I want to spread it around. Pippa Casaubon is a very rich woman but, as her fund manager, I think we can double that.'

Melanie put on her serious face and became all attention.

'I'm proposing a three-way division: UK, Far East markets, and a European growth fund.'

Melanie nodded. 'The Thai market seems a pretty good bet at the moment,' she suggested.

'Yes, but I don't want all our eggs in one basket.' Paul frowned as he found the file he was looking for and drew it towards him. 'I've done a preliminary outline here, which I want you to start following up. You've got authorisation to begin investment but, as authorised signatory of the trust, I'll need to countersign all cheques.' He began to explain in detail exactly what he wanted her to do.

Back at the rectory, Tom was trying to persuade Pippa that the course of action she was proposing was unwise. Mark had given up. He felt he simply could not get through to her these days. Every time he tried to talk to her she just seemed to look at him with a kind of angry contempt.

'You'll have to send him to a drug rehabilitation centre,' declared Tom.

'He's tried that,' responded Pippa. 'It didn't work. At least, it got him off temporarily, but then he started to go back. He speaks about drugs as if they're something external controlling him. He's frightened. He wants to be free.'

Tom threw his hands in the air. 'Pippa, you know absolutely nothing about drugs. How on earth can you help him? If the experts have failed, what are you going to do? Wave a magic wand?'

Pippa stuck out her lip. 'Of course not. But I honestly believe God has sent him here.'

'God is probably going to send every sponger within a hundred-mile radius.'

This was too much and Pippa exploded. 'How can you be so hard?' she shouted angrily. 'Do you honestly want me just to tip him back on to the streets? What hope will there be for him then?'

Mark cleared his throat. 'Pippa,' he began sententiously, 'he's not a child, you know. You're not responsible for him.'

This was a mistake, because now she rounded on him too. 'Don't be so bloody selfish. I never said I was responsible for him. I simply want to help. And I believe I can, because I honestly believe God sent him.'

Both men gaped at her. It was not so much what she had said as the fact that she had sworn. Pippa never swore, and so the impact was dramatic.

'So what are you going to do?' asked Tom at last.

Pippa breathed heavily. 'Well, for a start I'm going to get Dr Forrest to have a look at him and see if there's anything he needs medically, and then Elaine and I are going to talk to him and then,' her chin lifted defiantly, 'I thought we could pray with him.'

'God help us,' muttered Mark. 'Take up your bed and walk!'

Pippa duly summoned Dr Forrest, who came round later the same morning and, having examined Daffyd, pronounced him severely malnourished and clearly in a state of emotional disturbance, most probably induced by drug dependency, but otherwise all right. Like Mark and Tom, he advised Pippa to seek professional help for the boy, and offered to section him. Pippa was appalled. 'He's come to us in good faith,' she said, 'and all you can suggest is that we have him committed!'

'Pippa,' said the doctor gently, 'he's in a highly volatile state. He needs help, and I'm not convinced you can give it. The first thing we need to do is get him off the drugs, and then he's probably going to need intensive psychiatric help. And to be perfectly honest, I'm not sure in any case it's going to be any good. He may be too far gone.'

Pippa's eyes filled with tears. 'No,' she said, 'it can't be too late. And if you really think the psychiatrists can't help, then he might just as well stay here.'

Dr Forrest shook his head. He thought Pippa had not the slightest idea what she was taking on, and that her good resolution would very rapidly collapse once she found herself face to face with the reality. He was also not entirely sure that it would be safe if Daffyd remained at the rectory. The young man might run amok. But he had to acknowledge that there seemed little sign of that, and so he decided that the wisest course was to let Pippa have her way for a few days. The time to suggest more reasonable measures was when she became disillusioned, as he felt sure she would soon enough.

Quickly he wrote out a prescription. 'I'm going to give him some methadone,' he said. 'It's a substitute. The idea is we reduce his dose gradually, until we get to the point when we can bring him off it.' He looked at her. 'I'm warning you, it's not going to be easy, and he's going to need a lot of watching. But if you do need any help, well, I'm at the end of the telephone.'

Gratefully Pippa took the prescription. Elaine went to get it, while she herself cooked Daffyd the most enormous breakfast. When he had eaten, the three of them sat down to talk. The night's rest, in a clean bed and without fear, coupled with the food, had done Daffyd good. He seemed calmer, and they found he was able to talk. 'Thank you,' he said, when they first sat down. 'You must think I'm nuts, but I guess you're my last hope, and something honestly did tell me to come to you.'

'Why don't you begin,' Pippa suggested, 'by telling us how you got into this mess in the first place.'

Daffyd stared at his hands, still slightly grey in spite of the bath. Yet scrubbed, and in clean clothes, with his hair cut (which Elaine had insisted upon, given the lice), he seemed transformed. He had dark curly hair, and a gaunt, rather beautiful face, with deep, sad, brown eyes. But his skin was chalky and rather crepey and, despite what Dr Forrest had said, he looked ill.

'I've been living on the streets since I was eleven,' he said. 'My mum walked out when I was a kid, and then my dad got banged up. They wanted to put me in a home, but I ran away.' Faltering sometimes, as if the memory still hurt, he told them how he had been picked up in King's Cross by an older boy who had told him that, for those who knew how, it was easy to make a living. He had become a rent boy, selling his favours for money, food and, increasingly, drugs. The drugs, he said, had made it all bearable, at first. They had been a way of escape. A cushion for his mind when he had had to endure the indignities to his flesh.

Pippa and Elaine were horrified. They had heard such stories before in the press and on television, but that wasn't the same as hearing it first-hand like this.

'Why didn't you go home,' whispered Elaine, 'if it was all so awful?'

He looked at her and gave a tired smile. 'There wasn't a home to go to.'

'Shall we pray with you?' asked Pippa at last.

He looked slightly apprehensive, but nodded. 'If you want.'

Pippa and Elaine stood and laid hands on him. Pippa tried to remember everything she had ever read about praying with people for healing, but she found her mind had gone blank. Daffyd sat with an expression of intense concentration on his face, eyes closed, hands rigid on his knees, and it was clear he expected them to begin. Pippa glanced at Elaine, who stared back at her questioningly and then gave a little smile of encouragement. Elaine was obviously also expecting her to begin. 'Dear Lord,' Pippa began uncertainly, 'thank you for bringing Daffyd here.' Then in a rush she went on, 'Lord, I don't really know how to pray here, but you're God and I guess this isn't such a very big deal to you, so please, just heal him and set him free.'

A convulsive shudder ran through Daffyd's body and he opened his eyes and looked wildly around. 'I don't like it,' he said, starting to his feet. 'Please stop. I'm frightened.' To their intense surprise, he seemed suddenly to revert to the way he had been the night before. 'You've got to be quiet. It'll hear!'

'What will?' asked Elaine.

But Daffyd's face was now contorted with terror. 'It!' he said urgently. 'My beast. It'll hear. It'll know what you're trying to do. It'll hurt me.'

'But . . . Jesus is here,' said Pippa. 'It'll be all right.' She had no idea whether this was actually true or not. She had never really thought about the implications of such a statement before, but it seemed somehow the right thing to say.

Daffyd shook his head violently. 'I can't see him. But I can see It. Please stop, I'm scared.'

He did, genuinely, seem absolutely terrified and they sat down defeated. 'I've failed, haven't I?' he said miserably. 'I'm never going to be free.'

Later, when Pippa and Elaine were discussing what had happened, Elaine said, 'I guess it's going to take time. He's still in a bad way from being out on the streets. And of course he's still taking drugs.'

'Only methadone,' said Pippa. 'Now.'

Elaine shrugged. 'But how long does all that stuff take to work through the system? I think maybe we've got to go gently and build him up physically. And win his trust. That's terribly important. He's still really scared at the moment. Maybe he thinks we're going to let him down the way everyone else has. Maybe subconsciously he didn't want us to pray because he thought that then we'd just turf him out again, and he'd be back to square one.'

Pippa looked unconvinced. 'Maybe,' she said. 'But I thought it was more than that. He seemed terrified, and he seemed to be looking for something all the time. I began to think *I* was going to see something!'

Elaine laughed. 'That's the product of an over-active imagination, my dear. Let's just wait a bit and see how it goes. He certainly seems very determined to stick to this methadone programme and try and get himself off the stuff. Let's take it one step at a time.'

Elaine had actually found her time with Daffyd helpful. Somehow, seeing his plight, it had put all her own troubles more into perspective. She began to feel that Melanie really was rather a silly little girl. And with the thought, Paul somehow seemed to shift from the centre of her world, so that his actions no longer dominated her mind in quite the way they had before. She was deeply angry with him but, bordering her rage, was contempt. Lately she had gone from the overwhelming conviction that the marriage had to survive to a feeling of intense hatred that had made her for a while seriously consider sprinkling rat poison on his cornflakes. But now she felt only a great weariness, and was rapidly coming to the conclusion that Paul and Melanie deserved one another. With a sense of liberation, she discovered that though she still could not leave him, she would not mind very much if she woke up one morning and found that he had gone. She would manage. It would not be the end of the world.

She arrived back at Gentillesse at three, to be there for when the boys arrived, and discovered that the answerphone was flashing. When she played back the first message, a man's disembodied voice crackled out into the room. 'Hello, Jim Browning here. Sebastian's housemaster. I wonder if one of you could come in and see me. We've had a spot of trouble.' There was a pause, and then the voice added, 'Nothing to worry about – he's OK, but I feel we need to talk.'

Elaine went cold. She had never had such a message before, and her first thought was that something terrible must have happened. Her hands shaking slightly, she dialled the school, but the number was engaged. Spinning on her heel, she headed for the door. She got to the school by three twenty-five and discovered the younger boys already beginning to pour out. Suppressing the urge to run, her fear now growing, she headed quickly for the school office and asked the secretary where she could find Jim Browning. The secretary, who had recognised her immediately, looked solicitous, and Elaine's panic grew. 'Ah, yes,' she said, 'he was hoping you'd come in. If you'll just take a seat outside, I'll get him for you. He should be just finishing.'

Elaine sat in the tiny anteroom for perhaps ten minutes. It felt like an eternity. Finally, the housemaster arrived, looking flushed and slightly out of breath. 'Mrs Dufrayn,' he said immediately, holding out his hand, 'thank you for coming in. I felt we needed to talk. Sebastian's in the sick bay at the moment.'

Elaine sprang to her feet. 'Why?' she asked wildly. 'What's happened? Is he going to be all right?'

Jim Browning looked wary. 'He's perfectly all right,' he said cautiously. 'There's been a bit of a fight, that's all. He's got a black eye, but nothing worse. Please, Mrs Dufrayn, sit down. It's not Sebastian's injuries I want to discuss.'

Elaine sat, and Jim Browning took the chair opposite. He seemed to be searching for the right words. After a moment he said, 'Mrs Dufrayn, I don't really know how to say this, but I'll be honest with you. Sebastian's behaviour this term has been a bit strange, to say the least.' He looked at her inquiringly, obviously expecting some sort of response.

'Strange?' she said. 'How? What do you mean?'

He again glanced down, as if he found her frank stare disconcerting. 'Sebastian has always been such a nice little chap. Very open. A bit mischievous. But this term, I don't know, it's been difficult. It's the devil's own job trying to keep him in control these days. This fight today is typical.'

'Are you saying he started it?' asked Elaine, shocked.

He shrugged. 'I honestly don't know. I don't really think it matters that much. What does matter is that these days he always seems to be in some kind of trouble, and the other boys are finding it very hard to get along with him. He's even been picking on some of the younger boys.' And then he dropped his bombshell. 'Mrs Dufrayn, I must ask this, is there any kind of trouble at home? Has something happened that would account for this change?'

Elaine froze. 'No, of course not,' she said immediately.

'I think he's a very unhappy young man, Mrs Dufrayn,' Browning said. 'He's exhibiting all the characteristics of a dysfunctional child, and it's all happened very suddenly.' He looked at her. 'I'm worried that if things don't change we're going to lose Sebastian, the old Sebastian, and I'm not sure any of us like this new one. Especially himself.'

Ten minutes later Elaine was allowed to go and collect Sebastian from the sick bay where, Jim Browning said, they had kept him more as a precautionary measure than anything else, to help him regain control. She felt stunned. It had never occurred to her that the problems she and Paul were experiencing might be having an impact on the boys. She had always prided herself that they kept their differences hidden.

'What on earth have you been doing?' she asked, as soon as the matron had gone and left them alone.

He turned a frightened face up to her, and she felt a sudden, quite irrational, spasm of fear. 'I'm sorry, Mum,' he said, his voice catching. His face was blotchy, and he looked as if he had been crying; his eyes were red and puffy. Around his left eye a deep purple bruise was beginning to show. It looked awful. 'It's all right,' he said, catching her look, 'it looks bad, but it doesn't hurt. Matron says it'll be fine.'

Not knowing what else to do, she folded her arms round him and hugged him to her. 'Oh Sebastian,' she muttered, 'why? How on earth did you get into this mess?'

In silence they collected Harry, waiting for them at the school gate, and then began the short drive home. 'Don't tell Dad. Please,' whispered Sebastian from the back of the car.

Elaine kept her eyes fixed on the road ahead. 'He's going to have to know,' she said grimly. She was still torn between anger and fear. 'What happened?'

'It was Stebbings's fault,' said Harry suddenly. 'He started it.'

'Why?' asked Elaine. 'What did he do?'

In the mirror she saw the boys glance at each other. A kind of coded signal seemed to pass between them, and then Sebastian just shrugged and turned his face to look out of the window. 'He just did,' he said. 'That's all.'

She could get no more out of them. When they got back she sent them both out into the garden to play while she began to prepare tea. She had no idea whether she ought to send Sebastian up to bed or what, but Jim Browning had advised her to be gentle with him, and she was worried, too, what Paul would say when he discovered what had happened. As she moved about the kitchen, her anger towards her husband grew. This was Paul's fault, she thought. His crass selfishness was spoiling all their lives.

Out in the garden Sebastian sped off, running to hide in his favourite tree, the one Harry could not climb. His brother watched him uncertainly but then, seeing where he was headed, decided he was probably better off alone. Shrugging, he went to play down by the river.

It was in the same tree that, over an hour later, Stripe found him. It was a huge old oak, with spreading boughs that hung down almost to the ground below and seemed to reach the sky above. The branches on the left brushed the garage, so that the leaves made a gentle shushing sound against the windows. Sebastian's hiding place was in a fork some twenty feet off the ground, adjacent to Stripe's living room. From below, Sebastian was completely hidden, but inside the flat, when Stripe flung open the window, he found himself staring straight into Sebastian's tear-stained face. 'Wot ye doin' there?' he asked. 'Wot's up?'

Sebastian sniffed. 'Nothing,' he said.

Stripe looked at him more closely. 'That's a real shiner ye got there,' he remarked.

Sebastian sniffed again. 'I got it in a fight,' he volunteered.

'Did ye win?' inquired Stripe.

Sebastian shrugged.

'Do ye want to come in?' Stripe asked.

'Yes please.'

Holding out his hand and leaning out, Stripe grabbed his arm and almost bodily lifted him in through the window. Sebastian was surprised at how strong Stripe was; he seemed to catch him up as if he was a feather, and the next moment he was standing inside the room.

'Ye can tell me about it if ye like,' said Stripe. 'I've got some biccies somewhere.'

They sat companionably, munching biscuits and drinking Coke, which appeared to be the only thing Stripe ever drank. 'I started it,' said Sebastian suddenly.

'Why?'

Sebastian shrugged. 'I don't know really,' he said. 'At least . . . Stebbings was going on about Mum. He said she looked sour, and so I hit him.'

Stripe looked at him. 'She does look a bit sour sometimes,' he remarked.

'I know.' Sebastian took another biscuit. 'She's not really like that though. It's Dad, I think. I don't really know what's going on, but they always seem to be arguing these days, or not talking to each other, and Mum cries.' Stripe waited. 'They neither of them seem to take much notice of us these days.'

'You and Harry?'

'Yes. We seem to be in the way all the time. That's the way they act. Stripe, what do you think's going to happen? Do you think they're going to split up?'

Stripe set down his drink carefully and regarded him. He felt that his answer was important. 'Is that's wot's worrying you?' he asked.

Sebastian nodded. 'Yes,' he whispered. 'I keep thinking they're going to break up . . . and what's going to happen to us then?'

Looking at the boy, Stripe felt, for him, a most unexpected emotion. Concern. 'Hey,' he said awkwardly, 'it'll be all right. You'll see.'

'But what if they do break up?' said Sebastian intently. 'Where will we go?'

Stripe frowned. 'You'll be all right,' he said again. 'They both love ye, ye know. Even if they do split up, they'll still look after ye.'

'But I don't want them to split up,' said Sebastian passionately. 'I want things to be the way they used to be. I want us to be a family again.'

# Chapter Thirteen

Mark looked down at the floor, puzzled. At his feet lay a tiny bat, its black wings crumpled across its body, which in turn lay twisted awkwardly underneath. He had come over to the church to make sure that the pews had all been replaced properly, and that Mrs Stibbins's flowers were back where they ought to be. He suspected he had not yet heard the last of that lady's anger, especially as, for the last couple of days, no one had been able to find the pedestal which, Oogi swore blind, they had put safely in the church hall. It had finally been discovered only earlier today, in a broom cupboard adjoining the lavatories, and Mark was reliably informed that Mrs Stibbins's rage, when she heard, had been great.

It had not, however, been Mrs Stibbins who was on his mind as he came up the church path, but his wife. He was due to go the following day to Porthcawl with Tom, to start preparations for the church weekend that Tom had said Chalice would lead. Initially it had been planned that Pippa would go with them but now, because Daffyd was there, she had refused. Mark felt distinctly uneasy. He understood that Daffyd could not go with them, and that it was equally impossible that the boy remain in the rectory alone, but what he did not understand was why they did not simply pack him off to a drug rehabilitation centre. He was worried that if Pippa stayed with him alone, Daffyd might go berserk and attack her, or something even worse, while they were away.

He had felt so upset that he had even called on Dr Forrest for a chat and had come away, if it was possible, feeling even more alarmed. The good doctor had taken the opportunity to raise the issue of fertility tests, and Mark had felt so affronted that he had left abruptly, not even bothering to finish the cup of coffee he had been given. Pushing open the heavy oak door to the church, pondering these things, he had hardly taken two steps inside when he had come across the bat.

St Saviour's had a problem with bats. A colony of them had lived inside the church ever since Mark first arrived and, for all he knew, they might always have been there, installed by Alfred the Hermit himself. Sometimes, if there was a quiet spot in a service, they could be heard squeaking, but by and large they stayed out of sight, and

Mark suspected that the majority of the congregation were rather fond of them. The only drawback was their droppings which they deposited everywhere as they flapped backwards and forwards across the church at night. In the mornings, the first person in would find traces of their presence everywhere – over the pews, on the floor, even sometimes on the altar. Mark, not overly green by temperament, would have liked very much to have got rid of them, but they were protected by law, and so instead they packed away all the books, hid the kneelers under the pews, and regularly scrubbed down the aisles. But never before had he found one dead.

Stooping down, he picked it up distastefully, carried it outside, and deposited it under a bush in the graveyard. Then he went back in and prepared to resume his inspection. Hardly had he taken another three paces before he discovered another bat, and then, a little further on, two more, their wings entangled in each other, as if they had collided in mid-flight. Feeling even more puzzled, he walked all round the church and discovered five more. He was just putting the last of them outside, thinking that he would bury them later, when Tom arrived. 'What's that?' asked Tom curiously.

'Bats,' said Mark briefly, straightening up and stretching. 'I've just found nine altogether. All dead. It's quite extraordinary, I've never even found one before.'

'Maybe they've got bat flu.'

Mark looked at him. 'It's not funny, Tom. I'm wondering if all the noise on Sunday has affected them. If it has, there could be trouble – they're protected, you know.'

Tom grimaced. 'Highly unlikely, I'd have thought. I've never heard of anything like that happening before.'

'Well, something's killed them.'

Tom fell into step at his side, and together they went back into the church. 'Everything all right?' he asked facetiously. 'Flowers back where they ought to be?'

Mark grunted. 'As far as I can see,' he replied. He stared intently up at the roof, as if expecting to find the answer to the bat mystery up there, but Tom was not interested in the bats.

'Good,' he said absently. 'Very good.' He kicked at the stone flags, and then began to hum quietly to himself. It was an irritating habit he had whenever there was something on his mind. He said abruptly, 'Mark, I've had an idea.'

Mark's eyes transferred themselves from the roof to Tom, and he blinked apprehensively. He felt he had heard rather too many of Tom's good ideas over the last few weeks. Tom, however, appeared not to notice.

'Last time I was over in the States,' he said, 'I met this evangelist, Chuck Gibbons. He's got this huge church out on the West Coast, but he tours around a lot. Very into healing, and signs and wonders, but he also heads up a Christian TV channel, and they're just about to move into satellite. I thought Chalice could maybe get involved in that.'

Mark stared at him. He had a sinking feeling in the pit of his stomach that this was going to be even worse than he had anticipated. 'What do you mean?' he asked carefully.

'Well, Chuck was talking about coming over to Britain. They had a prophecy or something about eighteen months ago that Albion would experience revival. Chuck says that's us, England, and he said he wanted to come over and see what the Lord was going to do for himself. But most of all,' here Tom's face grew really excited, 'most of all, he said he felt a real call to help by opening up a satellite channel over here. The trouble is, he hasn't got any contacts.'

Mark swallowed, feeling his worst fears were about to be confirmed. 'So?' he asked.

'Well, don't you see?' exploded Tom, his excitement erupting like an over-active volcano. 'I thought Chalice could be the British end. We could link up with Chuck. He could even come over and do a mission for us. We could hire an arena somewhere and have a really big rally. Wembley maybe!' His face was animated. 'Something like that would really put Chalice on the map!'

Mark was appalled. 'This sounds expensive, Tom,' he said, desperately playing for time, while casting around for an objection that would effectively dampen Tom's enthusiasm.

'Oh, come on, Chalice can afford it, and think of the returns. Like the Bible says, Mark, cast your bread on the water!'

Mark had the sudden disorientating sensation that he was swimming through mud. He felt he was being sucked into some terrible mire from which there was very little chance of escape. He had not, he realised, the slightest desire to link up with an American tele-evangelist but he could come up with no convincing reason why not. At the same time it suddenly struck him that whatever he felt was irrelevant anyway, because Tom, if he thought it was a good idea, would simply go ahead and do it, confident that Pippa would foot the bill. Mark felt redundant. 'Have you spoken to Pippa yet?' he asked heavily.

'No, not yet. I wanted to sound out how you felt first. But now I know you like the idea, I will. Come on, let's go and find her now.'

Pippa was at the rectory, having just taken Daffyd on a long medicinal walk. She had had the feeling that a gentle ramble through the coutryside might go a long way to giving him some kind of calm, but she had been disappointed because Daffyd had given every appearance of finding the open spaces disturbing, while for some reason wood pigeons had filled him with dread. 'Go and lie down,' she said authoritatively as soon as they were safely back inside, 'and I'll bring you a cup of tea.' She had just made the tea and taken him some when Mark and Tom arrived.

'I don't know what on earth to do,' she said to Mark despairingly. 'Everything I suggest seems to be wrong. He was petrified up on the Chase.'

'Perhaps he's agoraphobic,' said Tom helpfully.

'Perhaps.' In the act of filling the kettle again, Pippa paused and glanced at them uncertainly. 'I wondered if maybe it wasn't something spiritual.' They both looked at her. 'I thought perhaps it might help if you two prayed with him. You know,' she added, her cheeks going pink because she knew Mark disapproved of all that sort of thing, 'priestly authority and all that.'

Mark contrived to look offended. 'Don't be ridiculous, Pippa,' he said. 'You make it sound like magic.'

'No,' said Tom. 'I know what Pippa means. Men have more authority.'

Mark weighed this. 'Well, yes, theologically I agree,' he said, 'but . . .' He suddenly became aware that Tom was staring at his wife with the oddest expression on his face. It was all sort of dewy and tender, utterly revolting, thought Mark, and he glared at Tom narrowly. It occurred to him yet again that Tom paid Pippa rather too much attention.

Pippa was staring back at Tom gratefully and saying, 'Oh, thank you, Tom. I knew you'd understand. That's exactly it, and you've both been anointed for this, haven't you?'

Tom looked deprecating. 'It's our calling, Pippa,' he said, 'that's all. But you're right, in a case of obvious spiritual conflict like this, it's men who are called upon to pray.' His expression grew even more tender. 'Your role is far softer. You're called to nurture and protect, and . . .'

Mark felt he had heard quite enough. The unwelcome suspicion that Tom was making up to his wife was hardening inside him. 'Yes, well,' he said savagely, stepping forward and interposing himself physically between them. 'I hardly think that new woman priest over at St Ethelburga's would agree with you.' They both stared at him amazed. Slightly embarrassed, he went on hastily, 'What's her name? Antonia Henty-Fitzgerald or something.' Tom and Pippa continued to stare at him, and he had the sudden feeling he was making a fool of himself. 'She's very charismatic, I hear,' he babbled. 'Prays with people all over the shop.'

'Perhaps I should take Daffyd over to her then,' said Pippa.

'No!' said Mark and Tom together. They looked at each other measuringly. There was a warning in Mark's eyes and they both knew it. Now he said with dignity, 'Quite unnecessary, Pippa.

126

We're quite up to praying with anyone the Lord cares to send along, thank you.'

'Does that mean you will pray with Daffyd then?'

Mark realised he had just talked himself into a corner. 'Let's not be hasty,' he began. She looked at him and he crumpled. 'All right, we'll have a chat with him and see.'

The phone shrilled and they all jumped. Mark went over and picked up the receiver.

'Hello,' he said, 'St Saviour's vicarage . . . Yes, I see . . . of course . . . Straightaway? Are you sure that's entirely necessary? . . . Tomorrow morning then.' When he replaced the handset, he looked crestfallen. 'That was the Bishop's chaplain,' he announced. 'Bishop Bob wants to see me as soon as possible.'

'Why?' asked Pippa.

'I don't know,' he replied. 'He wouldn't say, but it sounded serious.'

Tom was the first to recover himself. Being something of a nonconformist by temperament, he had not the same awe of the Bishop's authority as Mark, and he did not appreciate quite what such a summons might mean. 'It'll be all right,' he said airily. 'I expect he's heard about Chalice, that's all.'

'That's what I'm worried about,' said Mark.

This was lost on Tom. 'Let's go and have a chat with Daffyd,' he said, looking adoringly at Pippa, 'and then afterwards we'll tell her about our brilliant idea.'

They found Daffyd slumped against the wall of his bedroom, his tea untouched on the table, clutching to his chest one of Mark's old sweaters that Pippa had given him. Seeing yet another article of his clothing gone, Mark scowled, but Pippa smiled brightly. 'He needed it,' she explained, 'and you can always get another one.' She crossed over to Daffyd and knelt at his side. 'Daffyd,' she said. Her voice was gentle, as if she was speaking to a child, and she laid her hand on his arm. 'It's all right,' she reassured, 'Mark and Tom would just like a word, that's all.'

He turned terrified eyes on her. 'Why?' he asked.

She smiled. 'Because they want to help you,' she said softly. Then she straightened up and slipped quickly from the room.

'Well,' said Tom heartily after a moment, 'here we are then!'

'Yes,' agreed Mark. They pulled over a couple of chairs and sat down facing Daffyd. From his seat on the floor, he stared at them suspiciously.

'What's the problem then?' asked Tom.

'Yes,' said Mark, like an echo, 'tell us and we'll see what we can do to help.'

A few minutes later Pippa, peeling sprouts in the kitchen, heard a loud howl, followed by a lot of banging and a crash. Then there was another crash, and she ran as fast as she could upstairs. The sight that met her eyes would have been comical if Daffyd had not been in such obvious terror. He was perched on the dressing table, clutching a table lamp and panting slightly. Tom was lying on the floor, looking stunned, and Mark gave every appearance of being about to launch himself at Daffyd in a rugger tackle.

'They're trying to pray with me, Pippa,' said Daffyd wildly as she came in. 'They started as soon as you went out. I told them I didn't want them to but then they went for me.'

Pippa gaped. 'Good God,' she said, shocked. She turned to Mark. 'What on earth are you doing?'

'We were trying to do what you asked!' spat Mark. Like Daffyd, he was breathing heavily and he looked tense.

From the floor Tom groaned. 'My shoulder hurts,' he announced.

They all ignored him and Pippa crossed over to Daffyd. 'Come on,' she said soothingly, taking his arm, 'they're not trying to hurt you. It's all right.'

Daffyd gave one brief look at her face and burst into tears. 'I'm scared,' he sobbed, burying his face in her chest. 'I was frightened what they were going to do.'

Pippa refused to talk to either Mark or Tom for the rest of the night. She made it plain that she was very angry with them both and later, on the phone, Mark overheard her saying, 'Honestly, Elaine, it was like bedlam. The simplest thing and they make a hash of it! They went straight in like a bull in a china shop. Poor Daffyd was terrified out of his wits. A woman would never have done that. I sometimes think men haven't got the sense they were born with.'

The next day, straight after matins, Mark set off for his interview with the Bishop. He felt distinctly uneasy, and wished forlornly that Pippa was not quite so cross with him, but there was nothing for it; this particular bullet, he knew, he had to bite alone. Wishing that he had not traded in his little Fiesta quite so promptly, he climbed into the new pink Mercedes and set off nervously for Church House.

The Bishop was one of that younger breed of bishops who were all working hard to drag the Church into the twenty-first century. He had only been in office in Carbery a couple of years, and he was a dynamic liberal who believed in everything except belief – and he liked all his clergy to call him Bob. His most passionate conviction was that nothing and no one should ever rock the boat – the Church's position in society – and to that end he had set up an inter-faith working party, chaired by a lesbian priest, and was currently involved in negotiations with the local pagan group for a joint eucharist at the summer solstice, at the standing stones that lay on the edge of the diocese. He and Mark had never really got on, but never before had the Bishop had anything obvious with which to fuel his dislike. Mark had always been such an exemplary, hard-working priest of the old school; an evangelical of the traditional kind, who disapproved of everything that was not specifically endorsed in the Bible, as well as quite a few of what he saw as the more modern things that were. By and large, however, Mark had always kept his head down and, although the Bishop knew Mark disapproved of him, since he had not as yet done anything that could be openly construed as a criticism or a challenge, he had felt constrained to maintain at least a facade of friendliness. Until now.

'Mark,' he said, coming forward as Mark stepped in through the door to his office, and holding out his hand. 'Glad you could spare the time.'

Mark felt the full force of the implied criticism and wilted. Nervously he walked across the thick and expensive shag pile that was the Bishop's carpet, and sat down in the cream leather armchair that faced the desk. The Bishop sat down too and stared at him, his fingertips resting lightly together across his chest. 'I'll come straight to the point, Mark,' he said severely, as the silence became uncomfortable. 'I've had one or two complaints.'

Mark swallowed, and his thoughts reverted instantly to Mrs Stibbins. He waited, breath becoming more shallow.

'Yes,' continued the Bishop, pursing his lips, 'I've been hearing about some very odd goings-on at St Saviour's, and I hear your wife has won the lottery too.'

Mark flushed scarlet. He could not help himself. He felt the hot tide of colour flame up his neck and face, and across to the tips of his ears. 'Oh, er, yes, Bob,' he mumbled.

'Pardon?' barked the Bishop.

Mark cleared his throat. 'I said that's right.'

'I see.' The Bishop regarded him. 'I thought you were against all that sort of thing. At least, that was what you implied when the diocese was exploring the possibility of a grant from lottery funds to help with necessary repairs to the cathedral roof. If I remember correctly, we received a statement from your group stating that, as the spiritual root of gambling was demonic, you felt that to make use of such funds would be dishonouring to God.'

Miserably, Mark nodded. 'Yes,' he said, 'but, er, my wife was just carrying out some research . . . wanted to know how it worked.' The full banality of his reply hit him and he dried up.

'Yes,' said Bishop Bob. 'Quite.' He looked at Mark with dislike. 'Well, by all accounts she's certainly done that.' His eyes narrowed. 'But to return to the more serious issue, the complaints allege that complete anarchy has broken out at St Saviour's, and that the church has become a bear garden of,' he pulled a letter towards him on the desk and quoted, '"chaos and misrule". The complainant further says that last Sunday evening in particular, the service was more like a pop concert than evensong, and she says you have a most unsavoury black man playing for you, who appears to know nothing *but* pop songs!'

When Mark left, three-quarters of an hour later, he was reeling. The Bishop had suggested to him that, since he had access to such unlimited funds, he might now wish to consider whether or not his future really lay in the established Church. He implied that as they had already set up Chalice, Mark might wish to devote his energies there. He had made it clear that Mark could expect no further support from the diocese, and that all such shenanigans as had been going on at St Saviour's had to stop immediately. 'We have to be very careful,' he said ominously. 'It's a question of authority, and we can't have renegade priests declaring UDI. You're a loose cannon, Mark. The tabloids could have a field day, especially after all that fuss over at Sheffield. Some might even say we're perilously close to heresy.' And then, having lined Mark up in his sights, he discharged the full force of his episcopal guns. 'If you persist, the Archdeacon will have to make a visitation.'

The full injustice of his remarks had struck Mark like a blow. The Bishop had given him not the slightest chance to defend himself. He had seemed, indeed, completely uninterested in Mark's side, and had simply assumed that everything the letter had said was true. Mark felt certain it was Mrs Stibbins but, though he had tried to catch a glimpse of the signature, he had been unable to see, and when he had asked if he might know who the complainant was, the Bishop had said no, that that was irrelevant. 'So may I take it that you do intend to resign?' the Bishop inquired smoothly as he showed him to the door.

Mark, although shocked by the threat of a visitation, was not about to be dismissed so easily, especially by someone whom he felt, deep down, was unfitted for the office he held. 'No,' he said through clenched teeth, 'you may not. Please feel free to send the Archdeacon whenever you wish!'

Stripe also found himself faced with a dilemma. He was to travel down to Porthcawl the following day with Jack in the van, but he knew that he really ought to do something first about the two men who had assaulted Mark. He ought to go to Liverpool and clarify the situation, but he found himself putting it off. He was afraid of what he might discover, and that he might be forced to leave Little Wakenham.

It was not simply that for the first time in his life Stripe found himself with an abundant supply of honestly made money in his pocket, he had realised, too, that he was happy. He had thought about this, trying to discover the reason why, and had been able to come up with no very satisfactory answer. All he knew was that he was making music he loved, and that he was part of a group that made him feel at home. A rather odd group, it was true, and all of them displayed a disconcerting tendency to pray at the least excuse, but they treated him with a kind of accepting and ready camaraderie that made him feel he was one of them. And then, too, there was Sebastian.

Stripe felt genuinely sorry for the boy. He himself had never known his own father. He was not overly convinced that his mother had either. Before her conversion to Christianity a few years ago, her line of work had given her a varied life, and from his earliest years Stripe had never known her have any steady relationship. These days, of course, she was very proper, and had become vociferously disapproving of him, but in those days there had been a succession of men who had streamed by like so many oil tankers passing through the Suez Canal. That was how he had always thought of them, the image suggesting itself one day during one of the rare geography lessons he had sat in on at school – he had not gone in much for formal education. He had felt bitter as a kid and then, when he had grown older and himself embarked on the choppy sea of relationships, indifferent. His mother's change of lifestyle had been dramatic, but it had not impressed him. He could understand what Sebastian was feeling. He told himself it was daft, but he wanted somehow to help the kid get through whatever it was that lay ahead. To stay, however, he had first to make his own position secure.

Staring unseeingly out of the window he came to a decision. If he caught the next train to Liverpool, he could be back by nine that evening – time enough and more, he felt, to do what had to be done. He flung down the stairs of the flat and almost bumped into Elaine coming up.

'Oh, hello,' she said coldly. 'I wondered if we might have a chat.' She looked nervous and Stripe felt torn.

'What about?' he inquired, knowing what the answer was going to be.

Elaine swallowed and glanced nervously around, as if suddenly worried someone might overhear. 'Sebastian,' she said briefly.

Stripe resigned himself. 'Come up,' he said, 'but it'll 'ave to be quick. I've gorra train t' catch.'

Nervously, Elaine followed him up the stairs. She had been half hoping when she came over that she would find he was out.

'Sit down,' said Stripe, indicating the untidy sofa with a nod of his head.

Elaine looked round the once immaculate annexe and, with difficulty, repressed a shudder. She reminded herself that Harry and Sebastian liked him. 'It's Sebastian,' she repeated. A pair of Stripe's socks lay on the floor and she stared at them fascinated. They were grey, red, and grubby, and looked remarkably like uninhabited bean bags. She looked away quickly. 'Did he tell you what had happened?'

'Yeah,' said Stripe.

She hung her head. 'Paul and I,' she began, 'we're going through a bit of a bad patch.'

'Looks like World War Three from where I'm standing,' remarked Stripe conversationally.

Elaine blushed. 'Yes, well,' she said defensively, 'things aren't perfect, certainly, but the point is, Sebastian is very vulnerable at the moment.'

'I know.'

She looked up quickly. 'Has he been talking to you?'

Stripe nodded. 'A bit.'

'I suppose he told you about Melanie.'

'Who? Oh, the bird with the car. No, 'e didn't say anything about 'er. I worked that out for meself.'

'Does he know?' asked Elaine hollowly.

'Yeah, I expect so.' Stripe grimaced. 'She's been a bit difficult to miss lately.'

Tears welled in Elaine's eyes. 'I'm never going to forgive Paul for this,' she said bitterly.

In the quiet, the sound of a duck squawking from down by the river could be clearly heard. 'Where I come from,' remarked Stripe, 'we don't waste time moanin'. We get even.'

Elaine flinched. 'Quite,' she said tartly, recovering herself, 'but I haven't come here to ask for marriage guidance. I'm concerned about Sebastian. In particular, I want your assurance that you will not take advantage of his distress to lead him any further astray.'

'What yer on about?' asked Stripe, now genuinely puzzled.

'You know perfectly well what I'm on about,' she snapped back. 'I'm referring to that disgusting incident with what you call weed. I want your assurance it won't happen again.'

'Oh that,' he said. 'It may surprise you to know,' he went on belligerently, 'that I do actually feel sorry for the poor little sod. While you and Paul are busy carrying on your own private little war, he's feelin' he's bin dumped. I don't think I'm the one who's goin' to hurt him!'

Elaine sprang to her feet. 'I find your attitude offensive. Whatever happens between Paul and myself is none of your business. I simply want your word that you will not again lead the children astray with

132

drugs, drink, or anything else your warped little mind can come up with!' And with that she spun on her heel and flounced out.

Stripe shrugged and followed her out. He still had time to catch his train.

Elaine went back to the house and straight up to Paul's study. Stripe's words had struck home. For the past few weeks, she realised, she had been seeing herself as a victim and wallowing in self-pity. Her rage and distress had played straight into Melanie's hands. But now it was as if Stripe's words had released her, and she felt an overwhelming desire to go on the offensive.

She crossed over to the desk and began systematically to go through the drawers. Yes, there it was, a list of names containing Melanie's phone number and address. She took it out and took a photocopy, and then replaced the list where she had found it, in the desk. Next, she went into the children's TV and computer room and called up the shopping pages on the Internet. Then she settled herself down to have fun.

Two hours later, Melanie was the possessor of ten chemical lavatories, a dozen surgical trusses, a gross of incontinence pads, and two hundred bottles of hair restorer. She was also the subscriber to a pornographic magazine from Holland, and had had her details entered, with a few imaginative embellishments, with a computer dating firm that prided itself on offering sex to the over-forties without commitment. At this point, Elaine's imagination had taken flight, and next she had inserted an ad offering personal services on demand, but with particular attention given to sado-masochistic fantasies and massage. Mellifluent Melanie was given as the name to which to reply, followed by her address; the words TERMS BY NEGOTIATION followed in large black letters. Then, smiling evilly to herself, Elaine picked up the phone and dialled the police. 'I wish to report what I suspect to be a brothel,' she said.

# Chapter Fourteen

By the time Stripe alighted from the train in Liverpool it was two o'clock. The streets were filled with secretaries scuttling back to work and the first influx of afternoon shoppers who dawdled along, sticky-faced children clutching their hands, pushchairs marshalled in front like so many battering rams. 'I've told ye before, Jason!' screamed a raucous female voice as Stripe emerged from the station. 'Leave our Tansy alone, will ye!' There was a loud smack, followed by a howl. Stripe pushed his way past, narrowly avoiding falling headlong over the enraged child. He paused and sniffed the air, savouring it like an animal returning to its lair, and he suddenly realised that he was glad to be back, that for all the charm and peace of Little Wakenham, he had missed the bustling, seething untidiness of his home city.

Overhead the sky was leaden, brooding with a kind of premonitory threat and, unbidden, a shiver of dread ran up his spine. But Stripe was not given to feelings. He had long ago decided that mankind lived in an essentially chaotic universe, where events happened at random and nothing was either predetermined or ordained. His mother had believed in demons, he remembered, but then again she had believed in voodoo too, and all that that entailed, and her life had been bounded on every side by portents and charms, and the inescapable fixity of fate. But not Stripe. He thought all that was rubbish. So now, as the first heavy drops of rain began to fall and he hurried along the streets, he turned his thoughts to the more practical issue of what he had to do.

He was heading for the Green Flamingo, the club where his band used to play and which, for the past two years, had been like a kind of second home. He knew this was risky, and that there was every likelihood that the place was being watched, but old Samuel was there – Fat Sam, as they used to call him. Fat Sam had come to England some thirty years before from Jamaica; Kingston to be precise. As long as Stripe had known him he had talked longingly about going back, waxing lyrical about the Jamaican way of life, the climate, the people. But Stripe suspected that he never would go back now, he was too firmly rooted in the particular ash heap that he had made his own. And when all was said and done, it had proved a fertile compost for his growth, because Fat Sam had flourished down the murky side street in which he had planted himself. But it was undeniably a place where weeds grew too, and more tender blossoms were as often as not nipped in the bud by the slugs that infested the area. Yet Stripe liked it. He had been happy there.

The club was in the basement of a building in a faceless terraced street. The windows that looked out from both sides were blank and dark, and many had been boarded up. Iron railings flanked the entrance to the Green Flamingo, which was reached down a short flight of steps. From the outside, there was nothing to distinguish it, but invariably the railings were hung with young black kids in floppy hats and untidy jeans, who watched the passers-by with inscrutable eyes.

'Stripe! Hey, man!' cried one as Stripe came up. 'Where yo' bin, man?'

Stripe grunted and they crowded round him.

'We missed ye, man,' said another.

'Yeah,' added another. 'You comin' back now?'

To all their questions, Stripe merely grunted. 'Where's Sam?' he asked. 'I've gorra see 'im.'

They pointed inside and, wasting no time, Stripe ran down the steps and pushed his way in. The club was quiet at this time of day. No natural light penetrated down that far, and the murky gloom was hardly broken by the shaded lights on the walls. The club was small, with a tiny circular stage at one end, a cleared space of perhaps ten feet square in front, and tables dotted around against the walls. In the corner stood the bar and there, leaning up against the counter, was Sam.

The old man's face creased in a smile. 'Stripe,' he said, coming forward. 'Where yo bin, boy? I thought yo was dead.' For all that he had spent the last thirty years in Liverpool, Fat Sam had lost none of his accent and could still just as easily slip into the local patois he had spoken as a child. Now his eyes filled with tears, and he gripped Stripe's hand. They stared at each other, and then Stripe flung his arms round the old man's shoulders and gave him a hug.

'Hi, Sam,' he said.

'What yo want to drink, Stripe? Yo' usual?' He chuckled and called over his shoulder, 'Hey, Louis, get a Coke for Stripe.' Then, still gripping his hand, he led him over to a table. 'Yo shouldn't oughta be back here, Stripe,' he said sadly. 'This ain't a healthy place to be fo' some of us.'

Stripe nodded. 'Yeah,' he said. 'Did ye hear about Jimmy?'

The old man nodded. 'Yes,' he said, 'we heard. It ain't bin the same since.'

Louis deposited the Coke for Stripe and a coffee for Fat Sam, and then disappeared.

'Wot's happening, Sam?' Stripe said. 'I miss yer all. I want t' know.'

Sam shook his head. 'Bad, Stripe,' he mumbled. 'Real bad.'

They sat for a while in silence. Stripe noticed that the old man's skin looked grey, and his hands shook slightly. 'Who are they, Sam?' he asked.

In the half light, Sam's eyes flashed white. 'What for yo want to know that, Stripe?' he demanded. 'Them big trouble. Yo jus' keep out of it.'

Stripe shook his head. 'I'm not sure I can, Sam,' he said. 'I'm already in it. There's someone bin lookin' for me. They're followin' me.'

Sam stared down at his hands, the fat of his cheeks quivering slightly. 'I really love yo boys,' he said, 'you know that. All of you. When Jimmy . . .' his voice broke, and he raised a hand to shield his eyes. After a moment he said, 'I don't think I can stand it if anything happens to the rest of you.'

'Then help me to do something about it, man,' said Stripe. He leant forward and whispered earnestly, 'Tell me who they are. Tell me what you know.'

The old man stared at him in fascinated terror. A battle seemed to be going on inside of him. It showed in the fear that swept across his eyes. 'Dey's yardies,' he said. His voice dropped. 'Dey tryin' to take over. Dat why dey done Jimmy. Dey wanna be de power round here.' He shook his head. 'Dey ruthless, Stripe. Dey'll kill anyone dey tink's in deir way. Dey killed Hiram too.'

It was Stripe's turn to go pale. 'Ye mean they're tryin' to take over and wipe out all the opposition?'

Sam nodded. 'That's about it, Stripe. Safest for yo now jes' to disappear.'

'I can't, Sam. I've got Jimmy's gear.'

Sam's eyes grew round. 'Yo got it?' he said. He shook his head disbelievingly. 'Dat's bad, Stripe, real bad.'

'They've bin tryin' to get it, Sam.'

Sam stared at him. 'It's heroin, is it?' he asked and then, when Stripe nodded, he went on, 'Yo mean dat dey tryin' to steal it for demselves?'

'I reckon. Put everyone else outta business.' In the silence that ensued, Stripe could hear clearly the voices from next door. Somewhere a woman broke into song, and a baby began to cry. 'I thought that the people Jimmy was workin' for could maybe handle it, if I got in touch with them and gave them the stuff.'

Sam shook his head. 'You've bin away a while, Stripe. Dere was a bad shootin'. Most of dem gone to ground too.'

A feeling of hopelessness swept over Stripe. He had been reckoning that Jimmy's people would protect him and deal with the men, in return for the package Jimmy had entrusted to him. And then he would have nothing more to do with any of them. This seemed impossible now. 'I can't see any way outta this, Sam,' he said.

The old man looked at him, eyes narrowed. 'You say you got de stuff?' he asked. 'Yo not kiddin'?' Stripe shook his head and Sam lowered his eyes and blew out his cheeks. 'Well, den,' he mumbled, more to himself than Stripe, 'it may be possible . . .'

Stripe stared at him. 'Wot?' he asked. 'Wot do y' mean?'

Slowly, as if weighing every word, Fat Sam leant forward and laid out his plan. 'We get back to Kingston,' he whispered. 'We call in the family to help. Jimmy's got brothers, see? And dey real hard, man. We tell dem who did it to deir baby brother. We fight dese reptiles at deir own game.'

Stripe's eyes bulged. 'Ye talkin' gang war, man,' he said.

Sam nodded. 'Yes,' he agreed, 'but without dem, I'm talkin' dead.'

Stripe nodded. They were both desperate, Sam because he was on the brink of losing his club, and he himself because he stood to lose his life.

Half an hour later, when Stripe emerged, the rain had stopped but thick black clouds were now massed overhead and the air seemed to throb with suppressed menace. A sudden tongue of lightning crackled across the sky as he ran up the steps, and the next moment the air reverberated with a huge clap of thunder. 'Ye goin, man?' asked one of the boys.

Stripe nodded, pulling his coat more closely round him. He felt edgy after his conversation with Sam.

'It ain't the same since you bin gone,' said one of the others. 'And since Jimmy copped it.'

'Where yo hangin' out now?'

Stripe shook his head. 'Around,' he said vaguely. He looked into the boys' hopeful, forlorn faces and thought suddenly of Harry and Sebastian. Different kinds of wars, he thought, but all of them scarred. 'I'll see ye,' he said. He waved a hand and ran out into the street. As if at a signal, the rain suddenly unleashed itself, tipping in sodden fury on to the slate-coloured streets, while overhead the thunder rolled and crashed. In seconds Stripe was soaked and he took to his heels. Common sense should have dictated he run back to Sam's and take shelter there till the downpour was spent, but he rejected that. He wanted to get away now. It didn't feel so good any more. He ran as fast as he could down the cloud-dark, empty streets, water from blocked drains swirling and gushing around his feet.

Mark, too, rushed home, his one thought to tell Pippa about the appalling interview he had just endured. For once the fates seemed to smile upon him and he found her alone, sitting at the kitchen table trying to compose answers to the fresh pile of begging letters that Agnes had dumped on her as being of possible interest.

'The Bishop wants me to leave,' he said miserably.

'What?' she said, looking up. 'Why?'

He shrugged. 'He's had a complaint – from Mrs Stibbins, I think. He says he's heard about strange goings-on here.'

'Oooh, that woman!' said Pippa. 'She ought to be shipped off to a desert island!'

'He's not too pleased by your win on the lottery either,' he added dismally. 'He took enormous pleasure in pointing out to me that I had set up the anti-lottery group that had blocked his attempts to use lottery funds for the cathedral.'

Pippa looked crestfallen. 'Oh Mark, how ghastly.'

He sat down beside her, leaning his arms heavily before him on the table and, after a second, she slipped her own hand under his. Unthinkingly, he gave it a squeeze. 'It's all right,' he said, and then, 'but I don't really know why he wants me to go. He almost demanded that I resign.'

'That's outrageous. You've done nothing wrong. You're a good priest!'

Mark shrugged. 'He doesn't think so. He implied that I was a hypocrite, and that what I was doing was scandalous.'

They sat in silence and after a minute, in a small voice, Pippa said, 'It's all my fault. I really am so sorry. What are we going to do?'

'Well, I could just resign, like he suggests, and work at Chalice. I'd still be a priest, after all. I just wouldn't have a parish any more. I'm not sure I'd be an Anglican any more either.'

'But you'd hate that,' she said impulsively. 'You've always said your calling was to the Church of England. And you like parish work.'

'But if I don't resign, Pippa, we'll have a visitation. And I'm only priest in charge. I haven't got tenure, you know that. I could be sacked.'

Her chin lifted. 'That's not fair,' she said stonily. 'It's as good as saying you're entirely dependent on the Bishop's whim.'

The door burst open and Tom exploded in. 'There you are, Mark,' he exclaimed. 'We've been looking for you. We ought to be on the road.' And then he noticed their expressions. 'What's up?' he asked.

Briefly Mark explained, and Tom, too, sat down at the table. 'Well, I don't see it matters that much,' he said. 'I think maybe this is just another sign from God to dump that tired old dinosaur and go with Chalice.'

Mark's hackles rose. 'I wish you wouldn't refer to the Church of England as a tired old dinosaur, Tom,' he said stiffly. 'Some of us happen to believe we're called to serve the established Church, and that the wider communion benefits from that. That tired old dinosaur, as you call it, maintains tradition and guards the truth.'

The men glared at each other with real hostility, and Mark's hand tightened over Pippa's, so that his knuckles showed white. She stared at them both in surprise, and then Tom laughed uneasily and said, 'OK, Mark, don't take offence. It's just my way of talking. You know I care about the good old boat as much as you do.'

But Mark was not willing to be mollified. He was remembering all those times when he had caught Tom gazing at his wife, and remembering, too, all the little mocking barbs that Tom had been directing at him of late. 'I do take offence,' he said. 'And I am not at all convinced you care about the good old boat, as you call it, at all!'

Pippa continued to stare at him, astonished. 'If you really care this much,' she said, swallowing, 'I think we ought to stay and fight it, Archdeacon's visitation or not.'

Tom pulled a face. 'Look,' he said, 'I'm sorry. I'm really not mocking you, old chap, and I appreciate how serious this is for you. And of course I'll do everything I can to help, but I really do believe that Chalice is important too.'

Staring straight into his wife's eyes, Mark smiled at Pippa awkwardly. 'Do you really mean that?' he asked her, ignoring Tom.

She nodded. 'Yes, we can't just let him throw you out.' And then she looked at Tom. 'But maybe Tom's right too. Maybe our future, where God wants us to be, does lie with Chalice. After all, they threw Martin Luther out when he started reforms, and historically that often seems to be what happens when God's at work. But,' she turned back to Mark, her eyes intense, 'we've got to fight every step of the way, haven't we?'

A truce had been called between them. They both felt it. So did Tom, who glanced at Pippa with irritation, but he said no more.

Mark went and got his bag and, with a heart rather lighter than it had been an hour before, he, Tom and Oogi set off for Porthcawl. Still worried about Daffyd, he had insisted that someone stay behind with Pippa, and so it had finally been agreed that Jack should move back into the rectory over the weekend so that he could both keep an eye on things and continue his negotiations with Chuck's people, as he called them, over in the States. As they left, Mark gave Pippa a hug, the first he had risked in weeks, and whispered in her ear, 'If you still want, when I get back I'll go and see Dr Forrest.'

# Chapter Fifteen

'Is that Mellifluent Melanie?' wheezed a voice. It was rather an unpleasant little voice. It seemed to leer and ooze seedy suggestion and Melanie, who had not long got back from a very hard day at the office, felt her flesh crawl.

'I beg your pardon?' she said, outraged.

The voice began to outline, in lurid detail, exactly what it was it required. Melanie listened for all of two seconds and then slammed down the phone. She was already feeling awful. She had managed over lunch to have the most appalling row with Paul, who was proving unexpectedly obdurate in face of her demands that he tell Elaine it was all over. When she had said, 'If you don't tell her by next Wednesday, that's it!' he had retorted frostily, 'Fine, perhaps we'll both be happier that way.' And he had even gone on to suggest that maybe she ought to find someone unattached and nearer her own age. Melanie had been shocked, and it had taken all her feminine wiles to persuade him that she had not been serious, of course she had not meant it, she just loved him so, she ached . . .

By the time the coffee arrived, she had been beginning to wonder if older, married men were worth quite so much effort. Then, as if all that was not enough, when she had arrived back home some ten minutes earlier, she had discovered ten chemical lavatories piled prominently around her front door, together with an invoice asking for immediate payment.

Melanie lived in an extremely exclusive apartment block over-looking Canary Wharf. Her neighbours included a junior Cabinet minister who used the place as his Town base, an aspiring conductor who always seemed to be away on tour, and a young man who was 'something big' in Disney. Melanie had clawed her way into this flat. The mortgage was costing her an arm and a leg, but she thought that it was worth it because, once installed, she felt her feet were firmly set on the corporate ladder of success. She did not, however, feel very secure in this new world to which she was aspiring, and she lived in dread that something might happen to damage her fragile standing. Chemical lavatories, it occurred to her, might well be it.

Pushing her way through the offending sanitary ware, she discovered behind it several large cardboard boxes with Safewise Incontinence Pads stamped all over the outside. She felt sure that this was all a mistake, and was just beginning to allow herself the first faint stirrings of amusement, wondering to which of her unfortunate neighbours the goods actually belonged, when her glance fell on one of the labels. Ms Melanie Brownloe, she read, URGENT. Hastily she had dragged the boxes into her narrow hallway, praying that no one would wander by before she had got them all safely inside. She had just finished the task and mixed herself a stiff gin and tonic, when the telephone had rung.

As she replaced the receiver, she noticed that the answerphone was flashing and that it had twelve messages for her. Surprised, and wondering who on earth could have wanted to get hold of her so urgently, she pressed the rewind button and then stood to listen. After the fifth instalment of heavy breathing and indecent request, she turned it off in disgust and in fury phoned Paul. 'Has this got anything to do with you?' she demanded as soon as he answered.

Paul hastily pushed the study door closed with his foot and hissed, 'I keep telling you not to phone me here.'

'Sod that,' said Melanie, her anger from earlier in the day resurfacing. 'I want to know if it's you who's sent all these chemical lavatories!'

'Chemical lavatories?'

'Yes, ten of them.'

'Of course not.'

'What about the incontinence pads?' she demanded.

'Don't be so ridiculous,' he snapped.

From the kitchen Elaine shouted, 'Dinner!' and he broke off to call back, 'Coming, dear.'

He turned back to the phone. 'You must stop calling me like this. Elaine always knows!'

'Did you send them?' repeated Melanie.

'Of course I didn't,' said Paul. 'Why the hell should I?'

'Well, if you didn't, who did?'

Paul breathed heavily. 'Look, Melanie, I haven't the remotest idea, but I can't waste time like this. I've got to go. Elaine's calling me for dinner.'

'Will you phone me back later?'

'No,' said Paul angrily, 'I won't. Speak to me tomorrow.'

'If you don't,' said Melanie, dangerously quiet, 'I'll call you every ten minutes. I might even send another fax.'

'You wouldn't.'

'Try me.'

Paul tried another tack. 'Look, I can't phone you back tonight,'

144

he said. 'Elaine watches me like a hawk these days. As it is, she'll want to know who's on the phone.'

Silence, then, 'OK, come and see me when you've finished eating.'

Paul almost choked. 'I can't do that!' he said. 'I haven't got any reason to go out again tonight.'

'Then make something up. Tell her you've left some papers at the office and they can't wait.'

'No,' said Paul.

'If you don't . . .' The threat hung in the air.

'All right,' said Paul desperately. 'I'll come over. But only for half an hour. And only if you don't phone back.' He slammed down the receiver.

By the time he got to the flat it was half past nine. Melanie had received eight more phone calls; and a very persistent individual had even called round. When Paul finally arrived, she was very slightly drunk. 'I think the world's gone mad,' she said as she flung back the door.

Paul edged his way past the lavatories and incontinence pads, eyeing them warily. 'Are you sure they've not just been delivered to the wrong address?' he asked.

She shook her head. 'No, they're all addressed to me. But it's the phone calls that are really driving me mad.' She switched on the answer tape.

'Good God,' he said, when he had listened the whole way through. 'What on earth's going on?'

'That's what I want to know,' she said grimly, removing the tape from the machine. She poured herself another drink and then, as an afterthought, poured one for him too.

'How many of those have you had?' asked Paul.

'This is my seventh,' she replied. 'I think.'

'You ought to lay off that. Have you eaten yet?'

She shook her head. 'Would you feel like eating if you got back and discovered all that lot, and then had a string of perverted calls?'

'How do you think they got your number? It's not just one person, after all – they all seem to be different.'

'Yes,' she agreed, her face wooden. 'I've worked that one out too, and the only answer I can come up with is that someone has given it to them.'

'Yes, but who? And how?' He frowned and she continued to stare at him. 'Oh, come off it, Melanie,' he exploded. 'Why should I do anything like that?'

There was a ring at the door and Melanie went pale. 'Oh God,' she said, 'I can't stand this.'

'I'll answer it,' offered Paul.

But Melanie was already on her way.

She pulled open the door as far as the chemical lavatories would allow and found herself confronted by two men in long, rather grubby macs. 'Miss Melanie Brownloe?' asked one. Melanie glared at him, her eyes narrowing, and the man said, 'May we come in? We'd like a chat.' He fished in his pocket and held out a police identity card.

'Sergeant Pratt?' she said faintly.

'That's right. It's just a chat.'

With a growing sense of unreality, Melanie stood back to allow the men in. 'Going camping?' asked one of them with interest, taking in the boxes. 'Blimey, you've got enough for an expedition here.' And then he saw the incontinence pads stacked up behind. 'Hmm,' he said. 'I see.'

Melanie felt even more enraged. 'Go through into the lounge,' she said frostily.

Paul had taken off his jacket and loosened his tie, and he was standing at the window taking a sip of his drink as they came in.

'They're from the police,' said Melanie quickly, noticing his startled look.

'The police?' echoed Paul, and then he recollected himself and came forward, hand outstretched. 'Ah good evening, Constable.'

'Sergeant, sir,' said the policeman, ignoring his hand. Uninvited, both men sat down, and the sergeant stretched out his legs. Melanie blinked and Paul looked surprised. The sergeant gave a thin smile. 'We've had a complaint, madam.'

'A complaint?' Melanie looked totally lost.

'Yes. We've had a report that you are using these premises as a . . .' his eyes swivelled to Paul, 'brothel.'

'A brothel?' Paul was stunned.

The sergeant nodded. 'And who may you be, sir?' he asked smoothly. 'A client?'

Melanie looked as if she was about to pass out. 'This is outrageous,' she said faintly.

'I agree, madam,' said the sergeant, 'if the allegation's true.' He rose suddenly to his feet and crossed over to the telephone, his eye on the tape. Swiftly he inserted it in the machine and switched it on. The oily voice again wheezed out into the still air, then another, and another. In frozen silence they listened to all twelve messages, and at the end the sergeant said, 'Sounds like you're going to be a bit busy tonight, doesn't it, luv?' He looked again at Paul. 'Are you one of these gentlemen, sir?'

'No,' said Paul, revolted, 'I'm not.'

'Look here,' Melanie snapped, 'how dare you come here making these nasty insinuations. Those calls are a most disgusting hoax—'

'Of course they are,' said the second policeman reassuringly.

146

'What do you mean?' shouted Melanie.

'Look, Melanie,' said the sergeant, 'this is just a friendly warning, OK? You're a working girl, right? We understand that. We don't much mind you plying your trade, if you're discreet, but we're not going to have you setting up a business. This is a respectable area.' He glanced quickly round. 'Anyone else here?' Melanie shook her head, speechless, and the policeman nodded. 'Right. Keep it that way.' Then he looked at Paul, letting his eyes travel slowly down to rest on his left hand still wrapped round his glass. 'And I'd advise you to be a little bit more discreet in future too, sir. Associating with known prostitutes is not the most obvious way of promoting conjugal bliss, if you take my meaning.'

'Known prostitutes!' spluttered Paul. 'Now look here! I'd advise you to be very careful in what you say. Miss Brownloe happens to be a respected colleague and—'

'Is she?' The policeman looked at him with renewed interest, and then fished in his pocket for his notebook. 'Can I have your name, sir? Just for the record.'

'No you bloody can't!' said Paul.

'Paul,' said Melanie desperately, 'please tell them who you are so that they can get this ridiculous mess sorted out. They're obviously confusing me with someone else.'

The policeman continued to stand waiting and, after a moment, Paul said grudgingly, 'Paul Dufrayn.'

'Address, sir?'

'Look here,' exploded Paul, 'is this really necessary?'

The policeman eyed him. 'Well, it rather depends on your point of view. If Melanie here is a respected colleague, as you maintain, then it rather depends what line of work you're in, doesn't it?'

'I'm a banker!' shouted Paul. 'So is Miss Brownloe. This whole thing is ridiculous. She's obviously the victim of some very elaborate hoax.'

'Um . . . hum.' The policeman crossed over and took the tape from the machine. 'You may well be right,' he agreed, 'and we shall certainly check up on what you've said. But just in case, you won't mind us taking this tape as evidence.'

'Evidence of what?' asked Melanie numbly.

The sergeant smiled. 'Well, Melanie, if what you say is true, there's nothing to worry about, is there? But if, on the other hand, our informant is telling the truth,' he held up the tape, 'and things don't look too encouraging at the moment, do they? If our informant is telling the truth, well, we've got evidence now, haven't we?' He nodded to the other officer. 'We'll be off now, but just bear in mind what I've said. We'll be keeping a close eye on you for a while.'

As the door closed behind the officers, Melanie and Paul stared at each other.

'It's not true, is it?' asked Paul.

She looked as if she was about to hit him. 'Of course it's not!' she snapped.

He had the grace to flush. 'Sorry,' he mumbled. 'It's just, well, it is all a bit odd, isn't it?'

Melanie glared at him. 'I'm going to find out who's responsible for this if it kills me,' she said grimly. 'And when I do . . .'. She crossed over to her desk and wrenched out a notepad and pen.

'What are you doing?' asked Paul.

'I'm making a list of everyone who could possibly have something against me, and who might have done this.' She settled herself on the sofa and began to write and, after a moment, Paul sat down beside her and proffered a few suggestions of his own. By the time they had finished she had twenty-five names on her list, going back even to kindergarten and including the little girl whose plait she had cut off in a fit of pique and who had refused to speak to her ever again. Elaine's name was not on the list. 'I'm going to have all of these checked out,' said Melanie nastily. 'And when I find out who's responsible, they're going to wish they'd never been born! No one does this to me and gets away with it.'

Elaine was sleeping peacefully. She had not the slightest interest in where Paul had gone and at ten thirty, having checked that the boys were safely asleep, she had gone to bed. When Paul came in at one, she was lying on her back and snoring gently, the picture of untroubled peace. For the first time in weeks, Paul abandoned the spare room and heaved himself into bed beside her. He slid an arm round and under her shoulders and pulled her towards him. Elaine, surfacing groggily from a pleasant dream where she had been sunbathing in the Caribbean, opened an eye and peered at him. 'Oh, it's you,' she said, unenthusiastically.

Paul slid closer towards her and planted a kiss on her cheek. 'Hello, pumpkin,' he whispered seductively. He used to call her pumpkin in the early years of their marriage. Elaine went rigid. She had always hated being called Pumpkin. Paul did not notice. Paradoxically, his evening with Melanie had made him yearn for the rather more tranquil home comforts provided by his wife. It had never occurred to him that she might not respond. Elaine always responded. It was the price she paid for his continued support – a part of her job description. Besides, she loved him.

He pulled himself on to her and began to nuzzle her neck. Elaine, now fully awake, turned her face the other way and stared glumly into the dark. Something, she realised immediately, must have happened.

Paul had not made any kind of move like this towards her for weeks. She found herself faced with a dilemma. Her faith told her that she should welcome this unexpected development and respond, and in this way win him back. But as she thought of Melanie and remembered the atrocious way Paul had behaved over the past few months, she found she did not want to. She despised him.

Paul slid down and began to slobber across her breasts. 'Have you had a good evening?' Elaine inquired.

'What?' Paul abruptly stopped what he was doing and peered up at her face.

'I said, have you had a good evening?'

Paul swallowed. 'Not really,' he said. 'The papers weren't where I thought.' He lowered his head, preparing to resume.

'Where were they?'

'What?' He stopped again.

Elaine was cool. 'I said, where were they? Did Melanie have them, by any chance?'

'No,' Paul lied, and then he changed his mind. 'Well, yes, she did have them, as a matter of fact. When I found they weren't at the office I went round to her place to see if she'd taken them home. And she had, but she was terribly upset. That's why I'm so late. She's been getting a lot of obscene phone calls and strange deliveries and was really quite distraught, so I hung around to see what I could do to help.'

In the dark, Elaine's ears pricked up. 'What sort of strange deliveries?' she inquired.

Now thoroughly disconcerted, Paul sat up. The last thing he had intended was a concerned discussion about Melanie, and yet Elaine sounded simply interested rather than annoyed. 'Well,' he said uneasily, wondering if she would believe him, 'chemical lavatories for one thing, and I think there were boxes of incontinence pads too.'

'Really?' said Elaine.

'Yes, but the worst thing was someone had told the police she was keeping a brothel.'

'Oh dear.' In the dark Elaine smiled. She had not expected her orders to be delivered quite so promptly, but it sounded as if things were going rather better than she had anticipated. 'And you rode to her rescue,' she murmured. 'Just like Sir Galahad.' She rolled over and away, turning her back to him. 'How sweet.'

'No,' said Paul, nonplussed. Anger he could deal with, or even tears, but Elaine's indifferent unconcern had him floored. 'It wasn't like that, honestly. I just happened to turn up.'

'Of course you did,' agreed Elaine. She burrowed further down the bed, and then her muffled voice said, 'I'd go to sleep if I were you. You must be tired. You can tell me all about what happened tomorrow.'

# Chapter Sixteen

The weather felt slightly warmer to Roseanne. The appalling rain that they had had over the last couple of days had stopped. The morning had dawned, if not exactly clear, at least dry, and now the pale sun trickling through the clouds suggested to her a definite turn for the better. As she sat on the five-bar gate just down the lane from the rectory with her face upturned, drinking in the warmth, she felt a mood of happy expectancy, although why she was not quite sure.

She was waiting for Pippa. She had been there all morning; she wanted news of Daffyd. She felt sure Pippa would have to come past at some point. And when she did, she would simply leap off the gate, plant herself firmly in her path, and demand to know how he was. Roseanne liked Daffyd. He was her friend. She had come down with him from London at his request, knowing he was incapable of making the journey alone, but she was not really sure why they had come. His certainty, however, that Pippa would help him had been infectious. It had not been very difficult to find her, what with all the publicity about her lottery win, and the closer they had come, the more Roseanne had found herself praying that he was right.

Daffyd, she knew, was in a bad way. For some time she had been wondering how much longer he would be able to survive and the thought, lurking at the back of her mind, had caused her real terror, because she felt he was the only friend she had. There had been a vacancy about him lately; half the time he hadn't seemed to know where he was, or even who she was any more. And he had taken to conducting conversations with an imaginary person and Roseanne had felt frightened, cowering back when he raged at the air. But she had refused to leave him, even when he became violent and began to shout, lashing out at some unseen assailant with his fists, terror in his eyes.

Since that Sunday night five days ago when she had left Daffyd in the church with Pippa, Roseanne had stayed in the area, haunting the rectory, unseen, hoping that she would catch a glimpse of her friend and see for herself the improvement she had convinced herself was taking place. But she had not seen him once, and so now she was determined to waylay Pippa and ask her straight out how he was.

All morning she had watched the comings and goings at the

rectory, but Daffyd had remained out of sight. Then at around eleven she saw three cars drive off in convoy, the first of them containing the man she had come to identify as Pippa's husband. He had glanced at her as the cars swept past and she had stared back hopefully, but there was no answering flicker of recognition. And then, as the last car disappeared from view, the lane had fallen strangely quiet, and a feeling of abandonment had settled over Roseanne.

Now, however, a sudden noise from the direction of the rectory made her start up from her perch on the gate, and the next moment Pippa herself appeared, pedalling quickly down the lane on her bike. As soon as she came near, Roseanne leapt down from the gate waving her arms. 'Hi!' she called. 'Stop, please stop.'

Pippa braked hard, the wheels of her bike sending up a shower of little stones. 'Watch it,' she said testily, and then she recognised Roseanne. 'Oh, hello,' she said. 'You're Daffyd's friend, aren't you?'

Roseanne nodded eagerly, feeling ridiculously pleased that Pippa should have recognised her. 'That's right,' she said. She gazed at Pippa, biting her lip. 'How is he?'

Pippa's heart sank. She had actually just been thinking about Daffyd. After the fiasco with Mark and Tom the other night, he had refused to allow anyone other than herself to talk to him. That worried her, and left her feeling totally inadequate. When she had tried gently voicing her concern to Daffyd, he said, 'Don't worry, you'll know what to do. It's OK.' But the plain truth was that she didn't have the slightest idea what to do. She swallowed unhappily. 'Not too good, I'm afraid,' she said. 'But he seems a bit calmer.'

Roseanne's face fell. 'Isn't he any better then?' she demanded.

Unable to think of anything to say, Pippa shook her head. She saw hopelessness, anger, and what finally looked like despair pass in quick succession over Roseanne's face, and then the girl suddenly crumpled and sat down heavily beside the road. Pippa leant her bike up against the nearest tree and squatted down beside her. 'We've got him on a methadone programme,' she volunteered, putting an arm round Roseanne's skinny shoulders.

A muffled sob came from Roseanne. 'That won't 'elp,' she said. ''E's tried that before. That's not the problem.'

'What is then?' asked Pippa.

Roseanne raised her head and stared at her. Her skin was slightly olive, stretched almost transparently over the delicate bones of her face. Her thick chestnut hair had been hennaed to a bright orange colour at the tips. Most of it hung long and loose, but round the crown she had a layer of thin plaits, interwoven with brightly coloured strands of ribbon. 'I think 'e's 'aunted,' she said seriously, 'or possessed or something. 'E's always talking to something, and 'e's terrified. 'E says it won't leave 'im alone, but that 'e'll be all right if 'e can only get it to go away.' She looked at Pippa earnestly. ''E's really nice, you know. 'E really cares about people, and 'e'd do anything to 'elp.' Then her face again crumpled. 'Please, you've got to 'elp 'im. 'E said you could.'

'But how?' Pippa asked. 'What does he expect me to do?'

''E said you could deal with it. 'E said you'd *know* what to do.'

A feeling of despair swept over Pippa. 'Oh God,' she said, 'I wish I could. But I'm not Jesus, you know.'

That brought Roseanne's head jerking up. 'No,' she said fiercely, 'but you believe in 'im, don't you? And the Bible says Jesus 'eals people, and casts out unclean spirits, and that 'e gives the same gift to 'is followers. So you've just got to ask 'im, 'aven't you?'

Pippa stared at her appalled. 'It doesn't work like that,' she said hollowly. 'We're not in the New Testament now. People don't just get cured like that any more.'

'Why not?' Roseanne's huge luminous eyes filled with tears. 'The Bible says they do, dunnit?' she said stubbornly. 'And Daffyd believes it too. So why can't you do that? Why can't you just ask Jesus, or whatever it is you do?'

Remembering Daffyd's terror, a great tide of misery swept over Pippa. How could she explain to Roseanne his mystifying reaction, with which she had no idea how to deal? 'Would you like to come and say hello to him?' she asked gently.

Roseanne nodded. 'Yes, please.'

They found Daffyd sitting where Pippa had left him in the rectory lounge, with a pile of books at his side and a cup of coffee on the small table in front of him. He had not touched the coffee but he had dutifully picked up a book and now had it open on his knees. Pippa saw he was looking at pictures of the Holy Land. A great barren expanse of desert stared up at her as she leant over to tap his shoulder. In the foreground of the picture trailed a scrawny little flock, with a shepherd walking in front of them leading the way. There did not appear to be any very clear path before them, but in the far distance there rose a steep hill, with a building that looked like a medieval castle on top of it. Underneath was printed the caption, 'He shall make a path through the desert'. Daffyd looked up, and an expression of joy flooded his face as he took in Roseanne. 'Rose,' he said, 'you've come. I've been thinking about you.'

She ran to him and hugged him fiercely. 'Hi, Daffyd,' she said. 'I come to see 'ow you're gettin' on.'

Quietly, Pippa withdrew. She went into the kitchen and stared bleakly at the row of mugs hanging suspended under the cupboards. In her mind she heard again Roseanne's voice, 'Why can't you just ask Jesus?' Yes, she thought hopelessly, why not? Why was it all not as simple as that?

# Chapter Seventeen

'OK, team,' said Tom, 'let me lay it on the line. Cards straight.' He was becoming increasingly American as the days went on and had adopted a kind of mid-Atlantic drawl which he felt befitted his new status. He leant forward, placing his hands squarely on the table, and looked round intently. 'Chuck likes it!'

A small explosive sigh went up from the company assembled in the church hall, and Jack, who the previous night had been banished back to his hotel, sat back, a look of pleasure on his face. He had worked hard over the weekend, so hard in fact that when Tom and Mark had arrived back late on Sunday night, he had been able to tell them, with barely concealed triumph oozing through his voice, that Chuck Gibbons was on board. Tom had been overjoyed, but Mark had sighed heavily and announced he was going to bed. 'Forget the C of E,' Tom had said gaily, immediately and correctly divining his friend's thoughts. 'We're on the way. It doesn't matter what the Bishop does. Besides,' he added judiciously, 'he'll come round fast enough when he sees we're really taking off. He'll be all for us then.' He sniggered. 'Probably even tell the press it was all his idea!'

Mark had looked miserable. He did not share Tom's optimism. In fact, he thought the Bishop was far more likely to come out with a public condemnation of American-style evangelism, especially if it had anything to do with the media.

Mark was tired. He had done a lot of thinking over the weekend. So far he had not arrived at any very precise conclusions, but of one thing at least he was sure: he wanted to salvage his marriage. He had told Pippa as much that night, as they lay in post-coital exhaustion, and she had stared up into the dark and then said carefully, 'I want that too.' But she had not voiced it with the same unthinking and accepting enthusiasm that Mark felt she would have put into it only weeks before and, although he felt encouraged, he had become even more aware of the gulf that yawned between them.

Now, as the low buzz of excitement broke out, he stared at the table expressionlessly and wondered if this really was, after all, such a good idea.

'OK, OK,' said Tom after a minute, 'quieten down, everyone. Let's give Jack a chance to tell us all about it.'

Jack cleared his throat noisily. 'Yeah, well,' he began, 'as Tom says, I've had a chance to speak to Chuck. In fact we were on the phone for over an hour on Saturday night. The base line is, he's very interested. Very interested indeed. He says if we'll fix it up, he'll come over with his whole team next month, and we'll take it from there.'

An even more excited hubbub broke out. 'Next month!' said Oogi. 'That doesn't leave us too long.'

Tom held up his hand. 'Oogi's right. It doesn't leave us too long. But we need to remember, time belongs to the Lord! If he wants it, we can do it.'

Pippa grimaced. She, too, felt rather uneasy with this new development, partly because of what Mark had told her of the Bishop's reaction, but also because she had the unwelcome sensation that Chalice was spinning out of control. Despite what Tom said, she did not really feel that God was involved in what was going on. He was lurking around, certainly, but none of what they were doing really made sense to her. As for the wonders and signs Tom kept banging on about, all she could do was look at Daffyd and cringe.

Jack was speaking again. 'Chuck's got thirty-two people on his team, and of course there are the wives as well. Cherilee Gibbons is pretty big in her own right. Does a lot of counselling and marriage teaching, and she sings too. I thought maybe we should take over a floor at the Dorchester or something for them all.'

Mark went pale. 'The Dorchester?' he repeated. He looked stunned.

Tom waved a hand. 'Don't get hung up on that, Mark,' he said loftily. 'These guys are major league. Everything's on a bigger scale over in the States, and Jack's right. It's what Chuck will expect. The Dorchester's exactly the right kind of place. I mean, just think about it, Chuck's one of the biggest evangelists that the world has seen in the last ten years. He runs rings round Wimber or Graham. He's got his own TV station, a mega-healing ministry. And . . .'

Pippa stopped listening, her attention riveted by Tom's sudden and unexpected reference to healing. Chuck Gibbons had a healing ministry! She had not known that. She had assumed that he was simply an evangelist, along the lines of all the other superstar evangelists who seemed to be erupting out of the States these days. Her thoughts swung back to Daffyd whom she had left only ten minutes before, sitting hunched and broken in the rectory kitchen, staring dismally into one of his interminable, untouched, cups of coffee. Maybe Tom was right after all. If Chalice was to function as some kind of healing ministry, then they had to learn what to do, fast. Chuck Gibbons might be the very man to show them. They had failed so dismally with Daffyd. All of them. Not one of them had had a clue what to do. But it occurred to her that maybe God had sent the boy along for that precise purpose, to demonstrate to them their limitations so that someone with an already established ministry in that area could teach them. Maybe Chuck Gibbons could heal Daffyd! At least, not him of course, she amended silently, aware that there was something potentially blasphemous in that particular line of thought, but the Lord, through him.

And with the thought, her face suddenly glowed. 'I think it's an excellent idea,' she said loudly, her expression radiant. 'Chuck Gibbons sounds exactly right to me.'

Mark, who had just been explaining at length and in great detail that he felt the exotic lifestyle espoused by some of the more prominent American evangelists was out of line with Biblical principles, faltered.

'I'm sorry, Pippa?' said Tom, his tone registering surprise.

Pippa, who had heard not a word uttered by her husband, blinked. 'I said I thought Chuck Gibbons sounded a good idea,' she said, less certainly.

Tom beamed, while Mark cast her a look of wounded affront, and Pippa stared at them both, puzzled.

'Well, I think that settles it then,' said Tom. He turned to Jack. 'The Dorchester it is. See what dates they can manage, and then get back to Chuck.'

Mark immediately pushed back his chair and rose heavily to his feet. 'Very well,' he said, white-lipped. 'I can see my opinion is entirely redundant here, so I shan't waste my breath. But I would like it to be noted that I strongly disapprove of such profligacy and unnecessary luxury when there is so much suffering in the world, and when the money could be put to so much better use.' And without giving anyone a chance to respond, he turned on his heel and marched out.

Pippa stared after his retreating back, stricken. 'Mark . . .' she began. But it was too late. She winced as the door slammed.

'Don't worry, Pip,' said Tom airily, 'he'll come round when he sees how things work.' And then, seeing her stunned expression, he said, 'He's not right, you know. Chuck does tremendous work, and to a large extent it's made possible by the high profile he adopts. It's like he says, he aims to make sure that people know he's around, and that he matters. And out in the big wide world, that means status. He's just playing them at their own game to get their attention.'

Pippa bit her lip. 'Yes,' she said, 'I see.' But as she gazed at the closed door she was not at all sure that she did. And, even worse, she found herself wondering whether Mark would ever be able to forgive what he so obviously saw as her betrayal, yet again. She thought of their fleeting reconciliation the night before and sighed. It almost felt, she decided, as if fate itself these days was conspiring against them.

'Yeah, well,' said Stripe, his voice breaking into her thoughts. He had been sitting over in the corner ever since the meeting first began but, unusually for him, had up to that moment kept silent. Now he said reflectively, 'Sounds like this bloke's got it sussed to me. Wish I cud come up with a scam like that!' The remark did not help.

Elaine stared frostily at Paul. 'I fail to see why the expansion of Chalice means that Melanie has to move down to the village during the week.'

'It's a big account,' Paul explained for the third time. 'And what Tom's proposing now is going to take some expert financial handling. We need someone on hand.'

Equally patiently Elaine said, 'But does that someone really have to be your mistress?'

Paul sighed. 'This is purely a business arrangement,' he said plaintively. Over the last few days his life appeared to have become extremely complicated. It was not simply that he was finding Elaine increasingly difficult to understand, he was also aware that on the issue at that moment under debate he had been very deftly cornered by Melanie. He had already given her far more responsibility for the Chalice account than he knew he ought to have done, and when he had attempted to remedy the situation the week before by bringing in someone else to help administer the funds, Melanie had refused point blank to give access to the files she was steadily building up. Paul had been shocked, but in the bitter argument that had ensued – in her bed – Melanie had accused him of trying to oust her out of spite, and of being tired of her, and she had threatened that, if he did anything now to jeopardise her, she would blazon the full details of their affair round the office. 'You're just going to have to trust me,' she said nastily. 'You've already given me investment authority, and I want joint responsibility for the entire account from now on. I want to be an authorised signatory of the trust, just like you, with delegated authority to deal with the funds direct. Equal standing. I'm perfectly capable of administering Chalice. You know that, and it's time in career terms that I moved on.' Then her eyes narrowed and she added softly, 'I would hate to have to tell people about the abortion.'

Paul stared at her aghast. 'What abortion? Are you trying to tell me you're pregnant?'

She looked at him enigmatically. 'Well, now,' she said, after a minute, 'I might be.' Her eyes became slits. 'Oh dear, did I forget to mention I hadn't taken my pill?' Then she laughed. It was not a nice sound. 'That would be embarrassing for you, wouldn't it?'

Paul swallowed uneasily. He was not disturbed by Melanie's suggestion that she might be pregnant – he had had a vasectomy over eight years ago and had yearly check-ups to ensure it was still working properly – but he was worried by her threat to start gossiping in the office. He remembered with dread the fallout after his entanglement with Rhona, and was not sure he could survive another scandal. He stared unseeingly into the shadows in the corner of the room. He was becoming extremely tired of Melanie, but he knew it was going to be very difficult to break free without having a large amount of dirty linen washed in public. She gave a phut of annoyance when he did not respond and he glared at her sharply, on the verge of telling her to go to hell. And then she had dropped the bombshell that it was her intention to move down to Little Wakenham during the week and return to her flat only at weekends.

Melanie had actually been finding life in London rather hard. She had had five more packets of pornographic pictures delivered, and three gross of flavoured condoms. Even worse, the phone calls showed no signs of stopping and she had been driven to ask the phone company to intercept all incoming calls. Somehow, however, some had still managed to get through, and she found she was living in constant dread of who or what she would find waiting on her doorstep when she got home at night. The plan to move down to Little Wakenham had occurred to her one evening as a rather neat means of getting her away from a situation that she was finding increasingly difficult to handle. The idea had further appealed, not so much because of proximity to Paul – she was in fact beginning to see him as something of a lost cause – but rather because it had occurred to her that, if she presented the move as connected with work, she could get the bank to foot the bill. After all, if she could demonstrate that the move was solely to facilitate her accessibility for important clients, and at a time when large sums of money were going to be moving around, it was not unreasonable for the bank to pick up the tab for her expenses. She felt sure that if she could only get away for a few weeks, the whole unpleasantness would simply die down quite naturally and her life could return to normal. After which, she could address more confidently the problem of Paul.

However that, for her erstwhile lover, left the problem of his wife, who, not unreasonably when she was informed of the plan, hit the roof. 'You've got to see,' Paul now found himself saying desperately, 'that, quite apart from work, Melanie is under the most enormous strain from all those awful phone calls she keeps getting. And those deliveries. She's volunteered to give up her own home like this not just from dedication to work but because she's feeling she can't cope. She needs help.'

'I don't bloody care,' shrieked Elaine. 'Send her to Aberdeen!' She was beginning to feel her malicious little stab at revenge was rebounding on her. Unable to help herself, she burst into tears and Sebastian, who had chosen this moment to come into the kitchen in search of a biscuit, stared at her appalled. His frightened eyes took in the situation at a glance. He went white and then, without saying a word, spun on his heel and ran out.

'Now see what you've done!' said Paul.

The first moment she could, Elaine flew round to see Pippa. She found her in the kitchen, staring glumly into a bowlful of beans that she was supposed to be topping and tailing for dinner. 'Oh God,' said Elaine, flinging herself down, 'my world's falling apart!'

'So is mine,' said Pippa, throwing down her vegetable knife in disgust. But she roused herself sufficiently to ask, 'Why? What's happened?'

Elaine, temporarily checked by what she felt was Pippa's lack of response, sniffed. 'It's Paul,' she said with dignity.

Pippa grimaced. 'Of course it is,' she said. And then, seeing Elaine flush, she felt a sudden stab of guilt. 'I'm sorry,' she said. 'What's he done?'

Elaine told her. 'But it's all my fault,' she ended, giving a wail. And then, having first made sure there was no one else around, she poured out what she had done.

'You did what?' asked Pippa, round-eyed.

Elaine obligingly repeated the wording of the adverts she had inserted on the Internet.

In spite of herself, Pippa's lips twitched. 'Golly,' she said, 'you have been busy, haven't you? Honestly, Elaine, what on earth put the idea into your head?'

'Stripe,' said the other woman tonelessly. Pippa looked at her questioningly. 'It was something he said. He said that where he came from they didn't waste time whingeing, they got even. And I suddenly thought, why not? She's acting like a whore, so treat her like one.'

'Does Paul know that it's you who's behind it all?'

'No, not yet. I think he suspects Melanie might be making it all up, and I think he might even have been trying to give her the brush-off.'

'That's good, isn't it?'

Elaine's face grew even longer. 'No,' she said, 'it's not.' Then, as Pippa stared at her, she burst out, 'I feel so confused. It's all very well his coming crawling back with his tail between his legs like a disobedient puppy, but I can't stand him any more. I'm not sure I want him back.'

They sat for a while in silence as Pippa digested this. Then, in a small voice, she said hesitantly, 'But Elaine, marriage is for life. That's what the vows mean, for better or worse.'

'I know,' said Elaine despairingly. 'I know all the arguments, and all the stuff about forgiveness, but I'm finding I just can't do it. After all he's done, I think I loathe him.'

160

Pippa thought of Mark. She thought how petty he seemed to be these days, and how he always seemed to be living in a kind of permanent self-righteous sulk. She thought about his steadfast refusal ever to talk about things with her, and she thought about how very lonely her life had become. A great abyss of self-pity yawned at her feet. 'You can't, Elaine,' she said woodenly. 'You mustn't think like that.'

Elaine looked down at her hands and burst into tears. 'I know. God knows, I know. But it's so hard. And I'm just not sure any more that I can do it.'

Sebastian went to see Stripe, but he found the flat empty when he got there and the door locked. Stripe used to leave the door open and Sebastian had fallen into the habit of going over and waiting for him if he wasn't there. Recently, however, Stripe had begun to lock the door behind him, and Sebastian wondered if he was growing tired of him. He had tried putting this to Stripe, and Stripe had laughed. 'Don't be so daft!' he said, and he cuffed him jocularly around the ear. But the faint prickles of doubt would not go away and Sebastian had resolved after that not to bother Stripe quite so much.

This morning, however, for all his good intentions, things were different. Sebastian was devastated at having found his parents in the middle of yet another row, and he felt a real need to find Stripe and pour out all his woes. Determinedly he walked round the side of the garage to his tree and looked up. Relief flooded him as he saw that Stripe had left the living-room window open. Not pausing to think, he took a firm grip of the lower branches and began to shin agilely up the trunk. Five minutes later, panting slightly and with his trousers torn, he was standing in Stripe's front room.

It was gloomy inside because the curtains were still half drawn, and in the murky light Sebastian gazed about him curiously. The room looked as if a hurricane had hit it. There were clothes everywhere, an overspilling ashtray on the floor, empty Coke cans on every available sticky surface, and a plate of half-eaten toast perched precariously on the edge of the sofa. Sebastian, a fastidious child, wrinkled his nose in distaste, but then it occurred to him that he could help. He could tidy up for his friend while he waited, and then Stripe would be pleased, and would listen to all he wanted to say. He wasted no further time. He flung back the curtains and began to pick up clothes.

He had just made a trip down to the bins and then filled the dishwasher when he heard the outer door of the flat open. Stripe, he thought joyfully, and rushed to the top of the stairs. But the dark face that stared up at him belonged to a stranger. 'Hello,' said Sebastian uncertainly. 'Who are you?'

The big man below looked up at him, his face inscrutable. He was tall, about six foot three, as far as Sebastian could judge, and his hair was clipped short. He wore what looked like very smart designer jeans, and he carried a jacket slung negligently across his shoulder, revealing on his bare forearm a heavy Rolex watch. 'Where's Stripe?' he asked, his voice rich.

'I . . . I don't know,' stammered Sebastian. He felt afraid. 'He's out,' he said.

The man's gaze never shifted. 'Who are you then?'

'Sebastian. I live here. At least, over at the house. My parents own the flat.'

'Uh-huh. Nice place,' the man remarked. 'Your parents must be well-off.'

The door behind him opened and Stripe appeared silhouetted against the light.

'Stripe,' blurted Sebastian with relief.

The man swung round and Stripe tensed like a cat. Sebastian saw his eyes fix on the intruder. The air seemed to crackle with suppressed violence. But then, just as suddenly, and to Sebastian's enormous relief, the big man laughed.

'I take it you're Stripe,' he said. 'Relax, man. I'm Enoch, Jimmy's brother.'

For Sebastian it was almost like watching a play. Stripe let out a whoop. 'Enoch!' he cried. 'Hey, man. Y're 'ere.' And threw his arms round the big man, his dreadlocks bouncing, and gave him a huge, relieved hug.

Then Stripe looked up and his eyes for the first time seemed fully to register Sebastian staring down at them. 'Wot you doin 'ere, Seb?' he asked. 'Why aren't ye at school?'

Sebastian shrugged, his face pinched. 'I just wanted to talk,' he said bleakly, 'that's all.'

Stripe looked at him. 'Not now,' he said softly. 'I can't.'

Sebastian bit his lip and looked down. 'OK,' he mumbled. 'It's OK.' Tears started to his eyes, and he prepared to run down the stairs.

'Come back later,' offered Stripe. 'We'll talk then.'

'Yeah,' said Sebastian. 'Sure. OK.'

He flung down the stairs, brushed past the two men and ran out of the door. Stripe, staring after his retreating back, felt a stab of pity. The poor kid was obviously upset. Still, he had bigger worries just at the moment.

Sebastian fled from the garage back to the house, hot tears spilling down his cheeks. No one seemed to have any time for him any more, not even Stripe. The house, when he ran back in through the kitchen, felt empty, and there was a depressed feel to the air, as if it, too, was still reeling from the row. Sebastian stared about frenziedly, and wondered what on earth he should do. He felt he could not take much more. His home seemed to have become a battleground over the last few weeks, pockmarked with craters of seething hate. And he and Harry were stuck in the middle of no-man's land, wandering chaotically around in a wounded daze, or so it felt to him. Harry, he thought bitterly, was still so young that he seemed neither to know nor care exactly what was going on. His younger brother had retreated into a world of football and fantasy, and refused to talk about anything else. But Sebastian was desperate to talk, only no one took any notice of him any more.

Standing there in his mother's flawlessly streamlined kitchen, he came to a sudden decision. He could stand it no longer, so he would go. He would run away, just like Stripe had told him he had done years ago.

Sebastian ran upstairs to his room, pulled his rucksack down from on top of the wardrobe, and began hastily to stuff in as many clothes as he could. Then he went back downstairs and took some food from the kitchen. Lastly he went to the study and took all the spare cash that he could find from his father's desk. This sum was not inconsiderable because Paul, so precise in his working life, was casual, even cavalier, about his own money. He had never been selfish with personal possessions because he knew that anything lost or damaged was easily replaced. He had never gone short of anything in his life. He treated money in the same way. It was replaceable. And so, long ago, he had got into the habit of just leaving it around the house – abandoned on windowsills, shoved into drawers, unheeded in the pockets of trousers, even piled beside his bed. Consequently, Sebastian managed to collect a grand total of £310, as well as an assorted pocketful of foreign change. He would have enough, he felt, to survive.

Next he wrote a brief note telling his parents that he was going because he was fed up with all the rows, propped it up in the kitchen against the cafetière and then, without a backward glance, hoisted the rucksack on his back and set off in the direction of the railway station.

When Elaine got back in the late afternoon, all hell broke loose. 'Sebastian's run away, Pippa!' she shrieked, as soon as she had recovered from the shock sufficiently to remember the rectory phone number.

'Surely not,' said Pippa.

'Yes he bloody has,' yelled Elaine. 'Do you think I'm imagining it? He's left a note.'

'Oh God,' whispered Pippa. 'What does he say?'

'He says he can't stand all the rows. That he doesn't like living at home any more, and that he's running away.'

'Where to?' asked Pippa.

'How the hell should I know?' shrieked Elaine.

Pippa thought for a moment. 'You must phone the police,' she said. 'See if they can pick him up somehow.' She paused. 'Have you told Paul?'

'No,' said Elaine miserably. 'Not yet. I tried, but he's at a meeting or something, and they're not expecting him back.'

Pippa swallowed. Her brain felt numb. 'Stay where you are,' she said finally. 'Give the police a ring and tell them what's happened, and I'll be round as soon as I can.'

As she replaced the receiver, Mark came into the room. He made an elaborate pretence of ignoring her, walking stiffly across to the small table, his face averted.

Pippa glared at him angrily. 'That was Elaine,' she said loudly. 'Sebastian's run away.'

Mark, in the act of picking up his Bible, froze. 'I beg your pardon?' he said.

She repeated the statement, and he turned and stared at her blankly. 'What on earth do you mean? Why?'

With difficulty Pippa fought down the rising tide of her anger. In spite of herself, she could feel all the pent-up frustration and unhappiness of the last few weeks bubbling again to the surface. She was inexpressibly frightened by Elaine's news. The image of Daffyd and all he had told them about life on the streets gripped her, and she had the most appalling vision of Sebastian, abandoned and alone, facing the same terrible perils. What she would really have liked at that precise moment was for Mark to have put his arms round her and tell her everything would be all right.

'Why do you think?' she spat. 'Because his father's having an affair with another woman, as I've been trying to tell you for weeks, and he's fed up with all the rows.'

Mark went very white. He glared at Pippa as if she had struck him. 'Rubbish!' he said loudly. 'I simply do not believe it. I'm perfectly aware of all this garbage Elaine's been spewing out, but I do not believe that Paul is carrying on an affair at all. It would be completely out of character. The woman's an hysteric. She's neurotic.' They glared at each other aggressively. 'If Sebastian really has run away, I expect it's because he can't stand any more of his mother's manipulation. Elaine's an emotional menace!'

Tom came in. 'Hey-ho,' he said breezily, 'anything up?' Then he looked at their faces. 'Ah,' he said.

Pippa burst into tears. 'Elaine's just phoned,' she said. 'Sebastian's run away and she can't get hold of Paul. She's upset.' She cast a vicious glance at Mark. 'And all Mark can say is that she's an hysteric!'

Mark now went red. 'Look here—'

'Run away, has he?' Tom butted in. His nose seemed to twitch. 'Does she know what he's taken with him?'

He was rewarded by Pippa's full attention and he smiled, inordinately pleased and feeling a small spurt of triumph over Mark.

'She didn't say,' Pippa answered.

'Well, I'm sure she doesn't need to worry. Kids often do this, but they soon come back.'

'You of course would know,' said Mark nastily. Seeing the look Pippa cast upon Tom, all his jealousy once again erupted. He wanted to hit Tom.

Tom started, and then recovered himself. He looked at Mark with dignity. 'Yes, as it happens,' he said, 'I would know. Working with kids is my job, remember?'

Mark snorted, but Pippa had had enough of this. 'Would you come round with me now?' she said to Tom, turning on him the full force of her gaze.

Tom was lost. All his good intentions to put Pippa firmly out of his mind dissolved. 'Of course,' he said meltingly. 'I'd be happy to.'

By eleven o'clock that night Pippa was absolutely exhausted. True to his word, Tom had gone round with her to see Elaine and had proved unexpectedly competent. He had soothed Elaine, telling her that this often happened with adolescents and that it was not her fault, and that she must not worry. And then he took her upstairs and did a quick inventory of all Sebastian could have taken. After that he phoned up the railway and bus stations in Dorchester, which was the nearest place of any size, and asked them if anyone had seen any sign of Sebastian. Nobody could say with absolute certainty, but a porter rather thought he had seen a young lad answering Sebastian's description board the three thirty train for London. Elaine was quite irrationally delighted at this news even though, as Tom pointed out, the train would by now have arrived and it was therefore too late to try and stop him. She seemed to feel, however, that knowing where he had gone at least gave them something definite to work from. By the time the police arrived, she was able, with extraordinary calm, to give them details, and had even rooted out a photograph of Sebastian that had been taken last year. Paul arrived back while all this was going on, and looked aghast. 'What the hell's going on?' he demanded, bursting in through the front door after having almost driven into the back of the Panda parked in his drive.

Tom took charge. 'Nothing to worry about, old chap,' he said. 'Just a slight problem with Sebastian. He's gone missing.'

The colour fled from Paul's face. 'What do you mean? He's been abducted?'

'No, no.' Tom managed to produce a laugh. 'Nothing as dramatic as that. He's run away, that's all.'

'My God,' said Paul. He sat down heavily on the nearest chair. He looked dazed. 'Why?' he said. 'Why should he run away?'

Elaine, who had been sitting on a sofa in the lounge, giving details to a young WPC, now rose to her feet and came into the hall. 'I think he was upset, Paul,' she said carefully. 'He left a note. He said he couldn't take all the rows.'

Husband and wife looked at each other. 'Oh my God,' said Paul again. He staggered clumsily to his feet and threw his arms round Elaine. 'I'm so sorry,' he said. 'I never meant this to happen. What on earth have we done?'

Locked in his embrace, Elaine stood rigid. She endured it for perhaps five seconds, and then pushed him firmly away. 'The main thing now,' she said coldly, 'is to get him back.'

Pippa and Tom finally left at about ten o'clock. Mark had looked in at around eight but, seeing that he could do nothing and still smarting from Pippa's behaviour, he had left after about half an hour. Pippa felt even more annoyed with him. Later, coming out into the cold night air with Tom, she did not resist when he put an arm round her shoulders and drew her towards him as they walked slowly down the lane. She was too tired. 'Chilly tonight,' remarked Tom. She did not reply and after a moment he went on, 'I'm sure it'll be all right, you know. The police have got all the details now, and they're pretty good at picking kids up in situations like this.'

'Have you known many situations like this, Tom?' she asked, rousing herself.

'Yes,' he said. 'A few.' He shrugged, and she felt his arm tighten round her shoulders. 'It's not easy being a parent,' he added unthinkingly. 'Kids get difficult at around Sebastian's age.'

He had touched a nerve. 'I wouldn't know,' said Pippa heavily.

Tom could have kicked himself. 'Oh God, Pippa,' he said, 'I'm so sorry. I didn't mean . . .'

'I know,' she said. 'Don't worry.' She sighed, and the misery always lurking at her feet uncoiled and slid upwards. 'Everything seems such a mess these days,' she added.

Tom hardly dared breathe. He had not intended it, but they seemed to be setting off down a path he had been dreaming of for weeks. 'It doesn't have to be,' he said at last.

Something in his tone made Pippa halt. 'What do you mean?' she asked worriedly, turning and staring up at his face in the dark.

Tom decided to grasp the bull which had placed itself so providentially before him by both horns. 'I mean,' he said carefully, 'that you don't have to stay with Mark, you know.'

Pippa felt as if a bucket of ice had suddenly been poured over her.

Ever since her conversation with Elaine earlier, that same thought had been hammering for admission at her brain. She had been fighting it all day, aware that she felt so confused she was unable to think straight, but Tom's words seemed to unlock the door and finally allow the demon in. In the dark she gazed up at him in horror, trying vainly to make out his expression in the shadows.

Tom gazed back at her. Although his face was hidden from her, in the moonlight he could see every curve and line of hers. He saw the shock and disbelief, and the confused misery that suddenly flooded her eyes. His arms slid up more firmly round her and the next moment he bent his head and his lips fastened hungrily on to her mouth.

Pippa went rigid. It occurred to her fleetingly that none of this was real and that she was dreaming it all, but then Tom's hand slid inside her coat and up under her shirt and she heard him whispering, 'Oh Pippa, Pippa . . . This shouldn't be happening to you.' And she knew that it was all horribly real.

A little voice inside her agreed with Tom's last words. This should not be happening to her. Not now. Not ever. She had been married to Mark now for all of eight years, and not once in all that time had she ever even thought of being unfaithful to him. The idea had always seemed so ridiculous. She simply could not imagine herself with anyone else, and she did not want another man to touch her the way Mark did. They fitted together. God had ordained it.

'Oh Pippa,' sighed Tom again, rubbing his face against her hair. 'I love you so much. You've no idea.' And then his lips again locked on to hers and his tongue forced itself into her mouth.

Pippa came abruptly to her senses. 'Stop it, Tom!' she said, pushing him violently away. 'You mustn't. Don't.' She felt suddenly grubby, and as if everything was her fault. 'Oh God,' she said, struggling free and burying her face in her hands.

With difficulty Tom dragged himself back from under the wave of passion that had been threatening to swamp him. 'Pippa,' he said thickly. 'Sorry, I'm going too fast, aren't I? I'm not trying to take advantage.' He could smell the light perfume of her skin and he swallowed. He was distraught that he should have frightened her but at the same time he felt a wild explosion of joy somewhere in the pit of his stomach. He had done it! He had taken the irrevocable step. He had told her that he loved her.

'Forgive me,' he said, more gently. He put up a tentative hand to her hair, but she brushed him away.

'Please, Tom,' she said, 'don't.'

He looked crestfallen. 'Don't you care about me a little then?'

'Of course I do,' said Pippa immediately. 'But not like that.'

'You don't love Mark any more.' It was a statement.

'Don't I?' she asked wonderingly. She explored the idea. Did she love him? Of course she did. But if she didn't – did it matter? After all, she was married to him. Love changed. But Tom seemed to be suggesting that she was wrong, and that she loved him instead. She shuddered convulsively. No, she thought suddenly, that was not at all right. She was no longer sure what the truth was, but of that at least she was certain, and there was no way she was going to separate from Mark and tumble into Tom's arms – at least, she thought that was right. 'I'm not sure whether I love him or not any more,' she said, in a small voice. 'I'm just so confused at the moment that I can't think straight.'

They stood awkwardly looking at each other and then, as if by consent, they turned and began to walk slowly on down the lane, Pippa very careful to keep her distance.

'I've been thoughtless,' said Tom after a minute. 'I'm so sorry. Of course you're confused. You need time.' He checked and looked at her, and this time she could see his face all too clearly in the silvery light. 'When you're ready,' he said, 'I'm here. You know that, don't you? Just think about it. Please.'

# Chapter Eighteen

Mrs Stibbins's chest swelled with self-importance. The Bishop had written her a letter. He said he had been most concerned to learn about the untoward developments at St Saviour's, that he shared her alarm and distress, and that he had had a chat with the Reverend Casaubon. He added that so grave was the situation that he still retained deep fears, and should she have any further cause for alarm, she was not to hesitate to contact him again. Indeed, the Bishop went on, should there be any further incidents similar to the ones she had already told him about, he would be most grateful if she could inform him as soon as possible, so that he could take immediate appropriate action.

Mrs Stibbins determined that she would.

Mark, coming into the church in the early morning, found another dead bat on the chancel steps. Wearily he picked it up and buried it with the others outside under the yew tree in the churchyard, and then he returned and flung himself despairingly on his knees before the tiny cross in the Lady Chapel. From the stained glass window above, the serene face of the Madonna gazed unseeingly beyond him, a little smile playing about her nerveless lips, clouds billowing around her feet like some kind of advanced technological transporter. Mark felt that God was a very long way away – or was he a long way from God? He was not really sure which, but just at that moment he felt terribly alone.

Pippa had come back very late last night. He had already been in bed, pretending to be asleep. She had crept into the bedroom, pulled off her clothes in the dark, and then slid under the duvet as far away from him as she could possibly get. He had ached to reach out and touch her, but somehow he found his fingers could not span the yawning expanse that lay physically between them – and besides, he was unsure how she would respond. He was baffled by Tom. He felt it was wrong to harbour the suspicions that were gnawing away at his brain. He felt they were unworthy. But they would not go away. Tom had been his closest and dearest friend for years. But Mark could not rid himself of the horrible feeling that there was some kind of contagion lurking around them all. Tom kept looking at Pippa so strangely. He had no right to stare at her like that. And then Mark shook himself, and told himself he was imagining things. Tom was like a brother to them both. It was all simply concern. But still, he found himself watching Pippa more closely, and the suspicious little demon strangling his mind began to read terrible meaning into every casual turn of her head.

Now he suddenly drove his fist down on to the stone flag on which he was kneeling. She was a harlot, he thought viciously. She was leading Tom on. He would have it out with her. And then, unable to help himself, he fell forward with a sob, a great tearing cry that seemed to rend his gut. That couldn't be right. What on earth was happening to them all?

Mrs Stibbins came into the church and saw the Vicar throw himself prostrate on the ground. 'Well!' she muttered huffily, obscurely outraged. 'I never did! What will 'e be adoin' of next?' Mrs Stibbins did not hold with religious ostentation. She felt it smacked of popery and would lead to excess. 'Morning, Vicar,' she called out icily. 'It's only me.'

Mark abruptly sat up, feeling rather stupid. 'Oh, good morning, Mrs Stibbins,' he called back. 'I didn't know you were there.'

Mrs Stibbins sniffed. 'No,' she said, 'I'm sure you didn't.' She bustled forward into the nave, casting a gimlet eye at the pews. Three paces from the chancel steps she paused and looked with grim satisfaction at her latest floral arrangement – a huge creation in red and gold, with trailing ivy round the base. She had decided, since her last efforts had been so ignominiously removed, to make the displays so large that no one would be able to move them without the greatest difficulty. 'I've done the flowers for Sunday, Vicar,' she called.

Mark, who had watched her progress with dread, swallowed. 'Yes,' he called back feebly. 'Very nice . . .' Privately he thought they were not very nice at all. They extended so far out into the chancel that it was difficult to get round them, and there was no way that whoever read the lessons on Sunday would be able to use the lectern. After their last meeting, however, Mark thought on balance that it was probably wiser not to antagonise Mrs Stibbins by pointing this out. He clambered stiffly to his feet and gave an embarrassed cough.

Mrs Stibbins turned and glared at him. 'I'm glad I've caught you,' she said, 'I was wanting a word. I just wanted to make sure the services this Sunday were going to be normal. Dolly and I don't want no more of this wailing and jumping around nonsense.'

'No,' began Mark, taking a step forward. But just at that moment something very odd happened. A bat seemed to materialise from just above Mrs Stibbins's head. One minute there was empty space, and the next this small black flittering body erupted out of the gloom. Mrs Stibbins, standing there with her chest puffed out in sanctimonious indignation, looked up and uttered a shriek. The bat, as if startled, turned a graceful somersault and then began a steep dive, straight at Mrs Stibbins's upturned face. 'Get it off!' shouted Mrs Stibbins.

Her hands beat wildly at the air and the bat curved upwards, launching itself in a startling aerial spin that took it upwards into the rafters. The next moment another bat materialised, and then another. Like the first, both launched into a bizarre aerial display around Mrs Stibbins's head.

In a frenzy, she began to leap up and down screaming. From his position over in the Lady Chapel, Mark could only stand in frozen astonishment. He had never seen anything like it. The bats looked as if they had gone mad, and besides, they never came out during the day. The air was suddenly filled with little squeaks and squeals. More bats appeared and, like the others, began to wheel and dive in an amazing aerobatic display through the air. 'I said get them away!' screamed Mrs Stibbins.

Her cries jerked Mark into life. He rushed forward and grabbed her arm. He could think of nothing else to do. Flailing off the bats with his other hand, he began to pull her roughly towards the door. Mrs Stibbins screamed again as another bat launched itself at her face. She staggered, and the next moment her shoulder banged into the flowers. For one heart-stopping moment they swayed and then they plummeted to the floor. Flowers shot in every direction, and a long plume of water spouted up and then cascaded over the carpet, before forming itself into a dark puddle. Mrs Stibbins shrieked again, slipped on a piece of ivy and sat down heavily, right in the middle of the wet.

As suddenly as they had appeared, the bats all went. There was another loud burst of squeaks, a dark form fell to the floor, twitched slightly and then lay still, and as if at a signal they all disappeared. Where they went Mark was not sure. He peered apprehensively up into the gloom of the church roof, but the air was still now.

'You did that on purpose,' spat Mrs Stibbins. Her hat had slipped down over her left eye; she pushed it up and stared at Mark malevolently. 'You set them bats on me deliberately!'

Mark stared at her shocked. 'Pardon?' he said.

But Mrs Stibbins was not about to be fobbed off by apparent idiocy. 'You made them attack me like that,' she hissed. She staggered to her feet, her breath coming in short, painful gasps. With dull surprise Mark noted that one of her stockings had fallen down and was now wrinkling tastefully round her left knee.

'How could I?' he asked weakly.

With surprising strength Mrs Stibbins thrust him from her and lurched away. 'Take your hands off me, you . . . you bully!' Then she became aware of her stocking and, enraged, clutched theatrically at her chest. 'Ooh. I'm going to have one of my turns. I know I am.'

Mark swallowed. Two scarlet spots of fury burned on Mrs Stibbins's cheeks and her eyes were blazing. He thought she was going to attack him, and found himself uneasily casting around for a way of escape.

'The Bishop's going to hear about this,' she said nastily, catching the movement and correctly divining what was passing through his mind. 'We'll see what he's got to say about your little antics.'

Pippa was just finishing off her breakfast at the kitchen table when Agnes burst in through the outer door. 'My office is knee deep in faxes,' twittered the secretary excitedly. 'They're all from Chuck Gibbons, and I think he wants to come over straight-away!'

Pippa gaped at her. She had been unable to sleep the previous night, tossing and turning as she had striven vainly to come to terms with the extraordinary developments with Tom – and to sort out exactly what she felt. The more her mind churned over, the more she had caught herself thinking how attractive an escape from Mark might be. He had been behaving so badly over the last few months. She was absolutely certain he no longer loved her. Their married life had become simply an empty shell, carefully maintained to hide the truth from the outside world. But there was nothing there.

Now Agnes's words, pouring over her like a cold shower from out of the blue, gave her the sudden horrible feeling that God had listened in to every one of her thoughts. He had listened and he had disapproved, and as punishment she was about to be exposed as a sinner and would-be adulteress by his agent upon earth. God was sending Chuck Gibbons for a purpose.

Poor Pippa felt herself shrivel before the ghastly conviction that this was a heavenly visitation of the worst kind. Sitting there in her kitchen she felt absolutely sure she was about to be denounced by this holy man of God. This man who, if all the rumours were true, had words of knowledge and insights into people's innermost sins the way other people had hot dinners.

'Isn't it exciting?' crooned Agnes ecstatically. 'I must find Tom. He needs to respond.' And with that she swept through the door that led out into the hall, a little current of cold air the only remaining trace of her presence.

Left alone, Pippa put down her toast carefully and considered what to do.

She had reached no conclusion two minutes later when Daffyd came in. He looked miserable, and he had Roseanne in tow. 'It's no good,' he said, flinging himself disconsolately down opposite her at the table. 'It's just not working. I was stupid ever to think it could. I'm never going to be free.'

Jerked out of her reverie, Pippa stared at him. 'No,' she began quickly.

But Daffyd ignored her. 'I've made up my mind,' he announced, picking up a spoon from the sugar bowl and beginning to dribble a meandering trail across the top of the table. 'I'm not going to stay here any longer. I'm only in the way anyway. None of you can help. I'm beyond help.'

Roseanne looked as if she was about to burst into tears.

'No, Daffyd,' Pippa said again. 'You can't go now. I'm sure it's going to be all right.' He looked up at her and she saw the misery in his eyes. 'Honestly,' she said quickly. 'I've just heard. Chuck Gibbons is coming over any day now, and he's got this incredible healing and deliverance ministry. I'm sure he'll know exactly what to do.'

'I've never heard of him,' mumbled Daffyd. He looked mulish. 'Besides, the Voice told me to come to you. Not him.'

'Yes, but don't you see? That was only the first part. I feel sure the Lord wanted you to come here to me because Chuck was coming. I don't have any gifts that way, you see, but he does.'

Daffyd looked unconvinced, but Roseanne said eagerly, 'Do you really think so? Do you think this bloke can heal Daffyd?'

'Yes,' said Pippa firmly. After all, there had to be some sense to all of this.

They sat for a second in silence, Roseanne staring painfully at Daffyd as if willing him to give it another chance.

'So when's he coming then?' asked Daffyd at last.

'I don't know,' said Pippa, 'but soon. Agnes says she's knee deep in faxes.'

'Please, Daffyd,' said Roseanne.

He looked at her, and then shrugged. His eyes seemed totally dead, as if all hope had been extinguished. 'OK then,' he said wearily. 'I'll stay a few more days and we'll see. But if it doesn't work, we're out of here.'

Roseanne nodded. 'OK,' she breathed.

Outside in the hall there was a sudden babble of noise, and then they heard Elaine's voice say loudly, 'I don't care! I'm not just going to sit here and leave it all to the police. I'm going to go to London and look for myself.'

'For heaven's sake, be reasonable!' came Paul's infuriated tones. 'You haven't a clue where to look.'

'Oh, shut up!' said Elaine. And the next moment she burst in through the door. 'Pippa,' she said violently, 'I just had to come to tell you I'm going to go and look for Sebastian myself.' She checked, becoming aware of the three startled faces turned towards her.

'What's up?' said Roseanne immediately. 'What's 'appened?'

'Oh,' said Elaine. 'Hello, Daffyd.'

Paul pushed his way in behind her. 'For God's sake, make her see sense, Pippa,' he said. And then he, too, took in Daffyd and Roseanne. 'Ah,' he said ominously.

'Sit down,' said Pippa, rising quickly to her feet.

'What's 'appened?' said Roseanne again.

Paul looked white with rage. 'What's happened?' he repeated. 'I'll tell you what's happened! Ever since you lot have arrived, the whole world's gone mad, and because of your example, my son has taken it into his head to run off.'

It was Roseanne's turn to go white. 'When?' she asked, in a small voice.

'Yesterday,' snapped Paul. 'He took off some time in the afternoon and just left a note.'

'Where did he say he was going?' she persisted.

'What the hell's it got to do with you?' shouted Paul, even more enraged. 'It's you lot and your filthy ways that put the idea in his head in the first place!'

'No it isn't!' said Elaine, dangerously quiet.

Husband and wife stared venomously at each other across the kitchen. 'Well, it's not my fault,' said Paul finally.

'It's him,' said Daffyd suddenly. They had all been ignoring him, caught up in the noisy row between Elaine and Paul, but now they stopped and looked at him. Daffyd staggered to his feet. 'It's *him*,' he said again hoarsely, horror echoing through his tones. 'I told you he mustn't hear.'

They all stared as if mesmerised, and then Roseanne said impatiently, 'Come off it, Daffyd. Don't be so stupid. Your imaginary friend ain't got nothin' to do with this.'

'He isn't my friend!' shrieked Daffyd, whirling on her. 'I hate him!'

Pippa stared nervously around at all the people who had suddenly clustered into her kitchen. She saw Agnes, looking scared, and Oogi and Jack, and behind them Tom who, alarmingly, looked as if he was on the brink of running to her aid. 'Yes, well,' she said firmly, in tones that she hoped would squash

174

that idea, and looking determinedly away from him, 'I really don't think Sebastian's running away can be laid at your door, Daffyd.'

But the young man shook his head. 'No,' he insisted again. 'It *is* him, he turns everything upside down.'

'Who?' said Paul, exasperated. 'Do you mean to say there's another of these long haired layabouts hanging around?'

They all ignored him. 'Where did he go?' said Roseanne again.

'London,' said Elaine.

The two women were looking at each other, an odd expression on both their faces. Pippa saw unconscious pleading on Elaine's and what seemed to her to be bleak resignation on Roseanne's.

'I'll go and find him,' said Roseanne abruptly. 'I'll know where to look.' She turned defiantly and glared at Daffyd. She didn't like all this talk of invisible presences. It frightened her. 'I'll find him and bring him back,' she said now. 'If only to show you how bloody stupid you're being!'

'Bats?' repeated the Bishop, surprised.

'Yes,' screamed Mrs Stibbins down the phone, by now almost apoplectic with rage. 'He set them on me!'

'Did he?' The Bishop felt a momentary stab of fear that Mrs Stibbins was deranged. If she was, and the sole grounds of complaint against Mark Casaubon turned out to rest on her precarious testimony, then there was every likelihood that his plan to rid the diocese of the irksome priest would fail. 'How exactly do you mean?' he asked, playing for time as he tried to think what to do.

'He had them waiting for me as I came in,' blubbered Mrs Stibbins, managing to produce a sob. 'And when I got up to the chancel steps, he set them on me.'

'Do you mean he gave some sort of signal?' inquired the Bishop.

'Yes! No . . . I don't know,' said Mrs Stibbins, now flustered. 'I don't know how he did it, but suddenly they all just appeared out of nowhere and began to dive bomb me.'

'Ah,' said the Bishop. Mrs Stibbins, he felt, required careful handling. Mark Casaubon, he knew, inclined towards the charismatic, but he was not aware of there being any particular spiritual gift in relation to bats. He thought perhaps he would try and inject a little bit of rationality into the conversation. 'Are you entirely sure?' he began. 'After all, bats are extremely hard to train. In fact I am not aware that anyone has so far managed—' He winced as Mrs Stibbins unleashed a torrent of abuse. 'No . . . no,' he said, 'of course I am not trying to cast aspersions on your integrity . . . Dear lady, please!'

175

'You told me to keep an eye on him,' she yelled back. 'You're the Bishop, so do something. Discipline him. I'm lodging a formal complaint. I'll sue.'

'Sue?'

'Yes,' banged back Mrs Stibbins. 'And I'll have him charged with assault – assault and battery!'

Visions of a charge sheet with 'assault by a deadly bat' written on it floated before the Bishop's mind and he found his lips curling in a grim smile. But this was not really very amusing at all. 'I can see you're very upset,' he tried again. 'Rest assured I shall look into the matter.'

'He's been killing them too,' confided Mrs Stibbins, slightly mollified. 'And that's a criminal offence, that is!'

Bishop Bob's ears pricked up. 'Killing the bats? Are you quite sure?'

'Of course I am, I've seen him burying them. There's a whole heap under the yew tree in the churchyard.'

When the Bishop replaced the receiver five minutes later, he looked thoughtful. Mrs Stibbins's wild allegations that Mark had set the bats on her he dismissed as pure fantasy, but her other accusation he felt could well be of interest. If, as she maintained, there really were a number of dead bats buried in the churchyard and Mark was responsible, then he would undoubtedly be in serious trouble. The Bishop was well aware of the legal penalties attaching to the killing of bats, and he was aware, too, of how much they were often disliked by those who had to put up with them, because of the mess they made. It was entirely conceivable Casaubon might have been trying to get rid of them. But the problem would be laying the blame for their deaths at his door.

The Bishop smiled as a plan began to unfold itself in his head. He picked up the phone and dialled the Archdeacon. 'Hello, Charles,' he said. 'Yes, we seem to have a little problem, over at St Saviour's. Apparently something very odd is happening to the bats. It seems someone may be trying to kill them.' There was a buzzing sound from the other end, and then the Bishop said, 'Yes, what with all this other business, I think you may be right. We may well need to have a visitation, but I think we ought to check our facts first.' There was another buzzing down the line, this time quite long, and then the Bishop said, 'Do you think you could get someone to go along there with a spade and see if there really are bats under the tree? If so, we should perhaps have them examined . . . Yes, quite right . . . Entirely possible they might have died of natural causes . . . I agree, we don't want to start accusing people before we're sure of the facts. But if they have been deliberately killed, this is of course very serious.'

176

When he put down the phone ten minutes later, his expression was wolfish. Let them but find the evidence now, he congratulated himself, and Mark Casaubon would be out. There was no way he would be able to get out of this.

# Chapter Nineteen

Three days later Melanie arrived in Little Wakenham and duly installed herself in the King's Arms hotel, along with Jack and Oogi. Wishing that he had been able to find some way of avoiding the duty, Paul brought her along to the Chalice staff meeting that had been called for later that day. 'Everyone,' he said at the beginning, 'I'd like to introduce Melanie Brownloe. She's one of my colleagues. She's come down from London today and she's going to be staying down here in the village for the next couple of weeks, to handle the account from this end as Chalice establishes the American link-up.'

Paul privately had his reservations about the American development. He felt it was all happening rather too quickly, but he had been too tied up with concerns on the home front to express his fears aloud, and now the moment to advise caution seemed past. Chuck Gibbon's faxes had all said how excited he was. The American had revealed that there had been a number of prophecies, all confirming the earlier ones about Albion's imminent revival, which was why he was willing to come over, with his team, straightaway.

Faxes and e-mail had flown backwards and forwards across the Atlantic. In panic, Jack had secured the entire seventh floor of the Dorchester, and Chuck had expressed himself well pleased. Seven, he said, was a propitious number. Then Wembley Stadium had been tentatively lined up for a two-day evangelistic and healing rally in four weeks' time (by some miracle, which Tom said was confirmation from the Lord, there had been a last-minute cancellation). And then, close on this development, Cherilee Gibbons had demanded a piano. Although no one had asked her, she intended, she announced, to sing a revivalist medley at the rally, and would therefore need to practise with the choir that she was planning to bring over. Fifteen more bedrooms had then had to be found for the gospel singers, and Jack had arranged to install them in another, smaller hotel a few streets away from the Dorchester.

It was then pointed out to Cherilee by Mark, who felt he had to do something to assert himself, that Stripe was Chalice's director of music, and that he had already begun work on the programme himself. Cherilee was annoyed. Having listened to a demo tape of Stripe that had been sent over to her, she rather sniffily expressed herself happy with his contribution as support, but insisted that his offerings should in no way detract from her own, and that she should still have a solo spot, backed by her choir, lasting at least forty minutes. She had also pointed out that in Christian circles she was an already established star and that it was her practice to accompany herself, whereas Stripe was unknown. Mark had caved in, and Oogi had been dispatched to find a Bechstein.

Stripe, however, was not so easily dismissed. When he heard the recordings of Cherilee that were sent back across the Atlantic to reinforce her point, he expressed the view that she was treacly and insincere, and that she had a lousy voice. He also said he didn't like that kind of stuff, and that he didn't think anyone else did very much either. And then he refused to play at all if she was going to be given the star spot when it should more properly have gone to himself. Tom had had to exert all his powers of persuasion to get Stripe even to begin to reconsider. Then Stripe said did they really want all this crappy American garbage anyway, and Tom said yes they did, if it meant Chuck came on board. At that point Mark again entered the fray. He said he agreed with Stripe, and he would really much rather dispense with Cherilee's songs. And then Pippa was appealed to, but she merely shrugged and said she didn't care.

The dispute rumbled on, and seemed for twenty-four hours to threaten to overturn the whole campaign, but then Meredith Galender, Chuck Gibbon's resident prophet, delivered a stinging word from the Lord, to the effect that he had seen the wranglings of his people, and that he wanted the harmonious clashing of cymbals and varied sounds of praise, and that both Cherilee and Stripe had to sing; and so a compromise was agreed upon. Cherilee Gibbons would have a twenty-minute solo spot, and so would Stripe, and then together they would lead the crowds in praise. The matter was settled.

Then another e-mail arrived, saying Chuck wanted posters throughout the capital to herald his arrival, and Jack had been put into a frenzy trying to organise a publicity campaign that would meet the evangelist's exacting standards. He had gone into lengthy sessions brain-storming with Oogi, and had finally come up with, 'CHUCK away your crutches . . . with GIBBONS'.

Pippa asked what on earth it meant, but everyone else, by now exhausted, said it was brilliant, and Jack came up with a picture of broken crutches and wheelchairs, surmounted by a blazing cross, with Chuck's face beaming from the intersection. 'Wow!' said Oogi admiringly. 'That's great.'

'I think it's crap,' said Stripe. ''E looks like a monkey.' But nobody listened to him, and Jack put in an order for posters for eight hundred hoardings, and two hundred and fifty thousand flyers which would

180

be given out to commuters over the coming days as they came up out of the Underground. The cost for the advertising budget was astronomical, but Tom pointed out that it was the Lord's money, and that it would all be worth it in the end.

Melanie was ignorant of all these disputes – Paul had had neither the energy nor inclination to brief her – and so it was with a feeling of smug satisfaction at having landed so cushy and potentially prestigious an appointment that she now took her seat at the table in the church hall and nodded curtly to the others sitting round. She looked extremely efficient and Jack, who had not met her before and who admired that kind of thing, sat up smartly and grinned.

Stripe, sitting by the door, was less impressed. 'God 'elp us,' he muttered. 'That's all we need. The businessman's bimbo!'

Jack glared at him. 'Why don't you just back off?' he said loudly. 'You haven't got a good word for anyone.'

'Not for 'er,' agreed Stripe, unabashed. But he subsided and, after Tom had formally welcomed Melanie to the meeting, they got down to the business in hand.

'We've got two days,' Tom announced, 'before Chuck arrives. We've people stationed all over London and they're going to begin handing out the flyers tonight. Also we're sending flyers and A3 posters out to every church in the UK, and inviting them to send along nominated delegates from their fellowship. We've fixed on a cost of ten pounds per head for the day sessions, and fifteen pounds for the evenings. We think the evenings are worth more because that's when the main healing sessions are planned – Chuck's expecting people to stay for the entire day. And Cherilee's going to be performing at night too.'

'And me,' said Stripe.

Tom ignored him. 'Pippa, Mark and I will go and meet Chuck and Cherilee at the airport when they arrive. And Jack, if we can have you already stationed at the Dorchester on Thursday to liaise with the team they're bringing across and make sure everything goes smoothly?' Jack nodded. 'Oogi, I want you to tie up Wembley. They're being a bit sticky over disabled access. We need far more than just three ramps – after all, we could have a lot of wheelchairs, especially at night . . .'

The meeting droned on. Stripe lost interest, and his thoughts reverted again to the plan that Enoch had outlined to him a couple of days before. The Jamaican's strategy was simple. 'We're not that much interested in the gear,' he had said laconically, 'although of course it will be a bonus. Primarily we just want to get whoever did for Jimmy.' There was something icily menacing about his absolute calm, and Stripe had found himself swallowing nervously, wondering what on earth he was about to unleash. He had been unprepared for quite how smooth Jimmy's brother would be. He had always suspected that a large part of Jimmy's downmarket street style and quirky accent was assumed, but he had never dreamt that it was so completely a mask. With a shock he realised that he had really known very little about his friend, and that in fact they came from different worlds. Jimmy's family were obviously big in Jamaica. Enoch's casual manner said that they mattered, and his glittering eyes suggested it would be unwise to get on the wrong side of them.

Curtis, Jimmy's other brother, would be over in a few days' time, Enoch told him. He himself was the advance party, whose job it was to assess the situation and report back to Papa. There were more of them, he said, coming over. All of this gave Stripe a feeling of mild apprehension, but that was nothing to the lake of cold terror that Enoch's next words plunged him into. 'We need you as bait, man,' he said smoothly. 'We want you out in the open.'

Stripe attempted to protest that he was no good in violent situations; that yellow was his middle name, and that they would be far better off just taking the drugs and entering into negotiations themselves, while he quietly dropped out of the picture altogether. Enoch smiled, his eyes glittering. 'No,' he said softly. 'We think it's better if they don't know we're around. We want our meeting to be a nice surprise.' And then he laughed unpleasantly. 'Relax, man,' he said, clapping Stripe on the shoulder, 'nothing's going to happen to you. We'll look after you the whole way.'

Stripe was not convinced, although he had the feeling that Enoch was kindly disposed to him because of Jimmy. But how long that would last if he did not co-operate he was unsure.

'First and foremost go and check on the gear,' Enoch said softly. 'And then fix up a meeting.'

'But how?' Stripe protested. 'That's the whole problem. I know they're around but I don't know who they are. I don't know who to contact.'

'Use Sam,' Enoch said. 'Just put out the word you've got the gear and you want to negotiate. They'll contact you.'

Stripe was sure they would, and the thought filled him with dread.

He escaped from the meeting as soon as he could, neatly dodging Paul who seemed to be edging towards him as if there was something on his mind. Stripe wanted to go over to the church if there was no one around and, as Enoch had instructed, to check on the drugs. But when he emerged into the chilly morning air, unconsciously taking a great gulping breath that painfully flooded his lungs, he found he could not.

The lane leading across to the churchyard was empty. From the

182

trees a bird was singing an untroubled song, and in the distance he could hear the river, the sound of the water unruffled and strong. But terror paralysed him. What if he was being watched even now? He could not go over to that cold stone church alone, knowing that something terrible might be lurking close by. He could not go into that eerie, watching silence.

He turned on his heel and began with determination to head in the opposite direction back to the flat. Halfway there, Paul caught up with him.

'Stripe,' he called, 'hang on.' He broke into a run the last few steps and came up panting behind.

'Wot ye doin', man?' Stripe asked. 'Wot d'ye want?'

'Just a word,' said Paul, breathing heavily.

Stripe stared at him a second, disgusted, and then turned and began to walk on.

Paul fell into step at his side. 'It's about Melanie,' he said. 'Miss Brownloe.'

'Pgh! I might 'ave guessed,' said Stripe.

'I just wanted to say,' Paul swallowed awkwardly, 'no need to mention all the trouble Elaine and I have been having recently . . . Melanie's jolly good at her job, after all, and a lot of unnecessary tittle-tattle's not going to help anyone, is it, old man?'

Stripe was not sure whether it was being referred to as 'old man', or whether it was what Paul seemed to be suggesting that offended him most, but whatever it was, he found himself reacting with a fury that surprised them both.

'Ye make me sick, man,' he spat, swinging his fist violently in the air as they turned in through the open gate. 'Ye turn yer family upside down because yer can't keep your grubby little hands off whatever it is you want! Ye destroy yer kids. Humiliate yer wife. And then y've got the nerve to bring yer bit of stuff down and pretend it's all all right!' Just in front of the garage, he swung back on his heel and glared at Paul. 'It's all show with you, isn't it, man? Outwardly everything's perfect, but inside yer nothing but a load of shit!'

'Now look here!' began Paul, outraged, and then he stopped, his gaze fixed in horror just beyond Stripe's shoulder.

Unnerved, Stripe half turned to see what he was looking at and then pulled back with shock. There, nailed to the front door of the flat, was a dead crow, impaled on a short iron spike that protruded some three inches from its body. Its head lolled brokenly, and the crushed feathers on its back ruffled gently in the breeze. There was not much blood – it looked as if its neck had been broken first – but there was something so unspeakably threatening and violent about it that Stripe found himself recoiling.

'Good God,' said Paul, revolted. 'What on earth is it?'

Stripe swallowed. His tongue felt as if it had frozen to the roof of his mouth. 'It's a crow,' he said hoarsely. 'A dead crow.'

'I can see it's a dead crow,' snapped Paul. 'What the hell's it doing on the door?'

With difficulty, Stripe found his voice. 'It's a warning,' he brought out.

'Of what?' Paul looked at him suspiciously. 'What's going on?' Then horror gripped him. 'It's not got anything to do with Sebastian, has it?' he asked, his breath catching.

Stripe shook his head. 'No.' His mother had told him of this kind of thing. Back in Jamaica, she had said, in the occult beliefs of his forebears, a dead crow nailed to someone's door was a sign of death, a curse.

'Hang on,' said Paul, 'there's something else there.' With distaste he crossed over and gingerly extracted from beneath the crow's broken body a slip of paper. 'It's a phone number,' he said, 'I think—'

Stripe snatched it before he could go on and stared at the paper in disbelief, then without another word he pushed roughly past Paul, grabbed the iron spike and wrenched it violently from the door. Without pause he flung the bird with all his might as far as he could beyond the bushes that lined the drive. There was a dull thunk as it landed somewhere away to the right in the neighbouring garden – and a strangled cry told Paul its arrival had been noted. Horrified, he turned back and stared at the door. All that remained were two feathers, glued to the door by the crow's congealed blood, and a ragged hole where the spike had been.

'Look at my door!' he said furiously.

Stripe gave him one withering look then wrenched at the handle and went inside, leaving Paul staring at the splintered panels in disbelief.

Stripe did not care. He rushed up the stairs two at a time and burst into the front room. A quick glance told him all was undisturbed and, breathing a quick prayer of thanks to whatever spiritual beings might happen to be around, he grabbed the phone and began to punch in the number that Enoch had given him.

He had to wait for what seemed like an age, and then at last the Jamaican's smooth voice came down the line. 'Yes?'

'It's me,' said Stripe, in strangled tones. 'Stripe. I've found a dead crow nailed to me door.' His hands were shaking, and he forced them to be still. 'It's the nutters that did for Jimmy, I'm sure!'

Enoch's voice was unperturbed. 'You mean they've made contact? Good.'

'No, it's not bloody good,' shrieked Stripe. 'It's a death threat, man. Voodoo. You know what it means.'

There was a small silence and then, with mild interest, Enoch said, 'You don't believe that rubbish, do you?'

'What's it matter if I believe it or not?' Stripe demanded, by now almost beside himself. 'The point is, they believe it. They'll make it happen.'

'Look, calm down,' said Enoch. 'It's just a threat, that's all. Was there anything else?'

Stripe forced himself to breathe deeply. 'A phone number.'

'Good. Have you checked the gear's OK?'

'No.'

'Why not?' Enoch's voice was very restrained.

Stripe could not believe his stupidity. 'Look, man, they're 'ere. They've been t' me flat. The number they've left is local. For all I know, they're following me.'

'So?'

'So I don't particularly fancy getting bopped on the 'ead by them. We wouldn't need to set up a meeting then, would we?'

'Then make sure you're not followed,' Enoch said with emphasis. 'But go and check it's all right.'

'No,' said Stripe. 'It's too dangerous. I've 'ad it. The stuff can just stop there. I don't want any part of this.'

'Now don't be stupid,' said Enoch, dangerously quiet. 'You asked us over in the first place, remember? You told us about these guys!'

'Yeah, but I didn't know it was goin' t'be like this.'

There was silence for a minute. 'Look,' said Enoch, 'do you want me to come with you?'

'Yeah,' said Stripe immediately. 'I do. You said you'd cover me, man.'

'OK. I'll come and hold your hand. Where is it?'

Stripe told him and Enoch whistled softly. 'You certainly pick your hiding places.'

They arranged to meet in a nearby pub at three that afternoon.

The Archdeacon phoned up the Reverend David Chalke, a newly ordained deacon and therefore unlikely, he felt, to question instructions, no matter how bizarre. The Archdeacon had judged well. The clergyman was an earnest, rather naive young man of Anglo-Catholic persuasion, and he appeared to find nothing odd in being told to take a spade along to St Saviour's and dig up any bats he might find under the yew tree in the graveyard. 'Oh, and by the by,' added the Archdeacon, 'try and make sure you're not seen, there's a good chap. We don't want people to get upset.'

What people? wondered the Reverend Chalke vaguely, but then his brow cleared as the Archdeacon went on to give him details of the precise location of the tree. The people were obviously parishioners, he decided, and if there was some sort of bat plague sweeping St Saviour's, which was what the Archdeacon seemed to be implying, then of course the dreadful news should be kept from them until the authorities had worked out what to do. There was no point in spreading needless panic. And so, later that afternoon, armed with his spade, he set out.

The churchyard, when he got there, was quiet. Insects gently buzzed between the graves, while overhead the graciously trailing, ancient trees gave a feeling of undisturbed and undisturbable peace. As he stood there at the lych gate, the spade clutched in his hand, he felt that this was truly a place of prayer. Men and women of holiness had worshipped here in this church over the centuries, he thought, and their devotions had left a deep and lasting mark. He could sense it. He breathed deeply and wriggled his toes. He liked this place, he decided. He felt at home.

As he set off towards the yew down the narrow winding path that led between the tumbling, weathered stones that marked the graves, he did not notice the two men sitting on a tomb over in the far corner, almost hidden by the overgrown bushes and weeds that, despite all Mark's best efforts to impose some sort of order, obscured that area. Over in that corner, in fact, were the most ancient of the graves, going back to the Middle Ages and beyond, and gradually over the years they had become almost swallowed up by a riotous profusion of wild flowers, ivy and weeds, as nature sought to reclaim its own.

'What's he doin' then?' said one of the men, raising his head like an inquisitive meercat over a clump of nettlewort.

'Dunno,' said the other. ''E's got a spade. Looks a bit odd.'

As if by common consent, both men heaved themselves down from the tomb and crept quietly forward. The first, Ulysses, was very large and very black. The second, following close behind and named Marty, was white and rough looking, and had an unbecoming three-day stubble on his chin. If Mark had been there, he might have recognised his assailants from what he still thought of as Chalice's first disastrous mission.

There was no sinister reason for their being in the churchyard at that precise moment. Following on their so far half-hearted reports about Stripe, their boss, an evil-minded Irishman named Seamus O'Flynn, had dispatched them down to Little Wakenham to discover the precise location of the musician and try to recover the drugs. Their efforts so far had been desultory. They had been rather enjoying their holiday in the country and had been prolonging it for as long as they could. When they eventually reported back that they knew where Stripe was but didn't think the gear was with him, O'Flynn had instructed them to open up negotiations. Fast.

The crow had been Ulysses' idea. Like Stripe, he was West Indian in origin, and he knew that the musician would recognise instantly what it meant. He himself knew nothing about voodoo, but he was aware of the fear it could inspire, and he thought that in this case fear might be no bad thing.

They had been observing Stripe closely for the last three days, and this morning they had watched him go to the meeting in the church hall. Then they had gone and left the crow nailed to his door. Later they had observed, with interest, his return, and had felt mildly pleased at his reaction. When he had failed to reemerge from the flat, Ulysses had become bored. 'Look,' he said, 'nuthin's goin to 'appen. Why don't we get a six-pack and go an' 'ave somethin' to eat?' Which was what they did. With a six-pack of lager from the off-licence and two bags of smoky bacon crisps and some peanuts, they had retired to the churchyard to take advantage of the late spring sun and enjoy their lunch. They were just finishing off their third can each when the Reverend Chalke appeared.

Arriving at the yew, the young cleric put his foot on his spade and pushed it deep into the earth. He found it surprisingly soft, and within minutes he had excavated a small hole.

''E's lookin for somethin',' remarked Marty.

'You thinkin' what I'm thinkin'?' asked Ulysses.

Marty nodded. 'Maybe. Maybe this bloke Stripe really 'as gone bananas. Maybe 'e's got religion after all, and given the gear to them. 'E looks dead shifty, this bloke!'

They crept forward.

The Reverend Chalke stood back, panting slightly with his exertions. His high collar felt tight, and he ran an earthy finger round the inside as he peered down into the hole. Then the next moment he gave a small cry of triumph, instantly silenced as he remembered the Archdeacon's enjoinder not to upset anybody.

''E's found it,' breathed Marty.

'Yeah,' agreed Ulysses. 'Let's go see. This job may be easier than we thought it 'ud be.'

They slid forward through the long grass like two disreputable snakes.

The Reverend Chalke reached down and began carefully to pick something up. In the gently humming quiet of the churchyard, he had no suspicion there was anyone else there. Ulysses quietly rose to his feet and slid an expert arm round the young priest's neck, almost throttling him with the sudden force. 'Let's see wot ye got then,' he breathed lovingly.

The Reverend Chalke looked wildly up and round, saw the huge black face grinning down at him and, overcome with terror, passed out.

''E's fainted,' said Ulysses in disgust, letting the priest slide none too gently to the ground.

'Never mind 'im,' said Marty, 'let's see what 'e's got.'

They both stooped down and peered with interest into the hole. With his boot Ulysses gingerly prodded a twisted little black form, almost unrecognisable from its covering of earth. 'It's a bat,' he said incredulously. 'It's not the gear at all.'

'Bleedin' nutter,' said Marty in disgust. 'They're perverts, this lot.'

'Wot was 'e bein' so secretive for then?'

Marty shrugged. 'I dunno, but it's not got anyfink to do wiv us.' He stood back. 'Come on, we've 'ad our grub. Let's see wot's 'appenin wiv our chum.'

Ulysses gave the inert form of the Reverend Chalke a dismissive kick with his foot, and then followed Marty.

Half an hour later Stripe and Enoch, coming warily into the churchyard, found the young priest still under the yew and just beginning to regain consciousness. Enoch would have ignored him and gone straight into the church, but over the past few weeks, almost unconsciously, Stripe had begun to rediscover some of the Christian truths he had taken in at his grandmother's knee and so, seeing the crumpled figure of a man lying on the ground, he went over to see what he could do.

'Wot's up?' he asked. 'Wot 'appened?'

The Reverend Chalke moaned softly and attempted to sit up. 'I was set upon,' he announced. 'Two ruffians pounced on me.'

Stripe took in the spade and the hole. 'Wot were ye doin'?'

The Reverend Chalke looked at the hole and shuddered. 'Digging for bats,' he said hollowly.

'I always thought they lived in trees or old buildings,' remarked Enoch.

'Dead bats,' said the Reverend Chalke, as if this explained everything.

Stripe looked puzzled, but he said nothing, and instead helped the young priest to his feet. 'Are ye OK?' he asked.

The Reverend Chalke did not reply. With immense dignity, he reached into his jacket pocket and took out a plastic bag. Then he bent down and very gingerly placed the bat inside and laid it on the ground. 'I need specimens,' he muttered, more to himself than his rescuers.

He appeared dazed, and they watched helplessly as he began again carefully to dig, uncovering three more bats.

A thought occurred to Enoch. 'Are you going to tell the police?' he asked casually. Stripe glanced at him sharply, but Enoch's face was expressionless.

The Reverend Chalke put two more bats into his bag, and then stood back. 'I don't think so. There's nothing gone, and no lasting harm done. And the police probably couldn't catch them anyway.' Then he mumbled, 'Just an unfortunate incident.'

'Quite,' said Enoch. 'Very wise.' He smiled a thin smile and picked up the bag from the ground. 'Your bats,' he said, holding it out.

The Reverend Chalke looked momentarily bemused. He was in fact still rather shocked, but it was clear that this large and imposing black man wanted him to go. 'Thank you,' he quavered uncertainly. He took the bag, picked up his spade, and hurried out of the churchyard.

'Come on,' said Enoch to Stripe. 'Let's get on.'

Stripe stared after the retreating clergyman. He knew that Mark had been having trouble with the bats, and he knew he had been burying them under the yew tree, but why someone else should now be digging them up again was beyond him. And the fact the man should have been attacked in this quiet little backwater of Little Wakenham seemed to him bizarre in the extreme. 'Who d'ye think did it?' he asked.

Enoch shrugged. 'Who cares?' he said. 'Kids, I expect.'

'But they didn't take nuthin'.'

'So? Come on.' He set off in the direction of the church and, after a moment, Stripe shook his head and followed.

The interior of the church was, as ever, cool and dark. Nervously Stripe led the way down the nave, glancing left and right into the shadows to see if anyone was there. He never came into the church alone now because of the disturbing sense that someone was watching him. He had it now but, as far as he could see, the place was empty.

Enoch seemed unperturbed, whistling softly under his breath. At the chancel steps they came to a halt. 'Over there,' said Stripe softly, indicating the wall with a jerk of his head.

Enoch stared around, puzzled. 'Where?' he asked. 'There's nothing there.'

For answer, Stripe climbed up on to the heavy stall. The light shining through the stained glass window over the altar made a curious multicoloured pattern on the floor that seemed to shift and dance as if it was alive. 'Up here behind the monument,' whispered Stripe, determinedly ignoring the shifting colours of the light. He reached up and groped with his hand inside the crack. Before, he had been pushing something in; it was far harder, he discovered, to reach up and pull it out. He began to pant slightly as he strained upwards, his fingers scrabbling ineffectually behind the hard surface of the stone.

'Here, let me try,' said Enoch, exasperated.

He pushed Stripe aside and clambered up on to the stall. He was taller than Stripe, and his long arm reached up more easily. Face pressed against the rough surface of the wall, he slid his fingers up and then down into the crack. There was a sudden flurry and an angry squeak, and the next second a small bat catapulted out through the hole. 'Shit!' said Enoch, staggering back and almost losing his footing. He ducked as the bat swooped low and then rose twittering up into the roof, where it was lost in the dark.

They both stared upwards, fascinated. 'It's only a bat,' said Stripe.

Enoch glared at him. 'I hate bats,' he said. His breath was coming rather more deeply now, and he looked annoyed but, bracing himself, he reached up again and warily shoved his fingers into the hole.

This time he managed to locate something that felt bulky and hard – not bat-like at all. With a small exclamation of triumph, he strained upwards and closed two fingers round either side of the package and then, very carefully, began slowly to try and withdraw it.

He was rewarded by a small cloud of dust and loose plaster billowing out on to his upturned face. He sneezed violently, and then rested against the wall, a thin line of perspiration forming along his upper lip. 'What the hell did you put it up here for?' he demanded.

Stripe sniffed. 'It's a good 'idin' place, man. No one would think of looking up there.'

'I wonder why not,' muttered Enoch into the wall. But he took a deep breath and braced himself, and then once again reached upwards. He tried to extend his grip further round either side of the package and squeeze it, so that he could more easily pull it out through the narrow gap. Ten minutes later his efforts were rewarded, and with a small *thwuck* the bag suddenly came free. A shower of white powder exploded into the air and, once again, cascaded around Enoch's head. 'Shit!' he said for the second time – and sneezed again.

'What's up?' said Stripe. 'Has the bag burst?'

Enoch leapt down, and they both stared at it in dismay. Down one side was a jagged tear, and through it the grainy grey powder inside was spilling across Enoch's palm.

'The stone's torn it,' said Stripe.

'I don't think so,' Enoch said slowly. 'Look. The edge is ragged.' He ran the fingers of his other hand gently down the tear. 'This looks more like teeth marks to me than a tear.'

'You don't mean the bats, do you?'

190

Enoch shrugged. 'I don't know. Maybe. Maybe not. But some-thing . . . look, the powder here is damp and clogged.' He shook out some more on to the palm of his hand. 'I don't think this stuff is much good for anything any more.'

'Good,' said Stripe. 'I 'ate that stuff.' He looked at Enoch. 'But wot do we do now?'

Enoch twisted the corner of the bag up and across, so that the tear was covered. 'It doesn't make any difference,' he said decisively. 'Our chums won't know what's happened. And by the time they find out, it won't matter.' He looked up and grinned, his teeth flashing. 'I think the next step is for you to ring them and tell them you've got the stuff, and that you want to negotiate. But I don't think we'll put the gear back up there again, or else the next time we come back there might not be anything there at all. Those bats have got an appetite.'

Stripe swallowed. 'But if I tell them I've got the gear, what's to stop them jus' jumpin' me and takin' it?'

Enoch ground his teeth, exasperated. 'So what do you want to do?'

'You take it,' Stripe said firmly. 'I don't want none of it. It's bin nuthin' but bad news from the beginnin'. I'll do as you say, but I don't want that stuff again. I don't feel safe.' This was true, but what really upset him was the sense that Jimmy's wounded spirit was lurking around, and his heart suddenly ached for his lost friend. Were it not for that stuff, Jimmy would still be here.

Enoch was glaring at him. 'No,' he said softly, 'that's not the plan at all. I've already explained to you that we don't want them to know we're involved – yet. If I take it, things might go wrong. Also they might want some confirmation that you really do have it. You might have to get at it fast.' He thrust the package back towards Stripe. 'You take it. Keep it safe.'

# Chapter Twenty

Coming into the bar of the King's Arms late at night for a quick drink before he went to bed, Jack found Melanie sitting in the far corner with a sheaf of papers spread out in front of her on a small table, and a large whisky in her hand. 'Hello,' he said, coming over and throwing himself down opposite her. 'Can I get you anything?'

Melanie eyed him narrowly, and then slowly drained the remainder of her glass. 'OK,' she said, 'I'll have another Glenfiddich.'

'Right,' said Jack admiringly. He took her glass and crossed smartly to the bar, to return a few seconds later with two large doubles. 'There you go,' he said, holding it out to her.

Melanie nodded and put it down by her side, and then very carefully began to draw together the papers spread out before her.

'What are you doing?' asked Jack, interested.

'Forward projections,' she answered briefly. 'Paul said Tom wanted a million available to cover Wembley and this American project, so I'm just trying to work out how to juggle a few overseas investments to make the most of returns so that we don't have to dig too deeply into capital reserves.'

Jack eyed her appreciatively. 'You know, I don't think I know any other woman who could do what you do,' he said.

They had the bar to themselves. Over behind the counter the lone barman, Steve, stared at them briefly and then pulled a wry face. The King's Arms had a lot of business types staying over during the week, on their way to and from important meetings in the two neighbouring towns. Little Wakenham, with its Historic Village award, had a reputation as a highly desirable place to stay, and the fifteenth-century coaching inn had been quick to capitalise on that fact, offering special overnight deals, and throwing in a health hydro and conference facilities as added lure. They were usually full, and Steve had grown used to turning a blind eye to the expense-account bedroom games that regularly went on.

He sighed and wearily placed the last glass up on the shelf. Not long now, he thought. Give them half an hour and they would be away to one or other of their beds, and he could go back to Mary, and his.

For once, however, Steve was not quite right. It was true that Jack's interest was aroused and Melanie, in the normal course of things, would not have been at all averse to a little extra-curricular activity, but right now she rather thought her life was difficult enough without added complications. Still, she found Jack attractive and sufficiently different from all the other men she knew for her interest to be piqued. She looked at him, trying to make up her mind what to do.

Jack functioned at a temperamental remove from Melanie. He was most certainly attracted to her, and had been from the first moment he had laid eyes on her, but he was also a young man of quite strong Christian commitment. He had not yet achieved the ideal of a totally celibate, pre-married life, but he was still very far from being promiscuous and did not enjoy the idea of casual relationships. Now, as he sat opposite Melanie, he found himself imagining what she might look like without her clothes, but that did not mean that he was mentally taking the quantum leap into bed. He simply wanted to get to know her.

Melanie replaced the last of the papers in her bag, drew the whisky towards her and leant back, gazing at him with narrowed eyes. It occurred to her that if Paul had not been such a pig over the last couple of weeks she would have sent the young man packing immediately. But in a sudden flood of maudlin self-pity – brought on in large measure by the whisky – she abruptly thought how horrible Paul seemed to have become. It was almost, she thought, as if her hold over him had completely gone. It would serve him right if she was pregnant, although she was fairly certain she wasn't. It was true she had failed to take her pill the last time they made love, but she frequently omitted to take it these days because ten years of not very careful sexual activity with not the slightest hint of an alarm had begun to form in her the suspicion that there was no need. There had, however, been no reason to share this detail with Paul, and she had enjoyed watching him squirm.

Thoughts of Paul led on to other even less pleasant considerations, in particular the obscene calls and packages she had been receiving. She had received a letter only the day before from the telephone company, warning her that in future all incoming calls would be intercepted and stopped unless she ceased forthwith to use her telephone line for immoral purposes. This of course was precisely what Melanie wanted – she had after all already asked them to stop such calls – but being informed of this move by the phone company watch committee because they had decided to classify her as a whore was rather different. It was not pleasant, and she shuddered at the thought of the recorded message that would greet callers in the future if the threat was implemented.

194

Watching her face intently, Jack saw a scowl flit across it, and wondered immediately if he had annoyed her. He could think of no other explanation, and was just preparing to retire from the field, cowed, when Melanie suddenly smiled, turning upon him the full force of a mega-watt beam that pinned him squarely like an affrighted rabbit in the light. In the act of getting up, Jack faltered, and then again sank back. 'So . . . tell me about yourself,' he said weakly.

With a conscious effort Melanie thrust away her gloom and focused her full attention on him. She came to an abrupt decision. Whether it was wise or not, she no longer cared, she just wanted to immerse herself temporarily in the oblivion of a night's forgetfulness. She wanted to surrender herself to the death of another's touch. And maybe that way she would be reborn. Whatever happened, she did not want to have to think.

Twenty minutes later, they both rose to their feet. 'I'm in room thirty-one,' said Melanie meaningfully. 'You can come and have another drink if you like.'

'Oh no, that's all right thanks,' began Jack. And then he gaped at her as the full import of what she was saying hit him. 'Oh,' he said. 'I see what you mean . . . I think.'

She smiled seductively. 'We could even have some champagne if you wanted. I do so like champagne before bed.'

Jack swallowed. His scruples rather feebly insisted that they did not yet know each other well enough, and that there was no commitment. A sudden strong feeling of lust, however, countered that a few more hours spent in each other's company would remedy both deficiencies. He grinned idiotically, resolutely throttling his conscience which was protesting loudly. 'OK,' he said, 'but I mustn't be too late. It's going to be a busy day tomorrow.'

Melanie smiled. 'Yes,' she agreed, 'but don't worry. I'll make sure we both get to bed in plenty of time.'

At Gentillesse the house felt appallingly still. Elaine had ordered Harry to bed at nine, and had then retired herself some forty minutes later, overwhelmed by the mind-numbing anxiety of the day. Paul had then attempted to move his things back from the spare room, and had compounded the offence by again trying to clamber into bed beside her. Elaine had been outraged and had screamed at him to get out. After staring at her briefly like a wounded dog, he had obeyed. After that, she had got up and stood in the doorway of Sebastian's empty room, stupidly hoping that it was all maybe a nightmare, and that she would find him there asleep after all, his tousled hair clammy on the pillow, his hand cradling his cheek. But he was not, of course, and the emptiness of the room seemed to mock her.

It suddenly occurred to her that perhaps she ought to pray. She had found prayer very difficult ever since the whole business with Paul had begun. It felt to her as if God had somehow gone away. When she closed her eyes, it was as if a great gulf of loneliness stretched all around her. She imagined herself in a kind of desert, but it was dark and cold, and she felt as if everything that had any kind of life had gone – apart from the beasts, that is. They prowled around voraciously, searching for prey, their roars echoing through the frozen silence of her mind. But where was God? Where was that hand in the darkness? That inner certainty that all was well?

Elaine crossed over to Sebastian's bed and sank down on her knees with her hands, palms down, on the pillow. She closed her eyes, and sank into the familiar swirling mists of mind-threatening chaos. She spiralled downwards on a noiseless scream of pure agony, and the fog churned around her. 'Oh God,' she whispered, 'where is he? Where are you?' The formlessness of silence answered her. 'God,' she began again, 'please, I'll do whatever you want, I'll even take Paul back. I'll be good . . . only, please, bring Sebastian back safely. Bring him back to me.'

She began to cry, and as she sobbed a great weariness stole over her until she found she could no longer think clearly. It was as if she had fallen into a kind of abyss without form, but at the same time it felt oddly comforting. She tried to remember why she was so upset – and found she couldn't. Her mind could not even form itself into thought, but there in that huge immensity of light-filled weariness that seemed to be blotting out her mind she suddenly found that she was not alone. In the tiny bedroom where Sebastian had once slept, she gave a long, shuddering hiccup of total surrender, then she let her head fall forwards on to the bed and sank into oblivion.

The Bishop received the report from the laboratory to which the Reverend Chalke had taken the bats with surprise. The head of the lab, Dr Biffin, actually phoned him up. 'Your bats would appear to have been heroin addicts,' his voice crackled down the line. 'They overdosed!'

'I beg your pardon?' said the Bishop.

'Yes,' agreed the voice, 'does take a bit of taking in, doesn't it? But there's no mistake, I assure you. We've checked and doublechecked. The bodies were absolutely full of the stuff. Total tissue saturation, in fact.'

'But how?' queried the Bishop.

'Couldn't say. I've never seen anything like it before. Didn't even know bats would take heroin like that, but the evidence points to prolonged use. In fact, we can definitely say this wasn't just a freak,

196

one-off accident. We've got molecular changes here consistent with advanced addiction.'

'Good God,' said the Bishop, stunned.

'Quite.' The voice sounded cheery. 'But what I really wanted to ask was, do you mind if I write a monograph on it? Come over and take some more samples, photographs – you know the kind of thing. We may be able to learn some important things about addiction. All very exciting really!'

The Bishop thought rapidly. He was not entirely sure about the excitement value. 'I'm not convinced as to the benefit of a monograph,' he brought out at last. 'After all, we don't want the kind of adverse publicity this sort of thing might bring if it ever got to the ears of the press. And we do have to be very careful of image.'

'Oh, you don't need to worry about that,' said the voice blithely. 'We wouldn't be suggesting one of the congregation was supplying them or anything. It's the scientific value. Don't you see, if bats really can become addicted like this, then not only does it tell us some very important new things about bat life, but it may have enormous potential for treating people with an addiction problem.'

The Bishop came to a decision. 'By all means go across to St Saviour's and carry out further investigations,' he said carefully, 'but as to writing a monograph, well, we'll just have to look at the results. I will not give permission for anything that might cast adverse light upon the Church.'

When he put down the phone five minutes later, he looked thoughtful. There really did appear to be some odd goings-on at St Saviour's, and maybe Mrs Stibbins's accusations were not so wild after all. But if the bats really had been taking heroin, how on earth had they got it? Presumably they would have to have sniffed it – he could not imagine anyone would have injected them. But if they had sniffed it, was it remotely possible that the congregation might have sniffed it too? Had Mrs Stibbins, for instance, unknowingly ingested it? And had the young people she complained of brought it in? Or was Mark somehow responsible? How in the world could the bats have died of an overdose?

Baffled, the Bishop shook his head. It was completely beyond him. But one thing at least was clear, the Archdeacon would have to be brought in. He phoned him up and asked him to come over immediately. 'I've had a very disturbing report about St Saviour's,' he said. 'I'm afraid I simply cannot ignore it any longer. Distasteful as all this is, I am left with no option. You will have to carry out a visitation.'

Thursday morning Mark received a letter. 'Oh good God,' he said, staring at it aghast. He looked across the breakfast table at

Pippa, but she was engrossed in the newspaper and so he swallowed and looked down.

'What's up?' asked Tom, indifferently. There was a curtain of veiled frostiness between the two men now. Outwardly they planned and talked and, to the undiscerning eye, carried on much as before, but both were aware of a constant undercurrent of tension, and they prowled around each other warily.

'Nothing,' said Mark abruptly, and he put the letter down.

Pippa looked up and realised something was wrong. She leant across and picked up the letter. 'Goodness,' she said, reading the contents. 'He can't do that, can he?'

Mark bit his lip. Just a month ago, he thought bitterly, she would have come to him and put her arms round him. 'Of course he can,' he said, 'he's the Bishop.'

'What is it?' Tom asked, no longer indifferent.

'See for yourself.' Pippa held out the letter. 'It's from the Archdeacon. He says the Bishop has asked him to carry out a visitation. He wants to come the beginning of next month.'

Tom gave a low whistle. 'That's a bit premature, isn't it?' He scanned the letter. 'Don't they normally give you a bit more notice?'

'No,' said Mark hollowly. 'Not in cases of extreme urgency. I'm just surprised they've given me as long as they have.'

'But I don't understand,' said Pippa, bewildered. 'What's suddenly so urgent that they dump this on you now?'

Mark thought back to his last interview with the Bishop and shuddered. Although, like Pippa, he did not know the precise cause, he had been half expecting something like this. The Bishop, he felt, was out to get him, aided by Mrs Stibbins. Not for the first time, a feeling of utter desolation swept over him. His whole life, he thought, was in ruins. His marriage was in a state of terminal decay. His career was a mess, and nobody, but nobody, seemed to give a damn.

Daffyd wandered in through the kitchen door. 'Morning, everyone,' he mumbled.

All three of them jumped, and then Pippa seized the coffee pot. 'Good morning, Daffyd,' she said, striving vainly to keep her voice normal and hoping the young man would not notice anything amiss. 'Would you like some coffee?'

Mark's shoulders slumped even more. He felt he had been rebuffed. 'Excuse me,' he said, rising heavily to his feet. 'I think I'd better go and phone the Archdeacon and try and sort this out.'

'Don't be too long,' called Tom after him, 'we've got to leave in half an hour for the airport, don't forget.'

They were to meet Chuck, Cherilee and Meredith Galender at

Heathrow at twelve thirty. Pippa had told Daffyd that he had to stay in Little Wakenham but that as soon as the Gibbons were safely installed at the Dorchester, she would take him up to see them. 'You're going to be all right,' she had promised him again. 'Chuck Gibbons will know exactly what to do. He's got a real ministry in this area. He's famous.'

Daffyd remained sceptical, but he had given his word that he would give Chuck a try, and besides, Roseanne was still away in London looking for Sebastian, and he had said that he would wait for her here. He accepted the coffee and stared glumly into its murky depths, so sunk in his own private hell that he was totally oblivious of his surroundings.

Tom, seeing his absorption, abandoned all pretence of indifference and followed Pippa hungrily with his eyes as she moved about the kitchen. He had not been able to get her on her own since their walk back from the Dufrayns. He knew he had taken her by surprise then and that she was confused, but he assumed her apparently equivocal response had been simply that, surprise, and that once she got over the initial shock and guilt of having what he felt certain were her inmost thoughts voiced aloud, then she would acknowledge the truth of what he had said and respond. It would help, of course, if he could off-load Mark from Chalice, leaving Pippa to follow her own emerging ministry with the group – and with him. But so far he had not managed to work out how to achieve this.

It had been decided that both Mercedes should go to the airport – they would need the space – and Oogi was also bringing the Chalice van to collect the luggage. Tom hoped that Pippa would ride with him, but in the event she chose to go with her husband and, after a second's annoyance, Tom felt forced to acknowledge she was right; it might have looked odd to Chuck and Cherilee if they realised she had arrived with him.

They got there with only minutes to spare and went straight to the arrivals area. Pippa took the opportunity of the drive to try and mend some fences with Mark but he refused to respond. He had not managed to get hold of the Archdeacon and had had to content himself with leaving a message on the answerphone, simply saying that the date the Bishop had suggested would be all right. That had not helped his mood, and he ended up saying no more than three words to Pippa for the entire journey.

They found the arrivals area crammed with people, all waving boards and cards and jostling each other roughly in their attempts to get to the front around the barrier. 'Good grief,' said Tom, 'this is ridiculous. We're going to miss them at this rate. Why on earth is it so busy?'

A foreign-sounding voice announced something unintelligible over the tannoy, and then people began to spill out through the double doors ahead. 'Gosh!' said a shrill voice. 'It's him! It is . . . It's Sean Hebron.' There was a flurry of movement and then a bevy of photographers seemed to erupt out of nowhere, followed by a blaze of lights.

'Who on earth's Sean Hebron?' gasped Pippa as she was elbowed roughly aside in the flood that now surged forwards.

'An actor,' replied Tom briefly. 'That must be why it's so crowded. Just what we need!' He peered round distractedly and then began to shove forwards, trying to battle his way through the milling crowd.

Pippa found herself abruptly abandoned and Mark, seeing her stumble and half fall as she was jostled against the wall, shouldered his way across and planted himself firmly in front of her, shielding her with his body. 'You all right?' he asked grimly as more newsmen swept by and there was another explosion of lights.

'I think so,' she replied. 'What a madhouse. I've never even heard of this bloke they're trying to photograph.'

'Neither have I,' said Mark. He stared about over the heads of the crowd, obviously ill at ease, and then suddenly turned back to her and smiled.

Pippa's heart lifted. 'Thank you,' she said gratefully and slipped her hand into his.

Tom's voice suddenly rang out across the crowd. 'Chuck! Cherilee! Over here!'

'Oh Gohd!' came an answering female shriek. 'Tom!'

As if Cherilee's cry had been a signal, the actor disappeared off at a run towards the exit, hotly pursued by a gaggle of shrieking girls, and the newsmen, having got their photographs, evaporated as suddenly as they had come. Then, in the wake of them all – like an after shock after the devastation of the initial quake – came the Gibbons.

Pippa heard, rather than saw, their approach at first. 'Oh, it's so nice to see you!' shrilled Cherilee's voice. The next moment Pippa found herself enveloped in a suffocating hug that almost winded her, while a pair of lipsticky lips were planted on her cheek in a smacking kiss.

'How do you do,' she replied feebly.

Cherilee laughed. 'Oh my. Don't you look wonderful!' She stood back and surveyed Pippa's outfit – the one Jack had chosen. 'My Go-hd, is that Armani? Oh, I just love Armani!' Then she seized Pippa's arm. '*We have got to shop.*'

Her husband came up behind and slipped an arm round his wife's shoulders. 'Now, Cherilee,' he chuckled indulgently, 'just give the poor girl a chance to draw breath. She's looking stunned, what with the photographers an' all.' He appeared to think that the barrage of newsmen had been for them, and he turned and winked at Tom. 'That was quite a welcome you organised there, son!'

'Oh,' said Tom, 'yes.'

'Oh, Chuck!' Cherilee said. 'You just slay me – and I don't mean in the Spirit!' She gave a ringing peal of laughter, flinging her hands up in the air. 'Don't be such an ol' stick-in-the-mud an' try an' spoil our fun. Pipakins and I are gonna get along just fine. We girls like this kinda thing.'

Pippa winced at the transformation to her name, and took a step back. She felt as if a twenty-foot wave had swept over her, but when she looked at Cherilee more closely, she discovered she was tiny, only about five foot two, and there was an air of almost porcelain, doll-like fragility about her. What Cherilee lacked in stature, however, she more than made up for in presence. She had, Pippa noted, extremely large breasts and her hair was an amazing platinum blonde, bouffant and heavily curled, like some kind of sugar spun helmet. She was wearing an extremely tight, shocking pink suit that emphasised her ample curves and left very little to the imagination.

Pippa blinked as a feeling of rather distasteful unreality swept over her. Cherilee, Jack had said, was the Stateside doyenne of Christian womanhood, emulated by millions striving to fulfil the Biblical ideal. The embodiment, he had further insisted, of the joyous affirmation that womanhood, by virtue of the benign lordship of her husband, was redeemed. A frozen expression settled on Pippa's face as she remembered this, together with Jack's assertion that, properly handled, she herself would in time become a similar figure in Britain. No, she thought, shuddering, absolutely not.

She transferred her stunned gaze to the stocky, thickset man standing grinning at Cherilee's side. He seemed slightly more restrained but still, to Pippa's rather prim eyes, he glittered like an over-decorated Christmas tree. He was about five inches taller than his wife, rotund and well-scrubbed, with twinkling eyes that seemed to look piercingly out on a world that he found immense fun. Pippa was not sure she liked him. She felt awed after all that she had heard about his ministry, but to her eyes there was something self-satisfied and almost unctuous about him. He seemed oily, and she felt instinctively that he was not to be trusted. His suit was very obviously expensive, and his shoes looked Italian, but what struck her most was that he seemed to be hung with jewellery. There was no other way of describing it. On his wrist glittered a heavy, very shiny, gold Rolex watch, while on his cuffs sparkled large, equally shiny, gold cuff links, with a big 'C' embossed on either side. On the third finger of his right hand was a heavy signet ring – again gold, and on his tie sat a narrow clip, in the centre of which sparkled

201

a huge solitaire diamond that glittered and winked annoyingly in the fluorescent light.

'Hello,' she said, feeling even more confused.

'Oh Go-hd,' said Cherilee again, 'she's so English. And to think she's won all that money!' Then she turned from Pippa and flung herself over Mark. 'I just know you're the husband!'

It was a mistake. There was an awkward silence as Mark froze, and then he smiled stiffly and held out his hand, pushing Cherilee firmly away.

Tom looked disgusted, and to cover the moment ushered forward Meredith Galender who had travelled with the Gibbons and was now standing quietly behind. In the flurry of introductions, Mark recollected himself. 'Glad you could come over,' he managed, shaking the American's hand, but at the same time he stole a quick glance at Cherilee's hair and involuntarily shuddered.

All the way into London Pippa found herself staring, first at Cherilee sitting in the back beside her, then at Chuck in front. On the way to the car Tom had whispered to her, 'Great, aren't they?'

She had smiled weakly and replied, 'They're not quite what I expected.'

'No,' he had agreed, 'that's what's so marvellous about them. They're so totally unexpected. So normal!'

Normal was not quite the way she would have described them, but Tom had looked so pleased with himself that she had not had the heart to disagree.

Now, sitting in the back of the car and staring at the Gibbons, she could not help but remember all the tales she had heard about the powerful ministries they exercised. Not for the first time it occurred to her that, if so many people spoke so highly of them, there must be something about them that she was blind to – and that probably said more about her own spiritual state than theirs. In a trice, all the guilt that she had been so determinedly pushing away flooded back, and she found herself staring at Chuck's back apprehensively. How long, she wondered, before she was unmasked by one of those dreadful words of knowledge he was so famous for?

They crawled slowly through the heavy London traffic. Chuck kept up a steady monologue about how excited he was, and how he was convinced God was moving in power. He seemed hardly to notice Mark's lack of response. And then, as they at last turned into the Brompton Road, Cherilee let out a shriek – she seemed to do a lot of that. 'Oh Gohd!' came her now familiar ringing tones. 'Will you jus' look at that! Oh Chuck, baby, it's you.' The car again slid to a halt in the traffic and, as if on cue, they all four turned and stared. There, gazing down from the intersection of the huge cross on the hoarding above them, beamed Chuck's grinning face. The pile of broken wheelchairs and crutches from which the cross rose looked like some kind of metal Calvary.

'Oh, Chuck . . . ba-by.' Cherilee sounded awed. 'Chuck away your crutches – that's jus' so powerful!'

'Yeah,' agreed her husband. 'An' I look pretty good, don't I?' He gave a loud chuckle and, reaching over, gripped Mark's knee. 'Son, we're on the way. Let's take Great Britain for the Lawd!'

At the Dorchester, however, a problem awaited them. Cherilee expressed herself enchanted with everything. The foyer she said was just dinky, and the elevator boy adorable. But as they emerged on to the seventh floor, they found Jack waiting by the lift doors, looking worried. As soon as they appeared, he drew Tom aside and they had a hasty muttered conference. Then Tom looked up and called distractedly, 'Mark, come over here, will you? I think you ought to hear this.'

Whatever it was, Mark went white and Tom threw up his hands in exasperation.

'What's up?' asked Chuck as they came back. 'Problems?'

Tom frowned. 'A small one,' he admitted. Then he stopped, staring at Mark and biting his lip.

'Well, heck! Don't keep it to yourself,' exploded Chuck. 'Tell all of us, and then we'll see what we can do. There's nothing Satan likes more than a bit of fear!'

Pippa saw Mark swallow, and then Tom said, 'Actually, we're having a bit of negative feedback about the posters.'

There was a moment's silence, and then Cherilee said, 'Gee, I think that's good, isn't it? We're obviously hittin' where it hurts, and Satan don't like that.'

'Hushup, Cherilee,' said Chuck. He stared first at Tom, and then at Mark. 'Exactly what *is* the problem?'

This time it was Mark who answered. 'Apparently we're having protests from disabled groups, because they feel they're being devalued as human beings uniquely gifted in the sight of God. And we're having objections from evangelical groups, because they feel the emphasis is on you rather than on God, and they say that's blasphemous. Also they say they're not happy with the theological overtones implied by all the emphasis on miracles. We've also had protests over what people are labelling our prosperity gospel mentality. In particular, one group maintains that you, Chuck, regularly ask for money with the promise that if people give, God will give them far more. And they say that that's contrary to the Gospel.'

There was a moment's stunned silence. They all looked expectantly at Chuck. 'But, son,' he said at last, staring at Mark as if the objections were coming directly from him, 'it says in the Bible that if you serve Gohd an' are pleasin' to him, then he'll bless you, an' that means materially. An' Cherilee an' I are livin' proof of that. You folks over here maybe need to see the truth of that for yourselves.'

'Yeah,' chipped in Cherilee. 'Gohd wants us to be happy. He wants us to be rich.'

Mark looked at her. 'But people are complaining,' he said evenly, 'that your wealth is at the expense of others' poverty.'

'Then let them come an' see the miracles!'

'That's another thing, Chuck,' said Tom apologetically. 'Some people are saying your rallies are emotionally manipulative, and that there aren't any miracles at all. Apparently, the Christian Medical Association are calling for scientifically verifiable proof, and the press have got on to it and are demanding to be allowed free access to all our meetings.'

Chuck went purple. 'This,' he said in thundering tones, his voice managing to boom down the long, thickly carpeted corridor, 'is the work of the Devil! And we must resist it!'

Mark looked unhappy. As he was opening his mouth to respond, Meredith Galender cleared his throat and stepped forward. 'The Lord warned me of this,' he announced, his voice ringing eerily through the quiet that suddenly fell. 'We are in a spiritual battle for the soul of this land. The forces of darkness are gathering because the time of redemption draws near.' He swung round and slowly raised his hands into the air, palms upwards, fingers outstretched. 'We must fear not,' he cried loudly, 'but be still. The battle belongs to the Lord and he will defend us. He claims this land as his own. Only trust and fear not, and we shall see his glory shine!'

There was perhaps five seconds' absolute silence, and then Cherilee, the first to recover, said, 'Oh Meredith, that's jus' so beautiful. Ah know the Lawd won't let us down!'

'Bless you, sister,' said Meredith, his hands falling.

Chuck beamed round at them all, his expression radiant. 'Praise the Lord,' he said throbbingly. 'Jus' praise the Lord!'

In spite of herself, Pippa felt oddly stirred. There had been something so intense and so real in Meredith's outburst, which had been delivered with such absolute conviction, that she had found herself, entirely against her better judgement, believing him instinctively. She could easily see how he had earned a reputation as a prophet. As she stood there, his words resonated through her: 'The forces of darkness are gathering because the time of redemption draws near. The battle belongs to the Lord!' She felt it was somehow a promise to them all. But the next instant her mood of quiet assurance was shattered by her husband's sniff.

'Yes, well,' he said drily, 'that may well be right, but I don't see how it answers the immediate problem of how to respond to the combined demands that we immediately take down all the posters.'

His words fell like ice, and Pippa saw Chuck blink and then frown. 'Son,' he said, 'away with doubt! I shall write an open letter and meet with any critics who may wish to talk to me personally. We have nothing to hide, an' we have nothing of which to be ashamed.'

# Chapter Twenty-one

The Communications Officer for the diocese, the Reverend Tony Burrows, received a phone call. 'Would the Bishop care to make a comment?' inquired a voice. 'This rally at Wembley with the Reverend Chuck Gibbons *is* being spearheaded by a priest from his diocese, isn't it? But I understand there's some question over the validity of the Reverend Gibbons's ordination. There have been suggestions that he bought his theological title and that he's untrained. Is this true? Does the Church of England endorse this kind of thing these days? And how does the Bishop feel about all these protests from disabled groups?'

The Reverend Burrows, who was all too well aware of the controversy, swallowed nervously. 'The Bishop wishes it to be understood,' he began carefully, 'that in the current climate of controversy, and until matters have been more satisfactorily arranged, the diocese entirely dissociates itself from this initiative.'

There was a derisory snort from the other end. 'I'll bet it does, given what's happened, but it's a bit late for all that, isn't it? This priest, Mark Casaubon, is an Anglican vicar, isn't he? The fact that the money behind all this is coming from his wife's lottery win doesn't alter the fact that he's under the Bishop's authority, does it? So exactly how does the Bishop feel about the Reverend Gibbons? And again, how does he respond to all the protests there have been?'

The Communications Officer shuddered. He had had enough of this. 'Look, sunshine,' he hissed, 'why don't you just push off? Take your nasty little innuendos and shove them . . .' And he proceeded to outline in graphic detail exactly where he considered would be most appropriate.

Tony Burrows had been in ministry for all of five years, following on an extremely promising career in advertising. He was generally thought to be rather good at his job, and was well used to having to hush up scandals with the media, but never in all the time that he had been with Bishop Bob had he ever come across anything so completely uncontainable as this present situation. Each time he quashed a rumour in one place, another sprang up somewhere else. Mark Casaubon was a renegade, and having all that money at his disposal made it almost impossible to keep him reined in.

'Well, that's very interesting,' said his caller agreeably. 'Thank you.'

Something in the tone made the Reverend Burrows check. 'Exactly who am I speaking to?' he asked.

There was a silence, and then the voice said, 'Radio Brecon actually. You're on air.'

'Oh, shit,' said the Reverend Burrows. He hung up.

The Bishop heard the broadcast. He was driving with his chaplain to an engagement to open a new hostel for the young homeless on the outskirts of the diocese, and happened to have the radio on in the car. What he heard made him almost drive into a tree, an accident that was forestalled only by the chaplain's grabbing the wheel at the last moment, and jerking them drunkenly back on to the road.

'That bloody Casaubon is going to bring disaster on us all!' exclaimed the Bishop furiously, pulling sharply into a layby. Shaking with rage, he reached out for his mobile and punched in the number for his unfortunate Communications Officer. 'Tony,' he bellowed, 'what the hell do you think you're playing at?'

'Ah, Bishop,' said Tony Burrows weakly, 'it's you.'

'Of course it's me,' shouted the Bishop. 'What's going on? What on earth possessed you to give that interview just now?'

The Reverend Burrows decided, for once, to take refuge in the truth. 'I didn't realise it was on air,' he said lamely. 'There have been so many of those calls over the last few days.'

'And is that how you normally respond to people?' inquired the Bishop.

'No, of course not. I just felt I couldn't take any more. None of them ever believe what I say. It was just unfortunate, that's all.'

'Very,' agreed the Bishop. In the confines of the car, he clenched and unclenched his right fist. 'What's all this stuff about Chuck Gibbons having bought his title, anyway?' he demanded, controlling his rage with an immense effort of will. 'Do we know anything about this?'

'No, Bishop,' said the Communications Officer in a small voice.

'Why not?' rasped out the Bishop. And then, growing impatient, he barked, 'No, don't bother to give me any more of your feeble excuses. I'm not at all surprised we don't know, but find out. And fix up a meeting for me as soon as possible with this Gibbons character and the Chalice team. We can't have any more of this going on. This rally has got to be stopped. I will not have that charlatan using my diocese to create mayhem.'

Two days later Pippa drove Daffyd to London to meet Chuck.

208

For all the doubts she had had at first, beneath the ostentation and razzamatazz that surrounded the American there was, she now felt, a man of unshakeable and abiding faith. Certainly, the way he had handled the crisis at the Dorchester had impressed her. Even if, in real terms, it had done little to ease the situation. That had been left to Mark and Tom, who had both had to stay on in London to try and deal with the protests and complaints that were pouring in.

Upsetting as all the growing opposition was, much to her surprise, Pippa found that she did not feel worried. Cherilee had said that whenever the Lord was at work there was bound to be opposition and that the best thing both she and Pippa could do was simply to support their menfolk in this their hour of need. And, rather uncharacteristically, Pippa had taken her at her word, and so felt not the slightest qualm as she drove back with Daffyd.

Indeed, she was feeling rather hopeful on all counts this morning. Elaine had rung just before they left to tell her she had spoken with Roseanne on the phone. After her near hysteria of the last few days, her manner had seemed strangely calm. The girl had not yet found any trace of Sebastian, she reported, but still she had the oddest feeling that her son was all right. She said she felt God had told her so.

They drove at a snail's pace through the early morning traffic into the West End. Pippa, taking in the bundled, cardboard-covered forms still huddled untidily up against the doorways, found herself praying devoutly that Elaine was right. Her friend, she felt, could not take much more.

As they nosed their way into the car park, at long last, she determinedly pushed away these thoughts and focused her attention instead on Daffyd.

'Come on,' she said gently, taking in the obtuse set of his jaw and twitching fingers. 'You've come this far – why not try and have a bit of faith?'

'Huh,' he rejoined. He seemed unimpressed, but obediently undid the seat belt and clambered out. All his resistance seemed to have gone.

Pippa discovered the seventh floor of the Dorchester had undergone a transformation while she had been away. Several of the rooms had taken on the quality of a large and bustling office, teeming with young men and women with scrubbed faces and shining eyes, and there were tracts pinned up all along the walls: 'Jesus loves you! The battle belongs to the Lord! Go out with joy!' After the first half-dozen she got bored reading them.

She found Mark in one of the outer offices, perched on the edge of a desk and looking worried as he scrutinised a long fax. 'How's it going?' she asked, going up to him and slipping a hand on his knee. Ever since the Gibbons' arrival, and what she had perceived then as a faint thawing in Mark's mood, she had been making a determined effort.

If he was conscious of it, he gave no sign. He pulled a face. 'Not sure,' he replied briefly. Then he drew her to one side and lowered his voice. 'The posters are still up at the moment – you'll have seen them as you came in – but I don't know for how much longer. And we've had to stop the flyer distribution. Apparently there were a couple of nasty incidents around an Underground exit last night and one of our distributors got hurt.' He sighed. 'Everyone still wants to go ahead with Wembley – or at least Chuck and Tom do, though to be honest I believe we should have a rethink.' His shoulders slumped. 'That's not the bad news though. The worst thing is that the Evangelical Fellowship have now come out openly against us. They say they want a meeting and that they don't want to be associated with us any more. And Bishop Bob is on the warpath. He's due here in about an hour to meet us all. Heaven knows what's going to happen.'

Despite her optimism, Pippa felt shocked. She looked into his pinched face with concern. He looked tired and strained, as if somewhere, deep inside, all hope had been quenched. She wondered how much that was her fault. A flicker of fear begin to uncoil in her stomach. 'Don't worry,' she said, the words sounding trite even to her own ears, 'it'll be all right, I'm sure.'

He gave the ghost of a smile. 'I wish I had your faith,' he said heavily. But then he shook himself, as if trying to make a physical effort to concentrate on something other than his own problems, and looked up towards the door where Daffyd was still standing, fidgeting uneasily. 'You've brought him then,' he remarked.

'Yes,' said Pippa, following his gaze. 'I had a terrible job getting him here. He said it was stupid, and that his Voice knew.'

'I'm surprised you managed it, in that case.'

'He didn't seem particularly frightened, like the way he was with us. He just said it was all a load of rubbish, and he didn't think it was going to work. In fact, I'd have said he was bored more than anything else – except he's still so nervy about everything.'

They stood for a second in silence, both staring at the boy.

'You don't give up, do you, Pippa?' Mark said with a weak smile 'I think he's going to be OK, if only because you're going to drag him through despite himself.' And as he stared down at her, something at the back of his eyes seemed to ignite, a tiny little flame. 'Pippa . . .'

The door to the bedroom beyond was flung open and Chuck erupted into the room, with Tom close on his heels. 'I don't care,' he was shouting. 'They're wrong. They don't see miracles because they don't believe. We've got to stand out against them.'

'Yes,' agreed Tom, almost skipping in his efforts to keep up, 'but we need to work *with* these people. We can't simply . . .' and then he registered Pippa and Daffyd and stopped. 'Hello,' he said, surprised. 'I didn't know you were here.'

Pippa took her courage in both hands. She was unnerved at seeing Chuck so obviously angry, but it occurred to her that if she did not act now, she would not be able to persuade Daffyd to come with her again, and she had expended so much effort in getting him this far, she was unwilling to see it all go to waste. Daffyd's response, however, did not seem propitious. He had flinched as Chuck stormed in, and now gave every impression of trying to climb into the nearest wall. 'Yes,' she said firmly, grabbing his hand to prevent his escape. She turned and looked Chuck straight in the eye. 'I've brought someone along I'd like you to see.'

A shadow of annoyance crossed the evangelist's face. 'Pip, honey,' he began patiently, 'can't you see we're a bit busy here? Why don't you bring this young man back later and we'll—'

'No,' said Pippa. It took all her nerve because she could see how irritated Chuck was becoming. 'Please, he needs to see you now. It won't take long.'

She was unexpectedly helped by Mark, who suddenly stepped forward and said quietly, 'I think you should see him, Chuck. This young man says he was brought to Pippa by God. He's got an addiction problem, and he wants to be free. We've all tried to help and failed, so Pippa would like you to pray with him.'

Chuck stared at him. 'I see,' he said slowly. 'You should have said.' He turned and faced Daffyd, who squirmed and cringed back, trying desperately to withdraw his hand from Pippa's restraining grip.

'No, Daffyd,' she said commandingly. 'You promised.'

A look of complete and utter misery swept over Daffyd's face. 'I don't like it here,' he complained.

Chuck came forward till he was standing only some three feet away and peered into Daffyd's eyes. He was a short man, but in that moment he seemed much larger. 'Son,' he said, his voice throbbing with power, 'I discern a spirit of fear over you. Come into the bedroom with me and we'll cast it out.'

'I'm only coming if she comes too,' brought out Daffyd, suddenly clinging as desperately to Pippa as a moment before he had fought to break free.

'Fine,' said Chuck soothingly. 'We'll all go in, only let's get out of this office.' He nodded to Mark and Tom, and obediently they all trooped behind him into the bedroom beyond. 'Cherilee, honey,' said Chuck as they came in, 'give us a moment, will you?'

Cherilee, sitting doing her nails on the bed, gave a quick glance at them, registered immediately what was going on, and smiled.

211

'Hi, Pip,' she said, rising to her feet. And then to her husband, 'Sure thing, honey. Just let me know when you're through.' She disappeared through the door.

'Now come and stand over here by the window,' said Chuck. 'What's your name, son?'

Mark and Tom pushed Daffyd forward. He went unwillingly, still clinging to Pippa's hand, so that she found herself standing in line behind him, facing Chuck.

'Daffyd,' whispered Daffyd.

'What's that?'

'Daffyd,' said Pippa.

'David?' repeated Chuck.

'No,' said Daffyd. 'Daffyd.'

Chuck obviously decided to dispense with the name. 'OK, son,' he said, 'just tell me what's wrong.'

Daffyd seemed unable to speak, so Pippa briefly explained the problem, relating how Daffyd had found his way to them, and his belief in the promise that had been made.

'That's mighty interesting,' said Chuck when she had finished. He frowned. 'Son, Jesus can help you.'

'I know that,' Daffyd managed to whisper.

'That's great,' said Chuck encouragingly. 'So all we've got to do is ask him.' And then, without warning, he launched into a loud and powerful prayer that thundered through the room as if it was a shout for admission at the very gates of heaven itself.

They all jumped, and Daffyd screamed. Chuck seized him in a vice-like grip and clapped the palm of his hand to his forehead. 'I abjure you,' he bellowed, 'in the name of Jesus, to come out.' And then he gave Daffyd a violent shove, so that he stumbled back and fell into Pippa, who in turn lost her footing.

Mark and Tom leapt forward and linked arms under Daffyd's shoulders, catching him. Pippa scrambled free and then, very gently, Mark and Tom lowered Daffyd to the floor.

Chuck beamed. 'Praise the Lord,' he said with satisfaction, standing back.

Daffyd appeared stunned. He sat up, and gingerly rubbed his head. 'It's not gone,' he announced.

'Yes it has, son,' said Chuck firmly. 'You just don't realise it yet.'

'No,' protested Daffyd.

'Yes,' said Chuck. He turned away as if the matter was settled. 'Now, about this Bishop guy . . .' He made a move towards the door.

'Hang on,' said Pippa desperately. 'What about Daffyd? What should we do?'

'Do?' repeated Chuck, pausing in mid-step and turning back. He looked at Daffyd staring owlishly up at him from the carpet. 'Oh, yeah, I see. Well, just give him a few minutes, and he'll be fine. Sign him up for some sort of follow-up, and make sure he gets linked into a fellowship. But don't worry. He's cured.' Then he blew out of the room, signalling Mark and Tom to follow.

'How do you feel, Daffyd?' said Pippa hesitantly.

'I don't know,' said Daffyd lamely. He thought for a bit. 'Weird. My head feels all light. I'm OK, I think . . .' And then suddenly he crumpled and burst into tears.

'You're better,' said Pippa desperately. 'Chuck says it's gone.'

Daffyd stopped crying and stared at the carpet. 'Maybe,' he said. He sounded unconvinced. 'I think I'm going to be sick.'

Out in the office there was more confusion. The Bishop had just arrived, together with his chaplain, the Archdeacon, and the unfortunate Communications Officer. Chuck hastily shrugged on his expensive jacket and ushered them all through to the reception room of his suite.

'Well now,' he said, 'it's real nice to meet with you all.'

The Bishop sniffed. 'I find it hard to return the compliment,' he said icily. 'I am gravely concerned by the controversy your visit seems to have provoked.'

The door opened and Meredith Galender slid into the room.

'Meredith,' said Chuck heartily. 'Welcome. Come and meet Bishop Bob and his little group. Bob,' he went on, turning back to the Bishop, 'I'd like you to meet Meredith Galender, my right-hand man over in the States and a real warrior for the Lord.'

The Bishop did not appear overly impressed, but he duly rose to his feet and held out his hand. When they were all once again seated, he went on, 'My office has been inundated with complaints. It's not simply that the style of your ministry is causing offence, but claims are being made that none of your so-called miracles can be validated.' He looked grim. 'And doubts have also been cast on your personal integrity. It's been alleged that you have never received any formal training, and that your title is fictitious. Also it's been pointed out that the Shining Star Ministries is answerable to no one but yourself and—'

'Whoa!' said Chuck, holding up his hand. 'Now hold on there just a bitty. That's a lot of serious charges you're bringing there, sir. I'd like to know exactly who's making them.'

'They're from reports in the media,' said the Bishop stiffly.

'I see.' Chuck nodded. 'May I ask if there have been any complaints from the people who've been helped?'

The Bishop looked dour. 'Well of course not,' he said sharply,

213

'but the sum of these charges is that people have not been helped! Your claims, Mr Gibbons, are bogus!'

'Is that so?' replied Chuck, dangerously quiet.

The Bishop swallowed. The unwelcome thought occurred to him that it was just possible that he might for once have met his match.

'I'll have you know, son,' Chuck went on – the Bishop noticed that the 'sir' had disappeared – 'that I was out savin' souls when you were still in high school. My trainin' ground was the world, and the Lawd himself gave me my commission. The Lawd heals today just as much as when he walked upon the earth. He heals through me, pawr muddied vessel that I am! But he does. Over the years, we've seen thousands healed and set free of all manner of diseases. Your doctors are perfectly free to try and check whatever they want. There's no trickery involved in the Shining Star Ministries. You're not the first person to try and cast doubt on the work, and you won't be the last, but you've yet to prove it. And while the Lawd goes on workin', and the miracles keep happenin', then Chuck and Cherilee will just keep right on goin'. And I don't care who it offends!'

The Bishop went purple. 'Do I take it,' he grated through clenched teeth, 'that you are unwilling in any way to modify your campaign or the ridiculous claims that have been made by your ministry?'

'Yes, siree, Bob. I guess you could say that about sums it up.'

'Have you any idea,' interjected the Archdeacon, 'of the damage that will be done to people and to their faith if they come along to one of your meetings looking for some kind of healing and nothing happens?'

Chuck turned and looked the Archdeacon up and down, as if he had suddenly become aware of a rather annoying insect. 'I'm sorry,' he said. 'Exactly who are you?'

'Charles Prendergast,' said the Archdeacon stiffly. 'I'm Archdeacon to the diocese. I serve the Bishop.'

'Ah,' said Chuck, 'you look after the money, do you?'

There was something almost insulting in his tone and the Archdeacon flinched, but Chuck ignored him. 'People get healed,' he said, 'in the Lawd's time. If they come to one of my meetin's and nothin' happens, then that's the Lawd's will. People have jus' got to accept that. But they mustn't come with doubtin' hearts because that'll stop the healin', even when God wants to do it!'

Meredith cleared his throat. 'Chuck, I feel the Lord has a word here.'

Chuck blinked. 'Sure, Meredith,' he waved a hand, 'go ahead.'

Meredith Galender looked at the Bishop. For perhaps ten seconds he said absolutely nothing and, under his clear gaze, the Bishop shifted uneasily and looked away. Meredith sighed, a gentle sound, as if he found the world indescribably sad. 'To the shepherds,' he intoned heavily, 'I have seen your ways, says the Lord. I have seen you give stones for bread, and lay on others burdens that you yourselves take not up.' He stared at the Bishop intently. 'I have seen the imaginings of your heart, your desire for glory. You speak peace, but your heart is not peace. You speak love, but your heart is not love. You say truth, but lies breed on your lips.' He paused and then said suddenly, 'Bishop, do you speak to your wife any more?'

The Bishop started as if he had been stung, and then his face flamed. 'What the hell's that got to do with you?' he demanded.

Meredith smiled gently. 'With me, nothing. I think maybe this is between the Lord and you. But I have a feeling the Lord is saying your wife is sick. She's turned away from the path because she's lost and lonely, and you have let her go.'

'Now look here,' blustered the Bishop, 'just because you've heard my wife has had some problems and has had to go into hospital does not justify your—'

'I've heard nothing,' interrupted Meredith smoothly. 'Why should I have done? I've never met you before today. I just feel the Lord is saying that, and he's reaching out to you.'

The Bishop spun round in his seat and glared at Mark. 'This is your doing, Casaubon,' he spat. 'You've been spreading gossip, and this charlatan has picked it up.'

'No, I haven't,' said Mark, indignant. 'I didn't even know your wife had any problems.'

Chuck smiled at the Bishop. 'I feel I should say, son, that Meredith here has a real gift. The Lord gives him insights and prophecies in order to help people.'

'And what prophecy are you going to give me then?' asked the Bishop furiously.

All of them turned and looked expectantly at Meredith. Meredith gazed back at them levelly. 'Yes,' he agreed, 'the Lord does have a word for you. A warning, but I'm not sure you'll hear it.'

'Well, do tell me,' the Bishop said nastily. 'I don't think I can stand the suspense.'

Meredith did not blink. 'Repent,' he said quietly. 'The impulses of your heart are evil. Stop opposing the will of the Lord. Return while there is still time and seek his forgiveness.'

There was a moment's stunned silence. The Archdeacon looked as if he was about to faint and Tony Burrows had gone an interesting shade of green. The Bishop's face was stony and on the arm of the chair his fist clenched. Then he said, 'Thank you for sharing that very interesting opinion with us. I think perhaps there's no more to be said. It's obvious what your position is.' He rose stiffly to

215

his feet, and behind him the Archdeacon, the chaplain and the Communications Officer all jumped smartly up. The Bishop took a step forward but then seemed to change his mind. Pausing, he turned back and glared at Mark. 'I hold you entirely responsible for this, Casaubon,' he said through gritted teeth. 'Don't think you're going to ride this one out. I've got enough dirt on you now to smash you.'

Mark paled. 'What do you mean?'

'I've had the report on the bats from St Saviour's. I know all about their interesting little problem.'

'What?' said Mark. 'What problem? What on earth are you talking about?'

'The heroin problem,' said the Bishop. He had not intended to mention this quite yet. He had been saving it for the visitation, after which he had determined to demand Mark's immediate resignation. But his rage was stronger than all his carefully laid plans.

'I haven't got the faintest idea what you're talking about,' said Mark.

'Well, you will have,' the Bishop assured him. 'I'm initiating a full inquiry.' And with that he stormed out of the room, his little band following hard on his heels.

# Chapter Twenty-two

'Phone them up,' said Enoch.

Stripe swallowed uneasily. 'I don't want to. I'm scared.'

'Who are you more scared of? Them? Or me?'

'Wot do ye mean, man?' Stripe's eyes bulged. 'Wot ye saying?'

'I'm saying if you don't, I could get extremely displeased.'

They were in the living room of the flat. Enoch had brought in the telephone extension from the bedroom, and it now sat on the small Italian coffee table, next to the main phone. Jimmy's brother, Stripe decided, was not very nice. Then he remembered Enoch's promise that Curtis and the rest of the boys were due to arrive the next day, and he shuddered.

Enoch noticed, and smiled.

Stripe glanced unhappily at the photos Enoch had placed beside the phone in front of him. Marty and Ulysses, caught on camera, stared up at him. Enoch had been checking them out, he had explained, so that there would be no mistakes. 'Are these the guys?' he had asked, and Stripe had nodded, too terrified to speak. Calling in Jimmy's family for help, far from setting him free, was only drawing him ever more deeply into the whole sordid affair, and it occurred to him to wonder whether Jimmy, too, had been trying to escape. Stripe found it hard to believe that Jimmy, so feckless and gentle, could ever have had a brother like Enoch. The men who were chasing him were bad, it was true, yet in Enoch there seemed to lurk something infinitely worse; something that was cold and relentless and hard, that would destroy without qualm. He should never have listened to Sam; he should have followed his instincts and simply disappeared.

'Phone them,' repeated Enoch impatiently. He brought his face close up to Stripe, his hot breath moist on his cheek. 'If you don't, you're on your own, and you'll have them as well as me to deal with.'

His fingers trembling, Stripe punched in the numbers, and then placed the handset to his ear. Enoch picked up the extension. Stripe let the phone ring seven times and then said, 'That's it, they're not there.'

'Wait.' Enoch's grip on Stripe's arm was like iron.

There was a click as the phone was picked up, and a voice said, 'Look, Mum, I've already told ye, I'm not comin' 'ome this weekend. I can't. Right?'

Stripe felt sick.

'Speak to him,' hissed Enoch, covering the receiver with his hand.

Stripe's mind went blank. He could think of absolutely nothing to say.

'Mum? Is that you? Who is this?' The voice at the other end was getting annoyed.

'H-hello,' Stripe quavered. 'You left me your number.'

'Wot?' said the voice. 'Who is that?'

'It's me,' said Stripe, stupidly. 'Stripe. You left yer number on me door.' He faltered and shut his eyes. If only this was all over. 'I think we ought to talk,' he said lamely.

'Oh.' Comprehension dawned. ''Ang on a mo.'

Stripe could hear a whispered consultation, then a rustling noise, and then another voice said, 'OK. Let's meet.'

Enoch made a downward sweep with his hand, his face tense.

'No,' said Stripe, swallowing. They had talked about this. 'Not you. I want to meet the guy at the top. I'm not dealin' with you.'

Enoch made a thumbs up sign.

The voice at the other end snorted. 'Who the 'ell do you think you are? You'll deal with us.'

'No,' said Stripe. 'Your boss wants the gear. I've got it. But I wanta deal with the organ grinder, not the monkeys. If he won't meet, that's it. You'll never get it.'

There was a pause, and then, 'OK, we'll see what we can do. We'll 'ave to speak to 'im. Phone us again tomorrow. Same time.' There was a click, and the line went dead.

'There you are,' said Enoch smoothly. 'It wasn't so hard after all, was it?'

Stripe was shaking. 'Wot if they say no?'

Enoch shook his head. 'They won't,' he said. 'They want the gear. We know that. Either that, or they're planning to eliminate you.'

Stripe went pale. 'Yer not serious, man?'

Enoch shrugged. 'You'll be all right. After all, we'll be there too.'

Stripe was not reassured.

Melanie found Stripe desultorily playing the organ in the church hall early the following morning before the group met for daily prayer. She was rather intrigued by him. He had, it was true, made his dislike plain, but Melanie thought she could get round that. 'That sounds nice,' she said, planting herself firmly in front

218

of the keyboard as the last note vibrated and hung shimmering in the air.

Stripe grunted, but did not look up.

'What was it?' she tried again. 'It sounded vaguely familiar.'

'I shouldn't think so,' said Stripe. He flicked off the switch and stood back.

'You don't like me, do you?' said Melanie.

'No,' said Stripe.

'Why not?'

He shrugged. 'I don't like bimbos who pinch other women's blokes.'

'I'm not a bimbo,' said Melanie, stung.

He looked at her. 'Oh no, I forgot. You're the wannabe who turns everything she touches into gold. Sweet.' He turned on his heel and walked to the back of the hall, leaving her standing staring after him with her cheeks on fire.

'Don't take any notice of him,' said Paul, on his way in. 'He makes a virtue of being rude to everyone.'

'Is that how people here see me?' she asked through clenched teeth.

'I really haven't the faintest idea.'

Paul shrugged dismissively. At that moment, he felt he lacked the energy for Melanie. And the days passed and there was still no news of Sebastian, he felt as if his world was falling apart. The totally unexpected loss had caused him to re-evaluate everything and, more than anything else, he discovered that he wanted his family restored. Like Elaine, he had begun to pray. But unlike her he had not yet found any reassurance. He looked grey, with all the unexpressed fear churning round inside him reflected in his face. Without a glance he sank wearily into the nearest chair.

He and Melanie did not normally come for the morning prayer meeting – Melanie, indeed, had no Christian belief at all – but Tom had sent round a memo asking everyone to meet that morning to pray, because of the problems that were emerging over the rally. Paul had come for two reasons. One, because he was frightened and wanted to do anything which might persuade God to help – and Paul felt he had rather a lot of ground to make up here. And two, because he was making a real effort to get back into Elaine's good books. And Melanie had come because Jack was going to lead the group that day, and when he had tumbled out of her bed she had surprised herself by saying that she would come along too. She had not, however, thought that Paul would be there, and she looked at him sourly. Over the past few days he had made not the slightest effort to get in touch with her, and when they had met up in the course of work he had been cold and remote. It had annoyed her, and she had begun to think viciously of ways of paying him back. Jack, she felt, was only the beginning, although there was little point if Paul remained totally unaware of the development.

Jack arrived, along with Oogi and a few of the others. He looked in surprise at Stripe and Paul, and then said, 'Hey, great! Could you play something for us, Stripe, to get us into worship? And then we'll move into prayer.'

Stripe shrugged, and flung himself back down before the keyboard. The rest of the group began to drift in and arrange themselves in a large circle. Melanie sat as far away from Paul as she could possibly get, and then looked across and smiled meaningfully at Jack. He beamed back. He had begun to consider the possibility that, under his influence, Melanie might become a genuine Christian, and that then they might even marry and have kids – and serve the Lord together.

As Stripe began to play, people rose to their feet and sang, many with their eyes shut, arms upraised. They didn't sing any words as such – at least, not ones Melanie could recognise – they just seemed to voice various harmonies. Someone had explained to her that when they did this they were singing in tongues, but Melanie just thought it sounded rather discordant. She looked round and mentally groaned, and then the most awful sick feeling seemed to rise in her stomach and, unable to help herself, she sat down. It was no good, however. The feeling of nausea that had suddenly overwhelmed her rose in her throat. Oh my God, she thought, I'm going to be sick. Mentally cursing the fact that she had had so much wine the night before, she ran from the room and headed for the lavatory. Slamming the door behind her, she threw up noisily and comprehensively into the sink.

By the time she had recovered sufficiently to go back, they had stopped singing and were now deep in prayer. Some were standing, arms upraised, others were sitting, and three people were on their knees. Melanie registered that Pippa had slipped in and joined them. She caught Pippa's glance as she came in and looked away, but Pippa seemed hardly to register her. She appeared troubled. Feeling a small measure of relief – Melanie was rather in awe of Pippa – she crept back to her seat.

On her right, Oogi launched into a long prayer, calling upon the Lord to subdue the forces of darkness mobilised against them, and in particular to fetter the press who seemed to be taking such delight in trying to discredit Chuck and Cherilee. Melanie shut her eyes. Oh God, she thought, this was boring. What on earth had possessed her to come? Jack prayed that the Lord would be even then preparing the ground, and that many would come along to the meetings at Wembley and be touched. He prayed for miracles and mighty signs, and then Pippa prayed for an end to the chaos that seemed to have beset them all. Over in his seat, Stripe raised a hand to his face and shaded his eyes. He felt such inexpressible misery he could have cried. He opened his eyes and looked up, and caught Pippa staring at him. She smiled and, quite spontaneously, his face twisted with grief.

Afterwards she caught up with him as he was leaving the hall. 'Are you all right?' she asked, concerned.

Stripe grunted and looked down. He still liked Pippa. 'Yeah,' he said. 'No . . . I dunno.'

'Do you want to talk about it?' she asked. 'I'm very good at listening.'

He looked at her, his heart wracked. 'I can't,' he brought out. 'I wish I could.'

She stared at him, taken aback by his obvious distress, and then impulsively raised her hand and laid it on his arm. 'Oh Stripe,' she said, 'there's nothing that bad. The Lord can help.'

'I don't think so,' said Stripe bitterly, and with that he turned and walked away.

True to his word, Enoch arrived just before three, when Stripe was due to make the second call. 'OK?' he said, smiling. 'All set?' But his eyes remained hard.

'I guess so,' said Stripe hollowly.

This time the phone was picked up after only two rings. 'Yes?' said a strange, clipped voice.

'It's Stripe,' said Stripe. 'What's the answer?'

'You're on.'

'When?'

'Next week.'

Enoch shook his head.

'Er, no,' said Stripe. 'When then?' he mouthed at Enoch.

Enoch pulled a small notepad towards him on the table and wrote, 'Three days, 8 May.' Stripe goggled. He grabbed the pad and wrote, 'No. That's Wembley!' Enoch nodded. 'Exactly,' he mouthed. 'There'll be people there. They won't expect anything.' Stripe looked at him as if he was mad.

'When do you want to meet then?' said the voice at the other end of the line, irritated.

Stripe swallowed. 'Three days,' he said. 'May the eighth. We've got a gig on at Wembley.' He cringed at the sound of his own voice. 'Tell yer boss I'll meet 'im then.'

Enoch wrote, 'Eleven o'clock, behind the stairwell going up to the players' entrance.'

'Eleven o'clock,' said Stripe obediently. 'Behind the stairwell going up the players' entrance. I'll be waitin'.'

There was a silence and then, 'OK, we'll be there.'

The phone went dead. Enoch exhaled noisily, and then very carefully put down the extension. 'Ye – es,' he said triumphantly. 'We're on the way. We're going to get those bastards!' And then, almost as an afterthought, he added genially, 'Curtis is here, by the way, and the rest of the boys. They arrived this morning. They'd like to meet you.'

Stripe sat there feeling dazed. A shiver of icy prescience ran down his spine. Whatever happened now, he thought, was going to change his life, and it did not feel good.

# Chapter Twenty-three

Roseanne was still in London. She kept in touch with Elaine by phone, but so far she had had nothing to tell her. She had visited all her old haunts but nobody had seen Sebastian. Yesterday the police had informed Elaine that someone had reported seeing a boy who fitted his description near Paddington, so that was where Roseanne was now. She had a kind of forlorn hope that she might just find him there, out on the streets.

Gazing about, wondering which direction to go, the sheer impossibility of her task rose up before her. She had offered to go and look for Sebastian only because Daffyd had insisted that it was his Voice that was causing all the trouble. She had thought it was all so stupid, she could have hit him. His increasingly barmy statements these days made her angry because there seemed to be no practical way she could counter them. In Pippa's homely and rather battered kitchen, finding Sebastian had seemed to her the perfect answer. Find the boy and bring him home, and it would prove to Daffyd once and for all how idiotic – how mad – his nightmarish ideas were. But right now the idea that she had even the faintest chance of finding Sebastian seemed just as mad. As she walked across the station and out towards the open air she found herself praying, 'God, I don't really know if you exist or not, but Daffyd says you do, and Pippa believes in you too . . . so if you really are out there, couldn't you maybe do something to help? I don't mean to trouble you, God, and I guess you must be really busy – if you do exist – but could you please take me to Sebastian? Now?'

'Hi, Roseanne! Hey! It's me!' Footsteps pounded up on the pavement behind her, and a hand caught her arm.

Roseanne whirled round, startled, and found herself gazing into the ashen face of a kid whom she had befriended a few months before and who, like herself and Daffyd, lived on the streets. Matt was maybe five years younger than she was. She did not know his story. She had purposely avoided asking him, but she had come across him one night after he had been beaten up near King's Cross. She had felt sorry for him, and so had taken him back to the squat where she and Daffyd were living then. Like Daffyd, he had a drugs problem but, unlike Daffyd, he was in the early stages, and some fierce spirit of protectiveness in Roseanne had made her try to pull him back. It had been useless. Whether he had a home somewhere or not she did not know, but what was clear was that there was no way he would ever go back.

She looked at him now with concern. He had become a lot thinner since she had last seen him. His hair looked lank and dirty, and his skin had taken on an unhealthy, pasty sheen. He looked ill. 'Are you all right, Matt?' she asked.

He grimaced. 'Could be better, could be worse, I s'pose.' Then he grinned idiotically. 'I'm so pleased to see you. Is Daffyd about too?'

She shook her head. 'No, I'm on me own.'

'Is 'e all right?' The question was far too quick, and from the cloud in his eyes she knew he was asking if Daffyd was still alive.

'Yeah,' she said. ''E's . . .' she had been going to say OK, but realised that would not be true. ''E's staying out of town,' she amended.

Relief flooded Matt's eyes. 'That's good,' he said seriously. 'Probably 'elp 'im that, won't it?'

She gave a wan smile. 'Yeah. I 'ope so.'

They stood for a minute awkwardly, Roseanne's thoughts reverting to the immediate problem of how to find Sebastian.

'Do ye want to come and 'ave a coffee?' Matt asked suddenly. 'I've got dosh – my treat!'

It was on the tip of her tongue to say no, but something restrained her. He looked so pathetically glad to see her, and so battered and fragile. Half an hour would not make any difference, she thought. 'Go on then,' she said. 'But I gotta be quick.'

Matt kept up a steady stream of chatter. He seemed unable to stop, and something in his manner reminded her painfully of Daffyd. 'Matt,' she said at last, growing tired, 'shut up, will you? You're doin' me 'ead in.'

'Sorry,' he said. 'I'm just really pleased to see yer. I've missed you both.'

She smiled. 'Yeah, Matt. I know. Where are yer livin' now then?'

He pulled a face. 'I've got a place in the underpass. It's quite warm, but sometimes, when I'm 'ungry, I go to the shelter wot's opened over at the Bank.'

'I've never 'eard of it,' she said.

He looked down into his plastic cup. 'It's good. It's jus' for kids – you know, no one over twenty. It's OK.'

She nodded, fully aware of the unspoken horror Matt felt for the normal shelters where everyone up to the age of ninety was crowded into dormitories made foul by the fetid smell of smoke and unwashed bodies. But far worse, for him, was the abuse, both physical and sexual, that sometimes went on under cover of dark. The helpers tried to stop it, and anyone found bringing alcohol or drugs on to the premises, or abusing a fellow guest, was summarily turned out. But sometimes, for all their efforts, they failed, and young, pretty boys like Matt had learnt to avoid such places if they could.

Roseanne suddenly stared at him. 'Just kids?' she asked.

'Yeah.' He glanced up, surprised. 'Some church group's started it. There are only thirty places and you 'ave to say grace at night before they feed you. But it's good. They've got a doctor comes in too.'

'Are you goin' there tonight? Could I come wiv yer?'

He looked even more surprised. 'I could do,' he said, 'if you want. D'you fink they'll let you in?'

She shook her head. 'I'm twenty-three, but they're not to know that, are they? I'll say I'm nineteen.'

He grinned. 'Go on. Forty, more like!'

An odd hope was growing in Roseanne's breast. She told herself if was ridiculous, but somehow, the closer it got to night, the more excited she became. The shelter did not open till ten, and so they had to hang around aimlessly on the streets. Matt said he wanted to work, but Rosanne glared at him and said firmly no, not while she was there. Rather sulkily he agreed. But she could see from the bubbling little glow that flickered occasionally in his eyes, how glad he was to have her with him, and she felt maybe that he was even relieved at the embargo she had placed upon him.

Night fell, and the streets became quiet. A bitter wind blew and Matt, in his thin grey top, shivered. Roseanne undid her rucksack and handed him the thick sweater Pippa had given her. He put it on gratefully, and the frozen pallor that had gripped his face receded slightly.

The shelter he took her to was under a Christian bookshop, down a rather seedy side street. They arrived slightly late – ten minutes after the place had been due to open. Matt had been insistent that they should get there in plenty of time. People would be queuing, he said, and if they got there late there might be no spaces left. Roseanne, however, had needed to find a loo, and they had wasted valuable time trying to find a Ladies for her. 'Why don't you just use the pavement?' Matt said in disgust. 'Squat down. No one'll see.' But she had refused.

By the time they reached the shelter the street was empty. 'I told you,' Matt said. 'We're too late. They've gone in now. There won't be any room left. There never is if you get 'ere after they've opened.'

'Let's try,' she urged.

He sighed and pushed back the rickety wooden door.

A narrow flight of stairs led down into darkness and Roseanne stared at it uncertainly. 'Down 'ere?' she asked.

Matt nodded and, repressing a growing sense of unease, Roseanne began to feel her way slowly down. At the bottom she found a door, and beyond she could hear voices and laughter. 'Go on,' said Matt, clattering down behind and giving her a shove. 'Open it.'

Roseanne put out her hand and, very nervously, pushed open the door. Immediately smoke swirled out, and the dull glow of a single sixty-watt bulb trickled feebly on to the grubby staircase. She went in and found herself facing a small wooden counter. Behind it sat a young man. He was laughing, and had some kind of register spread out in front of him, with a cup of coffee at its side. 'Hello,' he said, looking up. 'You're new.' And then, looking beyond her, he caught sight of Matt and grinned. 'Hi,' he said. 'Didn't think we'd see you here tonight.'

'I've brought me sister,' said Matt.

'Really?' said the young man. 'Hi.'

'No,' said Roseanne. 'Joke. We're jus' mates, that's all.'

'Oh,' said the young man, disappointed. 'Never mind. It's nice to see you.'

'Any places, Jake?' asked Matt.

'As it happens, yes. The Lord must be smiling on you tonight!'

'Yeah,' said Matt drily. 'Sure.'

They registered – Matt checking in the small packet of drugs he was carrying and the half bottle of vodka that he dragged out of the back pocket of his trousers – and then went on through into a long narrow room which, at first sight, seemed to be almost bursting with bodies. As Roseanne's eyes adjusted to the dim light, however, she realised that this impression was wrong. There were perhaps twelve young people already there, two who looked hardly into their teens, the rest any age between fifteen and twenty. Looking at them, Roseanne felt indescribably old.

'We're pretty quiet tonight,' remarked the young man, coming in behind them. 'It's the weather, I guess. It's a bit milder. They're staying on the streets.'

Matt grunted and Roseanne peered closely at the faces around her. She had only seen Sebastian once, but she felt sure she would recognise him; besides, Elaine had given her a photograph. But stare as she might, she could see no sign of the boy.

Matt seemed to know almost everyone. Greetings were called out, and she followed him over to a small wooden table pushed up against the long wall, at which a noisy and rather violent card game seemed to be going on. In the opposite corner a small black and white television, with the sound turned off, flickered with some unintelligible film. Roseanne sat down on a rickety chair and watched it idly, while Matt joined in the game. The air felt damp and rank, and glancing at the white painted, brick walls, she saw they were running with wet.

'It's not ideal,' said Jake, following her glance. 'But we're on a shoestring as it is. Not sure how long we're going to be able to stay here, actually. The council are already threatening to close us down unless we can do something about the damp.'

'Where are you from?' asked Roseanne, feeling something was expected of her.

Jake took her response as an invitation to talk and sat down at her side. 'We're a charity,' he said. 'The guy who started us is a clergyman, Father Jackson. He felt the kids from the streets needed somewhere of their own to go. It's his church who owns the bookshop up above. They've been involved with the homeless for years – there's a soup kitchen that operates out of the crypt. But they noticed that far more young kids were turning up, some as young as seven and eight, and they were having a really rough time in with the adults, and so he set up this place for them. It's completely anonymous and there are no strings attached, of course. The kids know they can come here and get help, and that no one'll try and pressurise them into anything they don't want. That's why it works. The only rules we lay down are no drink, no drugs, and everyone's got to respect everyone else.'

Roseanne nodded. She had heard it all before. 'So how do you fit in?' she asked.

He grinned. 'I'm a volunteer, that's all. I'm on my gap year before university. I came to work with the main homeless project about three months ago, and then got drawn into this too. It's good. I do a couple of nights a week here now, and I'm getting to know a lot of the kids. Sam, that's the guy who started it all – Father Jackson – he'll drop by a bit later, just to say hi to everyone.' There was a commotion over by the door at that moment, and they both looked up. 'Ah,' said Jake, 'more clients by the look of it. Excuse me a sec. I'll just go and check them in.'

He rose to his feet and ambled through the smoke to the door. Two minutes later a group of three came in, two boys of about eleven and a girl, her body childishly thin but with heavily made-up, smudged eyes and a sparkly top. 'She's on the game,' said Jake, coming and throwing himself back down beside her. 'She's only thirteen. Bloody awful, isn't it?'

Roseanne nodded, and came to a sudden decision. She fished in her pocket and brought out Sebastian's photo. 'Do you know 'im?' she asked, thrusting it under Jake's nose.

He looked surprised, but he took it and scrutinised it carefully.

'Don't know,' he said at last. 'I might do. There was a kid here a couple of nights back who might have been him, but it's a bit difficult to say.'

'His name's Sebastian,' said Roseanne.

He looked at her and smiled. 'You must know they don't give their real names.' He regarded her a moment longer and then said, 'Why are you looking for him anyway? Is he a brother or something?'

'No,' said Roseanne. 'He's the kid of a friend, that's all. I said I'd keep an eye out for 'im.'

Jake looked at the photo again. 'He looks a nice kid,' he remarked. He stared at the house in the background. 'Looks, from this, like he's got it all.'

'Yeah,' said Roseanne drily. 'Got the world, 'e 'as.'

More kids arrived, but still there was no sign of Sebastian, and after a while Roseanne began to lose hope. Jake had told her that at quarter to twelve they would close the doors and no one else would be allowed in that night. At half past eleven Father Jackson arrived. He was a big, burly clergyman, with a bushy grey beard and twinkling eyes. To Roseanne he looked a bit like Father Christmas. All the kids obviously knew and liked him; his arrival was greeted with good-natured shouts and cheers. He went round everyone in turn, saying a brief hello. When he came to Roseanne he paused, a great beam on his face. 'Hello, someone new.'

'She's looking for someone,' remarked Jake, coming up behind. 'She wondered if we might have seen him.'

'Really?' Father Jackson looked interested. 'Tell me about him. I know most of the kids round here.'

Roseanne again fished out the photo and showed it him. The priest raised it to the dim light and stared at it intently. His huge shadow, flickering on the wall, seemed to dominate the room, giving a peculiar impression, thought Roseanne, of security and peace. He gave a small exclamation. 'Yes,' he said, 'I think I might know this lad. How long's he been gone?'

'A week,' said Roseanne, her heart transferring itself to her mouth. ''E ran away.'

'Did he?' The priest stroked his chin and looked pensive. 'If it's the kid I think it is,' he said slowly, 'he hasn't been here but I came across him yesterday morning.' He glanced up at her suddenly, a peculiar expression on his face. 'He was being beaten up. I chased the sods off. He's a bit of a mess, I'm afraid. I took him to hospital.'

'Wot was 'is name?' asked Roseanne, hardly daring to breathe.

The priest grimaced. 'Now there's a question. He wouldn't give his name. Not to me. Not to anybody. But then he was having difficulty talking. Broken jaw,' he explained, seeing her look.

Rosanne felt her throat grow tight. 'Is he still there, in 'ospital?'

228

The priest nodded. 'I think he's going to be there for quite some time,' he said gently. He hesitated and then went on, 'It wasn't just his jaw, you see. He was assaulted too.'

She went pale. 'Wot do you mean?'

'I mean what you're thinking. He's in a bad way.'

She stared at him, torn, and then said, 'Will you take me to him? Tomorrow? I'll know if it's 'im.'

He regarded her evenly. 'You say you're a friend?'

'Of 'is mother's.'

He nodded slowly. 'OK,' he said. 'I can't see as it'll do any harm.'

Roseanne could hardly wait for the next day. She veered wildly between elation at having at last found so positive a lead and despair at what Elaine would say if it really did turn out to be Sebastian. She thought, too, of Daffyd, and wondered how he would react to the news. Illogical as it was, she thought that he might well once again blame himself – or at least, his Voice.

True to his word, Father Jackson came for her early the next morning, immediately after the Daily Office. Roseanne said goodbye to Matt, promising to meet up with him later in the day back at Paddington, and they set off.

The walk to the hospital seemed to go on for ever, and then at long last they turned into a narrow side street and ahead Roseanne saw a huge, rather dirty Victorian building. Its main entrance, up a flight of shallow steps, was set behind forbidding wrought-iron gates, over which were inscribed the words, 'St Anthony's Hospital for the Poor'.

In spite of her eagerness to get there, Roseanne shuddered. She hated such places. She loathed the smell of antiseptic and sickness, and the feeling she always had when she went in that she would never be able to get away. Father Jackson, however, seemed totally at ease. Without pause, he pushed in through the large mahogany doors and led the way to the ancient lift, and up to the fifth floor.

The lift doors slid back to reveal a long grey corridor. On the right, Roseanne's eyes took in an immense cartoon figure of Mickey Mouse stuck to the wall. Underneath, in brightly coloured letters, were the words, 'Welcome! You are in the children's ward.'

'They do try, you see,' said Father Jackson, grimacing.

He led the way down the long central corridor. Roseanne found herself walking past, in turn, Goofy, Donald Duck and Minnie. In side wards she saw children, some lying or sitting up in bed, one or two tumbling noisily round the floor. 'Morning, morning!' called Father Jackson. 'How are we all today? Causing mayhem as usual?'

At the end, he stopped outside a closed door. He turned to her.

229

'Whatever you do,' he said gently, 'whether you recognise him or not, don't look shocked. This laddie's OK, all right? Just remember that.'

She nodded dumbly and he gave a quick nod and pushed open the door. The room was dark. Roseanne followed the big priest in, feeling very small. He went straight over to the bed and leant over and, with great tenderness, Roseanne heard him say, 'I've brought someone to see you, laddie. Someone who thinks she might know you.' And then he stepped back and to the side, and Roseanne went nervously forward.

She looked down into a chalky-white, rather frightened little face that seemed to be covered with wires and bandages. She recognised Sebastian instantly. His corn-coloured hair was spread on the pillow, and his huge, deep blue eyes stared at her unblinkingly. 'Hello, Seb,' she said, unable to think of anything else to say. 'It's Roseanne, Daffyd's friend.'

His eyes seemed hardly to register her and the priest whispered, 'He's still very shocked, but keep talking, he knows we're here. He'll react in a minute.'

'Yer mum asked me to come,' babbled Roseanne, unable to think of anything else to say. 'She asked me to try and find you, she—'

'Hush a minute,' Father Jackson commanded softly.

Roseanne stared, and the next second she saw Sebastian's eyes fill with tears. 'Mummy,' he whispered. 'Mummy.' He could hardly move his jaw and the words were indistinct, but they both knew immediately what he was trying to say.

'Bingo,' said Father Jackson softly. 'This *is* your boy.'

'I've found 'im,' Roseanne said baldly into the phone.

Elaine gave a shriek. 'Oh, thank God!' she exclaimed.

Without giving herself time to think, Roseanne said, ''E's not too well. 'E's 'ad an accident.'

'What do you mean? How bad?'

Up against the wall of the phone box, Roseanne shut her eyes and cringed. ''E's all right,' she said. 'It looks worse than it is.'

'Oh my God,' said Elaine. 'What's happened?'

''E's broken 'is jaw.' Roseanne checked, wondering if it was wise to tell Elaine the rest. But then she knew she had to. ''E was assaulted,' she said.

'You mean he was beaten up.' Elaine sounded stricken.

'Yeah,' said Roseanne, 'but more.'

'What more?'

Roseanne shut her eyes. 'Some bastard tried to rape 'im.'

There was appalled silence at the other end of the line. Then

Elaine's voice came back, close to breaking. 'Tried? Did they succeed?'

'No,' said Roseanne, 'not quite. Someone stopped them. A priest.' She discovered she was crying.

'Oh God,' said Elaine. She, too, began to cry. 'Where is he?' she asked, as soon as she could speak.

Roseanne told her.

'Stay with him,' said Elaine. 'Please. I'll be up straight away.'

Elaine asked Pippa to collect Harry from school, left a message for Paul at the office, and then caught the next train. She rushed, but even so it was a good three hours before she arrived at the hospital. Following Roseanne's directions, she went straight to the children's ward and found Father Jackson standing waiting for her at the desk. 'I checked the time of your train,' he explained. 'I'm the one who found your son. He's all right. You've got to believe me. But I wanted to prepare you.' He laid a hand on her arm. 'He looks a bit of a mess, but it's mostly superficial. However, he is in shock, and you might find that a bit difficult too.'

Elaine gazed at him with strained eyes. 'Are you sure he's all right?' she asked.

He bit his lip. 'He'll mend,' he said tersely. 'With a bit of care. What he most wants at the moment is you.'

'Oh God, why on earth did all this have to happen?' whispered Elaine. Father Jackson did not answer, and after a second she said, 'Take me to him, please.'

He led her down to the side ward and pushed open the door, standing back to let her in. Staring past him, Elaine saw Roseanne sitting beside her son's bed, holding his hand, talking softly. She looked up as Elaine came in, and immediately rose to her feet, relief flooding her face. 'It's your mum, Seb,' she said. 'I told you she was coming.'

Elaine crossed quickly to the bed. 'Hello, darling,' she said. She stared down at his open, fixed eyes, and then stopped, horrified. Her boy, her beautiful boy, lay there, broken and crushed. She felt a great, swelling tide of grief.

'Talk to him,' said Father Jackson softly, coming up behind. 'It's what he needs.'

She controlled herself and, with a tremendous effort, reached out her hand and very gently laid it on his head. 'Oh Sebastian,' she breathed, crying in spite of herself, 'it's all right, darling, I'm here now. Mummy's here.'

Paul arrived at seven. He had been out of the office, he explained. He had only just got back. He had come as soon as he heard. When they took him in to see Sebastian, he stared at his son's still figure, aghast, and then said, 'Who did it? How did it happen? Have they got the swine?'

In the intervening hours, since Elaine had first arrived, Sebastian had been slowly coming out of his shock. Her voice, calling his name, had been like a lifeline, pulling him back through the swirling, impenetrable mists that had seemed to be strangling his mind. He had been unable to get back before, incapable of finding the way, though he had tried. But her voice, calling out to him with such anguish, had reached out to him through the eddying dark, giving his mind a direction. And slowly, languidly, the effort almost too much, he had begun to grope his way back. Now he turned his head, perhaps a centimetre, and mouthed, 'Hello, Dad.'

'Who did this to you?' repeated Paul brokenly. He sank down on the chair beside the bed, tears welling in his eyes, and reached out his hand. But Sebastian looked so frail and broken, Paul was frightened to touch him in case it caused pain, and so he sprawled awkwardly instead, with his hand just hovering above his son's head as if in some kind of forlorn blessing.

From the other side of the bed, Elaine stared at him woodenly. She had come to a lot of decisions over the past few hours, sitting there beside Sebastian's bed, trying to keep up a steady stream of inane conversation, because the nurse had said it was helping. She had very little idea what she had said, she had just prattled, about school, about Harry, about a horse if he wanted one, holidays, and through it all she had kept repeating his name and telling him how much she loved him – and that she was so very pleased to have him back. After the first hour her brain had seemed almost to become detached, and while she still kept up the steady stream of words, she had thought. She remembered how she had promised God she would do anything, if only he would bring Sebastian safely back; she had even promised that she would take back Paul, and as she sat beside Sebastian's bed, it had seemed to her that God was saying, 'Fine, we'll try it then. Sebastian for Paul.'

Watching her husband now, she knew she was committed. She had to keep her side of the bargain. Sebastian moved his eyes slightly, looking to her for help, and in answer she gave his hand a reassuring squeeze. Then she looked across at Paul and said levelly, 'Sebastian's still having a lot of difficulty talking, but as far as we can make out he's been staying in a back street hotel. Some young men there saw the money he was carrying and jumped him when he went out to get something to eat.'

'The bastards!' said Paul. 'Any witnesses?'

Elaine forced herself to give a tight-lipped smile. 'Father Jackson, the priest who found him – saved him. He happened to come into the

232

street as the attack was going on. He chased the men off, and then he brought Sebastian here. And no, they haven't been caught.'

Paul sank his head on to his arms and burst into noisy tears. 'Thank God you're all right,' he said. 'Thank God.' After a moment he raised his head and said, 'I'm so sorry, Sebastian.' Then he looked at Elaine and repeated, 'I'm so very, very sorry. This is all my fault.'

Repressing the desire to agree, Elaine glanced down, incapable of responding, and after a moment he reached across Sebastian and very carefully took her hand. 'Will you forgive me?' he said. 'Please?'

Elaine felt Sebastian's eyes pinned on her, gazing at her imploringly. 'Mum,' he whispered, 'please . . .'

She swallowed. 'Yes,' she said. 'I suppose so. I usually do.' Immediately Paul gave her hand a squeeze, and then leant across and kissed Sebastian. Looking at them both, Elaine felt as if a nail had been driven into the lid of her coffin – but a promise was a promise, after all. God had honoured his part of the deal. Now it was her turn to honour hers.

# Chapter Twenty-four

Pippa was almost at her wit's end. She had duly collected Harry from school, as requested by Elaine, but had found it no easy task to impart to him the good news while withholding the bad. 'But why isn't Mum coming back tonight?' the boy kept asking. 'And why isn't she bringing Seb back?'

'He's had a slight accident,' Pippa found herself saying. But as Elaine had positively forbidden her to tell Harry exactly what had happened, she was at a loss to know how to justify both his parents' absence. So in the end she said lamely, 'They've just decided to stay over in Town, that's all.' But seeing his face freeze, and knowing intuitively what was passing through his mind, she immediately hated herself for the lie.

Harry sulked. He had long felt that Sebastian was the favourite, and clearly now imagined he was being excluded. After half an hour of belligerent silence, he shouted at Pippa, 'Everyone treats me like I'm a baby, but I'm not!'

They were in the kitchen at the rectory and Daffyd, whom Pippa had ordered to slice tomatoes in a half-hearted effort to get him to do something other than stare morosely at the floor, said unhelpfully, 'Well, stop acting like one then.' He had been in a bizarre mood ever since she had brought him back from the disastrous meeting with Chuck Gibbons. She had tried talking to him but, ever since Chuck had announced he was healed, he had withdrawn across some emotional divide which she was powerless to cross. It was patently obvious to everyone, not least himself, that he was not healed, but she could not even begin to guess at what was going on inside his head. Notwithstanding, he had been making a real effort to reduce his methadone usage but it was still, Pippa felt, horrifically high, and she knew that he was finding the whole process of withdrawal painfully hard.

She had tried talking about it all to Chuck a couple of days ago on the phone, when Daffyd was safely out of the way, but he had simply said, 'He lacks faith,' and sounded bored. Pippa had been annoyed. She felt the evangelist was somehow blaming Daffyd for his failure to be healed, and the full injustice hit her like a blow between the eyes. But there seemed to be nothing she could do, and so she had been reduced to watching Daffyd in apprehensive bafflement, overcome with fear in case he took it into his head, in despair, just to wander off. Without quite knowing why, she felt that that would be a disaster and so, unable to think of anything else to do, she had set herself the task of keeping him here, at least till Roseanne returned, and trying somehow to draw him back into normal life. That, however, was a separate problem from the one before her at this moment.

In the state Harry was in, Daffyd's comment was unwise. The boy eyed him malevolently and then said, 'Why don't you just shut up and mind your own business?'

'Your whingeing *is* my business,' said Daffyd, hardly bothering to raise his head. 'It's getting on my nerves.'

'I don't care about your sodding nerves!' shouted Harry.

There was a moment's shocked silence. Pippa, taken aback by his language, glared at him and his face flamed. Daffyd yawned and sliced another tomato.

'Well, I don't care,' said Harry defiantly, raising his chin. 'We're all supposed to be so careful what we say to him.' He indicated Daffyd with a jerk of his head. 'He's all you and Mum ever seem to worry about these days. But it's his own fault he's in the mess he's in.'

At that Daffyd sprang up, waving the kitchen knife wildly in the air, a piece of tomato skin hanging from the blade. 'Shove it!' he said violently. 'You haven't a clue what you're talking about! It's not my fault, and I don't *want* to be in the state I'm in at all.'

Harry, had he but known it, had achieved a minor miracle, he had got Daffyd to react, but Pippa was in no mood to appreciate the fact. 'Oh, be quiet, both of you!' she snapped, snatching the knife from Daffyd's hand before he inadvertently inflicted any damage. 'You're like a pair of five-year-olds, both of you! You're driving me mad arguing like this. Do something useful for a change. Here!' She grabbed a tea towel and stuffed it into Harry's shocked hands – he had never seen Pippa like this before. 'You dry the dishwasher.' Then she turned to Daffyd, who was now looking slightly puzzled, and glared at him in exasperation. 'Oh, set the table,' she said. 'And I don't want to hear another word out of either of you!'

Then she turned on her heel and marched quickly out of the room. She felt that if she remained, she would explode. She just wanted five minutes on her own. Halfway up the stairs, however, the phone rang, and she was forced to come back down to answer it. She paused outside the kitchen door, but all was now reassuringly quiet. 'Hello,' she said wearily, picking up the handset.

'Pippa,' said Mark's voice, 'I just thought I'd phone and let you know how things are going. I'm afraid I'm not going to be able to get back tonight, after all. This row just seems to be going on and on.' He sounded indescribably tired. 'We've had another meeting with the Evangelical Fellowship. They're still not happy. They're refusing to back Wembley, and they're still demanding that we take the posters down, even though the whole thing's only a couple of days away now.'

'Oh dear,' said Pippa, digesting all this. 'What does Chuck say?'

'He called them a load of small-minded bigots. He said they were stumbling blocks to the work of the Gospel, and he called on them to repent.'

'Good Lord,' said Pippa. 'And did they?'

'No,' he said heavily. 'And who can blame them? Honestly, I'm just not sure about any of this any more.'

'What does Tom say?'

'Tom?' Mark gave a small phut of annoyance. 'I think he's gone stark staring mad. He says it's high time the establishment got jolted out of its complacency and that it's better if they don't support us. He and Chuck egg each other on.'

'You don't agree with them then?' she asked.

There was a small silence and then, in a rush, Mark said, 'No, if you want to know the truth, not really. I want to serve the Gospel of course, but it's been absolute chaos since we started all this, and I agree with a lot of the criticism that's being made. There *is* too much emphasis on money and "signs". I know Chuck's got this huge ministry over in the States, and maybe the Americans really are different from us, but at heart I just don't believe God operates in the way Chuck and Tom say he does. It doesn't feel right, any of it. It's all too glitzy somehow.'

A swirling vortex of dark uncertainty opened at Pippa's feet. 'Has it all been wrong then?' she asked in a small voice, thinking of Chalice, and of Daffyd – and of the excitement, despite all the problems.

'I don't know,' said Mark brokenly. 'I just feel it's all gone pear-shaped. I don't know what to believe any more.'

'I love you,' she said after a moment.

'Do you?' He sounded surprised.

'Yes,' she said. 'We just seem to have lost sight of each other recently.'

He thought for a while. 'We have rather, haven't we?' Then he said, 'I'll be back soon. I promise . . . We'll find each other again then.'

It was not, however, Mark who returned later that same night, but Tom. At a quarter past twelve, after both Harry and Daffyd had gone to bed, his car scrunched up the gravel and came to a noisy halt outside the front door. Pippa, who had been about to go to bed herself, ran down the stairs, expecting to find her husband standing there. When she saw it was Tom, she stopped, disconcerted. 'Hello,' she said, with difficulty masking the disappointment in her voice. 'I didn't expect to see you here tonight.'

Tom, in the act of shrugging off his coat, turned and looked up, his face glowing. 'No,' he said, 'I thought I'd surprise you.'

Tom had had a terrific day. The latest news from small churches and fellowships up and down the country was that they could, so far, expect about three thousand people to turn up at Wembley on the first day. It was not enough to cover their expenses but Chuck said the numbers were good, and the general feeling among the Shining Star team was that this number might well quadruple over the next couple of days. The adverse publicity seemed to be having a good effect. Then in the afternoon they had met the Evangelical Fellowship, as Mark had already told Pippa, and Tom had felt that for the first time in his life he had talked to them from a position of real power. It had felt good and, like Chuck, he had dismissed their criticisms and objections as a species of sour grapes. They did not, Tom thought, enjoy playing second fiddle to their more obviously successful American cousins. And when they had left with their tails between their legs a mere half-hour later, he had felt a warm glow of triumph. It was then that he had begun to think of Pippa.

Mark, Tom felt, had been behaving rather oddly all day. For some time now Tom had felt his fellow director had not been entering into quite the same spirit of excitement that had caught up the rest of them; but following on the meeting with the EF that afternoon, Mark had seemed positively depressed. Staring at his stiff back as they filed slowly out afterwards, Tom had felt a sudden flood of annoyance. Why did Mark always have to be so gloomy? He should have been called Jeremiah! And hot on the heels of a flood of intense dislike, he had thought about Pippa, and how Mark did not deserve to have her as his wife.

Later, when he had overheard Mark talking to Chuck about a meeting he was trying to set up for later that evening with some senior Anglican clergy who, he said, might well be more favourably disposed towards them, Tom had realised that Mark would yet again be staying in Town. Tom could not imagine why Mark was bothering. It seemed to him irrelevant whether the Anglicans supported them or not, and Mark's constant insistence that they ought to have the backing of the established Church only fuelled his annoyance. He decided to make the most of the opportunity and go and see Pippa himself. He told himself it was all entirely innocent, that he was simply concerned about her, alone as she was with Daffyd. But the mounting tide of excitement that grew in his stomach the closer he got gave the lie to that particular piece of self-deception.

When she appeared on the stairs, Pippa had on her nightdress.

The light from the landing behind showed up the clear silhouette of her body underneath and Tom blinked, a hot flame of desire suddenly spurting up inside him. 'I just wanted to know you were all right,' he said thickly.

Pippa suddenly felt uncomfortable before his hungry gaze and tried to pull her nightdress more tightly round her. 'I'm fine, thank you,' she said, rather too quickly. 'No need to worry at all. I spoke to Mark earlier.' At the mention of his rival, Tom's face darkened and, seeing it, she said apprehensively, 'Have you had anything to eat? Are you all right?'

'Oh yes, I ate earlier,' said Tom. 'I'm fine.'

'Good,' she said. And for some reason she did not want to define, Pippa again felt a wave of embarrassment. 'Well, I'll go to bed then,' she said quickly. 'Night.' And, suddenly frightened what would happen if she remained, she turned and fled up the stairs, leaving him standing in the hall.

Tom gazed after her, perplexed. His first thought was to rush up the stairs two at a time and seize her before she could get to the top, but then, remembering Daffyd's presence in the house, he restrained himself. The last thing Pippa would want, he reminded himself, was a possible witness to any torrid declarations of love. But all the same, he was taken aback. He had rather thought, on the way down, that Pippa would fall into his arms, and was slightly puzzled that she had not. After all, he told himself, they had come to an understanding. She loved him, just as he loved her. He was sure of it. So why had she run off like that?

Tom slowly climbed the stairs after her and went to his room. It occurred to him that Pippa was maybe embarrassed out of prudishness, and that what she really wanted deep down was for him to go after her now and assert his rights. He undressed, had a shower, and slowly put on his pyjamas. Then he stood and looked at himself full-length in the mirror. His reflection stared owlishly back and, after a second, he picked up his dressing gown and with determination put it on. Then, swallowing nervously, he crossed the room and very quietly opened the bedroom door.

The landing beyond was dark, and a deep quiet lay over the house. From downstairs Tom could hear the loud ticking of the hall clock, and somewhere outside an owl hooted and then fell silent. He stood listening, and then very carefully stepped out onto the landing and pulled the door to behind him. Immediately he was plunged into inky dark, but a pale light filtering through the skylight overhead showed him the outline of the stairs and landing, and the doors leading off. Cautiously, feeling the way with his hands, he began to inch his way forwards, seeking the handle of Pippa's door. He knew roughly where it was, he had looked carefully before he shut the bedroom door and blocked off the light. For all his care, however, his foot banged into a bookcase and he swore softly – he had forgotten it was there. Then the next moment his fingertips located what he was seeking and, hardly daring to breathe, he pulled the handle gently down and went in.

Pale moonlight streamed through the open curtains into the darkened room beyond and, lying on the bed, Tom could just make out the faint outline of Pippa's body beneath the duvet. She was huddled up as if cold, and she looked so small and fragile, he thought, in that great bed, that he longed just to reach out and touch her, to fold her in his arms.

Breathing heavily now, his heart thundering so loudly he thought she would hear, he moved cautiously forward, terrified of falling over something. 'Pippa,' he whispered. 'It's me.' Silently he padded towards the bed, his bare feet making no sound on the carpet. At the edge he paused. 'Shall I get in?' he whispered again.

No reply.

Certain she knew he was there and was as nervously excited as he was, Tom raised the edge of the duvet and very carefully slipped underneath. It felt warm inside the bed and he stretched, for a second luxuriating in the delicious sense of her body only inches away from the tips of his fingers. Then, very carefully, he reached over and slipped an arm across her waist.

Pippa, who had slipped into a deep sleep almost the instant her head touched the pillow, was awakened seconds later by a body twisting heavily across her, and a cold foot lodging in the bend of her right knee. She started violently and jerked instantly awake, and the next second a mouth locked on to hers. As she swam groggily up into consciousness, her first thought was that it was Mark, and she obligingly slipped an arm round the body's neck. But then she remembered that he had said he would not be able to get back that night, and she went rigid as terror flooded over her.

Tom, in ecstasy at her response, moaned softly and slid his hand under her nightdress and up her naked thigh.

As she came fully awake, outrage swept over Pippa. If this was not Mark, who was it? In the eerie darkness of the room, silent now apart from the heavy breathing of the man straddled across her, she decided that someone had broken in and that she was being raped. With a furious exclamation, she jerked upwards, thrusting the man heavily aside, and gave a loud scream. At the same moment, she turned and flicked on the bedside light.

Tom stared up at her from the pillow. 'Good God!' said Pippa. 'You!'

Tom attempted a weak smile.

'What on earth do you think you're doing?' exclaimed Pippa furiously.

'I . . . I . . .' began Tom.

In one deft movement, Pippa sprang out of bed. 'Get out!' she said angrily, shaking with rage.

Tom blinked, and decided that the world had gone mad. He was not quite sure he recognised this harridan who was staring at him with such obvious rage. Sheepishly he slid out the other side, and they faced each other across the rumpled bed. 'I thought you wanted me to come,' he said foolishly.

'Wanted you to come?' almost shrieked Pippa, her eyes wild. 'You're mad! Why on earth should I have wanted you to come? I'm married to Mark.'

'But . . . we talked,' said Tom. 'The other night. You said you loved me.'

'No I didn't!' said Pippa, even more outraged. 'You're the one who talked about love, not me. I love Mark.'

There was a small sound from out on the landing, and the next second the door was pushed timidly open and a frightened little face peered in. 'I heard noises,' said Harry pathetically. 'I was afraid.'

They both turned and stared at him. Pippa was the first to recover. 'Oh, Harry,' she said. 'It's all right. It's nothing.' He looked as if he was about to burst into tears and she ran across the room and quickly gathered him in her arms. 'It's all right,' she repeated, 'honestly.'

But Harry had had enough of trying to be brave and pretending he did not care. All his upset of the last few weeks came flooding out, and he burst into noisy sobs. 'I was dreaming,' he hiccuped, 'and then I heard a noise . . . I heard you scream and I thought someone had broken in and . . .' He looked up suddenly and stared at Tom. 'What's Tom doing here?' he asked, puzzled. 'I thought he was in London.'

For one frozen second Pippa and Tom stared at each other, embarrassed, and then Tom went scarlet.

'Yes,' began Pippa, madly dredging her mind for some kind of excuse that might begin to make sense, 'that's right . . . he was.' She trailed off and stared at Tom desperately, willing him to say something to help.

Tom looked petrified and then swallowed. 'That's right,' he said lamely, and then dried up.

In disgust Pippa prompted, 'You heard something too, didn't you, Tom?'

'Did I?' Tom looked dazed, and then he started. 'Oh yes . . . a noise. Something strange.' Harry was staring at him in total bewilderment, and in a rush Tom went on, 'Terrible racket. I just thought I'd come and tell Pippa, and then go downstairs and take a look.'

Harry frowned. None of this made sense. 'But you were arguing. And Pippa screamed.' He looked round wildly as a thought suddenly occurred to him. 'There's not someone here in the room, is there?'

'No, of course not.' Tom looked flustered. 'It's just that, well, Pippa wasn't too keen on my going downstairs, that's all.'

Pippa gave him a look filled with contempt. 'That's right,' she agreed, through clenched teeth. 'Very silly really. Feeble.' Tom wilted. 'Off you go, Tom, and have a look.'

He gave her a look of anguish, and then bent obediently down and picked up his dressing gown from where he had let it drop on the floor. 'Right,' he mumbled. 'OK, I'll do that.'

Pippa held on to Harry as Tom walked past them and then went noisily down the stairs. 'Don't worry,' she said, feeling the boy beginning to shiver, though whether with fright or cold she wasn't sure, 'there's no one there, I'm positive. Would you like a hot drink?'

Harry looked up at her, his face crumpled like a distressed monkey, and attempted a watery smile. 'Yes please,' he whispered. 'I'm a bit scared to go back to bed.'

Pippa bit her lip and nodded. She thought longingly of her own bed and oblivion. She felt she wanted to blot from her mind all that had just happened with Tom. She wanted never, ever, to have to think of it again. A part of her whispered that Mark need never know, but another part, rather more loudly, said that would be a pretence that would be impossible to maintain.

Staring down at Harry's tear-stained face and hearing Tom clomping around down below, Pippa realised that she felt grubby. For some reason, inexplicable even to herself, she felt that all that had just taken place was her fault. She might not, in so many words, have asked Tom to come to her room but clearly she had done something to encourage him. Maybe, deep down, she had wanted him to make love to her. The thought made her freeze with horror.

# Chapter Twenty-five

Bishop Bob felt distinctly odd. It was really most strange, but ever since his appalling meeting with Chuck Gibbons and the Chalice team, he had been unable to settle. He did not feel exactly ill, or under undue strain, it was simply that he was restless. He would pick up documents needing urgent attention, for instance, and immediately his thoughts would begin to wander. He would sit down to prepare an address – he had long since ceased to give sermons – and it was as if some quixotic spirit simply whisked his mind away and he found himself mentally wandering through fantastic fields of Elysian escape.

The Bishop began to think a lot about life and the direction his profession had taken him in, and each time he saw his wife now (which was as rarely as he could make it), Meredith Galender's words echoed in his brain like an accusation. And then the Bishop began to feel angry. It was not his fault, he told himself. He was not answerable for the breakdowns she kept having nor her depression. He had married far too young. Elizabeth was unstable, totally unfitted for the rigours of being a clergyman's wife, let alone the fit helpmeet of a bishop. And with her woolly ideas on the New Age and reincarnation, and her selfish insistence on always being the focus of attention, he felt increasingly that she seemed to bear a grudge, not just against himself but against the whole world.

He could not be blamed for the way she acted, he raged. On the contrary, throughout his career she had been a liability, and he a model of saintly virtue. Whenever she had complained, or come up with the latest hair-brained scheme for realising her true self, he had never criticised. Even when he had disapproved most strongly – and there had been such a lot to disapprove of with Elizabeth – he had maintained his unflinching facade of stoicism and pained acceptance. Yet despite all his solicitous forbearance, the woman was still liable to erupt with that incomprehensible anger that bubbled away inside her and made her so difficult to live with. Really, if he had not talked to her as much as he should, it was only because he feared that if he said anything, he would descend to the same appalling level on which she herself seemed to live, and a vituperative slanging match, he thought self-righteously, would hardly benefit anyone. And then, as he thought a bit more about his wife and her intolerable shortcomings, his thoughts wandered on to Jean.

Jean had been everything Elizabeth was not. She was a teacher, he remembered. He had met her years before, when he was still a lowly parish priest and she a junior housemistress at the girls' public school on the fringes of his parish. They had met when he had gone to the school to lead a confirmation class, and he had been immediately attracted by her bubbly and so-obvious intelligence. She had been a looker too, tall and fair, in marked contrast to Elizabeth who was dumpy and dark. The Bishop had married at a time when he had been in love with the idea of being a priest, and had thought personal attachment did not overly matter. He had even thought it might be a sin, that God should not have a rival to his affection. Elizabeth, however, had clearly not felt that. From the beginning she had been possessive and demanding, and had even gone so far as to try and dictate to him what he himself ought to believe. In the long, dreary years of thinly disguised marital disharmony, the Bishop had felt his God slip further and further away, to leave only an empty space at the centre of his life. Elizabeth by then had discovered transcendental meditation, and into his life had crept a slowly spreading spiritual wasteland fuelled by disillusion and disgust. It was into this wasteland that Jean had come.

It had started off innocently enough. They had simply been friends. But as the weeks progressed, he had found himself looking forward to his visits to the school more and more, and then one day she had confided to him that she was seeking an appointment elsewhere, frustrated by the lack of opportunity where she was. He had been so devastated at the thought of this one tiny light passing from his by then wholly bleak life that he had begged her to stay and suddenly, he was not quite sure how, their innocent friendship had erupted into passionate love.

When he looked back on that time now, he thought it was almost as if he had been possessed. Jean had been like a fever in his blood but for the first time in his life he had been alive, so alive. The affair had ended as abruptly as it had begun, when she had announced she was pregnant. The Bishop had never been able to have children with Elizabeth – he had even pondered early on if this was not in fact the root of their problems together – but when Jean told him her news, he was appalled. In a moment of blinding clarity that had cut through all the self-deception, he had seen instantly that if she had the child, he would be ruined. He would no longer be able to continue as a priest. As his love for God had receded and dwindled, his love for the role had grown in proportion. He found himself presented with a choice: Jean and the baby, or the priesthood and Elizabeth. He had chosen the latter, and Jean had had an abortion and shortly afterwards moved away.

They had lost contact after that – at least, to be strictly accurate, he had chosen not to maintain contact, terrified by the swirling ripples of scandal that had threatened to overturn his life. Instead he had devoted himself to being a good priest, and fourteen years on had received his hard-won reward – his first bishopric. Throughout all that time Elizabeth had been like a troublesome thorn; he had even wondered once or twice if she had suspected what had happened, but she had never said anything, and over the years he had come increasingly to look on her as a kind of hair shirt, a deserved penance for the sin he had committed, but which, if patiently borne, would win him grace.

Now, however, before Meredith Galender's accusation, he paradoxically found his thoughts turning with longing once again towards Jean, and a deep antipathy for his wife grew and grew. He began to wonder what Jean was doing now, where she was, whether she had ever married, and if, like him, she ever regretted what they had lost together. And as he thought about her, the floodgates opened, and he began to wonder whether his determined pursuit of a bishop's mitre had been quite so worthwhile after all. There was only one thing to do: he found himself phoning the school she had moved on to and asking whether she still worked there. The secretary he spoke to was regretful. She remembered Jean Baynham vaguely, but she had only stayed a couple of years and had then moved to another appointment, down in the West Country, she thought.

The Bishop was tense with dread. Might she by any chance have the address? he inquired. It was really very important. The secretary searched the records and, when that yielded nothing, racked her brains, and finally came up with a name. The Lofthouse School, she said pensively; she thought that might be it – or maybe Barnhouse, she was not sure.

Frustrated, and his disappointment making him even more desperate to talk to her, the Bishop rang off and dialled directory inquiries. Two names, he said, the Lofthouse School and the Barnhouse School. He did not know the nearest towns, but he thought they were in the counties of Cornwall or Devon. The Bishop chewed his nails in an agony of apprehension while the operator searched. Finally, the voice at the other end said yes, there was a Lofthouse School, near Bridgwater in Devon. Trembling, the Bishop thanked her and took the number, and then, having buzzed his secretary and told her he was not to be disturbed for at least the next twenty minutes, he phoned it straightaway.

'Miss Baynham?' said the cool voice that answered him. 'Yes, she's still here, but she's in class at the moment. Would you like to leave a message or a number? I'll get her to phone you when she's free.'

The Bishop swallowed. 'Please tell her,' he said, his throat dry, 'that it's the Bishop of Carbery here, and that I'd be most grateful if she could phone me on a matter of some urgency.'

Immediately the voice became all cloying concern. 'Ah, Bishop, of course. I'll get her to phone you immediately. You should have said.'

Repelled, he left his number and hung up, but it was a good three hours before Jean finally rang back, and when she spoke, her voice sounded distant and steely. 'What do you want?' she asked.

'I just wanted to see you,' said the Bishop.

'Why?'

He swallowed, he had known this was going to be hard, but now it had come to it he found it almost impossible to know how to go on. 'There are things we need to sort out,' he brought out at last.

'No there aren't,' she said flatly. 'We sorted it all out twenty years ago.'

'Twenty years? Was it really twenty years ago?'

Her voice was scornful. 'I can give you the exact date if you want.'

'No.' He tried again. 'Jean, I'm so very, very sorry. I never wanted things to happen the way they did.'

'You got your bishopric though, didn't you?'

In the confines of his office, the Bishop hung his head. 'Some things,' he said quietly, 'are really not worth the struggle, only we don't realise till it's too late.' He paused, and then said, 'I'd really like to see you . . . try and put things right.'

When she answered he could tell she was crying. 'I don't think you can put things right now,' she said. 'It's all too late. He's gone.'

'He?' queried the Bishop.

'The baby,' she snivelled. 'He was a little boy. I've always called him Daffyd.'

He fell silent before the pain in her voice and then, the words so painful they almost hurt, he said hoarsely, 'Please, let's meet.'

She was silent for what felt like an age, so long in fact that the Bishop wondered if she was still there, but then, just as he was going to say her name, she said, 'Very well. Maybe you're right. Maybe we do need to meet. Lay everything to rest and all that.'

'Of course,' he said quickly. 'Give me your address. I'll come down.' They arranged to meet in four days' time.

Stripe was also facing a difficult meeting. He had learnt through Pippa that Sebastian was lying injured in hospital and so the next time he was up in London, rehearsing with Cherilee and the Shining

246

Star singers for Wembley, he took time off to go and see him. He discovered him sitting up in bed but still looking very forlorn, and with his jaw still wired. 'Wot's the other bloke look like then?' said Stripe, throwing himself down in the seat beside the bed.

Sebastian smiled weakly and tried to mouth something amusing in return, but Elaine cut in tartly, 'That's not really very funny in the circumstances.'

'No,' said Stripe ruefully. 'I guess not. Sorry.'

Elaine glared, but then relented. She had aged over the last week. Her skin looked papery and thin, and her eyes were sunken like two bruised pools above the stark line of her jaw. She had been crying a lot, although she had been careful not to show any distress in front of Sebastian, and she felt somehow as if her world had been tarnished at the core. She was overwhelmingly grateful to God for having restored Sebastian to them but she felt there was no longer any certainty about anything any more, and a deep, nameless fear seemed to have wound itself round her entrails and taken up residence somewhere in the inner recesses of her soul.

Staring at her, Stripe dimly realised all of this and dropped his eyes, suddenly ashamed. 'I really am sorry,' he mumbled.

Elaine attempted a smile. 'It was good of you to come,' she said. 'Sebastian's glad, I know.' She rose heavily to her feet. 'Look, why don't you two have a chat, and I'll go and get a coffee or something.'

They watched her walk from the room.

As soon as he had recovered himself sufficiently to take charge, Paul had said he wanted Sebastian moved into a private ward, but the doctors had said that there was not really any need because there was no way they were going to put Sebastian in with the other children, given what had happened to him, and the facilities would be exactly the same wherever he was. Paul, certain that private treatment would be better, had prepared to argue, but then Elaine had surprised everyone by saying she agreed with the doctors and that she thought it was all a waste of money, especially as she was hoping Sebastian would not be here very long. Paul, who still felt that with his wife at least he was treading on glass, had given way. 'No use arguing with her, old chap,' he had said conspiratorially to Sebastian, giving him a wink, and Sebastian, still teetering with fragile apprehension in case the crisis between his parents should not be past, had looked at him gratefully.

Paul, indeed, was being very solicitous to everyone, trying very hard, as he saw it, to make amends. Elaine watched him cynically but she did not waver in her new-won resolve, and when Paul booked them into a hotel close by, she allowed him to share her bed.

'So, are you all right?' said Stripe as soon as she had gone.

Sebastian very carefully nodded. 'I will be,' he mouthed.

'Wot 'appened?' asked Stripe.

Haltingly, Sebastian told him. All about getting the train, and booking into the small hotel and the peculiar men who had been friendly at first but who would not leave him alone. They had seemed always to be high on something, he said, and when he went out one night they followed him and then . . . Sebastian could not go on, and Stripe grimaced and looked away. He found it difficult to face Sebastian. He could not help but remember how Sebastian had come to him in such distress and how he had simply not had the time. And that made him think about Enoch and the deal that he had made with him, and about Jimmy. He had tried so hard to push the horror of his last memories of Jimmy from his mind, but confronted by Sebastian they all came flooding back in a spurt of anguish that was pure pain. As Stripe listened to Sebastian's stumbling and pain-filled voice, it occurred to him that lying behind both tragedies lurked the evil of drugs. From what Sebastian was saying, it sounded as if his attackers had been junkies.

Stripe shook himself and told Sebastian all about the preparations for Wembley, and the huge row that had broken out in the media. He told him about Cherilee and Chuck as well, and made Sebastian laugh with his cruel parody of the way Cherilee sang. When he left, he promised to come back again soon.

Wembley, and the meeting with Jimmy's killers, was only hours away now. Enoch seemed excited by it all, and as taut as an overstrung bow. But the closer it got, the more Stripe began to feel he could not go through with it. It was not simply that he was scared – he was terrified – and it was not that Enoch was planning cold-bloodedly to murder his brother's assassins – Stripe could not care less what happened to those gentlemen. What really got to him was the sight of boys like Daffyd and Sebastian. They were the net result of what he had inadvertently become involved with, and he felt a great and overwhelming shame.

In the few weeks that he had been with Chalice, he had discovered that his past life felt dirty, and his heart ached for the ruined lives of the young kids he saw all around him. He found himself thinking increasingly about God, and he began to puzzle over why people like Mark and Pippa should have given their lives to what was to him such an insubstantial dream.

As he trailed out of the hospital, his mind still filled with the image of Sebastian lying all wired up on the bed, he came to a decision. Whatever the cost, and even if it involved his own imprisonment, he could no longer be a party to what Enoch and Curtis were planning. In the cold light of day Stripe found himself for the first time really looking at what he had been instrumental

248

in setting up, and his heart plummeted. He realised that even if Enoch and Curtis successfully eliminated Jimmy's killers – as he had very little doubt they would – it was unlikely to bring an end to the business. Whatever the Jamaicans said to the contrary, Stripe suspected they would simply seize the opportunity to set up their own ring. There would be more Daffyds and more Roseannes – and more Sebastians who, though not a user himself, was undeniably a victim of the same vicious circle of filth.

Almost unconsciously, Stripe's footsteps took him in the direction of the police station he had seen earlier. In the pocket of his leather jacket he had the half-eaten packet of heroin that he had retrieved with Enoch from the church. Some impulse that morning had made him put it there, whether fear that his flat would be broken into while he was absent and the gear stolen, or an already half-formed plan to do precisely what he now had in mind, he could not tell; but whatever the reason, it was there.

Not giving himself time to think, he ran up the three steps that led into the police station and banged noisily on the bell for attention.

'Yes?' said a young constable, coming wearily to the desk. 'What do you want?'

Stripe took a deep breath. 'I want to see someone from your drugs squad,' he said. 'I've got some information they might be interested in.'

The constable took in his dreadlocks and frayed shirt and became instantly more alert. 'Right,' he said. 'Hang on, I'll get someone.'

Half an hour later Stripe was sitting in a small interview room, facing a couple of young detectives across a Formica table that was chipped at the edges. They looked bored. 'So what you got?' said one.

Stripe felt in his jacket pocket and dragged out the gear. 'This,' he said, banging it down heavily on the table.

The two detectives stared at it, and then one said with distaste, 'What is it?' He prodded it gingerly with the pencil he was holding and then said, 'It looks like animal droppings.'

'Not far off,' said Stripe. 'It's a hundred thousand pounds' worth of heroin, only the bats have been at it. Which is why it's such a mess.'

'Blimey,' said the detective. At the mention of bats he withdrew his hand quickly, as if frightened of catching something.

'Do y' want it, or don't you?' said Stripe.

The policemen looked at each other. 'Dunno,' said the younger. 'It looks like a bit of a health hazard.'

'Course it's a bleedin' 'ealth 'azard,' said Stripe. 'It's heroin, man, an' I can give ye names, dates, and a pick-up point. I can give yer the main men behind it.'

'Why?' asked the older detective suspiciously.

Stripe grimaced. He had been waiting for this. 'Well,' he began, 'it's like this, see . . .' He launched into the story of Jimmy and the gang war that had broken out. Then he told them about Enoch and Curtis and the revenge that was planned.

The older policeman gave a low whistle. 'You mean you set this up?' he asked incredulously.

Stripe hung his head. 'Yeah, I suppose I did,' he acknowledged.

Again the policemen looked at each other. 'So why tell us now?' one of them asked.

'Because,' said Stripe, 'I've seen wot it does. I don't want none of it. I never did, but I want it ended now, an' I think this is the only way.'

The older detective nodded slowly. 'You do realise this is dangerous?' he asked.

Stripe gave a hollow laugh. 'Man,' he said, 'you've no idea . . . I jus' can't live like this any more. I don't want anyone else to die.'

After that, events seemed to move with their own momentum. More policemen came in. There was excitement. Stripe discovered the Liverpudlian gang were already under surveillance, but the news of the Jamaican input was obviously new. The heroin was gingerly removed for closer examination and came back forty minutes later rather cleaner. 'You're right,' said a policeman, pushing it laconically towards Stripe across the table, 'it's good stuff, very pure – apart from the bat saliva. How did they get at it?' he added.

Stripe told him, and for a second the room rang with laughter. 'So you mean,' said one of the policemen, wiping his eyes, 'these religious nutters know absolutely nothing about any of this, but they're going to be used as a front for this supposed drop?'

Stripe nodded. He found he did not like his friends in Chalice being referred to as 'religious nutters'. A decision, however, seemed to have been made. A detective chief inspector was called in, and when he, too, had heard all the information, he said, 'OK, we'll go with it.' Then he looked at Stripe and smiled. 'You happy?'

Stripe nodded, although happy, he thought, was not quite the right way to describe what he was feeling just then.

Melanie glared at Paul. 'I tell you I'm pregnant,' she insisted. 'I've done the test.'

Paul looked at her coldly. 'That, my dear,' he said, 'is absolutely impossible.' Melanie stared at him and he went on, 'Eight years ago I had a vasectomy. Every year I have a check-up to make sure it's still good. I had one two weeks ago, after you dropped your last little bombshell, and I assure you there is absolutely no way I could have fathered any child you might be carrying.'

A feeling of cold swept over Melanie. 'You never told me,' she said nervelessly.

'Why should I?'

That stung. 'Didn't it ever occur to you that that little detail might have been important?'

'Why?' Paul was remorseless. He had had enough of Melanie. 'Don't let's delude ourselves, my dear, that what we had was ever going to come to anything. And there was never any harm in double precautions. Or any precautions at all,' he added after a moment. 'It seems you've been a little careless, doesn't it?'

Melanie opened and then shut her mouth, grappling feebly to take command of this new situation. She had known before, as soon as she had worked out dates, that Jack must be the father, but in her resurrected game plan to capture Paul – a far more attractive prospect financially – she had thought she could still claim the child was his.

'Are you quite sure?' she asked feebly.

'Of course I am,' said Paul icily. 'So exactly who is the father? Or don't you know?'

Melanie glared at him, going white. 'I don't think you're in any position to cast stones,' she said nastily.

Equally venomously, Paul said, 'If you're thinking you can still use this to get at me, forget it! I'll simply say you're suffering from delusions if you try and embroil me in this sordid little mess you've got yourself into.' He stood up and came round the desk till he was standing only about eight inches from her and said softly, 'I would advise you, Melanie, totally to erase our relationship from your memory. Don't forget, we have the interesting concern of the Vice Squad in your activities at the moment too. Just one word from me and all that's going to come out.' Melanie blinked and took a step back but Paul was remorseless. 'I would suggest,' he said, 'you get rid of the baby – if you can't get the poor sod who fathered it to acknowledge it – and then look for another job. But whatever you do, I want you out of here.'

'You can't do that,' spat back Melanie, some last remnant of spirit asserting itself. 'That's unfair dismissal. I could take you to a tribunal for that.'

Paul laughed unpleasantly. 'Try it. I think your dirty linen is rather worse than mine.'

Seconds later Melanie left his office, reeling. Her brain was in turmoil. Jack had been good for a bit of temporary relief from Paul but she really did not think she wanted to be saddled with him. She suspected he would be all too pleased to marry her, if he should ever find out what had happened, but at the thought of his trendy piety she shuddered. She could never, she knew, endure a

251

lifetime of sanitised jollity, which was what she felt a future with him would entail. So the only alternatives were either to abort the child and look for another position as soon as possible, or to have it, take a couple of months off, and then find another job – or even start up freelance. Melanie explored the idea of motherhood, and decided she did not like it. She rather felt the demands on her time would be too severe, and besides, she felt so ill it was simply not worth it.

But the thought of taking a break made her check. That did not seem such a bad idea, given all that had happened. She felt she needed time adequately to assess her future. The fact that the Vice Squad was, as Paul had so nastily pointed out, still interested in her was another reason to get away. And then she thought of the Chalice account, and of all that money invested overseas – to which she had access.

She gave an evil smile as a plan began to form in the back of her mind. Why not? she thought to herself. It would be easy. She had joint authority with Paul over the funds; by the time any of them discovered there was anything wrong, she could be long gone, and if she was clever they would never be able to find her. The reverberations for Paul would be appalling.

As she thought of his possible fate, the idea grew in attractiveness. He would almost certainly, she reflected, be sacked immediately for having made her an authorised signatory of the trust, and for allowing her to handle the account without any safeguards. They might even think that he, too, had been a party to fraud. Although of course they would never be able to prove it, she thought regretfully. Yet still, with that kind of slur on his integrity, it was obvious he would never work again. In career terms, Paul would be ruined.

That decided her. Pulling herself up straight and squaring her shoulders, Melanie headed determinedly for her desk. She flicked on the VDU and prepared to call up the markets. As lines and figures flashed rapidly across the screen, she flexed her fingers, an unpleasant smile on her face. She was ready, she thought, to play.

# Chapter Twenty-six

Mark phoned Pippa again. 'Why don't you come up here?' he suggested. 'I don't see any way I'm going to be able to get down there now before the rally starts. It just seems to be problem after problem.'

Pippa felt her blood run cold. 'Er, I'm not sure I can make it,' she temporised.

There was a small silence, and then Mark said disgustedly, 'It's Daffyd, isn't it? Honestly, Pippa, you've got to stop nursemaiding that boy. You're not responsible for him, it's not your problem. You've got to allow him to sort it out himself.'

'I think he is my problem,' she replied icily, and hated herself for it, knowing that she was seizing on Daffyd as an excuse. But although she wanted desperately to see Mark and knew perfectly well that she could leave Daffyd, at least for a day, she felt it was impossible. She still felt overwhelmed with guilt, and a tiny little voice whispered persistently to her that, as soon as she saw her husband again, he would know. The thought that perhaps he ought to know, she pushed resolutely away. If he should find out what Tom had attempted to do, it would rupture their friendship for ever and probably destroy her marriage in the process.

But the biggest problem of all was that she could not get clean. She had almost showered herself away in an attempt to cleanse from her mind the memory of Tom's weight on her body, and of his hand sliding up her skin, but whatever she did, it remained. She simply could not wash away the guilt, and because of that, she felt she could not see Mark. She knew she would have to soon, of course, but she would cross that bridge when she could no longer avoid it. Until then, she would postpone the evil for as long as she could, and so now she said more moderately, 'He's very upset after what happened, and I've got Harry here too, because Elaine still hasn't come back from London.'

Mark breathed heavily. 'Why does everyone always have to come in front of us?' he complained. Then, more softly, he said, 'I need you too.'

Pippa felt as if a knife was being driven into her. 'I know,' she said despairingly, 'and I want so much to come, it's just that . . .'

'Yes,' he said. 'I know.'

She rang off and stared about hauntedly. Daffyd was out in the garden with Harry. An uneasy truce seemed to have settled between them, and just at that moment they were attempting a rather lethargic game of football. Pippa, watching them through the hall window, decided they would be all right for a while, and that she could safely go and seek the solace of the church. She wanted to be there, in that cool building. Perhaps then, in that ancient place, she could find peace, and maybe even summon up the resolution to go and see Mark.

Strangely, she was not overly worried that seeing Mark would of necessity mean she would also see Tom. She felt, after all that had happened, that that particular chapter was closed. He knew exactly what she thought now. He would not bother her again. A part of her felt rather sorry for him, but she discovered also that a hard grain of anger still remained. How dare he treat her like that? Even if he was in love with her, as he maintained, how could he have put her in the position he had, given she was married to Mark? Then the old chestnut that maybe she had led him on resurrected itself, and so she stopped thinking about Tom and thought instead about Mark again.

Her footsteps took her slowly through the graveyard to the church. The early morning sunlight glinted off the tower, and not for the first time she thought what a pity it was that they no longer had any bells. Years before, they had had a full peal, but they had gone long ago and she doubted, even if they were restored, whether they could get the ringers now. So many things, she thought sadly, seemed to have died.

Pushing open the heavy oak door, she almost bumped into Mrs Stibbins, steam-rollering her way out. 'Oh, it's you,' said that lady dismissively. 'I was just checking the flowers were all right for Sunday.'

'And are they?' asked Pippa.

Mrs Stibbins's chest swelled. 'They are now,' she said, puffing herself out angrily. 'I've put them straight. Someone had disarranged them.' She looked at Pippa accusingly. 'There have been some very odd goings-on here over the last few weeks, and none of them good.'

Pippa wilted. 'Well, I wouldn't worry,' she said. 'Mark will be back next week and he'll get things straight.'

'Huh!' said Mrs Stibbins. 'If you ask me, he's been the main cause of it. But not for much longer. The Bishop'll see to that.' And with that sally she sailed on past, leaving Pippa staring after her, troubled.

The dark cloud that Mrs Stibbins represented fell away as Pippa stepped inside the church. The quiet seemed to well up and engulf her, like a surge of welcoming comfort, and she fell into it gratefully, letting all thoughts of Mrs Stibbins and the flowers and the chaos slip away. Here, she thought, was God. She would tell him about what had happened, and ask him if he could maybe help sort them all out.

She began to walk down the aisle, her footsteps echoing on the stone flags, but halfway down the main body of the church she paused, her attention caught by the dark figure of a man sitting hunched over in the shadows. He looked as if he was praying, and she made to move on more quietly, but then it occurred to her that he might be distressed and in need of help, and so she checked again and looked at him more closely. At that moment he looked up, straight at her, and through the gloom she caught the flash of something white. Although she could not make out his face, she could feel his eyes boring into her and she took half a step forward, uncertain what to do. He did not, she thought, appear upset, but it seemed somehow rude now just to walk on.

'Hello,' said the man. 'I was wondering if you would come.'

Curious now in spite of herself, she went forward. 'Hello,' she replied. 'I'm the rector's wife, Pippa Casaubon.' In the same moment she saw that the white that had caught her eye through the gloom was the small, neat inset of a dog collar. 'Oh,' she said surprised, 'you're a priest. I'm sorry, I hadn't realised. Mark's away at the moment.'

'I know,' said the man. Through the shadows she felt him smile, but she still could not make out his face. 'It was really you I wanted to see anyway,' he continued.

'Did you?' she said. 'Why?' And then she remembered the lottery win and sighed. 'Oh, I see.'

'Why don't you sit down?' he said quietly, indicating the pew with his hand.

'All right,' said Pippa resignedly. She assumed he was going to ask her for financial help for some worthy cause.

But the man surprised her. He sat for a while in silence and then said softly, 'Do you want to tell me what's wrong?'

Pippa's head jerked round. 'No,' she said offended, 'I don't.'

The man laughed and then said, 'Let's start again, shall we? You've been asking for help.'

Pippa stared at him. It was maddening. He was sitting at such an angle that she simply could not see his face. She twisted closer and peered into the gloom, and at the same moment such a wave of love seemed to roll out and enfold her that she gasped aloud.

'Tell me,' said the man simply. And to her intense surprise, she did. She poured it all out, keeping nothing back. Her problems with Mark and her desire for a child. The lottery win, Chalice, all the problems between Elaine and Paul, and Tom. As she told him about Tom, all the shame and humiliation that she had been feeling rose up and overwhelmed her, and she began to cry. And all the while she could feel the man's eyes fixed upon her, and sense, although not see, his gentle smile.

'Who are you?' she asked suddenly, breaking off in the middle of a sniff. 'Do I know you? Have we met before?'

Into the silence the man's sigh was like a stream of light – at least, that was the way it felt to Pippa. 'You haven't met me before,' he said, 'but I do know all about you. And I know Mark. Ask him. He'll tell you who I am.'

She digested this. His words seemed so comprehensive that she felt it was somehow rude to ask him anything more, and then suddenly a memory erupted into her mind and temporarily seemed to blot out everything else. 'Oh, there's Daffyd, of course,' she said impulsively. 'I haven't told you about him yet.'

'What about Daffyd?'

'He's in a dreadful mess,' and once again she launched forth on all the problems they had had. 'We've prayed for him,' she concluded, 'just like it says in the Bible, only nothing's happened.'

'Are you so sure?' asked the man mildly.

She thought about this. 'Well, nothing visible,' she amended. 'He seems just as bad as when he first came.'

'When you ask the Lord to heal someone,' the man said consideringly, 'you have first to be right with him yourself, so that you can be a channel, and so that his Spirit can flow through you. And then when you pray, it's not that you wrest something from God that he doesn't want to give – it's not magic. Rather you bring the one who is hurting or in pain to the Lord, and then you pray as the Spirit leads. God himself gives you the words, and you just follow what he says. Healing is an encounter of the one who is hurt with the living God.'

'Are you saying we weren't doing that then?' she asked in a small voice.

'I think you know the answer to that already,' he replied. 'For any great work, there has first to be training, and often God has to break us free of everything on which we've relied up until that point, so that we know his power and rely only on him.'

'I see,' said Pippa. She knew all this, of course, but she felt that she had never understood it before. Another thought occurred to her. 'Someone told me a few weeks back about a woman priest, Antonia something or other,' she said. 'They told me she has a powerful ministry, but Mark and Tom didn't want her to be involved. Do you know her?'

Again she felt the man smile. 'Yes,' he said, 'I know Antonia. She's doing a lot of learning too. You'll meet her one day, I'm sure, and you'll be friends.'

'Should we have asked her to pray for Daffyd?'

At this the man laughed aloud. 'Why are you so keen to take him to everyone else? The Lord brought him here.'

She considered. 'Yes . . . but we haven't helped.'

They sat companionably. Pippa became aware of the sound of birds, an extraordinary singing that seemed suddenly to erupt all around the church. 'Place your chaos into the hands of God,' advised the man softly. 'He knows *all* your troubles. Let him sort them out. And then let him use you.'

He made as if to get up to go and Pippa said urgently, 'But what shall I do? What ought I to do with all the money?'

In the act of rising, the man turned. 'Has it brought you any happiness?' he asked gently.

She shook her head. 'Not really. I only bought the ticket out of spite.'

He laughed. 'Did you indeed?'

To her intense surprise he reached out a hand and laid it on her head, and immediately she had the oddest sensation of warmth and peace flowing through her. It was so intense it almost made her reel and she shut her eyes. And then, as if from a long way away, she heard him say, 'The day of the Lord always starts in darkness, you know. Only listen to any command he gives you, and obey. He will bless you, and in time you will see this place again as a sanctuary of healing and joy. Only love.'

Through the swirling mists of light that seemed to engulf her she said again, 'Who are you?'

He did not reply. Instead he rose to his feet, and began to walk slowly down the aisle towards the door. As if returning from a great distance, Pippa forced open her eyes and stared after him. But she felt dazed, and all she could see through the quiet gloom was the shadowy outline of a man, tall, but somehow very real. Then at the door she saw him pause as if waiting. She saw the door half open, almost as if the person on the other side was afraid, and then she saw Daffyd slide in and fall down just inside the entrance on his knees. As he collapsed, as if all the strength had gone out of him, the man reached down with his hand and raised him gently, and together they went out.

How much longer she sat there she had no idea, but a feeling of such peace flowed over her that she felt she did not want to move. As she sat there, she discovered that she felt clean too, almost as if she'd been washed by a great wave of love.

At last she got up to go and found, incredibly, that the day was

257

fading. As she walked to the door, a smell of roses seemed to flood the air. She pushed back the heavy oak panels and passed out into the graveyard beyond. Sitting on a tomb just outside, she saw the dim outline of a man, his head bent, hands clasped before him as though in prayer. As she emerged, he straightened and looked round, and with a gasp of surprise she recognised Daffyd. But it was a Daffyd she had never seen before. He rose to his feet and smiled, and she realised suddenly how tall he was, and straight, while the eyes that stared back at her were clear and bright.

'He healed me, Pippa,' he said softly, in answer to her unspoken question. 'That man. He asked me if I wanted to be better, and when I said yes, he laid his hand on my head and began to pray. And then he said something like, "leave him, be free". I don't know exactly. I can't really remember.' She realised he was crying, unable to help himself, and he went on, 'It left me. I felt it go. Not violently or with some sort of terrible battle. It just went, as if it had to obey.'

They stared at each other in the fading light, and then Pippa felt the tears rise to her own eyes. 'Oh, Daffyd,' she whispered, 'I'm so glad. So very, very glad.'

Then they both ran forwards and threw their arms round each other, and Daffyd said, 'It's all going to be all right now, isn't it.'

It was not a question, simply a statement of fact, and she replied, 'Yes. It is now . . . Yes.'

# Chapter Twenty-seven

'Well, we managed to keep the posters,' boomed Chuck triumphantly. 'The Lawd sure has blessed us.'

Tom, standing a little apart leafing through his Filofax, scowled. It was eight o'clock in the morning, and there were just six hours to go now before they opened at Wembley, but he was feeling apprehensive. Pippa, he knew, had phoned Mark the night before and told him that Elaine had rung to say she was coming home and so she would after all be coming up, and that she would be bringing Daffyd with her.

Tom had not seen Pippa since the debacle of his attempted declaration of undying love. He had left early in the morning before she got up and, on the drive back to London, his humiliation and shame had hardened into hate. He felt he disliked her intensely now, and that in turn had solidified his feelings of antipathy towards Mark; but he had no idea what to do. He had committed himself heart and soul to Chalice but he was all too painfully aware that it was Pippa's money that was funding the enterprise, and that any open split would merely catapult him out into the cold. Tom did not want that. He had spent years trying to build up a ministry that no one seemed to take any notice of. He knew perfectly well that to many he was a lightweight and a bit of a fool, but Chalice, he felt, had been his long-overdue reward. He was loath now to throw it away.

However, when not thinking exclusively about himself, it also occurred to him to wonder what Pippa might do. He did not in all seriousness think there was any great probability she would tell Mark – he knew her well enough to guess she might be too ashamed – but he did wonder if she would try to winkle him out of Chalice. That, he determined, was at all costs to be avoided.

When Pippa arrived about an hour later at the Dorchester with Daffyd in tow, Tom was in a mood of belligerent antagonism and had already managed, by his off-handedness, to offend Mark and half the Chalice team still there. Cherilee, who had noticed his odd behaviour, whispered to her husband, 'I guess he's nervous, hon. You always hurt the ones you love!' And with that platitude, she went off to check that her sequinned dress had been packed properly for her appearance on stage later that afternoon.

'Pip, honey,' said Chuck as soon as she appeared. He threw his arms round her and planted a sloppy kiss on her cheek. 'We were beginning to think you'd deserted us.'

'No,' said Pippa, 'there was just so much to do back home.'

'Keepin' the ship afloat, eh?' said Chuck approvingly – he had decided he liked Mark's wife.

'Something like that,' agreed Pippa. She stood back to allow Daffyd to come forward and then said, 'I've brought Daffyd with me. He's healed.'

'Well, shucks, I already told you that,' said Chuck, beaming. 'I knew he was healed when we prayed. I told you it'ud be all right.' He pinched Pippa's cheek fondly and clapped Daffyd on the back.

Pippa gaped. 'Yes but . . .' she began faintly, but Chuck had already moved on.

Daffyd smiled wrily and shrugged. 'Don't worry,' he mouthed, 'we'll set the record straight later.'

Pippa, however, *was* worried. She wanted everyone to know the amazing things that had happened. In particular, she wanted to tell Mark all about the man in the church and ask her husband who he was. She wanted to set the record straight too. She wanted to tell Mark about Tom, and she wanted to tell Tom that it was all right, and that some chaotic spirit just seemed to have played havoc with them all, but that she understood now and it did not matter – any of it. She smiled radiantly, and Tom, intercepting the look she gave Mark, stared at her with loathing, feeling a sudden trickle of fear.

Pippa was oblivious. She went across to Mark and gripped his hand. 'I've got so much to tell you,' she murmured, reaching up and kissing him on the cheek.

'Ah . . .' said Cherilee coming back into the room just at that moment, a pair of pink stack-heeled boots clutched in her hand. 'Now ain't that sweet! I jus' love to see a husband an' waaf still so much in lo-ove.' She winked at Pippa conspiratorially. 'Romance, honey, it's what we all need.'

'Quite,' said Mark, embarrassed. He cleared his throat noisily and looked away, but the pink flush that crept up his cheeks betrayed his pleasure. 'Extraordinary,' he said, trying to change the subject and staring at Daffyd.

'Yeah.' Daffyd nodded, a huge, idiotic grin spreading over his face. 'It is, isn't it? It's great.'

Mark crossed the room and hugged him, then held him at arm's length and stared into his eyes. 'I'm really pleased,' he said sincerely. He turned back to Pippa. 'He really is better, isn't he?'

She nodded. 'It was wonderful.'

There was a commotion over by the door as Jack came in, the inevitable mobile phone clutched to his ear. 'Sorry, folks,' he said apologetically, 'but we really have got to make a move now. The team are in at Wembley, and the equipment's almost all set up, but if we don't go now, I simply can't guarantee that we're going to be there in good time.'

A ripple of excitement ran round the room. 'We're off!' shrilled Cherilee's voice. 'Ma Gohd, this is just so excitin'. Praise the Lawd!'

'Are you coming with us?' said Mark to Daffyd, still gripping his arms.

Daffyd shook his head. 'Not at the moment,' he said. 'I'll be along later. First I'm going to go and get Roseanne from the hospital. She doesn't know yet. I want to tell her.'

'Of course,' said Mark, releasing him. 'Have you got any money?'

'Yeah.' Daffyd nodded. 'Pippa's already given me some.'

Mark grinned at him. 'Good. We'll see you later then.'

'Yeah.'

Daffyd disappeared, and Pippa found herself herded with Mark down to the waiting fleet of cars. They were going to arrive at Wembley, it appeared, in style. 'Mark,' she whispered as they shuffled into the lift, 'we've got to talk. There's so much I've got to tell you. It's really important.'

Tom, who was standing on the other side of Mark and overheard, froze. She was going to tell him, he thought stupidly, almost spluttering aloud with rage. The silly cow was going to tell Mark what he had done! He would be a laughing stock. Without stopping to think, he exclaimed angrily, 'Don't listen to her, Mark.'

'I beg your pardon?' said Mark, startled.

'I said don't listen to her,' hissed Tom. 'She doesn't know what she's talking about. It's all lies.'

Mark gaped, and Pippa stared. 'Tom . . .' she began.

But Tom, now thoroughly aroused and desperate to save his own skin, was only further incensed by Pippa's open astonishment. 'It's all her fault,' he said viciously. 'She led me on. She enticed me!'

The whole lift turned and stared. 'Tom, what on earth are you talking about?' asked Mark. He had gone dangerously still, and beside him Pippa felt suddenly afraid.

'She lured me,' went on Tom recklessly. 'She kept telling me she loved me . . . leading me on! And then when I went down and threw myself before her, she spurned me.'

'When did you go down?' asked Mark.

'The other night,' almost screamed Tom. He found that once he had started, he was unable to stop. 'When you couldn't go back to Little Wakenham, I did. I got there late, I went to her room.'

'You went to her room?' echoed Mark. 'My room?' He sounded stunned.

'Yes,' said Tom. 'But only because she lured me.'

'Pippa lured you?' Mark turned and stared at Pippa and she shook her head wordlessly, too stunned to think of anything to say.

'She lured me into her bed!' Tom almost screamed. 'Your bed, Mark! I was weak.'

Over in the corner, Jack shuffled his feet and looked away.

'Now see here, son,' said Chuck suddenly, concerned, 'these here are serious things you're sayin'.'

'I know that,' shouted Tom. 'But that whore seduced me, and then when she'd got me where she wanted, she laughed at me and—'

*Smack.* Mark's fist connected with Tom's mouth. Under the impact of Tom's body catapulting back, the lift lurched, and then shuddered to a stop. Somebody screamed. For one frozen moment Tom glared at Mark, a hand clutched to his bleeding face, and then he lunged, his own fist upraised. The next second all hell broke loose. Tom hit Mark. Mark hit Tom again. Chuck tried to intervene, and got hit by both of them. Cherilee shrieked, and then hit both the assailants with her handbag – and Pippa, perhaps mercifully, fainted.

When she came to some thirty seconds later, the lift was still stuck, but Mark and Tom were being restrained either side, while Chuck, in the middle, held a bloodstained hankie to his face. 'Would you mind explainin' all of this?' he said, fixing a cold eye on Pippa.

She debated the wisdom of again passing out, but discovered she could not. 'It's all a bit difficult,' she said shakily, sitting up. 'I think Tom's a bit confused.'

At that moment the lift lurched, and a voice floated down the shaft, 'Don't worry down there, we'll have you out in a jiffy.' Then there was a grinding noise, the lift seemed to bump, and then very slowly began to descend.

Tom jerked and tried to break free. Panting with the effort, he hissed, 'She's a liar. Don't listen to her.'

The next second the lift shuddered to a halt and Chuck said urgently, 'OK, everyone, take five. There might be press out there. Just stand easy, and we'll sort all this out later.'

Immediately Mark and Tom were released and dusted down, and Pippa found herself hauled unceremoniously to her feet, while Cherilee smoothed her hair. Chuck straightened his tie, and everyone tried to assume an attitude of easy unconcern. 'Well, well, well . . .' laughed Chuck, with rather forced jocularity as the doors slid back, 'a little bit of drama for us all before the big event.' He stepped out into the foyer and seemed to shake himself. 'Come on then, folks, let's go into battle.'

Mark and Tom glared at each other. Pippa attempted to catch hold of Mark's hand as they left the lift, and found herself shaken roughly aside. In mutinous silence, they all trooped behind Chuck to the waiting cars.

Stripe was already waiting at Wembley. He was almost beside himself with nerves, fighting to keep calm, but it was not easy. Enoch had materialised the night before, along with Curtis and some half-dozen of 'the boys'. Stripe had thought they all looked like thugs – which was, of course, exactly what they were, but the knowledge did not help. Then the police, under cover of being music journalists, had insisted on giving him another briefing. 'Don't worry,' they told him, 'we'll have the place covered. Nothing can go wrong.'

Stripe was not so sure, and it had occurred to him to wonder if there was still time to run away. The temptation lasted only a second. He hardened his resolve. One way or another, he told himself, this was going to be sorted.

Chuck pushed his way through the huge double doors and into the corridors that ran under the auditorium, fuming. 'Keep them separated!' he snapped to his aides, indicating Mark, Tom and Pippa with a wave of his hand. 'We don't want no more trouble before the meetin'.'

Meredith Galender looked with studious unconcern down the rather murky corridor.

'What's up?' asked Stripe, intrigued in spite of himself.

'Don't ask,' said Cherilee. 'Jus' don't ask!'

They swept on past, and Stripe noticed that Chuck's nose was bleeding slightly. 'Wot's 'appened?' he asked again, catching hold of Pippa's arm.

She bit her lip, tears rising to her eyes. 'Not now, Stripe,' she said. 'I can't.' And then she, too, swept past him and through the door that one of Chuck's fixedly smiling assistants was holding open for her.

Mark made as if to follow her, but he found his arm firmly held and then he was propelled none too gently further along the corridor and through another door on the right. Tom was marched off under what, to Stripe, looked suspiciously like a guard. 'Blimey,' he said softly, 'that's a bit queer, that is.' But then, finding himself ignored, he shrugged. Whatever it was, he thought, it paled into insignificance beside his own problems. He set off morosely down the corridor in Chuck and Cherilee's wake, and then went on up the stairs at the far end and back on to the stage. 'No, not there!' he shouted, emerging just in time to see a couple of technicians pick up his keyboard and begin to move it back.

'Sorry, mate,' said the nearer laconically. 'That American bird just said to get it out of the way because she wanted her choir here.'

'Well, she bloody can't!' exploded Stripe. 'That's my place, that is.' He surged forward and placed his hands firmly on the front of the keyboard, shoving it back again. 'Purrit back.'

The workmen shrugged. 'Suit yourself, but she won't be 'appy.'

Down below, and finding himself alone in the dingy little room into which he had been so unceremoniously shoved, Mark sank heavily down on the nearest chair and gazed unseeingly into the mirror set opposite on the wall. His brain was in turmoil. Pippa, he thought, had been unfaithful. Tom had just said so. She had betrayed him. Then he thought more closely about what Tom had said, and a puzzled look came over his face. He had thought many things about Pippa over the last few weeks, and it was true that he had suspected Tom's behaviour towards her, but somehow what Tom had said just did not accord with the Pippa he knew.

Biting his lip, he thought about his wife's behaviour ever since the lottery win and decided that, although there had been obvious friction between them, try as he might, he could not detect anything odd or encouraging in her manner towards Tom. Then he thought of her expression in the lift when Tom had begun his accusations. She had seemed appalled, he thought. It was true she had made no attempt to deny what Tom was saying, but Mark remembered very clearly that Tom had said she had rebuffed him.

In the unnatural calm that seemed suddenly to have descended outside, the more Mark thought about it all, the stranger it all became. It occurred to him that Pippa might well have turned Tom out because she was as shocked by what was happening to her as he had been to hear of it. He suddenly remembered Pippa when he had first known her, her uncompromising honesty and desire for the truth – it had been that that had first attracted him – and he felt how out of character the deception Tom was now suggesting was.

He thought some more about the years gone by, and about Tom's past behaviour, and he realised with a sudden blinding sense of revelation that Tom had always been jealous of him. Tom had always, in so many different ways, been trying to take what he himself had already got. At college it had been records and clothes, and later his vocation. Now, apparently, it was his wife.

As he realised this, Mark suddenly thought about how horrible he had been to Pippa, how he had emotionally abused her and vented on her all his pent-up frustrations at what he had felt to be his failure. In the circumstances, who could blame her if she had gone off with someone else? Remorse swept over him. He let his head sink on to his hands and gave a great dragging sob.

There was a sound of footsteps rushing down the corridor. Mark looked up. More footsteps, a shout, and then silence. Wondering what fresh disaster was happening now, he stood up, crossed to the door, and carefully looked out. The corridor was empty. The 'guard' on Pippa's room, he noticed, had gone, as had his own. That decided him. Without pausing to think, he slipped quietly out and crossed the few yards to her door. Once there, he checked, and then very carefully reached out and turned the handle. To his immense relief it opened immediately, and casting one last glance round to make sure he was unobserved, he slipped quickly in.

'Pippa,' he called, staring round. His eyes came to rest on his wife slumped dejectedly across the dressing table built into the far wall, the harsh make-up lamps round the mirror casting an unforgiving brilliance on her bowed head.

She raised a tear-stained face. 'What?' she asked tonelessly.

He slid further into the room and stared at her uncertainly. Now that he had come this far, he found he was almost overcome with fear. 'It's not true, is it?' he asked, trembling.

She cast him a bitter look. 'How can you even ask?' she demanded.

Relief flooded over him. 'I'm so sorry,' he said in a rush. 'After all that's happened I just felt so confused. And Tom . . .' He trailed off and stared at her imploringly.

Pippa was in no mood to make it easy for him. 'Of course, what Tom says has got to be right,' she said angrily.

He flushed. 'No, that's not what I'm trying to say at all.' Then the next moment, unable to think of anything better to do, he rushed across, pulled her to her feet, and gathered her roughly into his arms. 'Of course I don't believe you "lured" him. I'd never believe that of you.'

Against his shoulder Pippa burst into tears. 'I never knew,' she said. 'He said he was in love with me, but I never realised.' She looked up at him, her face agonised. 'I never encouraged him. Not consciously.'

'I know,' he said shakily. 'Tom always gets hold of the wrong end of the stick.' Then he kissed her.

Minutes later, when they gently pulled apart, peace seemed to enfold them. 'Mark,' said Pippa urgently, suddenly remembering everything else that had happened, 'there *are* things I've got to tell you. There was a man in the church. At least, he looked like a man. He looked like a priest. But I'm not sure. He healed Daffyd.'

Mark looked at her fondly and stroked her hair. 'A man who wasn't a man!'

'No,' she said, 'don't laugh. This is real.'

'Like Chalice is real?' he asked wrily.

'No,' she said, shaking her head. 'Really real.' And then, unable to contain herself any longer, she told him all that the man had said and done, and the incredible sense of light that had seemed to fill the church when he left. 'And when I went outside,' she concluded, 'I found Daffyd sitting on a tomb. And he looked up and round as I came out, and he was better.' Her voice shook with excitement.

For a long minute Mark stared at her, and then he said abruptly, 'Pippa, let's leave.'

'What?' she asked uncertainly.

'I mean it,' he said, 'let's go now. This whole roadshow has been absolutely potty from the minute it started. I don't believe any of this garbage any more. I don't believe it's what God wants. It's total chaos. So let's just go. Let's take a few days off together.'

Her face went pink. 'But the cost . . .' She caught his amused expression and laughed.

'I don't think we need to worry about that,' he said. 'But I do think we need to get away and sort ourselves out, and discuss what God really wants us to do next.'

'All right,' she said. She smiled suddenly, a smile of pure release. 'Let's go. Maybe we could even have a few days abroad. France or something.'

'Maybe,' he agreed.

Suppressing their giggles, like two naughty schoolchildren about to play truant, they stole out of the door, down the corridor and away.

Up on the now crowded stage, Stripe and Cherilee were having a heated argument. 'I don't care,' Cherilee was shouting furiously. 'That there is where my choir is goin'.'

'You're mad,' Stripe replied. 'I want me keyboard there.'

'No!' said Cherilee.

'Now, darlin',' shouted Chuck authoritatively, rushing up – three of the choir had run distractedly to get him at the first sign of trouble. 'Now jus' hold on a minute, an' let's get this sorted out a bit more quietly.'

'He's tryin' to take over the stage,' said Cherilee, spinning round indignantly.

'Rubbish,' said Stripe. 'You're barmy. I always go there. That's my spot, that is.'

Cherilee glowered. 'Not when I'm here, it's not,' she said emphatically. 'Ah need mah choir behind me.'

Chuck looked at them both consideringly, and then Stripe said suddenly, 'Ask Mark. I'm always there.'

It was on the tip of Cherilee's tongue to tell him to go shove himself but Chuck, mindful of whose money was behind the enterprise, intervened before she could open her mouth. 'OK, we'll do that,' he said firmly. 'I'm sure we can work out a compromise here.' He nodded with his head to one of his aides and muttered quickly, 'Go an' get him, son. These limeys are nuts.'

The aide ran off and returned two minutes later, breathing heavily. 'He's not there,' he announced. 'He's gone. His wife's gone from the room we put her in too.'

Cherilee's hand flew to her mouth. 'Lawd's sakes!' she breathed. 'What if he's murdered her?'

But the aide shook his head. 'I don't think so,' he said. 'I looked outta the window as I came back up an' I saw them crossin' the car park together. They were holdin' hands.'

Pandemonium broke out. Chuck immediately sent people racing after them to bring them back, but they were too late. By the time they got outside the stadium, Mark and Pippa had gone.

'Do you think they're comin' back?' Chuck asked Meredith.

The prophet shook his head gloomily. 'Don't look like it,' he replied. 'Not if you ask me.'

'Tom!' said Chuck. 'Go check on Tom, boys. We need at least one of them here to speak.'

Five minutes later a rather subdued Tom was brought out on to the stage. Like Mark, he had taken the enforced time alone to think, but it had made him feel only more angry and depressed than ever. He came now dragging his feet and looking mulish. 'Mark and Pip have gone,' Chuck told him.

Tom shrugged. 'Good,' he said.

Chuck breathed heavily. 'Son,' he said, fixing him in the eye, 'we got work for the Lawd to do here today, and I'm not findin' your attitude overly helpful.'

Tom had the grace to look ashamed. 'Sorry,' he mumbled, 'I just feel a bit low.'

For another minute Chuck regarded him. 'Well now, that's only to be expected,' he said at last. 'I reckon you've a deal of repentin' to do.'

Tom hung his head.

'The Lawd forgives sinners,' intoned Chuck. 'Don't he, Cherilee?'

'Oh yeah, Chuck honey,' she said immediately. 'Why when you—'

'Yes, thank you, Cherilee,' interrupted her husband hastily. 'Let's not go over that now.' He peered at Tom. 'Are you sincerely sorry that you lusted after another man's wife?'

Tom nodded. He was extremely sorry that he had lusted after Pippa. He thought she was a cow. 'Yes,' he said miserably.

'Are you prepared to give your testimony?'

Tom nodded again.

'Good!' said Chuck. 'Then the Lawd forgives you.'

An explosive little sigh went up from around the assembled group – with the exception of Stripe. 'Wot about my keyboard?' he asked plaintively.

'Over at the side, boy,' said Chuck magisterially. And Stripe, realising that he had lost his allies, subsided.

# Chapter Twenty-eight

The afternoon session was a rather lacklustre affair. About four thousand people turned up, and they sang enthusiastically enough but, as Meredith said later, it was somehow as if a shadow hung over them. Chuck was so upset that he ordered the combined Chalice and Shining Star teams to fast and pray during the interval, before the evening event was due to begin. 'I'm jus' not inspired,' he said plaintively. 'The Lawd ain't givin' me nothin' to say. We gotta disperse this cloud.'

Stripe scowled and went and bought a hamburger.

When the evening session began, the atmosphere was again tense. From the stage Stripe located Enoch and Curtis in the second row of the audience. They nodded at him, and Enoch made a thumbs-up sign. Stripe swallowed uneasily. Glancing beyond them and round, his eye fell on Ulysses, standing with a small group of men over at the side of the auditorium, easily distinguishable from the crowd milling excitedly around them by the dour expressions on their faces.

'Oh God,' muttered Stripe fervently, 'please 'elp us.'

He stared wildly around, wondering where the police were, but in the chaotic throng that now churned below him he could make out no other faces that he even vaguely recognised. He felt very alone.

More people poured in. They were like a great surging tide. The evening crowd, Stripe realised, was rather different from the one that had come along in the afternoon. Looking down the length of the stadium, he saw what looked like a positive flotilla of wheelchairs advancing relentlessly towards the stage, while behind came people with crutches, white sticks, arms in slings. To Stripe, staring at them all in fascination, it seemed as if the audience was comprised entirely of walking wounded, and he blanched, feeling suddenly rather scared.

'Move aside, punk,' hissed Cherilee, coming up behind him. 'This is mah spot.' She pinned a huge smile on her face and walked forward, hand upraised, and the crowd, who had not the slightest idea who she was, nevertheless exploded in a great wave of frenzied clapping and cheers. Stripe dutifully tried to push himself further back into the shadows. He would have liked at that moment to have been invisible.

269

'Play something,' said Tom, coming up behind him just at that moment. 'Let's have some praise.' He seemed to have recovered a lot of his bounce over the last few hours and Stripe looked at him with dislike, but he complied, and soon the vast arena was echoing to the sound of loud choruses, led by an exuberant Cherilee. She seemed to be in her element now, gathering up and focusing the crowd's mood of excited expectation. By the time she held up her hand and shouted into the microphone, 'Ah can feel miracles tonight! Let's pray!' Stripe felt as if the whole arena was about to erupt. He looked down and saw Enoch singing with a bored look on his face, but Curtis next to him was swaying and waving his arms. He looked as if he was having fun. Obscurely terrified, Stripe stared back up the length of the stage, trying to calculate how long it would take him to get away, should the need arise.

After Cherilee, Meredith came on as the warm-up spot. He spoke movingly about God laying tables for repentant sinners. The crowd looked mystified, but then Tom came on. He told them that he was a sinner. That he had harboured the twin sins of fornication and lust in his heart – that he had desired another man's wife! At this point he sank movingly to his knees and raised an arm above his head, his other hand still clutching the microphone to his mouth. The Lord had convicted him, he bellowed. He had shown him the enormity of his sin, but he had forgiven him. Cheers from the crowd. Tom leapt to his feet. He had been cleansed, he shouted, by the blood of the Lamb. The crowd went wild. Yes, he screamed, by now almost hoarse, God had forgiven him. And he would forgive all such sinners. All it needed was true repentance of heart.

It seemed at this point as if he was going to go on. He appeared to be enjoying himself, but Chuck suddenly exploded on to the stage at his side and, gathering him up in his arms, seized the microphone. 'Yeah, brothers and sisters,' he shouted, holding Tom in a grip of iron. 'If Gohd can forgive a sinner like our brother here, he can surely forgive you, and he's a-comin'. HE'S A-COMIN' NOW.'

His voice shuddered with emotion and there were cries of 'Amen!' 'Alleluia!' and 'Praise the Lord!' from all over the auditorium.

'Welcome him,' shouted Chuck.

'We welcome you, Lord,' screamed the crowd obediently.

'Do any of you wanna be healed?'

Shouts of 'Yes' and more alleluias, and then Chuck said, 'Then come on up here all you who want the Lawd's healin' tonight.'

Out of the corner of his eye, Stripe saw Ulysses rise menacingly to his feet and begin to move towards the stage. At the same moment Enoch, who had noticed, also rose to his feet, staring round in consternation. This was not part of the plan. Then, as if at a signal, wheelchairs began to be pushed forwards and in their wake came a mad surge of people, all pushing and shoving in their eagerness to get to the front.

'Whoa there,' shouted Chuck. 'Take it easy. The Lawd ain't in no rush.'

Ulysses was at the foot of the stage. Stripe saw Enoch glance round, looking seriously worried now, and nod, and then head towards the stage after Ulysses. Stripe wondered if this might not perhaps be a good moment to disappear. Before he could move, however, Chuck skipped over to him and said, 'Play, boy. This is what you're here for.'

Stripe swallowed and began to play, rather inappropriately, 'Moon River'. It was all he could think of. Chuck looked at him askance and scowled, but the crowd was now clambering excitedly on to the stage and, without another word, he scuttled away back towards the centre. 'Make way,' he shouted. 'Let the wheelchairs up first.'

Six wheelchairs were pushed up the ramps on to the stage, and after them came a small knot of hungry-looking people, among them Ulysses. At the last minute Enoch shouldered his way through and jumped up behind. He nodded at Stripe as if to reassure him. Stripe was not reassured. Totally oblivious, Ulysses shuffled forward till he was standing only three feet away from the keyboard. Chuck was talking to the men and women in the wheelchairs, one or two of whom were crying. The Shining Star team now also came on to the stage to hold back the audience, entreating them to be patient. Under cover of the noise and confusion, Ulysses edged closer and hissed at Stripe, 'If yer thinkin' of doin' a runner, forget it.'

'Wot ye on about?' said Stripe, playing on for dear life.

Ulysses jabbed a finger in his ribs. 'Ye look edgy to me,' he said nastily. 'But jus' remember, we got every exit covered.'

Stripe felt his brow break out in a cold sweat. 'Come off it,' he protested. 'I'm not goin' nowhere.'

Over in the centre of the stage Chuck laid his hand on the head of a young man in a chair. 'You can walk, son,' he shouted.

Enoch, who was watching the exchange between Stripe and Ulysses with increasing concern, suddenly lunged forward and across as he saw Ulysses raise an arm. Ulysses had actually only been going to clap Stripe on the back, but he was edgy too, and catching the movement out of the corner of his eye, he whirled round and pulled out a gun, jerking it up and straight into Enoch's face.

Across the stage, the young man in the wheelchair suddenly leapt to his feet and raced forward. The crowd cheered, and in astonishment Chuck shouted out, 'Praise the Lawd! We ain't even asked him to heal him yet.'

The young man made a flying tackle at Ulysses' feet, bringing him to the ground. There was a loud report as a gun went off. Tom, standing at the side, looked surprised and collapsed. More men leapt up from the wheelchairs, pulling out guns, and then down below, Curtis pulled out from under his coat a sawn-off shotgun.

'Help,' screamed Cherilee, and then the whole auditorium exploded in a mass of thrashing and crashing, scurrying bodies.

By the time it was all over some twenty minutes later, the police had Ulysses and Marty and their group in handcuffs on one side of the arena, and Enoch and Curtis and the yardies in handcuffs on the other. By some miracle, no one, apart from Tom, had been injured. Tom had sustained a flesh wound to his upper arm and was complaining bitterly but, to his intense annoyance, no one was taking any notice – they were all too dazed.

'Gee,' said Cherilee plaintively, 'I know the Gospel's a stumbling block, but we ain't never had nothin' like this before.'

'Stay where you are, please,' said a middle-aged police officer. 'We need to take statements.'

Stripe was sitting over by the keyboard looking green. He rather suspected that, even if he tried to go somewhere, his legs would not obey. There was a scuffle off to the right, and then Jack burst on to the stage. He looked ashen and made straight for Tom. 'It . . . it's terrible,' he stuttered. 'I don't know how to tell you.'

Tom, who had been growing more irritated by the moment, glowered. 'For God's sake what?' he said nastily, clutching his arm.

Jack shook his head wordlessly, and then brought out, 'It's Melanie.'

'What about Melanie?' said Tom, exasperated. And then to his utter amazement Jack sat down heavily on the floor and burst into tears.

'She's gone,' he said brokenly, sobbing loudly. 'And she's taken the entire Chalice investment fund with her.'

# Chapter Twenty-nine

Pippa and Mark got back to Little Wakenham three days later. They had seen the newspaper reports and the coverage on television, but somehow there had not seemed very much point in coming back earlier. 'We can't do anything, after all,' said Mark. 'Better really just to let the police sort it all out, and then when we get back we'll tell them.'

They had talked a lot over those few days, and had come to several decisions. First and foremost, they were both agreed that Chalice was not, and never had been, right – although Pippa, remembering her conversation with the strange priest in the church, said that she thought what had happened had after all been a necessary part of God's plan, in order to train them.

'Who is he, Mark?' she asked impulsively. 'He said he knew you.'

Mark frowned. 'From your description,' he said, consideringly, 'it sounds very much like it might have been John Fotheram. He's a priest based over in Aylesbury, but he's very charismatic. He leads a huge church over there. Though why he should have taken it into his head to come over to Little Wakenham like that, I've no idea.'

Pippa digested this. 'Perhaps God told him to,' she said.

For once Mark did not look sceptical, simply puzzled, and when Pippa told him what the man had said, he frowned again, as if deep in thought. She felt he would have liked to have come up with a rational explanation, but in the end, he surprised her by simply saying that the lottery win had brought a lot of things out into the open that would otherwise have remained hidden, and that he thought therefore that the result on balance was good. And then really floored her by adding, 'Maybe God did send John Fotheram. Maybe what he said was a prophecy.'

For Pippa and Mark that time together was actually very good because, after all their inarticulate battling, they suddenly found each other again, and through that they refound God. They discovered again what was important in life, and in the soft clear light of their new dawn, they saw how far they had strayed. 'I don't understand how it could all have happened,' Mark said again in the early morning when they were lying in bed. 'We

273

were trying so hard, and we both wanted so much to get it right.'

'Yes,' said Pippa judiciously, 'but maybe that's why all of it *could* happen. We did both want to get it right, but there were so many things inside us that seemed to stop it. Maybe this was the only way God could bring them out into the open and make us face them.' Then she said seriously, 'What shall we do now?'

In answer Mark rolled over and smiled at her fondly. 'We go back and start all over again,' he said. 'And this time we listen to what God wants.'

'I don't want all that money,' said Pippa suddenly. 'It's too much. I haven't a clue what we ought to do with it, it seems to poison everything. Couldn't we give it away?'

Mark grimaced. 'I'm honestly not sure,' he said. 'After all, God did let you win it in the first place. Maybe he wants us to do something with it.'

In the end, they decided to wait and see, but they were unprepared for quite how speedy the resolution would prove to be. Jack was waiting for them at the rectory when they got back. He seemed to have aged considerably over the last few days and had lost all the bouncy rather arrogant self-assurance that Pippa had so disliked. He was, however, sufficiently in command of himself to tell them the details of Melanie's flight. No one knew where she had gone, he finished up bleakly. The police were investigating, and the general weight of opinion seemed to be that she was somewhere in South America. But wherever she was, it seemed she had taken over eleven million pounds with her.

Pippa looked stricken and asked, 'How?'

Jack, whose memories of Melanie were not without personal stain, looked down at his shoes and said hollowly, 'Details aren't clear yet, but it seems her signature was enough to transfer all the assets, which she did, to her own name.'

'Good Lord,' said Mark. He sat down heavily on the nearest chair. He looked stunned. 'That leaves only three million then.'

Jack was embarrassed. 'Er, no,' he said. 'Not quite.'

Mark regarded him. 'Explain,' he said evenly.

Two hours later Pippa still did not understand the details, but it seemed that the Wembley event had lost Chalice a grand total of one and a half million pounds. There were all the Shining Star expenses, Jack had explained – first-class tickets on Concorde, the entire seventh floor of the Dorchester – and then all the costs attached to Wembley on top of that. They would have made some money, he insisted, but after the gun battle, people had demanded their money back, and one or two had even threatened to sue for nervous shock.

Mark groaned and Jack, casting around for anything that sounded even remotely like good news, said brightly, 'There was one miracle though. A man who really was crippled got caught in the crossfire, and he stood up and walked. Well, he ran actually, but Chuck's claiming it as a genuine sign. He says it shows God really is with them. But he says he's not too sure about the British end, so he's gone back to the States with Cherilee.' He added, 'Apparently Meredith had a prophecy that Britain wasn't ready for them yet.'

'What about Tom?' Mark asked.

Jack grimaced. 'He's gone with them. Chuck said there was much joy in heaven over one sinner who repented, and that if he would keep on giving his testimony in public, he could have a job with them. So he went. He said he didn't think there was anything much left for him over here.'

'So how much is left?' Pippa asked.

Jack brightened. 'About eight hundred thousand, I think,' he said. 'And the police are hopeful they'll recover some of the money Melanie took. And, of course, although she was acting independently as an authorised signatory of the trust, Chalice could sue the bank.'

'I don't think so,' Pippa said. 'I don't think that would be right. I think it's gone – and better left.' She looked at Mark. 'You did say to leave it to the Lord, didn't you?'

So they prayed about it, and then Mark began to prepare the services for Sunday. They would be the usual sort of thing, he said, pretty much like it had been before they started Chalice and Tom had taken over. But later in the day, as he was putting the final touches to his sermon, Stripe arrived.

'If it's OK with you and Pippa,' he said, looking slightly embarrassed, 'I'd like to stay. After all that's 'appened, I really feel Chalice is right. I guess you could say I've found God – or 'e's found me, I'm not sure which. But whatever, this is what I want to do with me life now.'

Mark looked surprised. He had heard the full story from Jack and knew all about Stripe's part in the proceedings. 'But don't you want to go back to your music career?' he asked finally. 'Jack tells me you've had an offer from a recording company.'

Stripe shook his head. 'I'm through with that,' he said feelingly. 'I want to be 'ere. I want to use me music – it's the only thing I can do – but I want to use it in the right way now.'

Mark nodded, but then his face clouded. 'Stripe,' he said, 'we'd love you to stay, but I think I ought to tell you, St Saviour's is having a visitation next week. I may not be rector here for much longer.'

Three hours later, Daffyd and Roseanne arrived. They looked

radiant, and both of them hugged Pippa and then, after a second, Mark and Stripe too. 'We want you to marry us,' Daffyd said to Mark. He smiled at Roseanne. 'What's it say in the Bible?' He thought for a minute and then his face split in a huge grin. 'The Lord has done unto us great things . . . and we want to give something back.'

Roseanne nodded in agreement. 'Yeah. Daffyd's told me all about 'ow 'e got 'ealed, and I told 'im 'ow I got led to Seb, so we reckon this is the way we want to live.'

Mark looked across at Pippa and blinked. 'I'm absolutely amazed,' he said. 'Jack was telling us earlier how everything's gone wrong, but actually this is incredible. Of course I'll marry you. I'll be delighted to, only . . .' and he told Daffyd and Roseanne about the visitation too.

'Well, I don't see wot the problem is,' said Roseanne matter-of-factly. 'We jus' need to pray about it, don't we?'

Stripe nodded, and Pippa and Mark looked stunned. 'Of course,' said Mark. 'You're absolutely right. Why didn't I think of that?'

Jack stayed around for Sunday. He said he had nowhere else really to go. Stripe played, and it seemed to Mark, standing in the pulpit and looking down on the familiar sea of faces, joined now by the newcomers who had been coming along since Chalice had started, that a deep and abiding peace seemed to fill the air. It was almost as if there was a blessing on everything they did – and he uttered a fervent prayer of thanks that Mrs Stibbins was not there. She came, however, to evensong and stared at him throughout with a smug and rather nasty smile on her face and, in spite of himself and his renewed faith, Mark shuddered.

The following week Elaine and Paul brought Sebastian back to Little Wakenham. Elaine had been back at Gentillesse since the morning that Wembley was due to start and had been commuting up to the hospital daily, a couple of times taking Harry with her. He, seeing harmony apparently restored between his parents, had got over his upset and was overjoyed at the thought of his brother returning home, but Sebastian, when he arrived, still looked wan. He had had the wires removed from his jaw and the swelling was going down, but the bruises still remained, giving his face an unhealthy greenish tinge that shaded into a delicate yellow.

For the children's sakes, Elaine was still resolved to make the best of things. Only now, more than ever before, she was aware of a vacuum deep at the heart of her own life, which had nothing really to do with Paul but which needed as a matter of urgency to be filled. She began to toy with the idea of doing a course at university. Then the news became public that Melanie had taken off with all the money from the Chalice account and Paul found himself peremptorily summoned to answer questions from the police. They seemed to find it impossible to believe that he should have given her so much unsupervised authority. Then all the sordid details of his affair came out and it was suggested to him, in unflattering terms, that he was a party to fraud and his passport was confiscated pending further inquiries.

Paul got himself a solicitor, and Elaine went through the following days tight-lipped. Then Paul decided that honesty was the best policy. He admitted to his liaison with Melanie, something he had still been trying strenuously to deny to the police, but said that he had long been growing tired of her; that he was happily back with his wife now, and that he rather thought his erstwhile assistant had acted out of revenge. Elaine found she could no longer preserve her silence, because the police began to question her too. Then they decided to explore whether there was a link between Melanie's activities and those of the drug dealers arrested at Wembley. Stripe was questioned and categorically denied any link, but the police were not satisfied and Elaine found herself subjected to the humiliation of long interrogations centring on her husband's sex life. It almost broke her, but after each session she went back to Sebastian, and she remembered her promise to God.

When Paul was finally exonerated from any fraudulent involvement, he was summoned in to see his superiors at the bank. They asked him what on earth could have possessed him to give Melanie such authority, and all he could rather lamely reply was that he had trusted her judgement, and that to make her an authorised signatory of the trust had seemed the easiest thing to do. The managing director glared at him. 'We're giving you a choice,' he said. 'You can either resign now on a full pension, or you're sacked.' Paul resigned.

He found it almost unbearably hard to break the news to Elaine. He had rather imagined that, like him, she would be devastated, but she merely stared at him, her eyes cold, and then remarked, 'Not very surprising really, is it?'

Paul was astounded and then said tentatively, 'Maybe this is our big opportunity. We could spend more time together.'

Looking at him, Elaine mentally shuddered. To spend time alone with Paul was, she thought, the last thing she wanted to do. 'What will you do now?' she asked hollowly.

He looked at her for a moment and then said, 'Well, actually, I've always rather fancied the idea of a fish farm. Perhaps now the boys are getting older we could buy one.' Then he added hopefully, 'It might be fun.'

'I don't like fish,' said Elaine.

Sebastian and Harry, however, thought it was a wonderful idea and Sebastian even laughed. 'Wow,' he said, 'can we have trout?'

277

'Yes,' said Paul, laughing too. 'And salmon if you want.'

It was settled as simply as that, and in no time at all Gentillesse was on the market, and Paul was looking for land that could be converted into a fish farm close by.

'Mum,' said Sebastian, catching Elaine on her own one morning after she had shown the agents round the house, 'it is going to be all right now, isn't it?'

'Of course it is, darling,' she said, spinning round. 'Why ever shouldn't it be?'

He regarded her through narrowed, apprehensive eyes. 'You know,' he said.

She looked at him, taking in his still battered face and bruised eyes, and the stiffness with which he moved, and dread flooded over her. They had so nearly lost him, she thought; he had so very, very nearly gone. And she thought about her life, about her selfishness and the wasted opportunities, and the sheer futility of all the bitterness she had felt in trying to blame everyone, especially Paul, other than herself. She thought how irrelevant it all was. What really mattered, she thought bleakly, staring at her son, was that she protect the life of her children and give them the space to grow. After that, she had to make the most of all the opportunities in front of her. What she really must not do was wallow in the trough of self-pity that yawned in front of her, which was engendered by her hatred for Paul. She had to go forward now, whatever that meant, and in the going she had to ensure that the lives of those she loved most were not harmed. And Paul? She pondered the question. Well, in time maybe she would learn to forgive him, like it said in the Bible, and maybe she would even learn to like him a bit too, but for now, the best she could manage was to tolerate him. God could take care of the rest.

# Chapter Thirty

Pippa was not very well over the next few days, and Mark began to feel concerned, wondering if at long last the terrible stress of the last few weeks was catching up with her. She protested that she was fine, but she was unable to eat, and twice he caught her being sick. Then on the Thursday she fainted and, now seriously worried, he banished her to bed, phoned the surgery and asked for Dr Forrest to visit. 'He's very busy today,' the receptionist told him, 'but he should get to you by late afternoon.'

'She's not well,' Mark protested. 'Can't he come any sooner? She fainted, and she's been sick.'

The receptionist seemed unimpressed. 'Just keep her in bed,' she advised. 'If she gets worse, let us know. Otherwise Dr Forrest will be along later.'

Mark made Pippa breakfast on a tray, and took up the morning papers for her with the toast. It was a mark of his anxiety that he had not even bothered to read them first himself.

'Honestly, I'm fine,' Pippa protested as he appeared. 'I feel such a fraud lying here. I'm sure it's just a bug. I'll be perfectly all right later.'

'Stay there,' said Mark firmly. 'I've already phoned Dr Forrest.'

Pippa made a face, but subsided. She really did feel awful, while the sight of the toast made her want to vomit again. 'Have we got any Coca-Cola?' she asked suddenly.

He looked surprised. 'I think so. Why, do you want some?'

She nodded. 'I'm awfully sorry,' she said, 'I just don't think I can face coffee but I'd really love some Coke.'

He looked at her startled, and then went downstairs. Carefully, Pippa pulled herself up in the bed and explored how she felt. The world appeared to have stopped spinning, and so she pulled the paper cautiously towards her and spread it over the duvet. A headline leapt out at her, 'Bishop Runs Off With Lover', and there underneath she saw a large and none too flattering photograph of Bishop Bob, looking surprised. Appalled, she rapidly scanned the article. The Bishop had left a letter, she read, apologising but saying that he could no longer live the lie his life had become. He had been in love with another woman for twenty-five years, and so now he was

279

running off with her to start his life anew and to try to find the son they had had together over twenty years ago and lost.

'Have you seen this?' she asked Mark as he came back into the room, her voice shocked.

Mark, seeing his wife looking even paler than when he had gone downstairs, rushed to her side and laid his hand on her forehead. 'OK,' he said, 'don't worry. I'll phone the surgery again.'

She shook him off impatiently. 'Don't be silly,' she said, 'I'm fine. But have you seen this?' She picked up the paper and waved it in his face, and his mouth dropped open as he, too, took in the photograph of the Bishop.

'Good heavens,' he said. 'It can't be true.'

But it was, as they learnt later in the morning when the Archdeacon phoned. 'I just wanted to let you know,' that worthy said stiffly, 'the visitation to St Saviour's has been postponed. Indefinitely.' He sounded in a state of deep shock. 'You may have heard that the Bishop has gone away. All diocesan business that's not urgent has been put on hold.'

When Mark put the phone down he looked stunned. 'I don't believe it,' he said. 'There's not going to be a visitation after all. The Archdeacon says we've all got to pull together to keep the diocese going until they can sort the mess out. He says the last thing they want now is any more scandal.' He turned and looked at Pippa, who had come downstairs while he was on the phone and was now lying on the sofa in the front room. 'It means we can stay.'

By the time Dr Forrest arrived, it was five o'clock. 'Hello,' he said, taking in her wan face, 'you don't look too well. What's up?'

She told him, and he looked grave. 'I think we need to do a few tests,' he said. 'I'd like some blood, and then if you could do a urine sample for me . . . We should have the results back in a couple of days.'

Mark, who was standing behind him, looked aghast. 'What do you think it is?' he asked.

Dr Forrest shook his head. 'Can't say till we've got the test results back. Let's not try guessing.'

Stripe, Daffyd, Roseanne and Jack all gathered with Mark and Pippa in the rectory living room that night, and Mark told them the good news that there was no longer to be a visitation.

'So that means we can stay then?' said Stripe. Quite when the metamorphosis from 'you' to 'we' had taken place, Mark and Pippa were unsure, but take place it had and, looking at them, Pippa suddenly realised that God had put together a team.

'Oh!' she said aloud.

'What is it?' asked Mark, jumping up and wondering if she was going to be ill.

'Nothing,' she said. 'It's all right. It's just that I've suddenly realised.'

'What?' they all chorused.

She blinked. 'You're going to think I'm mad, but I've just realised that God has put us together.'

Mark stared at her in amazement, as if her words were blinding revelation, but Daffyd looked scornful.

'Oh that,' he said. 'Have you only just realised? All the rest of us cottoned on days ago. We've been praying about it ever since.'

'Have you?' asked Mark.

They all nodded, even Jack. 'Yes,' he said, speaking for all of them. 'After the fiasco of Wembley and all that's happened, we feel God must have a purpose. We're not completely sure what it is but . . .'

'But I think it's to do with homeless kids and junkies,' said Roseanne.

'And I think it's to do with music,' said Stripe.

'And I think it's prayer, and the healing and peace of God,' said Daffyd.

For a long moment Pippa and Mark stared at each other. Then, 'The priest in the church,' began Pippa, 'said that we'd see this place become again a house of healing and prayer. I think you're right, all of you, and that this is what God wants us to do, using all these things he's given.'

'Yes,' said Mark slowly, 'I agree. I believe God wants us to use this money you won, Pippa, to buy up, or maybe even build, a house of prayer that will become a community attached to the church.'

'Eight hundred thousand,' said Jack pensively. 'Do you think it will be enough?'

'I think it will be exactly enough,' said Pippa radiantly.

Two days later Dr Forrest called again at the house. He looked grave, but his eyes were twinkling. 'Brace yourselves,' he said when he had got Pippa and Mark together alone. He looked at Pippa. 'Are you still feeling rough?'

She nodded. She had been sick again every day since he last called and had lost five pounds in weight.

Dr Forrest shook his head. 'Well, I'm sorry,' he said, 'it's maybe going to be a bit rough.'

'What?' said Mark, by now almost paralysed with terror. 'Do you mean she's really ill?'

'Some people see it as a very serious illness,' remarked Dr

Forrest. Then he relented. 'She's pregnant, Mark,' he said. 'Pippa's pregnant.'

They stared at each other, and then Mark let out a great whoop of joy. 'Wow,' he said. 'How long? I mean how long has she been pregnant?'

Dr Forrest smiled. 'As far as I can tell it's still very early days, probably only about a couple of weeks, maybe even less.' He looked at Pippa kindly. 'It happens like this sometimes with some people. It'll get better.'

'I hope so,' said Pippa, and then she suddenly stumbled to her feet, a hand across her mouth. 'Excuse me,' she gasped, rushing from the room, 'I think I'm going to be sick.'